GF

The Bad Things

STO

Jane Riley spent many years as a BBC journalist and now broadcaster, covering some of the darker stories of last decade, including the Suffolk prostitute murders, the Cambridgeshire serial killer Joanna Dennehy and Operation Endeavour, the police operation to trap illegal gangmasters the Fens. She has had short stories published in women's magazines, including *Bella*, *Women's Weekly* and *That's Life*. Mary-Jane Riley is married with three children and lives in rural Suffolk. *The Bad Things* is her first novel.

D0807790

The Bad Things

MARY-JANE RILEY

an imprint of HarperCollins*Publishers*
www.harpercollins.co.uk

Killer Reads
An imprint of HarperCollins*Publishers*
1 London Bridge Street
London SE1 9GF

www.harpercollins.co.uk

This paperback edition 2015
1

First published in Great Britain by
HarperCollins*Publishers* 2015

A catalogue record for this book is
available from the British Library

ISBN: 978-0-00-815378-6

Set in Minion by Born Group using Atomik ePublisher from Easypress

Printed and bound in Great Britain

MIX
Paper from
responsible sources
FSC **FSC˘ C007454**
www.fsc.org

For Kim, Edward, Peter and Esme

FIFTEEN YEARS AGO

The stench was overpowering. Katie squatted on her haunches and pulled at the zip. The material tore; the metal teeth nicked her finger. Thoughts flashed through her mind: *should she wait? Could this be evidence?* She lifted the lid. The sightless, decaying eyes of a child stared up at her. The little boy, for it must have been a boy, was dressed in blue Thomas the Tank Engine pyjamas. His legs had been folded beneath his body so that he fitted neatly into the space. It rather looked, thought Katie, as if he'd been packed up, ready for death.

MON

1

The day Alex Devlin's life imploded for the second time was one of those bleak February days in Suffolk when the light never got above murky and spring seemed months away. Outside, whey-faced men and women were hunched inside their coats, trying to get their business done and move on. Shopping, working, maybe just passing the time in a warm coffee shop on the High Street. The streets of Sole Bay could be unforgiving.

Standing in the kitchen of her little terraced house with her third cup of coffee of the day, Alex rolled her shoulders, trying to ease the tension in them. She turned on the radio, hoping some background noise would help her relax.

'And now the news with Susan Rae.'

She hoped the couple of hours' work she'd put in polishing her news feature about an undercover policeman who'd infiltrated the murky world of Eastern European organized crime had been worth the early start. She'd been awake since four – Christ, always four; that time of night when everything seems to be at its worst – doing her usual bout of worrying about her sixteen-year-old and how she could make ends meet. Two hours of tossing and turning had been enough, and that was when she'd decided to get up and get on with some work.

'Five people have died in a multiple-vehicle accident on the M25. It happened during the rush hour in thick fog . . .'

Now she wanted a few minutes to herself before Gus blew in moaning and groaning.

Too late.

'So?' He glared at her, mouth a sulky pout and arms crossed, his slightly aggressive 'whatever' stance perfected.

It was as if the night, the dark, the four a.m. worrying hadn't happened; her son was carrying on the argument that had begun the evening before. Alex hoped he'd forgotten about it. Some hope.

She rubbed her temples, fighting against the headache that was slowly but inevitably building, pulsing behind one eye. 'Choose your battles' had been her mantra for the past two years, since her adorable boy with his blonde curls and loving cuddles had turned into a sullen teenager – all grunts and hormones.

'The Ukrainian opposition in Kiev say they have pulled out of the City Hall they have been occupying for the . . .'

'So no you can't go skiing with the school. I'm sorry. Nothing's changed overnight.' Alex said it as gently as she could. She would have loved him to go; of course she would if she had the money. Cash was tight, work not exactly coming in thick and fast. But it wasn't just the money. She had real difficulty letting her son go and allowing him to spread his wings. He knew it and resented her for it.

'Why not?'

Alex turned away and opened the fridge, taking out a bottle of milk and a tub of butter. 'Cereal or toast?' she asked, hoping an appeal to his stomach might defuse the situation.

'Mum. This is like, really important to me. Everyone's going. All my mates. And they need to fill up the places. If I don't go I'll really, really miss out. Like, I'll be the odd one out and you don't want that, do you?'

She took the bread out of the bread bin and put a slice in the toaster. 'You know why not, Gus.'

'It's just crap.' His sudden shout made her jump. 'I never get to do anything with my friends. Never get to go anywhere. It's like you don't want me to enjoy myself. Have mates or anything.'

She filled the kettle, opened the cupboard, and took out a teabag and a cup. She waited for the kettle to boil and for her irritation to subside. Pushing her hair behind her ears, she realized it needed a good cut and another home dye job. 'You know that's not true, Gus. I only ever want the best for—'

'Give it a rest, Mum.'

'Downing Street has welcomed a further fall in unemployment and the Prime Minister said . . .'

His slumped shoulders and look of defeat made her feel worse. Something shifted inside her, a realization that she had to loosen the ties just a little, had to put the trials and tribulations of the last few months behind her. Just be thankful he hadn't been expelled: joyriding and smoking cannabis not being on the school curriculum.

'Look,' she said, knowing she was going to regret it, 'when do you have to have the money by?'

'You can still pay in instalments. About five now, I think.' His sulky, cross expression had miraculously transformed into one of hope and she had to damp down the normal sinking feeling in her stomach that went with any mention of money. 'So it's not as if you've got to pay it all upfront. Mum?'

The kettle whistled and the toast popped up. Too dark. Alex poured the water onto the teabag and started scraping the toast. She breathed out, trying not to think of the electric and the gas and the phone that all needed paying. 'Get me the letter about it and I'll see what I can do.' She squished the teabag on the side of the mug with a spoon before fishing it out and plopping it into the sink.

His face lit up with a smile, the now habitual petulant look banished, at least, for the moment. 'Mum, you're the best.'

A woman jailed in connection with the murders of two children fifteen years ago has had her conviction quashed by the High Court in London. Jackie Wood had been . . .'

Alex froze. Oh God, Sasha, she thought. Oh God, oh God.

2

Detective Inspector Kate Todd was sitting in the doctor's waiting room idly flicking through a glossy magazine. She'd stabbed at the blasted machine on the wall that asked her personal questions in big letters, and confirmed it really was her for the appointment, before sitting down to wait; no doubt, in danger of catching some vile disease while she did so. The television murmured in the corner. She tried to focus on the magazine in her hands. Babies. Food for babies. Getting your baby to sleep. Bloody babies everywhere. She flung it down on the wooden table in front, eliciting a frown from the woman next to her.

'Sorry,' said Kate.

The woman gave her a small smile then shrugged. 'They're usually dead boring, those magazines. Years out of date, some of them. I'm reading about summer holidays three years ago.'

'Hmm. Yes.' Kate was being polite. Didn't want to get into conversation. Just wanted to get this over and done with and back to the station. Not that there was much excitement there, either. No major incidents to speak of, unless you counted the work that was going into planning raids in some godforsaken town in the Fens to try and combat the trade in poor sods being brought over to work and live in filthy conditions. Cannabis factories upstairs, three or four families downstairs. Trouble was, planning involved more than one force: the National Crime Agency and Uncle Tom Cobley and all. Had the potential to be a right cock-up.

Kate looked around the waiting room. No one she recognized. No one who looked as though they recognized her. That was the beauty of working in Ipswich but living in a small town some miles away – she was far less likely to come across any of her colleagues here.

'This little one . . .' The woman was talking again and Kate dragged herself back to the present. She noticed the woman was holding a bundle in her arms. A baby. How could she not have noticed? The woman carried on talking. 'She was born with a hole in her heart. Had to have an operation when she was so tiny. Didn't know if she would survive.'

Kate felt a sudden but familiar twist of fear in her chest.

'So we have to come for check-ups quite often, don't we sweetheart?' The woman cooed at the baby and smiled that smile that cut the pair of them off from the world.

The fear was now coiling around her heart. Whoever said the heart was just an organ didn't know anything. She took a deep breath and managed to put a pleasant look on her face.

'You got any?' asked the woman, who was now stroking her baby's cheek with the side of her finger.

'No,' she said. She must have sounded abrupt because the woman blushed.

'Sorry.'

'It's okay.' Kate picked up another magazine. This time it was *Designing Interiors*. Safer, she hoped.

She tried to concentrate on how to organize her living space better, what colour palette to use for a south-facing conservatory, and the 'beautiful home' created by some D-list celebrity. She tried not to think of the row she'd had with Chris last night. It was the same row they'd been having off and on with varying degrees of severity for the past ten years. This time, she had been about to turn the light off when Chris said, 'I wish you'd see someone.'

Her hand froze on the light switch. She was tired, had been doing paperwork for much of the day, and all she wanted to do was sleep. Now Chris had brought up the one subject guaranteed to make her tense and therefore lie awake for ages.

She gritted her teeth and looked over at her husband, who was lying in the bed, head on the pillow, hands crossed over his chest, his breath even. Eyes closed. Eyes bloody well closed. He always did that, so preventing her from having a damn good argument with him. She noticed lines around his mouth that hadn't been there before, and wanted to trace them with her fingers. Her irritation drained away. Chris loved her without any strings attached, and she loved him for that. He was calm, made her feel peaceful. She adored watching him work, how his hands, rough and calloused, fashioned the most beautiful objects out of wood. She loved him. But she had strings.

'Chris,' she said, propping herself up on her elbow, knowing it was going to have to be her making the first move, knowing that this time she had to give him some hope.

He opened one eye, reached out for her, pulled her down into his arms. 'Honey, I know how you feel, but . . .'

No, he didn't know how she felt, not really. He couldn't know the way her mouth went dry and her heart beat hard and fast whenever she thought about becoming pregnant, giving birth, having to look after another person who would totally depend on her. The emotional attachment scared her; the knowledge that, at some point, the child would leave and tear her heart out. Or worse, something – anything – could happen to him or her that would not only tear her heart out but stamp on it and throw it away. She knew it could happen. She'd seen it before.

'Can't we just adopt?' Even as she said the words, she knew she didn't mean them, and she knew what his answer would be.

'Surely we ought to find out first if there's any reason why we can't have our own?' His voice was gentle, and she felt hot tears gather at the back of her throat.

'Maybe it is all down to me. Maybe I'll never be able to conceive. Maybe I'm too old.' Or maybe she should just stop taking the pill.

'No, you're not. And if it doesn't happen soon, there is so much we can do. I just think it's a good idea to be checked.'

'Aren't we happy as we are?' she asked, guilt heavy on her shoulders.

'Yes.'

'Aren't I enough for you?'

'Darling, it's not about that.'

'I know,' she said into his neck. 'I know.'

He had gone by the time she woke in the morning – he often went for an early morning run, summer or winter, when he needed to clear his head, to give himself some thinking time.

As soon as she could, Kate rang the doctor's surgery.

Which was why she was now sitting on a plastic chair, flicking through a magazine without seeing any words, and wishing she was at the station, drinking filthy coffee out of a flimsy cup and enjoying the banter between colleagues.

The buzzer sounded and Kate saw her name on the electronic noticeboard. She got up, and the woman with the baby gave her an encouraging smile.

She was nervous because she knew she was going to have to say something to the doctor, but she hadn't worked out what yet.

She knocked on the door and went in.

The young woman GP, the appropriately named Dr Bones, looked up from her screen and smiled. 'Take a seat, Kate. What can I do for you today?'

Kate sat and blinked. What was she supposed to say?

'Kate?'

She cleared her throat. 'The thing is Doctor . . .' She thought of Chris and his kind face, the hands that worked so hard for her, the fact that he didn't ask anything of her, just this one thing. 'My husband wants a baby.' She stopped, feeling helpless.

'And?' Doctor Bones prompted her gently, her head cocked to one side.

'And I'm not sure I can.'

The doctor nodded. 'Okay. So you're . . . what —?' She looked at her computer screen, 'Thirty-eight and on the pill. No reason why you shouldn't get pregnant, you know. A lot of women are having children later these days—'

'It's not that,' Kate said. 'Sometimes I think that if you're not meant to have children then you shouldn't go down that route.'

Doctor Bones nodded. 'That's certainly a view.' She was waiting, wrists resting on the edge of her desk, for Kate to give her more. What else? 'I think there is so much misery in this world that I'm not sure it's the right thing to do.'

'The right thing?'

Kate looked at the walls, avoiding the doctor's eyes. Saw the brightly coloured children's paintings stuck up with Blu Tack, the height charts, the posters about healthy eating, even a chart to test eyesight. She gazed around the surgery, at the box of children's toys in the corner, a child's chair, everything catering for children. She refused to let the tears reach further than the back of her eyes.

'You know, getting pregnant just because I . . . we . . . want a baby. It seems a bit selfish, you know.' She shrugged, aware of how useless she was sounding.

'And what does your husband think?'

'Chris? Oh, he's desperate for them. I mean, he doesn't put it like that, obviously, but I know that's what he thinks.'

'But you're not sure?'

'No.' Her eyes began to fill with tears. For God's sake. She blinked furiously.

'Kate,' the doctor started gently, 'I'm not sure what I can do for you.'

14

'I only came because Chris . . .' She tailed off and stood up. 'Sorry, I don't know why I came really, I—'

'Sit down, Kate.'

'No. I've got to go back to work. Thank you for your time.'

Dr Bones looked at her computer screen. 'You have a stressful job, Kate. Are you coping?'

'Yes.'

'Look, I'm going to give you some very mild antidepressants. You don't have to take them, but they could help. And I'm going to put you on the waiting list for some counselling.'

Kate opened her mouth to object.

Doctor Bones held up her hand. 'It's just a waiting list. Have a think. It might be good to talk to someone other than your husband. An outsider. Okay? And I want to see you in a month.'

Kate could only nod.

Outside the doctor's room she leaned against the wall and took deep breaths. The air was stifling. It had been a mistake to come here, but at least she'd done it and she would be able to tell Chris. And she would tell him that the doctor thought she was a bit down about things. It would buy her some time. Things would resolve themselves, wouldn't they?

She hurried along the corridor and out into the waiting room. Luckily the woman and her baby weren't there. She made her way to the swing doors at the back.

'Ms Todd?'

Kate turned round. It was the pharmacist.

'I'll have your prescription ready in a minute, if you'd like to take a seat.' The pharmacist smiled at her from through the hatch.

'Right, thank you.'

Kate stared at the television still murmuring in the corner, sitting up when she saw the breaking news headline running across the bottom of the screen.

Jackie Wood wins High Court appeal.

She watched the pictures – Jackie Wood on the steps of the court, reporters waving microphones, cameras, people jostling one another, a self-satisfied man standing next to her, opening his mouth, talking, but Kate couldn't hear what was said. She hardly needed to, the inference was clear. Jackie Wood, one of two people responsible for the deaths of two small children, had finally won her appeal.

'Ms Todd? Your prescription is ready.'

Kate stood up automatically, walked over to the hatch, and took the paper bag handed to her by the pharmacist.

Then she went outside, got into her car, and rested her forehead on the steering wheel.

3

Sasha had always been the troublesome one. The needy one. The daughter their parents worried about. The one they spoke carefully to, treated with kid gloves. Alex had learned from a young age that Sasha had to be indulged. She was ten months younger than Alex, but when they were growing up Alex had often felt ten years older. 'Look after your sister' had been drummed in to her. The 'poor me' attitude Sasha cultivated had annoyed Alex all her life. Sasha was willowy, with fine blonde hair that curled attractively around her heart-shaped face. Whenever people saw the two of them together, they'd never believe they were sisters barely a year apart in age, because Alex was short with dark hair that was poker straight. She had also inherited her father's sallow – if she was feeling kind towards herself she'd call it olive – complexion. Sasha was the beauty and Alex was not. Or Sasha had been the beauty. That was the thing. Nowadays, she was still thin, still had blonde hair and the heart-shaped face and the blue eyes, but her thinness was of the bag of bones variety, the blonde hair was unkempt, her glacial features sharp and her blue eyes empty. She also had to wear long sleeves to cover up the scars.

Sasha had never got over the loss of her twins. They were four years old when they went missing. One boy, one girl; the complete set, and both with her blonde hair and blue eyes. Harry was a typical boy: loved rough and tumble and was always grubby. Millie was much the same, but with that cute girlishness that made everyone want to hug her. She smiled all the time. They were adventurous children; curious, inquisitive, loving. It was Harry who turned up a few weeks later; Millie was never found.

Harry's funeral was unbearable. The little white coffin balanced on the shoulder of Sasha's husband, Jez, and all the mourners; each and every one of them thanking whatever God they worshipped it wasn't happening to them. Alex had vowed to keep her own little boy safe. Unusually for that summer, the sky was grey and the drizzle didn't stop. God's tears, she heard someone say.

Alex wasn't sure that either she or Sasha believed in God anymore.

Their parents were there; shocked and bewildered that something like this could be happening to them. The church looked beautiful; a medieval place of worship in the Suffolk countryside. St Mary Magdalene. Sasha and Jez had chosen to bury Harry in their parents' parish because Sasha couldn't bear to be in Sole Bay at the time. And she wanted somewhere quiet for him, somewhere the birds would sing and the sunlight would dapple through the trees and warm the earth beneath. So she chose the next door village, where their parents had moved to when she and Alex left home. Someone – the good ladies of the parish, Alex supposed – had decorated the church with roses and willow and honeysuckle that scented the air. Harry was buried in the little graveyard at the back and it was overwhelming to see the tiny mound of earth that was going to hide his coffin forever.

But at least they were able to bury Harry; not knowing Millie's fate was unbearable.

And now Alex was on a mission to get to Sasha before she hurt herself again. Her sister had stayed in the house she had lived in with Jez and the twins. Couldn't bear to leave it, she said. Alex thought it was unhealthy, but despite her attempts to get her sister to either move in with her or find somewhere that wasn't jam-packed full of memories, Sasha refused. 'What if Millie comes back?' she said. 'What if she came back and I wasn't there?' And Alex wanted to say to her that Millie was only four when she went missing so she wouldn't even remember where to come back to, even if she was still alive. Naturally, she didn't say any of that to her. No one could say anything like that to her. At least, though, Alex was in the town and could look out for her sister, and, on a good day, she could run there in eight minutes.

This was not a good day – lack of sleep and not much food – but adrenalin would add wings to her feet.

'I have to go, Gus,' she said, running to the door. 'You finish your toast. There's a new jar of peanut butter in the cupboard.'

'But Mum – what's up?'

'I'll tell you later.' Alex felt breathless as she pulled on her coat and fumbled with the buttons. 'I have to go and see Aunty Sasha. Okay?'

He shrugged. 'Whatever.'

The radio carried on in the background.

The pavements were damp but thankfully not slippery. She ran, weaving through the people who blocked her way. Where was the family liaison officer? He'd said there wouldn't be a decision this early. She'd have time to prepare Sasha for the possibility of Wood getting off. What had happened?

Two old women pulling shopping trolleys were chatting, taking up the whole pavement. Trolleys with loud red and green spots, the sort that tripped up the unwary pedestrian. She hated them. She had to leap into the road to get round them; a car hooting as it just missed her. Then a woman with one of those pushchairs that could be used to haul babies up mountain ranges suddenly stopped, almost making her fall. A crowd of school kids laughing, pushing each other, appeared in front of her. Inside her head she screamed at them, wanted to shove them out of the way. She barged through.

19

Not too far now.

She skittered around the corner into Sasha's road.

She needed to stop, lean up against a wall and catch her breath, but didn't dare.

She weaved passed two black wheelie bins, noticing that one of them was overflowing with rubbish – cartons, cereal packets, chicken bones – that littered the pavement. She crossed the road, passed the public toilets, to Sasha's waist-high wrought iron gate. Alex wiggled the catch until it finally gave way, thinking she must get Jez to do something about that, then finally the five steps up the path to the front door.

She slipped her key into the lock, turned it, and pushed the door open all in one movement, almost falling into the hallway.

Sasha was in what passed for the sitting room; a room that had once been light and full of laughter, but with its faded blue and white striped wallpaper and cream carpet that had seen better days, was now oppressive. A two-bar electric fire in the fireplace pumped out a desultory amount of heat. There was a television in one corner, and a sofa pulled up in front of it. The curtains were half drawn and the place smelled fetid and unkempt: all a sure sign that Sasha was in one of her downward spirals. Some thirty pictures of the twins, in various stages of development, right up to the day they went missing, were arranged on every surface. One photograph had been taken in the clearing in the woods, the tartan blanket laid out, picnic basket ready to disgorge its lunch of dainty crustless ham sandwiches, slices of banana, apple, segments of tangerine. And the treat of lemonade to drink, with iced biscuits and little strawberry yoghurts to finish. A perfect day out. A few days later they were gone.

The television was tuned to *BBC News*, its red logo adding a bit of colour to the room. The breaking news strapline screamed out at Alex from the crawler across the bottom: *Jackie Wood wins High Court appeal – conviction quashed.* Pictures flashed up: Jackie Wood on the steps of the High Court smiling and waving, her solicitor by her side about to read out a statement. The words washed over her and around her.

'Held for fifteen years . . . an innocent woman . . . rebuild my life . . .'

She heard the viper's tongue in every word.

And the shouted questions from reporters: 'How did you cope with life inside?'

'What will you do now?'

'Are you going to try and get some compensation?'

The sound of the traffic and blaring horns obliterating some of the syllables.

Wood smiled, and Alex saw the smug look in her eyes. She could imagine the triumph the woman was feeling and she wanted to reach into the box and grab her round her scrawny neck. At least she didn't look great on prison life or food – she was alabaster pale and thinner than Alex remembered. Her skirt and jacket looked chain-shop cheap. She quite fancied strangling the solicitor too, though his neck was much less scrawny. In fact, the feeling was so visceral she could almost taste the air being squeezed from the man's body. How much of any compensation was the woman going to get? Alex looked at Wood again. Three appeals and finally she'd managed to get off. Three appeals, a campaigning television producer, and a discredited expert witness and there was finally enough evidence to make two out of three High Court judges feel her conviction for the abduction and murder of Alex's niece and nephew was unsafe. She was a free woman. At least, Martin Jessop, her accomplice, was dead and gone. Hanged himself in the first three months of his sentence.

'I have nothing more to say, thank you.' Wood turned and went back into the building. The newsreader moved on, unaware of the effect the news was having on both her and Sasha.

The telephone started to ring, making both of them jump.

Alex thought quickly, then picked it up.

''Allo?' she said in a bad imitation of a French accent.

21

'Is that Sasha Clements?' The slightly breathless, high-pitched voice of a journalist hoping to get the first interview.

'Non.'

'Is Sasha Clements there, please?'

'Non. She moved from 'ere three years ago.' She winced, unsure her days of am-dram had stood her in good stead after all.

'Oh.' Disappointment in the voice. 'I don't suppose you have a number for her, do you?'

'Non, sorry.'

'Do you know where she went?'

'I think she went to Spain.'

'Spain?'

'Spain.'

'Oh. I see. Well thank you for your time.'

'*Plaisir.*'

Alex cut the call and then put the receiver down on the table, wanting to laugh at the sheer absurdity of it all, and wondering if she'd done enough to delay the feeding frenzy. Only time would tell.

She turned off the television and looked at her sister properly. Sasha hadn't noticed her, hadn't realized there was no sound or picture coming from the television. She was sitting staring at the now blank screen, tears rolling down her cheeks and her arms hugged around her body, hands tucked in the sleeves of her shirt. The material was stained red. Alex wanted to cry.

She sat beside her sister and put her arm around her, trying to ignore the fact that she flinched. Alex didn't say anything for a moment, attempting to breathe evenly to get some saliva into her dry mouth. Then Sasha leaned her head on her shoulder and let out a shuddering sigh.

'Alex.' She said her name softly, like a small puff of wind. 'I didn't think they'd let her out. They told me the appeal would fail. They told me.'

Alex kissed the top of her head. 'I know, my love, I know.'

'I thought I was dealing with it, you know; living with the fact that Millie was gone, buried somewhere and we'd never find out where.'

Alex tightened her arm around Sasha. And me, and me, she thought.

'But now—'

'We will find Millie, you know, one day. I promise.' And she felt the burden of that promise settle on her shoulders.

'I don't want you here,' Sasha said suddenly. 'Not you.'

Alex closed her eyes, briefly, trying not to be hurt, telling herself that her sister was like that, had been for the past fifteen years; that Sasha couldn't hate her any more than Alex hated herself. That Sasha didn't mean what she was saying. She didn't answer.

They sat quietly for some minutes. 'Sash?' Alex said. 'Can I look at your arm?'

A shrug.

Gently, Alex lifted Sasha's head off her shoulder and took her arm, pushing up the sleeve of her sister's shirt. The gash down the side of her forearm glistened wetly, but she judged it didn't need stitches this time. She got up and went into the kitchen, finding a bowl and some kitchen roll. She filled the bowl with warm water, poured in some salt and went back to sit beside Sasha. She wiped the cut, thankful to see it had stopped oozing blood. Her movements were mechanical – if she thought too hard about what she was doing, about what Sasha had done, she wouldn't have been able to clean up the wound.

'Don't take me to hospital, Alex. Please. Otherwise, I won't be able to feel.' She rubbed her face with her other sleeve. 'I need to feel.'

Alex nodded. 'Okay, but you must take care of yourself.' She bit her lip. What she was saying was nonsense. She could never stop Sasha from self-harming. God knows, she'd tried. Their parents wouldn't believe it was going on, not even when Sasha had to stay in hospital because she'd cut herself so badly, and not even when

23

the local doctor had her sectioned after she'd cut her wrists – not self-harming, not a cry for help, but a real suicide attempt. But she hadn't hurt herself this badly for months and Alex had been beginning to hope she might be on some sort of road to recovery.

Sasha looked at her with dead eyes. 'How can I take care of myself,' she whispered, 'when I couldn't take care of my children? When the woman who murdered my babies is out there again?'

There was nothing Alex could say to that.

4

It was mid afternoon and the light was already leaching out of the day when Alex left Sasha, having bandaged her arm and made her lunch, which she picked at. Alex also tried to persuade Jez to go round and stay, at least for one night. That was hard work. She knew that statistics for a couple splitting up after the death of a child were higher than average – she wasn't sure what they were when two children were dead. But Sasha and Jez had disintegrated pretty quickly after Harry was buried, and not even the thought that Millie might come home one day was enough to keep them together. Anyway, Alex had always thought he ought to give his ex-wife more support, so she steeled herself and rang him.

'Yes,' he said to her, whispering fiercely down his phone, 'I do know about the court's decision. I am in the right place, you know.'

'And you hadn't thought to go round to Sasha's?'

There was silence. 'I couldn't, Alex. I thought you—'

'Yes, well, I'd been told nothing would happen before midday, but they were wrong there, weren't they? So you can imagine what she was like when I got to the flat and she'd been watching it over and over again on bloody 24-hour news.' She found she was whispering, too.

He sighed, and Alex imagined him raking his hair with his free hand, making it all stand up on end. 'Look, it's difficult enough for me to process this right now, and I'm in the middle of another case.'

'I'd have thought you would have been there. At court, I mean.' Alex couldn't help herself.

'Why weren't you?'

'They weren't my children.' No, they weren't her children, but they were her sister's children, and if it wasn't for her they might still be alive. But she had to stop thinking that or it would send her mad. 'Couldn't the police give you compassionate leave or something? Look,' Alex went for a more conciliatory tone, 'I'm not asking you to drop everything now. I just want you to go over later. Stay there for the night. I would if I could but I've got Gus to think about.'

Silence. 'I can't, Alex. I can't do it.'

'Why not? Don't you owe her something?'

'Owe her?'

'You were married to her.'

'And now I'm not, okay? I wish things could have been different, God how I wish it. I still—'

'Still what?'

There was more silence. 'Never mind. It doesn't matter. Besides, it's too late now.'

'Jez, I know—'

'No.' His voice was sharp. 'You don't know anything. I'm trying Alex, really trying to get over her; to deal with what happened all those years ago, but the pain is still so near the surface, you know? Even after all this time. Christ, it's even hard to go out with other women, even though I try. God, how I try.' He laughed bitterly. 'And I never thought I'd say that.' He paused. 'And I bet she's been cutting herself.'

Alex said nothing. Two could play the silence game.

'I'm right, aren't I? And I know I'm partly to blame. Look, Alex, I don't expect you to understand, but me and Sasha—'

'You and Sasha what?'

'Nothing. Me and Sasha are nothing.'

'If you can't go round, could you send another plod round just to, I don't know, stand outside the flat or something. I don't want her besieged by journalists.' She knew her play-acting on the phone wouldn't fool a determined hack for very long.

'I will ask,' he said finally.

She had to hope it was enough.

It was cold and damp and Alex hunched her shoulders as she put the key in the front door. Suddenly a pair of arms encircled her waist.

'Honey, you're home.'

She rolled her eyes and felt her depression lift just a little. 'Malone, you are so predictable.' She opened the door. 'And what are you doing? Waiting to ambush me?'

'And how else am I supposed to get into your house? You haven't given me a key yet.'

'Too soon, Malone, too soon.'

'It's not too soon for me.' Malone pushed the door shut behind them, grabbed hold of her hair each side of her face, and kissed her deeply. He smelled of whisky and smoke.

She pushed him away, trying to smile. 'Down boy.'

'Come on, sweetheart. And haven't I just given you all of myself so you can keep yourself in handbags and shoes?' He laid his slight Irish accent on thickly.

'Ha. As if. And you know I'm very grateful. But, to be honest, it's been a shit of a day.'

He stroked her cheek. 'Did they not like the piece?'

'I don't know yet, I haven't looked.' Alex rolled her shoulders and rubbed the back of her neck.

'So?'

'Sasha.'

'Ah.' Such a wealth of meaning in such a little word.

Alex hadn't known Malone that long. In fact, she met him while researching her latest article; he was the article – the mad man who'd worked undercover most of his adult life. He had posed as a member of a far-right group. His work had included exposing would-be terrorists. It had been a dirty job and his life had been in danger. Then there had been the infiltration of environmental protest groups of the flat sandals and vegan persuasion. Lord, he told her with his lopsided grin, he never wanted to see a lentil again.

'How close did you have to get to the protestors?' she'd asked him.

He'd shrugged at that. 'As close as I had to.'

'Sex?'

'As close as I had to.'

It had been a hard slog, but she had eventually been able to tease out more details from him, and her admiration for him had grown. It helped he was amusing, too, and made her forget herself.

And she told him about Sasha and her babies and how her marriage fell apart and how her sister needed her. She'd told him all that, but she hadn't told him what really kept her awake at night.

'Tea?' He picked up the kettle.

'Yes please,' she said.

'So what about Sasha?'

Alex shook her head, amused. It was what she liked about Malone. He might have thwarted terrorists and saved the world, but he had no interest in the news of the moment.

'Jackie Wood got out on appeal.' Alex thought if she just said the words in a matter-of-fact way it would be easier. She was wrong. There was a familiar stinging behind her eyes.

'Ah,' he said again. He put down the kettle and put his arms round her, holding her tight.

'Sasha was in a bad way.' Her voice was muffled by his jumper. 'I tried to get Jez to go and stay the night, but I don't know if he will.'

'He'll go.' He kissed the top of her head. 'I'm sure he'll go.'

'I hope so. Though there's no reason why he should. Although sometimes I wonder—'

28

'What?'

'I don't know. Yes I do. I wonder if he still loves her in some way.'

'Well, you can go back in the morning and see how she is, or later, if you want to. I can stay here with Gus.'

She pushed herself gently out of his arms, dashing the tears off her cheeks. 'Thank you. Now I know why I like you.'

'And it explains why the telephone wouldn't stop ringing.'

'How do you know it was ringing?'

'I could hear it during the long and lonely wait for you outside the door.'

'Bugger.'

And on cue, it rang.

'Alex Devlin?'

'Yes,' she said. She could try and protect her sister but when it came to herself it wasn't so easy.

'Hi, I'm Ed Killingback from *The Post* and I wondered if I could have a few minutes of your time to talk about Jackie Wood and her winning her appeal today?'

'Do you know what, Ed, I really am not up to it.' She made her voice as cold as she could.

'It won't take long, and if you give me your story as an exclusive then you won't have to worry about the others, will you?' His young, eager tone wearied her. 'We could put you up in a hotel so you're not bothered by any of the red tops and—'

'Look,' she cut in, 'I know how it goes and I'm not interested. Please leave me alone.' She put down the phone with a satisfying clunk.

Her mobile began to belt out some grungy piece of music she didn't know, but it had been set by Gus as her ringtone. She looked at the screen. Unknown number. She sighed and turned it off.

Malone switched on the kettle.

'I'm sorry,' she said. 'This is exactly what you don't want.'

'What do you mean?'

She gave what she thought was a wry smile but probably looked more like a grimace. 'You're trying to avoid publicity now you've done your bit, and here I am, bringing it right back to your door.'

'Hmm,' he said, the kettle starting to boil. 'I reckon I'm used to the parasites knocking on the door, don't you think?'

'I guess. But I don't want you bothered by it.' What she meant was she didn't want him so spooked that he would leave her just as she was getting used to him in her life.

'I won't be.' He poured water onto the two teabags. 'How's Gus?'

Bringing her into the real world. She looked at the clock. Football practice tonight. 'He's okay, I think.' And yes, Malone knew about Gus's patchy history. 'Wants to go skiing with the school.'

Malone raised his eyebrows. 'Expensive stuff.'

'Hmm.'

'And?'

'And what?' Alex knew she sounded defensive, and it was none of his business anyway.

Malone drummed his fingers on the kitchen unit. 'And are you able to pay for it?'

'That, Malone,' she said, 'is nothing to do with you.' He handed her a cup of tea: dark brown builders'; just how she liked it. 'I'm going up to my study to see if Liz likes you.'

'I hope you gave me a good write-up.'

Alex stopped, her hand on the doorknob. 'Sympathetic, I think you'll find.'

'And anonymous?'

'Malone. What do you take me for? It's an "all names have been changed to protect their identities" article. As you well know.'

He grinned. 'Just checking.'

She gave a wry smile. 'I'll be back in a minute, help yourself to a biscuit or something. Read the paper. Do relaxing things.' Then a thought struck her. 'What are you doing here, Malone? Shouldn't you be going deep undercover into a brothel or something? Saving people, being a hero?'

He gave a slow, gentle smile. 'Don't be flippant. It's important stuff. Anyway, I've told you already, I've done my bit. Rescued all I can. Thought I'd come and say hallo.'

'And see if my piece about you is going to be published in the *Saturday Magazine*. Egotist.'

Malone shrugged his shoulders.

Alex sat down in her study, switched on the computer and waited for it to go through its warm-up routine. She thought about Malone, lounging on the sofa downstairs, reading the paper, all relaxed and smelling of his organic soap, and she thought of Sasha alone in her flat with only the television and a razor blade for company, and she knew where she would rather be. She couldn't say she felt guilty. How could she when guilt was so much a part of her life? There is only so much of it one can feel.

She and Malone had hit it off as soon as they met. And meeting had been an exhausting task involving clandestine calls to men and women who she was sure wore balaclavas just to answer the phone. Eventually she was deemed worthy of meeting the Man Who Saved The World From Harm, and she presumed they'd also checked out her credentials and whether or not she really was a journalist and not an undercover member of the Russian mafia or a gangland boss. Anyway, they met in a spit and sawdust pub south of the River Wensum. It was down an alleyway in an unprepossessing part of Norwich, and she'd had to muster all her reserves to walk into it without feeling intimidated.

She didn't know what she'd been expecting – someone in a beanie hat and Jesus sandals she thought was most likely – but sitting at the table in the corner underneath the portrait of the Queen (yes, they still exist in pubs, and yes, that's where she'd been told he would be sitting) was a man in his early forties – dark jeans, light blue shirt with white polka dots, trainers – nursing a pint.

31

She held out her hand. 'Hi, I'm Alex Devlin. You must be Malone.' Another conceit: last name only. She had resisted the temptation to introduce herself as Devlin.

To his credit he stood up, shook her hand, and offered her a drink. She was impressed, and it only got better from then on. And when they finally got round to it, the interview went well too. He told her what motivated him, the chances he'd taken, like befriending one of the women who was the girlfriend of the leader of the group he was supposed to be a part of. By 'befriending' Alex understood that he meant more than having a chat over a cup of coffee. He told her how he kept a flock of geese in the garden as they were the best alarm against intruders, how he had infiltrated the whole subculture of gangs. Although she thought he was mad to have taken some of the chances he had, she ended up admiring him. Oh, and sleeping with him. Pillow talk was quite good for in-depth personality pieces.

Of course, being the good interviewer she tried to be, she let him talk about himself and said very little about herself. But she found it . . . what – interesting? amazing? – that the gentle, mild-mannered man she got to know had been responsible for some of the major high profile arrests in recent months, after years of work. When she ventured to ask why he was letting himself be interviewed, he said he wanted to publicize what was going on as much as possible while keeping himself in the background. 'Look,' he said. 'We have to be lucky all the time. People who are trying to destroy us and our way of life have only got to get lucky once. That's why I do it.'

He also, he said, hated to see exploitation of people, and was hoping to be able to play some part in the war against human trafficking. Organized crime. Too much of that was going on. Kids brought in to be held as sex slaves. 'All driven by the drugs trade,' he said. 'This area is rife with drugs factories. Houses on urban streets, isolated farms, sheds, barns – whatever.' But for the moment, he told her, he was resting, he thought he'd done enough. At least for now.

The two-tone noise of the computer announced it was ready for business, and Alex let the emails download. She decided not to go on Facebook or Twitter; it would only push her blood pressure sky-high. That was the trouble with being a freelance – she felt she needed to be readily contactable, which was easy in the era of mobiles and social media, but, boy, when she wanted to lie low, it was bloody difficult.

The emails were, as she suspected, a mixture of clothes companies, train companies, and supermarkets advertising their wares, and requests for interviews about her and Sasha from various magazines. She deleted them all. But the one she wanted from her editor was there.

To: *Alex Devlin*
From: *Liz Henderson*
Subject: *Malone*

Hey Alex – loved your piece on Malone, strikes just the right balance and gives us a good rounded picture of the man. The photographs all add to the mood.

The photos had to be done in shadow or from the back to keep Malone's anonymity intact. At least he hadn't insisted on wearing his balaclava.

You'll be pleased to know we've found an early slot for it in the Saturday Magazine *– should go in two weeks time. Please invoice as usual.*

Alex let out a breath she didn't know she'd been holding. Thank the Lord; she'd be able to eat for a little longer, though she still wouldn't have enough to pay for the skiing trip. Worry began to gnaw away at her again.

Keep coming up with the ideas, Alex, we love your pieces.
Best
Liz

That lifted a little of the heavy weight that was permanently on her shoulders. It was hard making a living as a freelance, and she was lucky to have found such regular work with the magazine supplement. She'd even done news stories for the main daily paper to earn some extra cash. Sometimes she felt like a jack of all trades and master of none, but her in-depth features seemed to chime with the *Saturday Magazine*'s ethos.

She looked at the time of the email. Liz had sent it just after the news broke of Jackie Wood getting out of prison. Keep the ideas coming. Sure. Easier said than done sometimes. News features didn't just fall into your lap; you had to keep your eyes and ears open. Be receptive.

Jackie Wood.

The thought flashed into her head. A thoughtful piece on her time in prison, reflecting on her life; all that bollocks.

She shook herself. Where on earth had that idea come from? Left field, most definitely. She sat back in her chair.

Absolutely not.

She gazed out of the window onto the scrubby courtyard that passed for a garden, the gloom pierced by the lights in the kitchen. The terracotta pots she had planted with geraniums and lilies in the summer looked defeated. They bore cracks from the frost and the plants were withered bits of brown stick. If she'd had an ounce of foresight she would have brought them inside before the winter. The grass was patchy and mostly mud and even the silver birch looked tired of life.

Picking up a pencil, she began doodling, making notes. Suppose, just suppose for one minute that she did get to talk to Jackie Wood, what were the pros and cons?

Pros: she really wanted to talk to Jackie Wood. She never thought she'd be able to and yet here it was. The opportunity. The woman had been let out on a technicality and she was still guilty. At least, in Alex's eyes. She must know where Millie is buried. She could tell her. She would tell her. And that would bring peace of mind to her sister.

34

Cons: Jackie Wood probably wouldn't want to talk to her. Wouldn't want to talk to any journalist. Would she know who she was? Would she remember her; her name? Not necessarily. It was fifteen years ago and Sasha had captured all the headlines. Sasha and Jez. Jez had managed to keep Alex's name out of it as far as possible, and, because he was a police officer, that seemed to be a long way. And then she'd kept her head down, not courting any publicity. But she did give evidence at the trial, so that was living in cloud cuckoo land. Jackie Wood would know who she was, there was no doubt about that.

And what about Sasha? And Jez? How would they feel?

But she'd be doing it for them.

And then there was the main stumbling block – her editor would never wear it. Liz was bound to say she was too close to it; it wouldn't be fair; it wouldn't be balanced, and all that. In truth, Liz would be worried about bringing the Press Complaints Commission down on the *Saturday Magazine*'s head.

But, what if she talked to Jackie Wood, managed to write the article and then pitched it to Liz, what about that? She'd done that many times in her career – written an article on spec. And if Liz didn't want it, she could tout it around. It would be a financial risk, but someone, somewhere would take the article. And there would be no deception involved. All above board. She would declare her interest and sell it as a personal story. Everyone wanted a personal story.

The words went in and out of focus. It could be the best chance she had to get the story out of Jackie Wood; the best chance to find out what happened the day Harry and Millie were taken. From her garden. While she was supposed to be looking after them. The day their family had been torn apart; the day she had let her sister down. And if she knew why Jackie Wood and Martin Jessop had taken the twins away and murdered them, then maybe she could find some sort of peace.

And she would go some way to paying her dues to Sasha; get rid of that guilt that had been eating away at her for the last decade and a half.

She turned back to her computer and opened up a document file entitled 'Jessop and Wood'. She'd kept all links to the case in one tidy place on her computer. Links to stories; links to people who claimed they'd known Jessop and Wood were evil; she'd even kept a link to the clairvoyant who insisted he'd be able to lead them to Millie's body, for a fee, naturally. Alex never found out if he went to the police in the end. She stared at the file. She would be adding new links soon, to today's story, but first—

There it was. A picture and contact number for Wood's lawyer. She picked up her phone.

Something like adrenalin surged through her. She'd had fifteen years of being passive, of believing that justice would run its course, of thinking that she could run away from it all. Now she knew she'd been wrong all along. She punched in the number.

5

After that, it was all plain sailing. Alex got through to Jonathan Danby easily, and the conversation went exactly as she hoped. He had heard of her, had read a few of her articles and even enjoyed them, he said in that oleaginous manner she knew he would have. Loved the *Saturday Magazine,* he said. She crossed her fingers in the hope that he wasn't great friends with Liz or something. She wanted the interview to be a fait accompli before anyone could say no. However, all Danby said was that he'd met the owner of the paper and the accompanying magazine at a couple of events. That was all right. Clive Lambert had little idea of who his staff were, never mind the freelancers. So when Alex broached the subject of Jackie Wood and an exclusive interview with her, she could hear Danby thinking in pounds and pence and not worrying about anything else.

'It would be a fair depiction of Jackie and everything she'd been through?' he asked. Alex heard the tippety-tap of his pen on his desk, or more likely on his blotter on what she imagined was his mahogany desk.

'Yes,' she said. It had to be fair otherwise it wouldn't get published. It was just that she hoped to get so much more out of it.

'I would need to be there.'

'No, Mr Danby, I'm afraid it doesn't work like that.' Alex kept her voice even. 'It needs to be just me, and preferably somewhere she feels comfortable and relaxed. I want her to open up.'

'I see.' She heard him breathing down the phone. 'And what's in it for my client?'

'The magazine can pay its standard rate.' She named the usual figure and crossed her fingers. It would be worth it to confront the woman who had brought such misery to their lives. 'But that's all. What she will get is publicity, which she would be able to use to her advantage.'

'She is innocent you know. Of conspiracy to murder.'

'As you say, Mr Danby.'

'We'd want that underlined in the piece.'

Alex gripped the phone. 'I can only work with what I get.'

'It would be sympathetic to her?'

If she wasn't careful she would break the damn phone. 'It all depends how she comes over. Another reason for talking just to me with no one else around.'

'Actually Ms Devlin, that's a very good reason for me to be there. I wouldn't want her to say something . . . inappropriate.'

Alex let the silence hang.

'You realize the media are this close . . .' She imagined him holding his forefinger and thumb apart so there was hardly any space between them '. . . to being gagged. And that includes you, Ms Devlin.'

'I'm sure,' she replied.

'And the fact you're Sasha Devlin's sister?'

Damn. How long had he been waiting to say that? Foolish of her not to expect it.

'Makes it all the more personal, Mr Danby. Obviously. There would be no deception involved. It'll be written as a first-hand account of meeting the woman who had been accused of being involved in the murder of my niece and nephew. And acquitted, of course.'

'Of course.' A heavy sigh came across the line. 'Leave it with me. I don't think it'll happen, though. She wants to keep a low profile. But I will be in contact with her and let you know, okay?'

'That would be great, Mr Danby, I appreciate it.'

Alex gave him her number before finishing the call and turning her phone off again, sapped by the effort of remaining civil throughout the conversation, but also strangely exhilarated.

'Hey you,' Malone's voice drifted up the stairs. 'Am I going to see you at all?'

She put her computer to sleep and went down to the kitchen. 'Sorry, I was just trying to fix up my next interviewee.'

Malone looked up from the paper he was reading. 'Oh? Am I allowed to know who?'

She put her arms around him and her chin on his shoulder. 'No.'

He turned and looked at her. 'Any particular reason?'

'Nope. Just the way I work.'

For some reason she wanted to keep it to herself. Was it because somewhere deep down she knew her motives for wanting to interview Jackie Wood were more than just to help Sasha? She wanted, she *needed* to see the woman up close and personal; to look in her eyes and see her guilt. Or perhaps, she reasoned, it was because the fewer people who knew, the less likely it was there would be a slip-up that would give away the woman's whereabouts.

'Look, I've made you a sandwich.'

He pushed a plate towards her and she realized she was hungry. In her efforts to get Sasha to eat she had neglected to eat anything herself. Cheese and pickle. Perfect.

The front door slammed. Gus was home. Alex looked at the clock – he was later than normal.

'Hi darling,' she called out, knowing she had to tell him that Jackie Wood was out of jail. Nothing. Just the sound of his size tens thudding up the stairs.

She looked at Malone. That was unusual. Gus normally came in and gave her at least a civilized grunt before disappearing into his lair.

'I'd leave him be,' said Malone. 'He's a teenager, probably wants a bit of privacy.'

She put down the sandwich. 'Nonetheless, I've got to go and talk to him.'

She went upstairs and knocked on his door. No response. She knocked again, harder this time, in case he was plugged into his iPod.

'Come in.'

Alex didn't think she'd ever get used to her little boy's gruff new voice.

As she went in, he minimized the web pages he'd been looking at and turned to her. She switched on the light. 'Did you bring the letter home about paying for the skiing by instalments?' she asked.

'What's that? A sweetener?' His lip curled.

'Gus?'

'Why didn't you tell me, Mum? About the woman? Jackie Wood.'

Alex suppressed a sigh as she went further into his room, stepped over the discarded books and DVDs that littered the floor, and sat down on the bed. She patted the cover. 'Come here.'

Avoiding her eyes, Gus sat down next to her.

She put her arm around him, trying to ignore the *tick tock* of the clock on the wall and the shock of stale booze on his breath. He leaned into her. She could feel the bones of his shoulder, his arm. Had he always been this thin?

'They said at school that she was out. Someone had seen it on their phone. They said her conviction had been overturned so that meant she hadn't had anything to do with it and so probably the bloke – Martin Jessop – was innocent as well, and we were all shitty liars.' His eyes glittered with unshed tears.

'She is out, Gus, but her conviction was said to be unsafe.'

'What does that mean?' he muttered.

'It means that they found some discrepancy in the evidence that was used to convict her of conspiracy—'

'What evidence?'

40

'Forensic evidence. Something to do with particles of dirt found at the scene and the particles found on her clothing in the flat hallway.'

Gus ran his fingers through his hair. 'You mean—'

Alex winced. 'Yes, sweetheart, where little Harry's body was found. Gus,' she knew she had to tread carefully, 'have you been drinking?'

He wiped his sleeve over his face. 'Bit.'

'In the afternoon?'

'Why, wouldn't you mind if it was in the evening?' he shot back.

She rolled her eyes, hoping to defuse the situation. 'Don't be smart with me. You know I would, that's not the point.'

'Look, I was stopped outside the school gates by some reporter scum who wanted to do an interview, take my picture and all that.' He plucked at the sleeve of his jumper. 'And I don't want it, Mum. I don't, like, want it to be anything to do with me. I was only a baby. I don't even remember Harry and Millie.' He sniffed. 'But they kept asking and asking and saying we were liars, that you were a liar. And I wanted to get away.'

'I'm sorry, love.' She pulled him closer.

'And then a couple of mates asked me if I wanted a drink.'

'Mates?' she asked, more sharply than she intended. Please don't let him have fallen in with a bad crowd again.

'Yes, mates.' He glared at her. She decided to leave it, for now. 'Anyway,' he carried on, 'I thought you'd be more concerned about the reporters than the half pint of lager I'd had.'

'I am concerned about that,' she said, trying to believe it really was just a half pint of lager. 'They had no right to stop you and talk to you. What did you say?'

'Nothing.'

'How did they know you had anything to do with her?'

He shrugged. 'Dunno. But there are a couple of them at the gate now.'

'What?' Alex jumped up and went over to the window. Sure enough, a man in a shiny grey suit and yellow tie and a woman in a black shaggy coat were standing just outside the gate under the streetlight and looking at her front door. Both of them on mobile phones and having animated conversations. She wondered which of them would be the first to come up with an offer. Vultures.

'Bugger,' she said, stepping back from the window before they saw her, heart thumping, 'I thought they wouldn't find us.'

'Come on, Mum, you know you can find anyone these days through the internet.'

Irritation crawled up her spine. She knew that. She damn well knew that, so why hadn't she given it a thought? 'They'll go away as soon as they realize we're not giving them anything. Or until they get cold or tired or hungry, or all three.' She half drew the curtain.

'How's Aunty Sasha?'

It was her turn to shrug. 'You know, coping.'

'Badly?'

She nodded. 'Yes. I've just got to support her through this.'

'We will, Mum. We will.'

Alex looked at her little boy. Taller than her with wisps of facial hair and that deep voice. 'Thank you, sweetheart.' She resisted the urge to lean over and kiss his cheek.

'So are you going to do anything about her?'

'Her?'

'Jackie Wood?'

'I—' No. She wasn't going to tell him. 'Look, there's nothing we can do. She'll be whisked to some safe house somewhere until the furore's died down and then she might change her identity and find somewhere new to live. The best thing we can do is to help Sasha through this.'

'Mum?'

'Yes?'

'What can you remember about that day?'

Alex drew him back into her arms and hugged him close to her, resting her chin on the top of his head. 'Oh, love, it's difficult to describe.'

'Try. Please.'

She closed her eyes. 'I remember the police coming round, making lots of notes. Everyone going to look for them. Not finding them.'

'They were taken from our garden, weren't they?'

A spear of pain lanced Alex and the guilt threatened to over-whelm her. 'Yes. Yes they were.'

She was responsible.

6

Kate shoved the pills to the back of the bathroom cupboard and closed the door. Her head was pounding; the picture on the health centre's telly of Jackie Wood on the steps of the High Court, smiling, going round and round in her head. The smug lawyer. The sentence quashed. A murderer's accomplice set free.

She thought back to when the judge had sentenced Wood and Jessop to life imprisonment for the murders of Harry and Millie Clements, and how she'd felt as though she could breathe again. Although she'd been the one to find Harry's little body all squashed up in the suitcase, abandoned behind a bin in a shitty lay-by as if he was just a piece of rubbish, she hadn't had anything more to do with the investigation, apart from celebrating in the pub when they arrested Wood and Jessop.

She'd had her day in court, of course, when she stood in the witness box and told the judge exactly what had happened the morning she had found the little boy, reliving it in her head as she kept her voice even and unemotional. She'd glared across at the pair of them in the dock; wanted them to look her in the eye so she could stare them down. But they didn't give her the satisfaction; just kept examining their hands, Wood occasionally

44

dabbing at her eyes with a white handkerchief edged with blue. Funny how she could remember the little things. And then she'd been in the public gallery when the professor of dirt and stones or whatever he was delivered his damning evidence. The unusual type of soil and gravel found in the corridor of the flats in Sole Bay matched that found inside the suitcase that had contained the body – that was the gist of it, and the jury bought it, every single damning word. So did they all, to be fair.

And now, fifteen years on, the great professor had been discredited. The evidence he had given in another trial had been called into question five years previously. After that, the convictions tumbled, and it was only a matter of time before the Jessop–Wood trial was scrutinized. And yes, the evidence was called into question. Unsafe conviction. The gravel and soil could have come from several places in Sole Bay. So Wood was now out in the community.

Kate found herself obsessed with Wood. She didn't believe for one moment that Jessop and Wood were not guilty, and she knew her colleagues would be of a like mind. There was no question of it being opened as a cold case, and it wouldn't be too long before the force would trot out the line: 'We're not looking for anyone else in this matter.' Subtext: they did it, and Jackie Wood has got away with it.

She turned on the cold tap and splashed her face, remembering too late the make-up she had put on earlier that morning. Bloody hell, she'd have panda eyes now. Opening up the cupboard again she took out her make-up remover wipes and began to clean her face so she could redo her mask.

'Is that you Kate?'

A door slammed as Chris's voice floated up the stairs. Her hand stopped its cleaning. Damn. What was he doing home? She thought he'd gone to source more wood for the table and chairs he was making.

'Kate?'

She put down the make-up remover wipes and gripped the basin, head bowed. Then she dragged in a deep breath and pasted a smile on her face. If she made herself smile, it would sound in her voice.

'Hallo sweetie,' she said, emerging from the bathroom and going downstairs. 'I thought you'd be out for most of the day.'

Chris enveloped her in a hug. With her nose pressed into his thick woollen jumper she breathed in the familiar smells of freshly-cut wood and linseed oil. There was a prickling in the back of her nose. 'Hah. So your secret lover could come and go with impunity.'

'Something like that,' she mumbled, not wanting to think about the visit to the doctor. 'What about the wood?'

'Bloke I needed to see won't be back until this afternoon. Bit of a wasted journey.'

She lifted her head up. 'Didn't you check he was going to be there?'

'No. I had some other stuff to do and I fancied a drive so took a chance.' He smiled down at her, his cornflower blue eyes wrinkling at the corners. 'Is that okay?'

''Course it is.'

Typical of Chris. Freewheeling; not worried about what other people thought; always able to go with the flow. Which was probably why she married him – a good contrast to her tendency to be uptight.

'Anyway, what are you doing home?'

'Meeting my lover, what else?' She laughed lightly. 'Have you had anything to eat? Do you fancy some toast?'

He grabbed her by the shoulders and planted a kiss on her lips. 'Toast sounds good. Unless you fancy something else . . .' He looked up the stairs and then back at her. Cocked his head to one side.

She thought of the pills she had got from the doctor and the pill she took every day, both shoved in the back of the cupboard, and felt guilty and irritated at the same time. She pushed him away. 'No time for that. I must eat and get going. So, toast?' She tried to make her voice sound bright.

Chris held up his hands. 'Whoa. Sorry. Just a thought. Toast would be great.'

Kate kept her head down – she couldn't bear to see the hurt look on his face. Instead, she went to the bread bin and took the loaf out, trying to undo the red plastic tape. 'Bugger, bugger, why do they wrap bloody bread like this.' She took a knife out of the drawer and started to hack at the tape.

'Careful, don't hurt yourself.'

'I won't,' she snapped, taking a couple of slices from the now open packet. 'See? It's done. But the sodding bread's mouldy.'

Chris was beside her, taking the bread out of her hands. 'It's only a bit of green along the edges. It'll be fine when I've got peanut butter and jam on the top.'

'Up to you.' Kate reached up into a cupboard and took down the pack of muesli, shaking some into a bowl, looking crossly at the dried fruit, seeds, and oats. 'Urgh, why can't I like this stuff?'

'Because it's rabbit food.'

'That's lettuce.'

'Well, some animal that eats oats and fruit and enjoys it.'

'Good for me though.' She poured milk out of the bottle onto it.

'Sometimes it's good to have things you enjoy.'

Kate looked at him sharply, then caught her breath at the sadness of his expression. She put down her bowl and went over to him, putting her arms around his solid waist. 'I'm sorry,' she said. 'I'm just a bit twitchy.'

'Any particular reason?'

The toast popped up and Chris began to slather it with butter. Kate's irritation flared up again. 'You'll give yourself a heart attack if you're not careful.'

'At least I will have enjoyed myself,' he said mildly.

'What are you saying?'

'Nothing. Nothing at all.' Out came the peanut butter and jam. He sighed. 'I don't know what's eating you this morning. I'm beginning to think I did disturb you and your lover.'

All the fight went out of Kate and she sat down. What the fuck was she doing, trying to pick a fight with him? 'I'm sorry, Chris. It was something I heard on the news today that's made me feel a bit out of sorts.' Understatement of the year.

'Oh?'

'A woman called Jackie Wood has been released from prison. Her sentence was quashed—'

'I heard about that on the radio. While I was driving. Put away for – what was it – conspiracy to murder or something? Her and some guy called Martin Jessop had murdered two little kids, is that right? I was abroad at the time so don't remember it really. But why has that made you so—'

'Bad-tempered? Irritable?'

He grinned. 'If you put it like that, yes.'

She sighed. How much to say? She had never told him about finding little Harry, about eventually holding him in her arms after the photographs, the examination of his little body, the forensics that had been carried out, and about the sheer and utter helplessness she had felt. She had never wanted to feel his pity. 'I was involved in that case.'

'Oh?' Chris began to eat his toast.

'Worked on it. Had to give evidence in court. It was a bit . . .' She hesitated. 'Upsetting.'

'But it was, what? Sixteen years ago?'

'Fifteen.'

'Right. Not your case now.'

'No. But I feel for the family. They must be pretty upset to see her coming out like that.'

'I'm sure. But it's not for you to get involved, is it? I mean, not personally.'

She shrugged. 'I just keep wondering what they're feeling, thinking. I wonder if I ought to go and see them.'

'Because you were on the case all that time ago? You were only a PC then, weren't you?'

Kate didn't heed the warning note of exasperation in Chris's voice. 'Yes, it was one of my first jobs after months on the beat.' She spooned some of the muesli into her mouth. 'I've had enough of this.' She walked over to the sink and dumped her bowl in it with a clatter. 'I ought to get to the station, I've got plenty to do.'

Chris stood and took hold of her hand. 'Can't you give it a few more minutes? You're out all the hours God sends and I'd really like to talk.'

'We do talk.'

'Properly, I mean. Without you falling asleep on me.' He smiled. A serious smile.

'I can't help it, you know. It's tough out there.' She shook her hand free of Chris's.

'Hardly the mean streets of New York though, is it?'

'You'd be surprised. And New York isn't like it used to be. If you listened to the news more often you'd know that.' She cringed inwardly at her own words.

'Kate—'

'No. I really do have to go.'

'Why is it you're so damned keen to interfere in everyone else's lives but keep our life together at arm's-length?' Chris asked, his tone deceptively mild.

'Interfering?' Kate let a note of self-righteous anger into her voice. 'What? You mean my job? I thought you were proud of me? I thought it was part of why you love me—'

'I'm sorry. I shouldn't have said that. I am proud of you, of course I am, because you're you. But I care about us, you and me. Not drugs or prostitutes or murderers. You and me, Kate. You and me. And sometimes—'

Kate stood still. 'Sometimes what?' It was like picking a scab.

Chris picked up his toast again. 'One day, Kate, we're going to have to talk about this. I mean, really talk.'

Kate went to the door. 'Chris?' Suddenly she wanted to tell him about the trip to the doctor's, the pills, the possibility of counselling, of finding Harry's body, how it had made her feel.

'Mmm?' He appeared to be engrossed in the newspaper that had been lying on the table, and he didn't look up.

Anger surged through her once more. 'I'll see you later,' she said.

7

Alex pulled the front door closed behind her and hunched down into her coat, trying to avoid the worst of the east wind and the rain lashing at her face. She loved Sole Bay with its jumble of terraces, semis, and mansions, and the B. & B.s, and the chi-chi shops that sold everything from designer clothes to plastic windmills, but, God, how she hated the winter weather. The wind and rain whipped off the grey North Sea, across the sand, around the beach huts, straight at anyone who dared get in the way. In the summer, the streets were clogged with visitors – the little train running up and down the pier doing good business; barrels of beer were transported to the pubs by a dray pulled by shire horses, and holidaymakers whiled away the day on the beach. But at this time of year the few tourists spent their money in the steamy tea shops or art galleries rather than brave the outside.

The wind pulled at her as she walked along the coast road, out of the main town, passed scrappy grass with its 'No Ball Playing' notices and the pub that still sold 'Austerity Lunches'. She was heading to her favourite part of Sole Bay – the trashy harbour end, with its caravan park, dodgy prefab houses growing shells and beach paraphernalia in the gardens, and the black rickety sheds advertising fresh fish for sale. Today, the boats were tied up in the harbour, the fishermen not foolhardy enough to brave the North Sea conditions. There would be no boxes of slippery silver fish or snapping crabs until the weather had calmed.

The call from Jonathan Danby had come a few days after she first spoke to him. Days that were spent going to and from Sasha's, making sure she ate something, even if it was only a bowl of soup. Days of going over and over the whys and the wherefores of Jackie Wood's release from prison. Alex tried her best to sound soothing and caring, but however much you love someone, however much you care, after a while your patience runs out. She couldn't risk her sister doing anything else stupid so she just gritted her teeth and carried on caring. Sasha's house became ever more claustrophobic. The one good thing was that Jez did come up trumps and was spending each evening there, and the occasional night. She managed to avoid him nicely.

So when Danby called, she was ready to do anything, go anywhere.

'This'll be a sympathetic look at her life?'

Not this again. She took a deep breath. 'As I've already told you, it'll be an honest one. That's how I've got my reputation. Whether it's sympathetic or not is up to her, in a way. I write as I see it.' She held her breath.

'Fee?'

'As we agreed.'

An inhalation and then a sigh. Smoking, Alex reckoned.

'Look, I'd be lying if I said I was happy about this, I'm not. But Miss Wood seems keen, for some reason. Says she likes your work.' Sure she does. 'Will only talk to you. Doesn't want me there.' Alex closed her eyes. All above board. Now there was no reason for Liz to get the jitters and say no. This interview could be gold dust.

'So the answer is yes, but with certain restrictions.'

'I don't do restrictions,' Alex said. Ground rules have to be set from the outset, parameters defined, otherwise you end up dancing to your subject's tune, and that just doesn't work. Alex

51

knew she'd done the song and dance thing with Malone, but that was an exception.

She heard the crackle of cellophane; the flick of a lighter, another inhale. 'Jackie doesn't want anyone to know where she is.'

'I understand that.' The dance continued.

'You know what this country's like; there'll be a lynch mob after her before you can say "not guilty". The *Mail* will be writing editorials about the death penalty and all the other red tops will be baying for blood.'

'Right.' She balled her fist. But she is guilty, Alex wanted to shout at him down the phone. She was found guilty. She was only let off on a technicality, some obscure legal thing; the expert witness making a fuck-up, being discredited. Alex had believed him, they all had. And she didn't see any reason to change her mind now.

'You won't have to travel far,' said Danby. 'She wanted to go somewhere she knew. Figured it would be easier for her.'

'So . . .?'

'She's in your neck of the woods, as it happens. Suffolk.'

Alex closed her eyes. She was so close. 'Fine,' was all she said.

Eventually she and Danby managed to thrash it out. She was to tell no one where she was going, who she was interviewing – apart from her editor, she lied – and for that Jackie Wood was going to grant Alex one or two mornings of her time.

Deal done.

It was half-term and Gus was at home. Alex had been trying to get him to do some schoolwork; to help her with shopping; to get him chatting to Malone: anything to keep him away from trouble. Smelling the drink on his breath had unnerved her, as had his run-in with a reporter. She didn't want him to be sucked into something else he couldn't deal with. And she had started paying for his skiing trip, crossing her fingers at the same time.

He was in the sitting room on his Playstation, swatting zombies. Malone was due round in a couple of hours.

'Gus?'

'Mmm?'

'I'm just off out.'

'Mmm.'

'Malone'll be here soon.'

'What to— gotcha!' She saw a splat of red on the television screen.

'Not to babysit you, no. He's come to see me, but I'm just off to interview someone for the magazine.'

'Anyone good? Yesss.' His fist punched the air. 'More points.'

She hesitated a little too long.

Gus took his eyes off the undead. 'Mum? You're looking shifty. C'mon, who is it then?'

Should she lie? Tell a half-truth? What? She sat on the arm of the chair. Tried to ruffle his hair. He jerked his head away. 'Listen, Gus, it's Jackie Wood.'

He turned away, his eyes now glued to the screen. More splats of red, more zombies' heads exploded.

'Why?' His voice was flat, his knuckles white where he gripped the games console.

'I think it could be useful, helpful even.'

'What are you going to ask her?'

She shrugged. 'You know, the obvious really.'

He stared at the screen. Even the undead were motionless.

At last he turned and looked at her, blinking slowly, coming out of zombie-land again. 'You've got your coat on.'

'Yes. Walking, saving petrol.' Bloody hell, she could have bitten her tongue.

He nodded. 'So she's nearby. Come back to the scene of the crime, as it were. How can she do that? How can she come and live here, of all places? Surely there should be some sort of law against it or something? I dunno. Anything?'

'Gus—'

'I know, I know, you can't tell me. Confidentiality and all that. But I don't reckon you'd make much of a detective.'

'What do you mean?'

'Didn't take me long to suss out she's come crawling back to town.'

Alex attempted a laugh, but it sounded hollow. 'Please don't say anything, Gus. Part of my contract is that no one knows where she is.' And she'd made a right fuck-up of that already.

'What are you going to ask her?'

She was on firmer ground now. 'I'll begin by asking about her time inside, you know, just to get her confidence. Nod sympathetically and all that. Ask about her childhood. How she met Martin Jessop. Draw her out, that's the plan.'

'Do you get to ask about, you know?' He swallowed, his eyes darting around the room. Not for the first time she cursed the fact that her boy had grown up defined by the murder of his cousins. But she believed in telling the truth. What was the point in shielding him when he would find out another way? And probably in a badly thought-out muddled way from his mates.

She gave a small smile. 'I hope so.'

Gus shuddered. 'I can't think of anything worse,' he said, turning back to his game. 'She doesn't deserve to be out, free, does she?'

Boom. Thud. Splat. Zombies started hitting the deck again.

'She won her freedom, sweetheart.'

'It was what? – quashed – isn't that what they say? Doesn't mean she's innocent.'

'That's the way it works.'

He sighed and turned to look at her. 'Is this gonna make you even worse?'

'Even worse? What do you mean?'

'Come on, Mum. You know what I mean. You don't let me have a life now. And if there's some murderer roaming the streets—'

'It's only because I care and want to keep you safe. Anyway, the courts say she's not a murderer.'

'Mum. I've said this before. Harry was killed fifteen years ago. Fifteen, you know? And Millie? Who knows what happened to her, but it happened. A long time ago. It wasn't my fault and it wasn't yours.'

Alex closed her eyes and let the guilt invade her body.

'Mum? Mum? Are you listening to me?'

She opened her eyes. 'Yes, of course I am.'

'No, you're not.' He turned back to the screen, disgust evident on his face. 'You never do.'

Alex looked at him. Did she have any idea what her own son was thinking or feeling? She saw more than the beginnings of fluff on his chin and wondered who was going to teach him to shave. Maybe he had already done it, guided by his friends. She ached for him inside and, for the first time, wondered at her wisdom in going it alone after she'd got pregnant. Not that she'd any choice, as the one-night-stand father hadn't wanted to know. But still.

His hands were busy with the controller. 'Besides. Me and my mates think they should bring the death penalty back. For murderers of kids. They don't deserve to live. Do they, Mum?' Another zombie bit the dust.

What should she say? Teenagers saw things in black and white – there was no grey or in-between in their world. But then, how could she disagree with him when she didn't? For most of her life she had been vehemently against the death penalty, arguing that it was plain murder by the state, and that the sign of a civilized society was the way it treated criminals. But that was then. Fifteen years ago she changed and believed nothing short of hanging would have been good enough for Martin Jessop and the same for Jackie Wood, even though she was only found guilty of being an accessory. But the pair of them made the family go through a long and tortuous court case, which completely destabilized Sasha. There had been no rest for any of them; every day they had to live with what had happened.

Now she hated her, Jackie Wood, more than him. That woman could have stopped Jessop. She could have not given him an alibi and saved them weeks of misery, of the police hunting for the bodies.

But although Jessop was dead, the guilt was still alive in her. Her house. Her garden. Her fault.

If Jackie Wood had any self-respect, any at all, she would reveal where Millie was buried.

'Do you ever wonder what happened to Millie?' Gus's voice broke into her thoughts.

She took his hand and squeezed it. 'All the time.'

'Ask her, Mum, won't you?'

She nodded, her throat all at once too full to speak.

8

The rain had eased off by the time Alex reached the caravan site at the harbour end, but still she pulled her scarf up around her face. The rain might have stopped, but the wind was still strong enough to make skin sore, especially when combined with the salt from sea spray. The sea looked rough and wild, too, and you couldn't tell where the greyness of the sky bleached into the greyness of the sea. Plenty of white horses rolled into the shore, only broken up by the groynes that stretched out like witches' fingers into the water. Seagulls swooped and screeched overhead, and in the distance the smooth, ping-pong dome of the nuclear power station rose like a modernist sculpture.

The caravan site, rather obviously called 'Harbour's End' was, as it said on the tin, at the end of the harbour road and opposite the lifeboat station. At its entrance were the public toilets.

She looked at the piece of paper that had the directions to the caravan on it; the cold air making her shiver. Number forty-four. Down the main bit of road, turn second left, and it was at the end of the row.

The wind moaned in and around the lines of static caravans. She saw the odd person in the distance, tending to the outside of the vans, but generally it was very quiet. A ghost town.

Jackie Wood's caravan, which was cream and green with a lick of decay, just like the other hundred or so, was opposite the river that ran into the sea, with a good view of the fishermen's ramshackle huts and the row upon row of fishing boats, some from Lowestoft, some from Aldeburgh, most from Sole Bay. There were net curtains at the windows, and a couple of terracotta pots either side of the door, sporting fronds of grass and dead twigs. Alex stopped, realizing she was shivering not just from the cold, but also because she felt lost, a bit frightened even. What was she expecting Jackie Wood to say? Come on, she told herself, treat this like any other interview.

She thought back to the last time she'd seen Wood, before the court case. She was being interviewed on the News Channel – *News 24* as it was then – sitting in her flat, Martin Jessop by her side. Mr Jessop from upstairs. Nice flats they were too; a well done Georgian conversion in a decent part of town. Nobody wanted to rent them after Jackie Wood and Martin Jessop were arrested for murder. They were holiday lets now; completely repainted, redecorated, rehabilitated. There was a campaign to get the whole block demolished and a memorial garden planted. But the Sole Bay Society put their boots in and saved the Georgian building. It didn't really matter to Alex – Georgian building or memorial garden – it was still where her nephew and niece had been murdered.

When they first went missing, there she was, Jackie Wood, sitting next to him – the murderer – and saying what a tragedy it was. How the community had to pull together, that they were pulling together, and were organizing searches of the town, the beaches, the dunes, the harbour. The local and national media were hungry for interviewees about 'the situation', and Jackie Wood and Martin Jessop fitted the willing bill. Wood, the local librarian; Jessop, a lecturer at the college in Ipswich. There was much speculation about their relationship. Again, something else the media wanted to romanticize; document every twist and turn.

If only they had known there was a much better story than that.

If she closed her eyes, Alex could still see her, head cocked slightly to one side, the furrowed forehead, the oh-so-sympathetic expression. He, meanwhile, just looked at his shoes. Then, suddenly, he gazed at the camera and shook his head.

'They were lovely children,' he said. 'So polite. Full of life.'

Past tense.

And she remembered knowing then; knowing absolutely that they were the ones who had taken the twins.

When they were arrested, the feeding frenzy really started.

'She is in,' said a voice from behind her, interrupting her memories. 'She's always in.'

Alex looked over her shoulder. A woman of about thirty with a cigarette in one hand, mug in the other, was standing in the doorway of the caravan opposite. The dark roots were showing in her hair, and her face had lost the fresh-skin look of youth. Alex wondered what she was doing in a caravan on the Suffolk coast in the middle of winter.

'I came this way looking for work.' The woman had read her mind. 'Thought it might be easier here than in the city.'

She wondered which city she meant. 'And has it been easier?' she asked.

The woman shrugged. 'No, not really. But I have got a few shifts at the Tesco's on the high street, so I reckon that's better than nothing.'

Alex nodded. The idea of a new supermarket in the middle of the town had caused a lot of local consternation when planning permission was granted. There were petitions, and placards, and letters to the planning office and the local MP, and God knows who, but it had lumbered forward like a boulder rolling down a hill squashing everything in its path.

'Anyway,' the woman went on, 'give her a knock.'

'Thanks,' Alex said.

'Do you know her?'

'Sort of.' She managed to give a rictus smile.

'She looks familiar.'

'Really?'

The woman shrugged. 'Tell her she can come over and have a coffee if she wants. Wouldn't want her feeling lonely here.'

Alex nodded. 'Okay.'

The woman shut her door.

Alex swallowed. Her mouth was dry and her heart was thudding. She pressed her fist against her breastbone. 'You can do this,' she whispered. The enormity of her actions had just dawned on her. She was about to come face-to-face with the woman who was – whatever some bloody judge said – complicit in the murder of Harry and Millie. And she was supposed to be carrying out an interview with Jackie Wood when all she wanted to do was to shake out the answer to the question that had haunted her family for more than a decade – where was Millie buried?

And why shouldn't she? There was no need to talk to Jackie Wood for any length of time; she could even ditch the idea of an article. Nothing lost, except more of her dwindling savings. And she would have had the chance to ask her about Millie. On another level, Alex was curious about the woman; about what had made her tick then and what made her tick now. How she could sit and blatantly lie to everybody; the lies she was still continuing to tell now?

Let out on a technicality. That was not innocence.

Squaring her shoulders, she lifted her hand up to knock on the door.

It opened before her hand made contact.

'I saw you standing outside. Alex.' Jackie Wood's voice was pitched a little too high and had the soft Suffolk burr that Alex remembered from the courtroom – both characteristics had been blurred by the television microphones. What was more startling was that the long black hair she had seen on the screen was now cut short and dyed blonde. Jackie Wood was dressed in an off-white fluffy fleece, faded, ill-fitting black jeans, and brown slippers with pom-poms on the toes. She was even more diminished than she had seemed on television and her skin had not yet regained a healthy colour. Alex guessed the woman opposite was telling the truth; Jackie Wood didn't venture out much.

She was so very *ordinary*.

Then Alex noticed the scar down one side of her face, the skin puckered, as though it had been sewn up by a child.

Jackie Wood blinked at her. 'Come in. I've been expecting you for ages. Let's not talk on the doorstep.' She opened the door a little wider while keeping herself inside the caravan.

For a moment, Alex was outside of her body. One part of her looking at what she was doing and wondering how the hell she could do it, the other part of her relishing the idea of talking to the woman. She wanted to sniff the air, see if she could smell evil.

Not evil, but fustiness. The smell of a tin box that rarely had its windows or doors opened. Stale cigarette smoke, too. Grease, fat; the lingering smell of fast food. The lightness in her head dissolved.

'Take a seat.' Jackie Wood waved to a cloth-covered bench to one side of the caravan. The table in front of it was crowded with papers, a plate with a piece of half-chewed toast on it, and an overflowing ashtray. Some sort of convector heater was pumping out warm air. She sat on the bench, sliding round behind the table.

'Sorry about the mess,' said Jackie Wood, whipping away the plate and putting it into the tiny sink. 'I should have cleared up before you came.'

'It's okay,' said Alex, noticing that she had quite an array of daily newspapers, from *The Times* to the *Daily Star*. Again, Jackie Wood saw her looking and began gathering them up into a pile.

'Something to do, isn't it?' she said, nodding towards the papers. 'I like to see whether there are any stories in them about me. Since I came out. Sometimes, you know, they get the facts about me wrong. One of the papers kept saying I was forty-four years old. I'm not. I'm forty-three. It's horrible reading really personal things about yourself in newspapers. And it's even worse when they're lies. Do you think I should write to the editor?' She stood still, looking at Alex, blinking slowly. Then she turned away and dumped the papers onto the floor with a thump. 'Are you warm enough? I've taken to wearing these thick fleece things, keeps the wind out.' She plucked at the material. 'It's so bloody cold in this part of the world.'

'Wind off the Urals,' Alex said, for the sake of saying something after the sudden change of subject.

'That's what they say.' Jackie Wood was nervous. Probably as nervous as she was, Alex realized. 'I'll make the coffee.' Pom-poms flapping, she made the short journey over to the sink, filled the kettle and set it on the top of the cooker.

Alex shrugged off her coat and put it down beside her, looking around the caravan. Not much to see, really. A small kitchenette, cupboards above the sink and cooker; a corridor that she guessed led to the bedrooms – two?– , and bathroom. A couple of paintings on the walls. One was a view of beach huts. The other of a few lonely sheep in the middle of a snowy field. Both had the corpses of insects preserved behind the glass.

There was silence while they both waited for the kettle to boil. 'Here we are.'

Jackie Wood set a tray down on the table. On the tray was a cafetière of coffee and two plain, white mugs. There was a plate with chocolate digestives. A jug of milk. A bowl of sugar. She hovered.

'Shall I pour?' Alex asked.

Jackie Wood nodded. 'Please.'

She pressed the plunger of the cafetière, hearing that pleasing sucking sound, then poured out two mugs of coffee. 'Milk? Sugar?'

Jackie Wood nodded again. 'Lots of milk. Three sugars. Please.'

Alex did the honours, wondering when the Mad Hatter was going to turn up. 'Here you go.'

'Thanks.' Jackie Wood lowered herself onto a plastic chair.

Alex took a sip of coffee and then reached into her bag, taking out her digital recorder. 'I hope it's okay to record our interview, Jackie.' She tried not to stumble over her name. She had never thought of her as 'Jackie', only 'that woman' or 'the murderer's accomplice', or 'Jackie Wood', both names together. To call her Jackie was implying an intimacy that she didn't feel. But then that's what she did all the time; that was her job. She had to think of this as another job. Money. Cash. Gus's skiing trip. Millie's grave. No, not that, not yet.

'I know who you are, you know.' The words were spoken quietly.

Alex switched on the recorder then looked up at her. 'Really?'

'I've known ever since Jonny Danby told me you were coming.' She smiled. 'You think I'd forget you? Sasha's sister?'

Alex held up her hand. 'Don't,' she said.

'Don't what?'

'Just . . . don't. Her name.'

'What? Sasha? What should I call her?'

'Not her name. After what you and Jessop did. It does not give you the right to call her by her first name.'

She looked startled. 'What Martin did. Not me. Not me. Anyway, I looked you up. Googled you. Found out about your work. I'd never read any.'

It didn't surprise Alex that Danby had lied. '*She likes your work.*' Please.

Jackie Wood smiled. 'We didn't get too many upmarket newspapers in High Top. And when we did, someone had always nicked the supplements.' She shifted herself and reached into the back pocket of her jeans, pulling out a squashed packet of cigarettes. 'Do you mind?' she asked, pulling one out and putting it between her cracked lips. 'Only it's a hard habit to break. Something to do when you're banged up.'

Alex shook her head, wanting one herself.

'Here.' Jackie Wood thrust the packet at Alex. 'You can have one if you want.'

How did she know? 'No thanks, I've given up.' Alex found herself smiling apologetically.

Jackie Wood shrugged, put the cigarette between her lips, took a lighter off the table and lit it. She inhaled deeply, then coughed – a great hacking cough that shook her whole body. Alex hoped the smoke was furring up her lungs, causing changes in the cells of her body. She hoped it was killing Jackie Wood.

'I missed my books,' she said, quietly.

'Pardon?'

'Books. Being around them all the time. Discovering new authors. Flicking through a book, deciding if I wanted to borrow it from the library. I missed that.'

'Right.' Alex was suddenly wrong-footed by a sudden feeling of compassion. 'But you had a library in the prison?' What did she know?

'Oh yes.' Jackie Wood waved her hand, a dismissive movement. 'Statutory requirement and all that. But it wasn't the same. I mean, I could look at books at all times of the day in my job. Savour them. There was a time limit in prison.'

'I see.'

'I miss the children.'

Alex's back stiffened.

Jackie Wood waved her arms. 'No, no, what I meant was the children in the library. I miss seeing them, reading to them, story time. You know.' She stubbed out her cigarette. 'Anyway, I expect you've got better things to do than spend all day with me. What did you want to know?'

A loaded question, but Alex restrained herself. She smoothed back her hair. 'You agreed to see me because you wanted to do the interview?'

''Course I did.' Jackie Wood blinked at her. 'Why else? It's a good chance to put my side of the story, to tell the world what really happened.' She leaned forward on her chair, put her elbows on her knees, and it was all Alex could do not to recoil. 'It'll be a good scoop for you as well. Don't think I haven't thought of that.'

Alex ignored the jibe. 'Your side of the story?'

She blinked again. 'That's what you told Jonny. That it'd be an opportunity for me to tell everyone what really happened. How I was only trying to help.'

'Trying to help?' Why was she echoing everything?

Jackie Wood put her mug down, leaned back again. 'Look, I hardly knew him, before, before the . . . you know.' There were tears in her eyes.

Alex tried not to move a muscle; if she did she would hit her. How dare she cry. How dare she.

Jackie Wood blinked harder than ever. 'Sorry.' She gathered herself. 'He – Martin Jessop – just came to my door and asked if I wanted to help, organize searches and stuff. Well, there was no question about it. I knew little Harry and Millie from the library. Sash – your sister – used to bring them to story time.' She gave a sad smile at a memory. 'They used to love the stories.'

Alex had a prickling sensation in her nose and was finding it hard to swallow. She hated hearing Jackie Wood say their names. Sasha's names, the children's names, all of it.

'But I want to start at the beginning. Can I do that, Alex? I can call you Alex, can't I? Even if I can't call your sister by her first name?'

She nodded, but she still didn't want to call her Jackie.

So Jackie Wood told Alex about her childhood – middle class, ordinary, lonely, brought up in Great Yarmouth by parents who were both teachers. She liked books, didn't want to go to university so she thought she would enjoy working in a library.

'You know, I was quite happy, in my own world. I even had a boyfriend.'

Alex must have looked startled. 'Surprised you, haven't I?' she said. 'And it wasn't Martin Jessop, whatever the papers might have said.'

'Who was it?'

Jackie Wood looked out of the window. 'I didn't say anything about him then, and I'm not going to now.'

'Come on, Jackie. It's been fifteen years.' Alex could scent a good story here. A different story. She didn't think she'd read anything about her having a boyfriend before.

She shook her head. 'It doesn't matter who he was. He wasn't involved, wasn't around when it was all happening.' She gave a harsh laugh. 'Certainly didn't want to know when I was arrested.'

Alex sensed she would not open up about this mysterious boyfriend. Yet. It was a case of gaining her trust and confidence, and to do that she really had to put any negative feelings aside. 'And then?' She tried the gentle probing, concerned face, furrowed brow.

'And then I was alone.'

Jackie Wood stubbed out one cigarette, but not before lighting another from its stub. 'When the children disappeared it was a dreadful day.'

A dreadful day. Alex shuddered inwardly and wanted to tell the woman how her sister's life had been destroyed that afternoon. How she had waited, not knowing what to do with herself while Jez hunted for the children, dreading Sasha's return. Then, after what seemed like days but was only hours, a police car picked her up and took her to Sasha's house. Jez white-faced, holding Sasha's hand saying over and over again: 'they'll be back soon, Sash, they'll be back soon.' Sasha crying. At first great screams that tore the air to shreds, then silent gulps, her face running with tears and snot and saliva. More police turning up, wanting a picture of the twins. Sasha scrabbling in her bag. Finding that picture taken on a sunny day in a clearing in the woods. They were having a picnic: Sasha, and her, Millie and Harry. Who took the picture? Must have been Jez. Then a policeman asking questions while a young woman police officer sat by, her notebook out, pen poised. She didn't take one note as far as Alex could tell. Endless questions. Questions she couldn't answer. Alex, not looking at Jez, keeping her arm around Sasha, comforting her, telling her it would all be all right. Their parents driving over from Mundburgh to stay. Then the endless searches, the false sightings, the weirdos who wanted a piece of the grief. How, as the days went on and there was no news, Sasha grew thinner and smaller. Insubstantial. When they found Harry it was a sort of tortured relief.

Then they found the clothes in Jessop's rubbish bin. More evidence in his flat. Evidence linking Martin Jessop and Jackie Wood. And the guilt that settled on her, suffocating her. So, yes, Alex wanted to tell her how her sister's life had been destroyed that afternoon.

'Why did you do it?' Alex looked at her properly then, for the first time. She looked past the scar and noticed how her eyes were dull, her skin lifeless. She had lines around her eyes – not so much crow's feet as bloody great emu feet – and there were smoker's lines around her mouth. Her forefinger and middle finger were stained yellow and her nails bitten down to the quick.

She took out another cigarette from the squashed packet. Lit it. Inhaled deeply. 'I told you, I didn't kill anybody.'

'You gave him an alibi.'

She smiled, the scar down the side of her face rippling. 'He didn't do it. Funnily enough, he was in the library that day, researching something or other, I can't remember what now.'

'Nobody else saw him.'

She laughed. 'For one thing, hardly anybody came in that day, and for another, he was tucked away in a corner behind one of the book stacks. Unless you went round there, you wouldn't see him. Anyway, I've been over that a hundred times. I was only telling the truth, and look what it got me. Accessory to murder.' She stubbed out the half-smoked cigarette and grabbed Alex's arm. 'I didn't do it. Nor did he. That's what I want you to say.' Her voice was earnest, a note of desperation.

Alex sat still for a moment, then shook her hand off. 'You were both put in prison. The police didn't believe you. Nor a judge and jury.'

Jackie Wood's mouth twisted in a parody of a smile. 'You think evidence can't be manipulated? That the police can't be corrupted?

That a jury can't be fooled? What are you? Stupid or something? Have you already forgotten that I got out because the evidence was suspect? The expert witness was *discredited*!'

Alex clenched her fists, tried to breathe evenly, not wanting to shout at Jackie Wood, not wanting to shake the truth out of her. She knew she had to be careful, treat her as though she were normal and that she thought she had a point. After what seemed like minutes but was probably only seconds, she got her breathing under control.

'Jackie,' she began gently, 'signs of the twins were found both in Jessop's flat and in yours. Items of their clothing were found in the rubbish bin. So much evidence.' She wanted to pick up her coffee cup but knew her hands would be shaking.

'I was acquitted.'

Alex thought she saw a sly look flash across Jackie Wood's face, then it was gone.

'The particles of dirt didn't add up,' she went on. 'Professor Gordon Higgs was discredited.' Professor Gordon Higgs. Such a competent name. One you would trust, don't you think? But he was wrong. Or lying.' She leaned forward. 'I wasn't involved.'

'Jessop was.'

'Jessop was what?'

'Involved,' said Alex, the lightness in her head threatening to come back.

Jackie Wood shook her head. 'I told you. He had an alibi.'

'No, the evidence was too strong.'

She shrugged. Silence opened up. 'He kept a diary, you know.'

'What?'

'A diary.'

Alex tried to look uninterested, as if her words hadn't made her heart beat faster, the palms of her hands sweat. 'Oh?' She hoped she'd hit a casual note. 'And what happened to it?'

Another shrug. 'Dunno.'

She was lying. Alex knew she was lying, she could feel it in her bones. 'Why did he keep it?'

'Said he'd always kept a diary, right from when he was young. Always told the truth in it, he said.'

'So,' said Alex, measuring her words, 'it might contain details of where he buried Millie.'

She shook her head. 'We didn't kill them.' She put two fingers either side of her temples and pressed hard. 'At least, I didn't kill them. Can you go now? Come back another time.'

Alex stared at her. She wanted to shout at her. Demand to know what Martin Jessop did, how he did it. Why did he put Harry into the suitcase – what was the point of that? Why they let Harry be found but not Millie. She wanted to grab Jackie Wood around her neck and shake the answers out of her. Shake the whereabouts of Millie right out of that horrible, thin, lying mouth.

But she didn't do any of that. She merely leaned forward and pressed the off button on the recorder, trying to stop her hand from shaking. She was going to have to be patient. 'So who do you think did kill them?' she asked quietly.

Jackie Wood leaned back, eyes closed, fingers still on her temples. 'I don't know. I don't know anything anymore. Sometimes I wonder what's real and what I've imagined.' She opened her eyes, looked into Alex's. 'But it's a long time. Fifteen years. You know?'

Depression washed over Alex. Was she ever going to get anywhere? Any nearer to finding out about Millie?

'I understand,' she said, getting up and putting her coat on. 'I'll come about the same time tomorrow, is that all right?'

'Yes. It's been good talking to you, actually. Cathartic. Maybe,' Jackie Wood hesitated, 'maybe we could go out tomorrow as well, have a coffee or something? There's a really good pastry shop in the town. They do lovely doughnuts and things. At least, they look nice in the window. I haven't dared go in. You know.' She sounded pathetic. 'Do you know, I don't even know how to use a smartphone?'

For a second Alex got an insight into what her life must be like. Not being able to do, or being used to doing, the things she took for granted. Just simple things like having a coffee. How the world had passed her by. 'Do you worry that people will recognize you?'

Her mouth twisted. 'You don't think the hair dye does much, then? You think people would know who I am?'

'Why did you come here?' asked Alex. 'Why not Scotland or somewhere really far away?'

Jackie Wood shrugged. 'Why not? It's where I grew up. I don't know anywhere else. Besides, I'm innocent aren't I? I haven't got anything to fear.'

'And the caravan?'

'Worried the taxpayers are footing the bill? Don't be. My parents died some years ago, one after the other. I think the shame got to them in the end. They'd bought this caravan so they could stay in it when they visited me. They loved this town. After they sold their house to pay for my legal bills they had to live in it. When they died it came to me. It was all they had left to show for forty years of marriage. They wanted me to have the best, but the best wasn't good enough, was it?' Alex could almost reach out and curl her hand around the bitterness in Jackie Wood's voice. 'They were hounded every day by people wanting to talk to them about me, about Martin.'

'That's the trouble though, isn't it? The families always suffer.'

She looked at Alex, obviously trying to gauge if she was being made fun of. But Alex was deadly serious and sidled along the bench, standing and putting on her coat. Jackie Wood sat very still, looking at her.

'I could tell you things.'

Alex stopped, mid shrug. 'Oh?'

This time the look on Jackie Wood's face was sly. Mercurial; she had changed from someone pathetic to a woman with a secret.

'What things?' Alex's heart was beating fast. 'What things?' Her voice was louder.

A quick smile and Alex saw in her face the reason she had survived prison for all those years. She had a shell; a toughness to her.

She rubbed her scar with her finger, up and down, up and down. At that moment Alex hated her so much that she wanted to slap her, hit her, rake her nails down her face; make her bleed. She had to clench her jaw and her fists to stop herself from launching at her across the bench.

'Things that might make you change your mind about me. Things that happened that you know nothing about.'

'The diary? Is it in the diary?'

'Come tomorrow,' she said, 'and maybe I'll tell you more then.'

'Tomorrow,' echoed Alex. How could she wait a whole twenty-four hours?

'My scar,' said Jackie Wood suddenly. 'Do you know how I got it?' That slow blinking again. She traced it with her finger. 'Someone took a shank to me a couple of years ago.' She shrugged. 'Probably one of the worst things that happened. I had the usual spit or piss in my tea. Punches here and there. Things stolen. People not talking to me. Even when you're on Rule 45 other prisoners try to get on it purely to do you. They don't like child killers in prison. Even ones who are innocent.' She smiled. 'Goodbye, Alex.'

Jackie Wood was in control; Alex had no option but to go.

She felt weightless, dizzy with Jackie Wood's words. She tied her scarf around her neck and opened the door. Breathed in the cold fresh air that smelled like freedom. Tomorrow.

But Jackie Wood wasn't finished. Alex heard her clear her throat behind her. Then she spoke.

'By the way—'

'Yes?'

'All those years ago, what were you doing with Martin Jessop?'

Alex pretended not to hear.

9

He'd held her hand a little longer than necessary when they first met, but Alex hadn't minded that. He was tall, with dirty blond hair just touching his collar. The sleeves of his white shirt were rolled up to his elbows, showing strong, tanned forearms.

They met, about six months before the murders, at a talk being given by a couple of well-known authors at the college in Ipswich. She asked a question – she couldn't for the life of her now remember what it was – but it must have ignited a spark of interest because at the toe-curling have-a-glass-of-warm-Chardonnay-and-meet-the-author event after the talk, he approached her.

'My name's Martin,' he said.

They chatted for a while, he asked her to go for a drink with him and she did, realizing that the attraction was mutual. He was clever and witty, and made her laugh. The drink led to dinner, dinner led to a hotel and a clandestine relationship. Oh, she knew there was a wife somewhere but she fell for the classic 'my wife doesn't understand me' line and that there was a 'messy divorce' going on, which was why he'd prefer to keep their relationship quiet for a while. It was Alex who found him the flat in Sole Bay, who was careful not to be seen when she visited, and was convinced no one knew about the two of them.

When she looked back and wondered why she had been drawn in, she realized it was because she'd been lonely. She was struggling to get her freelance career off the ground and look after a lively baby boy on her own. She was young, and having a clandestine lover made her life more exciting, which was why she never questioned Martin closely about his personal life.

It wasn't until after he'd been arrested that she found out he was spinning her one great lie. Several lies. There was a wife, but very much married to Martin (no 'messy divorce' in the foreground or background), and two teenage children living in a small village in Cambridgeshire. He stayed in Sole Bay two or three nights a week, sometimes weekends because of his job at the college. Not because of her. She didn't figure at all. She read all the details in the papers and knew she had been well and truly duped. The classic woman who believed everything her cheating lover told her.

At the time, it was all she could do not to fall apart. Something she had started for fun had been destroyed. She had brought a murderer into the family. The only reason she kept on living, kept herself together, was Gus. If it hadn't been for him, she wouldn't have been able to get out of bed in the morning. She also had to put on a show. No one had known about her affair with Martin and she wanted to keep it that way. How she managed to get through each day, putting one leaden foot in front of another, was now a blur. But she had done it.

Alex saw Martin's wife in court, not unexpectedly. Tall, blonde, always well turned out – well groomed, well dressed. She never said anything or displayed any emotion, not, that is, until Martin was sentenced to life in prison. Then Alex watched as a solitary tear rolled down her cheek. She didn't wait for him to be taken down.

The only emotion Alex felt when he was sentenced was thankfulness. He would be out of her life forever. Throughout the hearing she was terrified he would bring her into it, but he never did. Perhaps he thought she had suffered enough.

The last thing she could do was confess to anybody that she knew Martin Jessop.

But it was worse than that.

She walked quickly out of the caravan park and went to sit on a bench overlooking the sea. In its seeming infinity, the water always made her feel as though nothing was as bad as it seemed. And she sat there, hunched over, watching the grey waters dash against the harbour wall and feeling the wind tug at her clothes while the salt air scrubbed her skin, making it sore.

How did Jackie Wood know?

The question gnawed at her. She must have seen them at some point. Same block of flats. But why didn't she say anything at the trial? Why didn't she stand up and shout, 'the sister knew the murderer too!'

Why?

Alex arrived home to hear the grunting speak of teenage boys and the drone of the Playstation in the sitting room, and no sign of Malone.

'Hi guys,' she said as she took stock of the dirty plates and cups on the floor, magazines lying about, and the feral smell of male youth. It was good, though, she had to return to normal mode, forget about Jackie Wood and think about everyday life. To be honest, it was a relief. She didn't want to wrestle with her conscience any more and she didn't want to be going over and over in her mind what Jackie Wood might have meant by 'things' and what might have happened to Martin's diary.

'Hey, Alex. How's tricks?'

'Fine thanks, Jack,' she said, resisting the urge to tidy up. 'You?'

'Great.' He didn't look up from his laptop perched on his knee, fingers flying over the keyboard. Jack, gangly and yet to grow into his cheekbones and aquiline nose and full mouth; was a little different to Gus's other friends; into computers and gaming, though he did enjoy his sport. Alex liked him. He always said hi,

and when Gus was going through his difficult phase (the difficult phase that nearly gave her a mental breakdown), he stuck by
her son; helped him shake off the bad group of lads he'd been
hanging about with. Probably something to do with them both
being in the local youth football team and the fact that he didn't
go to Gus's school.

Gus stood. 'Hey, Mum, hope you don't mind a few of us hanging
out here.'

'Nope,' she said, counting, as well as Jack, two boys she hadn't
seen before and, sitting with slim legs curled under her bottom
in an armchair in the corner, flicking through a magazine, a girl.
She almost did a double take. This was the first time she had ever
known a girl penetrate the male circle of Gus's friends.

'Great. We might go to the cinema later.'

'Okay.' Alex hung on, hoping for some introductions, and trying
not to stare at the girl who was gorgeous. Curvy figure, masses of
auburn curls, brown doe-eyes which she turned on Alex now, her
bee-sting lips curved in a smile. Her nose, slightly too large and
a tad crooked gave her face character.

'Thanks, Mum,' Gus said in that dismissive voice, giving her a
fierce look, which meant she was supposed to leave.

'Okay,' she said again. 'Enjoy yourselves, won't you?'

She backed out of the room, and, although she was sorry not
to be introduced to the girl, she was pleased that the presence of
Gus's friends meant he wouldn't be able to quiz her on how the
interview with Jackie Wood had gone.

She made herself a coffee and sat in the kitchen, sipping it
slowly and watching the wind blow through the bare trees in the
back garden. All that was needed was a bit of tumbleweed rolling
on through. It was how she felt. Empty, spent.

Come on.

She needed to concentrate on the interview in the context of
the article she would be writing; make herself forget about any
personal connection between her and Jackie Wood.

Okay, so she'd discovered the woman had a boyfriend. Who? Surely someone local; and it was odd that Jackie Wood hadn't given up his name then or now. He might have been able to help her by providing some sort of character reference. Did he get cold feet? Not love her enough? Just wanted to have his name kept out of the whole mess, plain and simple? And she couldn't say she blamed him. Or maybe he had something to hide. Or Jackie Wood did. But now? Well, if she'd told her about him now it might make her seem more human to the readers. Elicit some sympathy, maybe.

Alex took her notebook out of her bag and started to write. It was the way she preferred to work, recording her first impressions on paper. Then she'd listen back to the interview. *So what were they?* She wrote. *I felt sorry for her. Why? Her time in prison? That and her life as it is now. Compared to then, when she had a life. But she doesn't deserve life now. Why not? Because she's guilty? Is she?* Before she realized what she was doing, she had underlined that last sentence twice. Her pencil had gone through the paper.

She needed a drink. She was guilty. Definitely. Judge, jury, the media – had all found her guilty. There was no question, no question at all. And her mission was to find out where Millie was buried. Then they could give her a proper burial. And the other thing she had to do was to write the bloody article. And then there was the diary. A bloody diary. She slumped back in her chair.

The front door opened. Voices. It slammed shut.

'Hi.' Malone came into the kitchen and kissed the nape of her neck, sending a delicious shiver down her spine. 'Gus let me in,' he said pointedly, before walking over to the fridge and taking out a can of beer. 'Want one?'

Alex shook her head. 'Glass of wine, though?'

He popped the can and took a deep swallow. 'Okay,' he said, wiping the foam moustache from his top lip, before going back to the fridge.

Did she mind how familiar he was around her house, treating it as his own? She supposed not, otherwise she wouldn't have allowed it, but still . . .

She was irritated. Her back itched and she wanted to squirm around on her chair. What did she really know about Malone? Damn all, really. Despite all the time she'd spent interviewing him she didn't feel she had got to the bottom of what made him tick. She knew he was holding back. There had been the tales of derring-do and infiltrating gangs and all that. She knew he was in his forties and bloody good-looking. And he'd told her he'd been born and spent his early years in a town near Dublin, before moving to England. But what made him risk his life like that? And although he said he'd finished with that kind of life – could she trust him?

And even if she didn't trust him, what was she doing bringing him into Gus's life?

'Here you go.'

He handed her a cold glass of something white. She took a gulp and immediately felt better. Not sure that was a good thing.

'How was it then?'

Alex froze, her glass halfway to her lips ready for a second swig. What did he know? She hadn't said she was going to see Jackie Wood, so how had he found out? Gus? Surely—

'Hey.' There was laughter in his voice. 'No need to look so worried.'

'Worried?'

'You look like a rabbit caught in headlights.'

'Oh?'

'Look. I don't know where you've been, and I don't particularly want to know. But my guess is that you've been somewhere interesting and spoken to someone important and I sort of thought it might be to do with your work.'

Alex looked at him: calm, steady, strong. No, she didn't know him that well, but she did know that he cared about her and that if she let it, their relationship could grow into something special. And she hadn't had anyone to make her feel safe for so many years. She had built a wall around her and Gus and not let anyone breach it. Perhaps now was the time to let the cracks widen that had come with Malone.

She let out a breath she didn't know she was holding. 'Jackie Wood.'

'That's who you went to see?' He gave a low whistle. 'Wow, no wonder you're uptight.'

'I am not uptight. Well, maybe a little. You mustn't tell anyone. If it got out where she was living then I'd be done for.'

'But I don't know where she's living; you haven't told me,' Malone pointed out, probably quite reasonably, she supposed.

'True,' she said.

'And I won't mention it again.' There was a pause. 'So what did she say?' Malone sat back, balanced the ankle of one leg on the knee of the other. Perfect relaxing pose.

She shook her head. 'Malone.'

'Come on, Alex, spill the beans. You know I won't say anything. I've worked under the radar, as well you know.'

Alex pursed her lips. Blew out some air. 'Said she didn't do it.'

'Do you believe her?'

She rubbed the rim of the glass with the tip of her finger. 'Not really.'

Malone lifted an eyebrow. 'Some doubt there, though?'

'I suppose I'm not entirely sure. She was pretty convincing.'

Malone put his drink down, went over to her and took her hand. 'Look. If I can help at all, I will. I've got contacts. Friends, you know?'

'Friends. Do I really want to know, Malone?'

He gave a twisted smile. 'Probably not. But then you wouldn't need to know; you could leave it to me.'

She gave a heartfelt sigh. 'I'm going back to see her tomorrow. For the final part of the interview.' She looked down at Malone's hands. Began to stroke the signet ring he wore on the little finger of his left hand. 'I'm sort of hoping that she'll have had time to think and that she'll trust me.'

'And she'll just happen to tell you where Millie is buried? Why should she do that? It would send her back to prison, wouldn't it?' His expression was kind.

'I thought I would tell her that I wouldn't tell anybody where the information had come from. Plead protecting my sources, that sort of thing.'

Malone cupped her chin. 'Is that going to work? Post Leveson? There are other people involved in this, you know. Sasha for one. Jez. Gus, too. And if she does tell you, it'd be tantamount to her admitting killing the twins. You'd have to tell the police.'

She gritted her teeth. 'I'm not telling the police. She has to be able to trust me on that. My only consolation there is that she has already served fifteen years. Not enough, but I'd accept it, if we could only know where Millie is. I just want to know, that's all.'

He kissed her lightly on the lips. 'No you don't, you want retribution. Love, Millie's gone. Buried in some wood or field. This woman is not going to put herself at risk by telling you anything.'

Deep down, she knew Malone was right.

'Look,' he said, 'I'll put in a couple of calls to some people I know, see if she said anything in jail. See if Jessop said anything before he topped himself.'

'Jessop?'

Malone gave a shrug. 'I know it's a while ago, but people who've been inside have long memories. It's worth a go.'

Alex took his hand. 'Thanks, Malone.'

'Now,' he got up, stiffly, rubbing the small of his back, 'I'm too old for squatting down on my knees. I suggest you go and write up at least the first part of your article while it's fresh in your mind.'

'You're right.' She put her glass down, thankful she had a clear head. 'By the way, did you see the girl who was with Gus?'

'*With* Gus?' He laughed. 'From his expression I think he would love that. She was quite a looker, I must admit.'

79

She punched his arm playfully. 'Too young for you, mate.'

'I know, I know. She did seem to be in the centre of the group, though.'

'Perhaps it'll do Gus some good, something to keep his mind off his more unsuitable friends.'

Malone frowned. 'You're still worried about them? He seemed to be pretty well in with the lot who were just here.'

'Hmm, I know. It's just I can't help—' she shook her head.

'You're just being silly. Go.'

She laughed. 'You're right.'

'Aren't I always?'

'No. But as you're sending me away—'

'Go and chain yourself to your desk, woman.'

She went.

10

The next day brought a change in the weather. The never-ending rain, easterly winds, and lowering grey skies were banished in favour of a crisp feel to the air, a watery blue sky, and a weak, clotted-cream yellow sun. On the radio the farmers were talking about how perhaps their winter crops would be saved if there was a bit of warmth and clear skies. Forecasters on the telly were talking optimistically of a low front having moved on. Alex was feeling pleased with herself; firstly, for not asking Gus about the girl and secondly, transcribing the first interview with Jackie Wood.

The walk to the caravan site was very different too. People nodded at her, one or two even commented on the change in the weather. It was all so British – a bit of sun and everybody's friendly. She almost felt sorry for Wood: not being able to walk freely, breathe in the air, and, yes, have a cup of coffee and a doughnut in the bakery.

And because of the sun, more people were out and about on the site, mainly older couples; the families would come later, starting in the Easter holidays and building up to a crescendo in August. Then the whole of Sole Bay would be filled with people of all ages and sizes, swelling the population and the economy.

Alex was at the door of Jackie Wood's caravan when a woman came out of another van. The same young woman she had seen yesterday, smoking another cigarette. This time she had headphones in her ears. She dragged them out and Alex thought she could hear the tinny beat of some music programme. Alex nodded to her.

'I haven't seen her today,' the woman said. 'Not a bloody sight.'

'Really?' said Alex, not wanting to stop and chat.

'Really,' the woman said, mimicking her voice. 'Did you tell her I was good for a coffee?'

'Yes I did,' Alex lied. 'I'm sure she'll be round when she's got a minute.'

The woman nodded. 'Great. Only I'm off in a couple of days. Got myself a flat in town so I don't need to live in this dump any longer. Who is she, by the way?'

'What?'

'Who is she?' She nodded towards Jackie Wood's caravan. 'Don't know her name.'

Alex opened her mouth, realizing she had no idea what name Wood was living under now. 'A friend,' she said eventually. 'Just a friend.'

'I went over there last night, just to have chat, maybe a glass of wine, and she didn't answer the door.'

'Perhaps she was out.' Alex tried to keep the impatience out of her voice.

'Nah. I could hear the radio and I'd seen her shadow against the curtains earlier. Thought you were there, too.'

Now Alex did look at her properly. 'Me? No.'

'Oh.' The woman shrugged her shoulders and then ground the cigarette butt under her foot. 'Well, don't forget to tell her I'm here.'

'I won't,' she said.

Alex watched the woman go inside her caravan and shut the door, before she knocked on the door of Jackie Wood's caravan. No answer. She knocked again, then tried to peer through the window to the side of the door. The curtains were drawn tight. Damn. Where was she? Alex listened for a moment and could hear talking from inside. Was somebody in there with her?

She looked around quickly. The last thing she wanted to do was to attract attention. She knocked once more, then tried the door. It was unlocked. 'Jackie?' she said, pushing the door open and stepping into the caravan. 'It's me. Alex.'

It was the smell that hit her first. Thick, cloying, metallic. The caravan was dark, just a crack of light showing through the ill-fitting curtains.

Alex covered her nose and tried to breathe just through her mouth as she went over to the windows and drew back the curtains, letting the sunlight filter through the nets. It was hot as well. She unzipped her coat, then looked around. A mug was on its side, the tea – she guessed it was tea – had spread across the table and dripped onto the floor. There was a plate of food upended too; congealed chips, white fish matter ground into the thin carpet, and blobs of what she guessed was tomato ketchup spread across the floor. Somebody was talking and then she heard the familiar jingle of *5Live* coming out of a radio on the side by the sink. She went over and turned it off.

But the smell, where was that coming from?

A pair of legs was poking out from a door in the tiny corridor that led, she guessed, to the bathroom and bedroom. They could almost have been legs from a mannequin.

Without thinking about it, Alex walked towards the legs. Looked inside what she then discovered to be the bathroom: a chemical toilet squatting under the window, and a corner shower with its curtain speckled with black mould.

At first she wondered what on earth had made someone want to lie in such a tiny, uncomfortable, smelly space. Alex wanted to tell her to get up, otherwise she would get too stiff. Then her head cleared, and the smell and the full horror of what, of *who*, hit her. Jackie Wood was lying at an angle, her head propped on the side of the shower tray. Her eyes were wide open, but empty and glazed looking. Her lips were drawn back over her teeth, and the scar on the side of her face was raised, twisted, looking like a white worm lying on her cheek. She was wearing what Alex thought was a red shirt, until she realized the red was blood and the shirt was white. There was blood on the walls, all over the floor. Who knew there could be so much blood? Blood that had come from wounds in her chest and stomach. That was the cloying, iron smell, and it was intermingled with the stink of piss and shit. Alex was light-headed, floating; the whole scenario was unreal. It was as if she was watching from a distance, needing to get the facts straight so she could write a balanced, thoughtful story. This was not her life that was becoming more complicated than she knew how to cope with; this was an interesting piece that needed to be written down for other people to read with a degree of Schadenfreude.

This was not normal.

Alex looked at her again.

Instead of the old black jeans she had seen her in the day before, Jackie Wood was wearing a skirt. Denim blue with crimson splodges. She tried to think of her going into a shop in Lowestoft or Yarmouth – she couldn't imagine her venturing to the swanky shops in Sole Bay. She would have had to take the bus. Or maybe gone to – what was she doing? Here was a woman lying dead on the floor of a caravan and she was speculating about her clothes. But her legs were splayed and the skirt was all twisted up over her hips, showing a glimpse of grey underwear. Alex didn't want to leave her like that, so she went down on one knee and tried to straighten it, trying to keep the tails of her coat out of the mess on the floor.

She had little room to move and she couldn't lift the body, so she pulled the skirt down as best she could, just to give Jackie Wood some semblance of modesty. As she did so, she knocked against something. She looked down. A bloodstained knife. Alex almost laughed. It was exactly as you saw in those detective programmes on television. The murder weapon lying by the body. And if she'd been following the script, that was when she should have picked it up. But she didn't.

Alex touched Jackie Wood's cheek. Her skin was cold, waxy.

Then she stood up, backed away, the confined space making her movements crablike, the stink of death all around her. She was aware of acrid-tasting bile at the back of her throat and she thought she might be sick. She wasn't, but she could feel beads of sweat on her forehead and her hands were shaking. Think.

Police. Ambulance. Somebody. She had to phone somebody. She took her phone out of her coat and went back into the main part of the caravan. She was just about to punch the buttons when she snapped out of her dream-like state. *Think.*

Who wanted Jackie Wood dead?

She did. Alex Devlin, aunt of the murdered twins; she wanted her dead. But after she'd found out where they had buried Millie. Sasha? Without a doubt, though Alex couldn't see it happening in her fragile state. Then there was Jez. What would he do? She felt in her bones that he would follow the letter of the law – well, he would – wouldn't he? Though he could surprise them all as he had in the past. Who else? Who else?

A knock on the door made her jump.

'Hello?' Another knock. 'Hello? It's me, Nikki, from across the way. Wondered if you two would like a coffee in town with me?'

This was Alex's chance to say 'call the police' or, 'something terrible has happened here, please help'. But she didn't. Instead she went to the door and opened it just a crack, putting her fingers to her lips as she did so.

'Sshh,' she said. 'Jackie's asleep. Got a migraine. That's why the curtains were closed. I've opened them, but the light's too bright. Hurts her eyes. Makes her feel sick.' She was babbling. She gripped the side of the door to stop herself until her fingers went numb. She tried not to think of Jackie Wood's sightless eyes and the way she lay on the tiny bathroom floor like a broken doll.

The woman – Nikki – shifted from foot to foot. 'Jackie,' she said, trying the name out for size. Alex kicked herself for giving it away. 'Oh. Okay. I thought she might like to come out, have a bit of fresh air.' Nikki tried to look round her, into the caravan. 'Maybe go to a caff or something?'

Then Alex realized she was looking at another lonely woman; somebody who wanted a bit of company to break up the monotony of her life. 'Look,' she said. 'I'll leave a note for her for when she wakes up. Say you called. I'm sure she'd love to see you sometime.'

'Tell her not to leave it too long because I'm off soon.'

'I will.' She managed a smile then shut the door, leaning forward until her forehead was touching its cold metal. She could feel Nikki still on the other side of the door. Eventually she heard her clumping down the steps. A few seconds silence as she walked across the grass and the path. Then the sound of her clumping up her own steps, the door shutting.

Alex sank down on her haunches and put her head on her knees. What the fuck was she doing? Going out of her mind, that's what. Then she realized what it was that had made her not call the police straightaway, not ask Nikki for help. She saw it again in her mind's eye. The knife. It was just an ordinary kitchen knife, and it was exactly like one of a set that was in Sasha's kitchen. Not that she used them much, if at all. Sasha wasn't a great one for cooking these days. Now maybe she was jumping to conclusions, adding up two and two and making ten, all that sort of stuff, but something nagged at her. She tried to think back to when she was last in Sasha's house. They'd sat and watched a film together – she couldn't now think what it was except that it was some romantic comedy that made them laugh. Sasha had been in a good mood, there had been no more self-harming incidents and they had managed to talk about Jackie Wood without Sasha dissolving into tears. She thought they'd even looked at a photo album of the kids.

Had she gone into the kitchen? Probably to get another glass of wine, some crisps, more dips. Did she look at the knife block?

Why should she have done? When Sasha self-harmed she used razor blades, a penknife; anything that was easy to buy, easy to hide, easy to dispose of. So she wouldn't have noticed if a knife was missing.

Groaning, she pushed the hair back off her forehead and then stood up slowly. She caught sight of herself in a flyblown mirror on the wall. God, what must that Nikki have thought? Her hair was all over the place and she looked as though she'd seen a ghost. Which she supposed she had, in a way. There was even a fleck of red on her jumper. Blood? Probably.

Had to think.

She heard a door slam shut and she peeped through the net curtains. Nikki was walking away from her caravan, off to have her lonely cup of coffee somewhere in town. She had, what, an hour?

Looking at herself in the mirror once more, she pulled her fingers through her hair, trying to make it look half decent. She looked down at her clothes and saw that the knees of her jeans were dark and sticky from where she had knelt down beside the body. The body. Bile rose in her throat again. No. Stop it. She did up her coat and looked around the tiny sitting area. There. On the shelf; a key. She picked it up and went to the door, opening it carefully. She looked out. No one. She stepped outside the caravan and locked the door behind her, then tucked the key into her pocket. She went down the steps and hurried along the path, her head down.

She was lucky. The skies had clouded over and the rain was beginning to fall again. No one was about and she left the campsite without seeing anybody and without, she hoped, anyone seeing her.

Alex kept her composure walking down the road. Then she crossed over, went up some wooden steps and into the sand dunes. Following the path, she went down to the beach and sank down onto the damp sand and marram grass in the lee of one of the dunes. The rain had stopped again and the sun was coming out. There was a magnificent rainbow, all the colours clearly delineated.

Richard of York Gave Battle In Vain. The old school mnemonic was going through her head. Where was the end of the rainbow? Where was the pot of gold? Round and round in her head. Anything to stop thinking of Jackie Wood lying crunched up on the floor, her body punctured with stab wounds. She breathed deeply, trying to get rid of the stink of the caravan in her nostrils, then she took her phone out of her pocket.

'Alex?' Malone's voice, mellifluous and cool, soothed her. She opened her mouth, but the words wouldn't come out, her throat was thick with tears.

'Alex? It is you, isn't it?' A note of worry in his voice.

'Malone,' she managed to say. 'Malone, I need you.'

'Where are you?'

'On the beach. Somewhere . . . not far from the harbour. Christ, Malone, it's . . . I don't know what to do.' Tears were falling freely down her face. She gulped down a sob. 'Please, Malone.'

'Stay there. I'll be with you as soon as I can. Don't move.' The line went dead.

She sat, watching the white horses race to shore, listening to the drag of the waves on the pebbles, and felt almost calmed.

11

Kate turned off the A12 at Martlesham and headed to the police headquarters. Built in the late 1970s, it was an unlovely building of corridors and offices. At least the new Police Investigation Centre had a bit more of an airy feel to it, with more glass and open spaces, but the whole area was utilitarian, not made any cosier by the bleak winter scene of leafless trees and mud where grass should be.

She pulled into a parking space – lucky to find one near the doors just before lunchtime – and sat for a moment, closed her eyes and tried to empty her mind. She leaned her head on the steering wheel. Christ, she was tired. She was going to have to stir herself and get out of the car soon enough, but she wanted to think about the monumental fuck-up that had happened earlier. This was what she liked to do; turn things over in her mind and then let them settle, rather like dealing with a compost heap.

Kate's day had begun early – three-thirty to be precise – and on a cold, drizzly, dark morning in a Fenland town. Even her trusty leather trench coat had difficulty keeping the damp air out. Sodium street lights – not yet the victim of council cuts – shone in the gloom. They'd pulled up at the end of a cul-de-sac of respectable middle-class houses. Semi-detached, solid, with front bay windows and probably, Kate guessed, built in the 1950s. Front gardens either paved over for car parking or sporting a patch of grass, and borders that had been put to bed for the winter. Bed. Kate yawned and sipped some of her thermos-flask coffee. That's where she should be now. Just her bloody bad luck to be the one left in the office when DI Howlett'd had to go and tend to his wife who was about to give birth on the kitchen floor. This was his case, his intel; he should be here. The coffee slithered, lukewarm, down her throat.

She stepped out of the car and looked around, trying to stifle a yawn. This was not the normal sort of place they came for a serious early-morning drugs bust. Usually they'd be on some run-down council estate or at a whole load of soulless industrial units. This looked too, well, *nice*. Though crime was no respecter of class. She started to move towards the target. Number forty-three.

'Are we ready then?'

Kate turned. Ed Killingback was standing beside her, notebook in hand, camera looped over his wrist. Behind him, a cameraman, reporter, and a guy she thought must be a producer, were fiddling with various bits of equipment. That would be the local BBC TV programme. She tried not to let the resentment grow. After all, they had been, in part, responsible for the success of the investigation; doing their own digging around and coming up with evidence they passed on to the police. So she'd had no choice but to say they could come along on the raid. Somehow Killingback had heard about it and turned up too. She tried not to sigh. Bloody press. A liability.

'We're ready,' she said, smoothly. 'Don't forget what you've been told. Stay back. Don't interfere. Don't get in our way. We don't know what we might find.'

'Understood.' Killingback touched a finger to his forehead in an irritating salute.

Eager young puppy. Kate's bones ached.

'Okay, let's go.' She signalled, and four officers in full riot gear jogged along the road and up the path of the house.

There were thuds as one officer pounded the white uPVC door with a battering ram to guttural shouts of encouragement.

'Put yer back into it.'

'Go, on, get in there.'

'Come on, get the door out.'

The door gave way and was tossed aside like a piece of cardboard.

The officers stood to one side to let Kate through; the house exposed to the chill, the dark, and the huddle of reporters and photographers staring in.

She shone her torch around and realized she was in a hallway. Parquet flooring. Old-fashioned red rug. Landscapes hanging on the wall. Fresh flowers on a half-moon table. The smell of polish. Motioning to her officers, she pushed open a door to her left, allowing them to bundle through with shouts designed to frighten and quell any resistance. Nothing. The same for the room on the right. And the kitchen. All perfectly normal; perfectly respectable rooms with everything as it should be.

'Upstairs.'

'Just get out of my house.' A tremulous voice came down the stairs. 'Now. I've called the police. They'll be here any minute.'

Kate shone her torch upwards.

Blinking in the beam was a man, probably in his seventies, Kate estimated, judging by his balding head and collection of wrinkles. He was clutching the edges of a dressing gown together with one hand and waving what looked like a brass statue in the other in what he clearly hoped was a menacing way. Behind him stood a woman of similar age, thinning hair, eyes wide with shock, lips trembling.

'I said get out.' Another wave of the statue. 'I've told you, the police will be here soon.'

'We are the police,' Kate said, feeling very weary as she took her warrant card out of her pocket and held it up.

'Come here. I can't see it.'

Conscious of the officers in their riot gear behind her, Kate climbed the stairs.

'Stop there. Now, throw your card up to me.'

'Mr—?' said Kate, trying not to let her exasperation show. Exasperation not just with the old man, but with the intel that was proving to be bollocks. This man did not look like the group of ten Vietnamese they had been told would be in the house. If this was the right house, which Kate was now seriously doubting.

'Williams. Jeffrey Williams.'

'Mr Williams, I can only apologize.' With the flick of her wrist she threw her card like a Frisbee and it landed at his feet. 'There seems to have been some sort of mistake.'

'A mistake? Mistake? I should bloody well think so.' He bent down with some difficulty and picked the warrant card up off the floor to examine it. 'And what about my door?'

'I can assure you—'

'And what about my suffering? And that of my wife?' Wife nodded vigorously. 'We could have had a heart attack, or anything.'

'Mr Williams,' began Kate, feeling at a slight disadvantage, as she was still halfway up the stairs. 'I am so very sorry for—'

Then she heard the screeching of sirens coming ever closer.

'There we are,' said Mr Williams, a note of triumph in his voice. 'The police.'

Kate nodded. 'Right.' Jesus. What a monumental fuck-up.

So it was no wonder she was dog-tired, with a sodding headache to boot. Another row with Chris hadn't helped, either. They had been more frequent since she'd seen Jackie Wood on the television, staring out of the screen at her, mocking her. Seeming to say, 'See? I told you I would get out. One day.' And she had.

The argument that morning had been a humdinger though. Chris had started to talk about some friends who'd been trying for a baby for years until they found out that she couldn't have children. Then they went for IVF, and now they had twins.

She'd whirled round, slopping muesli over the table – the bread had been mouldy again – and looked at him disbelievingly. 'IVF? You want me to pump myself full of hormones and have my eggs harvested in some vain attempt for a baby that'll probably never happen because there isn't that great a success rate and everyone I've ever spoken to about it, everything I've ever read about it says it is a hard, hard thing for couples to go through. Is that what you want?' God, she was so tired, she didn't want to be talking about this, thinking about this.

'Why not? Surely it's worth thinking about? Please? That's all I'm asking. Just to think about it.'

Kate had wanted to hurl the cereal bowl across the room and watch it smash into tiny pieces. Instead she set it down carefully and walked to the door. 'I wish you could just leave it alone.' She picked up her jacket. 'I'll be home later.'

Kate sat down at her desk, trying to push all thoughts of Chris out of her head. She was at work; she could do this. And she was good at compartmentalizing her life. The past in one compartment. Locked, key thrown away. Home life in another. That compartment was hidden in a corner. Work, on the other hand, was allowed to be right there in the front. Work she could cope with. As messy, despairing, and soul-destroying as it could be, it was better than anything else. Though when she let herself think this, she felt guilty.

'Hey, Kate, how you doing?' Steven Rogers, a stalwart of a detective sergeant brushed sugar crystals off the front of his shirt. He put a doughnut down on the greasy bit of paper sitting on his desk. Kate could smell his takeaway coffee. So much better than the rubbish the machine spewed out.

'Fine, Steve. Just fine.' She switched on her computer, not quite able to shake the feeling of doom that seemed to hover above her head. Maybe this time things were so bad that she couldn't tidy away those bits of her life she didn't want to think about. She was going to have to talk to Chris. Sort it out with him, tell him she'd been to the doctor. Hell, even go to counselling. Her marriage was important to her. 'Got a lot to get through.'

'Heard it all went tits up.' He sniffed.

'It did,' she said, grimly. 'I'm waiting for the flak.'

'Well, the Artist wants to see you.'

She jerked her head up. 'Already? I thought I might have some time—'

'When you came in, he said.' Steve nodded towards the closed door of Detective Chief Inspector Grayson Cherry, generally known as The Artist, not just because his name was similar to that of the famous cross-dressing artist, but because he also liked to paint and several of his 'works' hung in his office. Mostly blank canvases with a single blob of colour on them. It was the placing of that blob that was integral to his art. Apparently.

'Sit down, Kate,' said Cherry.

Kate sat in the chair across from his desk and tried not to stare at the new painting hanging on the wall behind him. It was obviously his first venture into nudes. Like Picasso, it had odd protuberances in odd places. Unlike Picasso, Cherry couldn't draw. So instead, Kate tried to keep her eyes fixed on his thick, straight eyebrows and hair that was beginning to show some streaks of grey. He was a handsome man, and sharp to boot. Idly she wondered if he plucked his eyebrows – they were so straight with not a stray hair in—

'Now, Kate.'

Kate blinked, dragged away from thinking about Cherry's facial hair. She tried not to yawn. Or think about the mountain of work she had to do. Or how much of her back she had to cover.

He steepled his fingers. 'This morning.'

'It was – er – unfortunate, sir.' She tried not to squirm.

'Unfortunate.' He raised one of his thick, straight eyebrows. 'I see. Is that what the Independent Police Complaints Commission will see it as? Hmm?'

Kate wanted to sigh. Only Cherry would give it its full name and not just use the acronym like every other bugger. 'Sir, I was acting on intel received.'

'And it was DI Howlett's case; I am well aware of that. And if he had not been called to minister to his wife he would be sitting in front of me now and not you. Isn't that right?'

'Yes sir.'

'But it is you.'

'Yes sir.'

He leaned forward across the desk. 'A cock-up all round, I think. We are left with egg on our faces and stern questions from above.'

'Yes sir.'

He blew some air out of pursed lips. Kate watched a few strands of hair jump in the sudden breeze. 'As yet, Mr and Mrs Williams have not employed lawyers, threatened to sue, or shouted for compo.'

'Right.'

'Right. Leave it with me, Kate.'

'Really?'

'Don't look a gift horse in the face.'

'Mouth.'

He shrugged. 'Face, mouth, you know what I mean.' He shuffled a couple of files on his desk. 'To more . . . ah . . . pressing matters. I know that you know we have an unexpected visitor in our midst. An unwanted visitor, we should say.'

Jackie Wood. All at once her tiredness and irritation vanished and her heart began to beat fast. This was the first confirmation they'd had that the woman was holed up somewhere in the area. Rumours had been rife at headquarters for the last few days and Kate was surprised it hadn't got out. The place was as leaky as a sieve when it came to secrets. But she guessed that the recent arrest and charging police officers for accepting bribes from the press had stopped up the leaks, at least for now.

'Yes, sir,' she said.

'And do you know where she is?'

Cherry liked to play guessing games. Kate played along. 'No, sir.'

He leaned across the desk and tapped the side of his nose. 'The bad apple never falls far from the tree.'

'Ah,' she said. 'So she's definitely back in Suffolk.' She nodded, as if she hadn't already guessed. It was the only logical thing for her to do, to come back to the place she knew. She would have been advised to change her name, go elsewhere in the country, but she would have been drawn back to the place where she grew up, and drawn back to the scene of the crime.

'Now, I don't have to tell you, Kate, that if anyone found out where she was, and by "anyone" I specifically mean the gentlemen and women of the press, then we would be in deep *shitenstrasse* – *comprende?*'

Kate nodded, willing her mouth not to twitch into a smile. 'I won't say anything, sir. Of course.' She bit her lip. 'Would it be a good idea for me to go and see her, sir? You know, tell her we're here, that we know she's there, and all that?' At last.

Grayson Cherry gave a deep sigh. 'Kate,' he said, not unkindly, 'I am well aware of your previous involvement in the Clements case, so, no, it would not be a good idea. We leave her be unless it becomes necessary to talk to her. Otherwise her bloody lawyer will be all over us like a rash.'

There was a knock and Steve's head poked around the edge of the door. 'Sir, we've got an incident. At the Harbour Bay caravan site. In Sole Bay. A woman's been found dead.'

Detective Chief Inspector Grayson Cherry closed his eyes and pinched the bridge of his nose before lifting his head to look Kate in the eye. 'Looks like we're already up *shitenstrasse*.'

12

'So you're okay? Know what to say?' Malone looked at Alex, and she knew he was willing her to be strong.

She nodded. 'Yes. I got here to do the second interview and found her like that.' She swallowed the bile that kept rising in her throat.

'And?'

'And when they ask if I saw a knife I say no. I say it's exactly as you see inside. I got out as quickly as possible.'

Malone nodded. 'Good.'

She looked at him, pathetically grateful for his help.

He'd come to her straightaway, taken her in his arms on the seashore and held her for a long time. Then he'd pulled away, stroked the hair away from her face and kissed her forehead. She told him about the caravan, the body, the knife, and her fears.

'Okay,' he said. 'Let's go back there now and I'll find the knife and get rid of it.'

'But what about DNA and fingerprints and all that sort of stuff?' She had watched plenty of *CSI* shows, along with the rest of the country.

'Yours will be all over the shop, but that's only to be expected. After all, you've been here once before and you were due to be here today. It's only natural that you'd've touched stuff.'

'And Sasha?'

He gripped her shoulders. 'Be logical. How would Sasha even know where to find Jackie Wood? Or be in any state to find her?'

'I don't know.' She tried to damp down the panic again. 'Perhaps she followed me or has been through my things or—'

'Look. If she has been here, unless she did a good clean up job, her DNA and fingerprints will be everywhere. But at least if we get rid of the murder weapon the plods won't have that crucial piece of evidence. And I can get in and out without leaving a calling card.'

Alex nodded.

But there was one other thing Alex needed Malone to do for her in the mess of the death in the caravan.

'Martin Jessop kept a diary.'

'And?' said Malone.

'I don't know where it is, but it could be in the caravan.'

'Is it likely? After all, Jessop's dead and his effects would have gone back to his family.'

Alex bit her lip. 'I know. But Jackie Wood intimated that she had it or knew where it was, so, just in case, could you have a look?' It was her first lie to Malone.

'Why is it so important?'

This was the tricky bit. She couldn't say that he might have detailed their affair between the pages and it could destroy her, could she? 'There could be some clue about Millie in there. I need to know.' That much was true.

'Wouldn't the plods have found it?'

'Possibly. Unless—'

'Unless what?'

'Unless he never had it in prison.' She looked him straight in the eyes, willing him to accept what she said. It wasn't that she wanted to deceive Malone, but she couldn't tell him the sordid truth. Not unless she had to.

'But—'

She could have screamed with frustration, but she took a deep breath. 'Please, Malone.'

He narrowed his eyes. 'Why do I feel there's something you're not telling me?' She stayed silent. Then he blew air through his lips. 'Okay. For you.'

'Thank you.'

Alex hadn't thought about CCTV cameras at the campsite. Malone had. He said that it was unlikely they were working at this time of year, if at all.

'These places put the cameras up to deter trouble; they don't necessarily have any film in them. And it would be too expensive for them to have the digital sort,' he said.

'Digital?'

Malone smiled. 'Don't worry about it.'

She was too scared to feel patronized, and supposed she shouldn't worry. If anyone knew how to dodge stuff like CCTV cameras, and the whys and the wherefores of them, then Malone would.

'It's like burglar alarms on houses,' he carried on, warming to his theme. 'There's hardly ever a real alarm in them. Deterrent, that's all.'

So here she was, perching on the steps, waiting for the police to arrive. Malone had been in the caravan and picked up the knife. What he did with it she didn't know and didn't want to know. There was no sign of any diary.

'Just this,' he said, handing her a key.

She took it from him. 'What is it?'

'It's a key,' he said, rolling his eyes.

'I can see that,' she snapped.

99

Malone held his hands up. 'Whoa, I'm only trying to help.'

Alex noticed he was wearing thin latex gloves, the sort that doctors wear, or criminals. She guessed he probably had a stash of them somewhere left over from his undercover days. For some reason the sight of them sent a shiver down her spine. She supposed it brought the reality home to her of what they were doing. She'd found a dead body and Malone was clearing up the mess. If only she'd got there sooner, would Jackie Wood be alive? When was she murdered? And was Sasha involved? It all went round and round in her head like some sort of horrible mantra. She rubbed her forehead. 'Sorry. Sorry. I . . .' Inexplicably, her eyes filled with tears. She composed herself. 'You think it's important?'

Malone shrugged. 'I thought it might be. It was hidden away at the back of the cutlery drawer and it's a key to one of the left-luggage lockers at the Forum in Norwich.'

'The Forum?'

'Yes, that place that houses the BBC and the library and some sort of café.'

'I know what the Forum is,' she said, testily. 'How do you know the key is from there?'

'Because it says so. On the fob.'

She peered at it. 'Right.'

'Worth a look, I reckon. Don't you? As you're so anxious to find this diary. You never know, it could be there. I could come with you, if you like.' His expression was neutral, as though he knew she wasn't telling him the whole story.

She closed her fist around the key. 'Thanks,' she said, leaning her head on his shoulder, trying to regain some of that feeling of safety she'd had when he'd embraced her on the beach. He put his arm round her, and she snuggled even closer – just as she heard the sirens in the distance. She realized she was shivering. She felt sick. What the fuck was she doing?

'Okay, here we go,' he said.

Then it was as if she was looking through a veil, everything was a blur. An ambulance, a police car, a van: all turned up. Why so many? The sirens which had gradually filled the air as the vehicles made their way down the harbour road had brought the few people in the other caravans out to gawp. Then a scene reminiscent of a television show unfolded, with a woman in a long black leather overcoat seeming to be in charge. Police officers scurried around her, following instructions, going back to the van, taking out boxes of equipment, all of them moving towards them.

'Alex Devlin?'

'That's me.' Alex stood up and clenched her jaw to stop her teeth chattering.

The woman in the coat frowned. She had coal-black eyes and black hair cropped close to her head, making her look like a hawk. High cheekbones, pale skin. Slash of red lipstick. As tall as Alex. She reached inside her coat and flashed her warrant card. 'Detective Inspector Kate Todd.'

Alex nodded.

'How long have you been here?'

'About half an hour. Maybe less. I'm not sure.'

She turned and looked at Malone, hesitated for a split second, eyes narrowing as if she knew him. 'And you are?'

'Malone.'

'Anything else?'

'No.' Belligerent. Alex sighed inwardly. 'Just Malone.'

Detective Inspector Kate Todd looked impassively at him for a moment before turning back to Alex. 'I would be grateful if you could both come down the steps, please.'

They did as she asked.

'You found the body, Alex, did you?' Her voice switched from brisk professional to professional kindness.

Alex nodded. Behind her an officer was tying blue and white tape from one bush to another, sealing off the caravan, the body, Jackie Wood, from prying eyes. Men in shapeless white suits and masks ducked under the tape and went into the caravan. She suddenly thought of all the police shows she'd seen, the crime books she'd read, and wondered about clues and fingerprints and contaminating the scene. She started to burble. 'Yes, I'd come to interview her for the magazine I work for. It's Jackie Wood in there.'

'We know.'

Well, they would, wouldn't they?

'Is it the first time you've been here?'

She shook her head. 'It was the second part of the interview.'

'Interview?'

'I'm a journalist. I do news features. Sometimes about people who've been in the news or who just have something to say. You know.' She felt stupid.

'And the magazine?'

'It's called the *Saturday Magazine*. Part of the *Saturday Herald*. Here.' She fished about in her pocket and took out a rather dog-eared business card. 'My number's on there.' She dug into her pocket again and brought out a pen and wrote on the card. 'And that's the number of the magazine.'

The DI took it. 'Thank you.'

'Look, Alex is exhausted and needs to get home.' Malone had that determined look on his face.

Kate Todd looked him up and down. 'I am well aware of how Ms Devlin must be feeling,' she said.

Was she? How could she be? How could she know about the way her guts were churning and how she felt as though she was about to throw up?

'I'll get someone to take a witness statement from you now, Ms Devlin, and perhaps you could come down to the police station later.'

'The one in the town? Why?' She tried not to look as panicky as she felt.

Kate Todd gave a small smile. 'I know it's not glamorous, but I'll be setting up an incident room there. And we'll need to take your fingerprints, please.'

'Fingerprints?' Now her heart was racing and she began to feel light-headed. Her fear must have shown on her face, because Kate Todd put her hand on her arm. 'It's just to eliminate you.' Her voice was kind. 'You've been in there. Your fingerprints will be in the caravan, we'll need to cross them off our list, as it were. You too, Mr Malone.'

'I didn't go in there.'

'Nevertheless.'

Alex could feel the stand-off building but instinctively knew the DI was not a woman to cross. 'Thank you,' she said.

'Would you like someone to take you home after Steve here has taken your statement?' She signalled to a stocky man in a uniform who came hurrying over.

'It's all right,' said Malone. 'I can do it.'

Kate Todd inclined her head. 'Very well. But while Ms Devlin is talking to my DS, perhaps you and I could have a word?'

'Sure.' They walked away.

It didn't take too long. Alex recounted her story to the police officer, as agreed with Malone. It was a version of the truth, much easier, he'd said, to keep the story as near to the truth as possible, then she wouldn't trip up in the telling. So she did just that. She said nothing about the knife or her fears about Sasha.

'So you didn't see a murder weapon then?' Detective Sergeant Steve asked, licking the tip of his pencil. She wondered what his surname was. Perhaps that was his surname. Perhaps—

'Ms Devlin?'

She shook herself. 'No.'

'And Mr Malone?'

'What about him?'

'Did he see the murder weapon?'

'He didn't go in. I told you he came along after.'

'When you phoned him.'

'Yes.' Alex was getting irritated. 'I thought it was my statement you're supposed to be taking?'

Stocky Cop Steve shrugged. 'Just want to get a picture, that's all.' But he didn't ask her any more questions about Malone.

'Okay?' DI Todd and Malone came back over to where she was standing, Stocky Cop Steve having gone away with her statement.

'Yes, fine thanks,' Alex said, looking at DI Todd, knowing she was familiar; the name was familiar. Then it struck her. How could she have forgotten? Although now she was older, more severe-looking. Her hair cut short, whereas then it had been long, passed her shoulders, in fact. She had been a young officer when— 'Excuse me, Detective Inspector, but we know each other don't we?'

DI Todd gave a brief smile, her expression softening. 'Yes, Ms Devlin, I'm afraid we do.'

'Come on,' said Malone abruptly, taking her elbow. 'We're done here.'

'But—' said Alex, wanting to talk more to the detective.

'Now, Alex. Please.'

'Good to chat with you, Mr Malone. As I said to you before, I'm sure we'll see one another again.' Kate Todd stared at him, then looked over Alex's shoulder, frowning. 'No Sergeant,' she shouted, 'not there.' She shot Alex a glance. 'Sorry, I have to go. See you at the station.' She looked at Malone once more, a slightly quizzical expression on her features. 'As I said, Mr Malone, I look forward to seeing you again.' She hurried off.

'Maybe,' muttered Malone. He began to frogmarch Alex away, just as she saw Nikki come round the corner, laden down with carrier bags. She stopped, mouth agape at the sight of the ambulance and police activity.

Alex had forgotten about Nikki.

'What's all this?' she called out.

'Don't say anything to her,' Malone said in her ear.

Alex pulled her elbow away from him. 'Malone, I have to say something. She saw me go into the caravan. I answered the door, for God's sake, when Jackie was lying dead in there. How am I going to explain that away?'

'You didn't say in your statement?'

The panic started again and her head began to hurt. 'No. I . . . but I told Nikki that Jackie had a migraine. How am I going to get around that? The police are bound to talk to her. She'll tell them I was there.' Oh God, what was she going to do?

'Okay.' Malone took charge again. 'Tell her you panicked. About the migraine. You'd found Jackie Wood on the floor and didn't know what to do when she came to the door.'

'She's not going to buy that, is she?'

'Try it. You never know. She's probably got something to hide, too. There must be some reason why she's holed up in a caravan in the middle of winter on the Suffolk coast.'

'And then what? Ask her to lie to the police?'

'All she has to do is not mention knocking on the caravan door and you saying about a migraine. That's all.'

That's all. There was nothing else for it.

'What's going on?' Nikki called out.

'Nikki, it's dreadful.' Alex hurried over to her, trying to ignore the fear gnawing at her.

Nikki put down her carrier bags. 'The police and everything. What are they doing?'

'It's Jackie.'

'Your friend in the other caravan?'

Alex nodded. 'She's dead.'

She whistled. 'Dead? What, the migraine see her off, did it? I'll never get that cup of coffee with her. I always felt she was a bit like me, a loner, you know?'

Alex did know. 'It wasn't the migraine, Nikki.'

She cocked her head to one side. 'Oh?'

'When you knocked, she was lying on the floor and I panicked; I didn't know what to do. I thought – I thought – actually, I don't know what I thought. As I say, I panicked.' She tried to give a little smile as if to say 'wasn't I silly', which was a bit inadequate under the circumstances.

105

A sly looked flicked across Nikki's face. 'Is that right?'

At that moment Alex could see that Nikki was not all she made herself out to be; that Malone was right. There was a reason why she was in this godforsaken place in the middle of winter. Alex still wished she'd done the sensible thing, though, and asked her for help when she'd come knocking. But perhaps she could get away with it, perhaps Nikki wouldn't want to get too involved.

'Yes and the thing is, Nikki, I didn't tell the police about that. I thought it would make me look—'

'Silly?'

'Something like that,' she said, breathing out carefully. 'And it was silly. Stupid. I don't know what I was thinking of. And now if I say something to the cops, well . . .'

'Look,' said Nikki, 'I have no intention of talking to them if I can possibly help it. Me and the police don't have too good a history, y'know? And if I do have to, it'll be short and sweet.' She squeezed Alex's arm. 'Don't you worry any more, I didn't see or hear anything anyway. I mean, she was dead and that was that. You didn't kill her, did you?' She laughed.

'No.' Alex laughed too, but she could hear a nervous tremor in her voice.

'Well then. Least said soonest mended, eh?'

'Thanks Nikki.'

''S'okay.' She picked up her carrier bags. 'And perhaps we could have that coffee I was talking about? When I'm in my new flat, yeah?'

'Right.'

'And I don't even know your name?'

'It's Alex.'

She started to walk towards her caravan. 'Okay Alex, don't worry. I won't say a word.'

Alex watched her go. Nikki had changed from being the lonely woman who just wanted to find a friend to someone who had a small measure of control over her.

Why did she think that was more of a threat than anything?

13

Kate finished her conversation with the sergeant who had been about to dump several thousand pounds worth of expensive equipment on to the damp grass and went to get a forensic suit from the back of her car. She took off her coat and pulled it on over her clothes and tried to find somewhere dry to slip on the bootees.

Out of the corner of her eye she saw Malone and Alex Devlin talking to a young woman laden down with shopping bags. She would have to make sure someone spoke to shopping-bag woman – from the expressions of the three of them there was something going on. Malone looked particularly fierce. He was a slippery one, that was for sure. When she had taken him to one side it had been to give some space for Alex to be able to talk to Steve without him glowering at them both. Influencing what she might say. A controlled menace had radiated from him that even his good looks couldn't disguise.

'I know you from somewhere, don't I?' she'd asked, getting straight to the point.

Malone raised an eyebrow. 'Do you?'

She studied his face, irritated at the slow smile spreading across his features. 'What's your first name please?'

'Mickey.'

'Mickey Malone? Somehow I don't believe you.'

'No?' He shrugged. 'Tough shit.'

She narrowed her eyes. 'If you don't come in and give a statement in the next couple of days, I'll bring you in myself. Is that clear?'

Again that infuriating smile. 'That should be interesting.' He looked at his watch. 'Shall we see how Alex is doing? I've got an appointment in half an hour.'

I'll bet you have, she muttered under her breath before smiling tightly. 'Remember Mr Malone, I will come and find you.'

Mickey Malone my arse, she thought as she went up the caravan steps. She'd soon sort him out when he came in to give his statement. But his face nagged at her. She knew she'd seen him somewhere before.

The air in the caravan was dank, fetid, and smelt of death and decay. Kate tried hard to breathe through her nose and knew the smell would linger on her skin and clothes until she washed. The police photographer was taking pictures of the scene from every conceivable angle, and other forensic officers were carefully bagging evidence, dusting for fingerprints, and testing for anything out of the ordinary.

She looked around the living area, seeing an overturned cup on the table and a brown stain underneath. Food was ground into the carpet, too. A couple of chain-store paintings on the wall, thin brown curtains pulled back from the windows. A small pile of books and newspapers on a chair. An open can of baked beans. She tugged at a drawer by the sink. Cheap cutlery. In the cupboards above she found white plates with a green line painted around the rim. Bowls, mugs, all with the same pattern. There was also a jar of mustard, salt and pepper pots, and a jar of pickle. She bent down and opened the fridge. A limp lettuce, three yoghurts, and a piece of cheddar. She stood up, her hands vaguely damp inside the police-issue gloves. Not much to show for a life. Someone had pulled the caravan door shut. She went to open it, to let death out and fresh air in.

Kate knew she couldn't avoid it any longer, and looked towards the toilet-cum-shower-room. She saw the splayed legs of Jackie Wood and the broad back and iron-grey head of hair of the pathologist, Jane Blake, crouched between the legs and taking samples from beneath Jackie Wood's nails.

'Nasty one, this.' Jane stood, her bulk filling the doorway. 'Blood everywhere. Quite a frenzied stabbing.'

'Time of death?'

Jane laughed. 'Come on, Katie, you don't expect me to tell you that without lots of uming and ahing do you?' However grim the situation, Jane never stopped smiling. She enjoyed her work, took great pride in it. She was good too. Experienced.

'And it's Kate these days, as you very well know,' said Kate.

'Ach, you'll always be Katie to me.' Jane smiled at her.

Kate grinned. Jane, with her round face, ready smile, and comforting presence was the only one allowed to call her Katie. They had known each other since Kate found Harry Clements and Jane had performed the post-mortem in a gentle, considered manner. 'Okay. Let's presume you've umed and ahed enough. What do you reckon?'

Jane wrinkled her nose though more in concentration than at the smell that curled around them both. 'It was a cold night but the heater had been left on. Rigor mortis had set in and is still in place. She died where she lies now – from blood loss in all probability – and maybe shock. I would say sometime between ten o'clock last night and seven this morning. Though until I've carried out a proper exam I won't know for sure.'

Kate looked down at the shell that had been Jackie Wood. That was all it was – a shell. Any sense of life had fled. It was at times like these that Kate thought maybe human beings did have souls, otherwise what was it that left the body at the time of death? And what sort of person – deranged person – could do this to another human being? Leave them lying on the floor of a smelly toilet after stabbing them multiple times. It was so *sordid*. But

109

then murder was sordid. She looked at Jane, trying to ignore the waves of nausea that swept over her.

'Weapon?' she asked.

Jane stared down at the body, pursing her lips. 'Knife. I'll know more after the post-mortem.'

'Thanks Jane.'

Jane smiled briefly. 'It never gets any better, does it? Seeing the body of someone who's had the life snuffed out of them?'

'No. It doesn't.'

Twenty minutes later Kate walked through the doors of the Sole Bay police station, which was on a side street in the town. The smell of hops from the nearby brewery permeated the air; a warmer scent than the stench of death that had followed her back from Harbour's End.

'Good to see you Ma'am.' The desk sergeant in the reception area stood a little straighter and looked as though he was about to salute. Kate smiled at him. 'Sergeant, I gather you have a room set aside for me while you get the incident room set up?'

'Incident room?' The sergeant looked worried. 'Incident room. Yes.'

'And?'

'The ... er ... incident room is in the yard, Ma'am. The Portakabin. It's just being cleared now.'

'Okay, I'll take a look.' She strode through the door on the other side of the desk into the cold. The makeshift building in the concrete yard looked as though it'd had several resting places before it had finally reached Sole Bay. Broken plastic chairs lay forlornly at the bottom of the steps. Bundles of newspapers tied up with string were strewn around, as if they had been thrown out of the building. A fact confirmed when a bundle sailed through an open window and landed at her feet. A couple of uniforms were coming out of its door carrying cardboard boxes in their arms. If she looked carefully, Kate was sure she could see mildew on the boxes. All in all, it didn't look like a great prospect. Oh well. She went back inside.

'Detective Inspector?' Alex Devlin was sitting on one of the hard chairs in the reception area, her hands jammed between her legs, foot tapping.

Kate stopped. 'Ms Devlin.'

'I thought I would come and get it over with. The fingerprints and all that.'

'Great. I'm afraid I'll have to take you into one of the interview rooms – my incident room isn't ready yet.' She looked at the desk sergeant. 'Can you ask DS Rogers to come through, please.'

'Yes Ma'am. Interview room is on the left.'

A few minutes later Kate was watching Steve Rogers as he manoeuvred Alex Devlin's fingers onto the ink pad, while apologising for not having the state of the art digital equipment used in more modern police stations. Next came the swab of the inside of her mouth; not that Kate thought either process would elicit any new information about what had happened in the caravan. The woman's prints and DNA would be all over the place.

'Interesting job you've got,' said Kate. 'How do you come up with what to write about?'

'Sometimes it's commissioned – my editor asks me to find out about so-and-so – other times I see an interesting story in a paper, hear something on the TV or radio, or read something online that piques my interest so I do a bit of research and pitch the idea to my editor.' Alex held her fingers in front of her face as if to examine her black fingertips.

'Don't worry, it will come off. Is that how you met Mr Malone?' She tried to sound as casual as she could, aware of Alex suddenly shifting on her chair.

'Sort of,' she said. 'I can't really say too much—'

'Confidentiality and all that?' Kate smiled. 'That's okay, I understand.'

'It's my next feature coming out soon. It's a bit under wraps.'

111

Kate smiled. Under wraps. Of course, that's where she'd seen Malone before, at Martlesham, disappearing into an office. Three or four years ago now and she hadn't seen him since. Probably worked undercover. Right. Cocky git. She filed the knowledge away for future reference. 'So, you were what? Wanting to write something about Jackie Wood?'

'Yes.' Alex licked her lips. 'I know it must seem odd to you, wanting to write about the woman who killed my niece and nephew—'

'She has been freed.' Kate said, gently, not wanting to stop Alex from talking.

'Yes, yes, I know. It's just that I wanted to understand her, try and find out what life had been like for her inside, that sort of thing.'

'And you thought she would talk to you rather than anyone else?'

'Yes. No. I don't know. It seemed like a good idea . . .' Her voice trailed off. 'Her lawyer set it up.'

'So today was going to be the second time you talked to her?'

'Yes.' She began to feel impatient. 'Look, I've already told your detective this. I've told him all this. Do I have to go through it again?'

'I just like to get it clear in my head, that's all Ms Devlin. From what you've said, you obviously still think she was guilty?'

'Yes.'

'So were you hoping to find out where Millie was?'

'It was an interview about Jackie Wood and her time inside. Her side of the story.'

She was a calm one, thought Kate. 'And your sister?'

Alex visibly stiffened. 'Sasha? What about her? She's got nothing to do with Jackie Wood's death.'

'I didn't say she had,' said Kate patiently, watching as Alex's eyes darted around the room, looking everywhere but at her. 'I was only wondering what she thought about you talking to Jackie.'

'She doesn't know. Not yet. I was hoping—'

'Yes?'

'I was hoping she wouldn't have to find out.'

'She would have when the article was in the magazine.' Kate pointed out.

'I know, I know. But I wanted to be able to tell her when the time was right. Now I suppose—'

'You'll have to tell her sooner.'

Alex jumped up, pushing the chair back. 'Do I have to stay any longer? Am I under suspicion, or what?'

'No, you don't have to stay any longer.'

'But I am under suspicion?'

Kate sighed. 'Everybody is until we can eliminate them.'

'I just wanted to talk to Jackie. Find out about her. I didn't want her dead. Stabbed like that with a bloody great kitchen knife. Now I want to go, please. I've done what you wanted. Given you a statement, fingerprints, DNA, and unless you're going to arrest me I'd like to leave.' Kate watched as Alex clenched and unclenched her hands.

Kate stayed sitting, looking up at her. 'You can leave, Alex. I'm not keeping you here. I just wanted to talk to you, that's all. Can I ask you to be discreet, please?'

'Discreet?'

'I know you're a journalist, but could I ask you not to say anything until we have traced any members of Jackie Wood's family.'

Alex stared at her. 'I thought there weren't any?'

'Probably not. But we have to be sure.' Kate thought it unlikely Alex would say anything – at least, not yet. This was her exclusive and she wanted to keep it that way.

'Okay. But in return could I ask you not to release the name until I've told Sasha?'

Kate was surprised. She thought Alex would ask her not to tell the media about Jackie Wood until she had filed her copy. She nodded. 'There'll be a press conference at about six and I'll have to do it then. There are various TV companies and newspapers sniffing around as we speak.'

'Thank you.'

'And I'm sorry you had to find the body like that. It can't have been easy.'

'No,' Alex replied. 'I shouldn't think it ever is, is it?'

Kate watched as Alex left the room.

She drummed her fingers on the table. Why did she feel that conversation had all been a bit of an elaborate dance? And the kitchen knife. How did Alex Devlin know the weapon was a kitchen knife?

14

Alex sat in her office and stared out of the window. The bare trees and neglected pots still wouldn't sprout any foliage or flowers, no matter how many times she glared at them. Even if she narrowed her eyes, they didn't look any prettier. It had taken her a while to stop shaking, but a large slug of brandy helped. She reasoned she needed it. She was finding it hard not to see Jackie Wood, lying at that awkward angle in the tiny bathroom with her dead eyes and the bloom of red over her clothes.

How was she going to find out where Millie was buried now?

The sky hung leaden again; threatening more rain and making the afternoon seem even shorter. Malone had gone back to wherever he went back to, saying he had things to do and would see her later. Thankfully, there was no sign of Gus, until she heard the door slam.

She went downstairs and braced herself.

'Hey, Mum,' he said, coming into the house and shrugging off his coat, leaving it on the floor; his mate Jack trailing behind him and munching an apple. 'Have you heard?'

Alex walked into the kitchen. 'What?' she asked, before she could stop herself, knowing what he was about to say.

'Her. The murderer. Jackie Wood. Someone's killed her.' His eyes were shining.

'Stabbed to death,' said Jack, almost, she felt, with relish. 'Lots and lots of stab wounds. I heard. Blood everywhere. Drowning in blood.'

What was it with these boys that death meant so little to them?

Alex opened up the fridge. 'Have you eaten? I've got ham, tomatoes, a bit of salad? I can make you a sandwich.'

'Muuum? Did you hear what I said?'

'I did, darling. Now, food?' She reached in and brought out a packet of ham, waving it in front of their faces.

She felt rather than saw the two boys look at one another.

'Okay,' she said, shutting the fridge and sitting down, peering at the packet of ham which looked as though it had a blue-ish tinge, 'I do know about it. I found her body.'

Alex swore their mouths dropped open. 'Really? You're not shitting me?'

'No, Gus, I am not "shitting you", as you so delicately put it. I went to do my next bit of the interview, and there she was, on the floor, dead.' She shivered at the memory. Perhaps she was wrong to feed their violent fantasies, but she did think they needed to hear what actually happened, from her. She could just imagine what gruesome spin active young minds could put on it. 'It was not exciting or thrilling; it was rather depressing and horrible to see someone dead like that. There was a lot of blood. It's the first dead body I have ever seen, and I don't want to see another one. Not like that, anyway.' She hoped her flat, even tone would discourage any macabre interest.

'Did you call the police?' asked Gus.

'I did. They arrived with forensic vans and tape and people put white suits on and they put a cordon around the caravan.'

'Wow.' Gus saw her face. 'Sorry. I know it wouldn't have been nice for you.'

'No it wasn't, sweetheart.' And she wanted to put her arms around her son and hold him close to protect him from the evil

116

in the world; to protect him from the knowledge that his mum wasn't perfect, that she had secrets she couldn't share. She felt overwhelmed by the love she felt for Gus right at that moment, and wanted nothing more than to shut out the world, keep them both safe. But she knew she couldn't do that. She'd learned the hard way that the world always came knocking on the door.

Jack took another bite out of his apple. 'Where was she?'

'What do you mean? In the caravan, I told you.'

'No, I mean, whereabouts in the caravan?'

'In the bathroom. Why?'

'Just wondered, that's all.' He grimaced. 'They're pretty small, aren't they, those caravan bathrooms?'

'Yes,' she said.

'So she was sort of squashed in there?' He swallowed his piece of apple, his Adam's apple bobbing up and down.

Alex shook her head. 'Jack, I don't think we need to go into all the grim details, do we? A woman has lost her life in the most horrid way and we shouldn't relish it.'

The crunching of the apple as Jack bit into it again sounded loud. 'No. Sorry, Alex.'

'Okay,' she said.

'But she's definitely dead, isn't she?' Gus suddenly looked anxious. 'She looked it to me.'

'That must have been awful for you, Mum.' His face twisted. 'But I'm glad she's dead, I really, really am.'

'What do dead people look like?' This from Jack.

Alex ignored him, and reached out her hand to Gus. 'I know you are.'

He nodded and squeezed her hand.

'And I had to give a statement and go to the police station and all that sort of stuff.'

'Cool.'

She sighed. 'No, Jack. It wasn't "cool". It was tiring and a bit frightening.' For a moment all she wanted to do was to close her eyes. She was more than tired. Exhausted. But she pulled herself together, all brisk efficiency again. 'Food?'

Teenagers, they were always hungry, so she made them a ham and salad sandwich and left them to it, going back upstairs to her office.

She had to regroup.

What had she succeeded in doing, besides getting herself into deep shit? How long would it be before the press got hold of the story? And Sasha? What was she to do about her sister? She hadn't told her she was going to see Jackie Wood, that was one problem. But the other was that she now wasn't entirely convinced Sasha hadn't had anything to do with her murder. What if Sasha had killed her? What if she confessed to her, then what should she do?

This was ridiculous. Her exhaustion was getting to her, making her get everything all out of proportion. If she looked at it logically, Sasha wouldn't even know where to find Jackie Wood, or have the strength to stab her in such a vicious way. Surely she could rule Sasha out of the equation. Couldn't she?

She examined the tips of her fingers, which still bore traces of the ink used to take her fingerprints, then ran her tongue around the inside of her mouth as if she could feel where they had taken the DNA sample. At the time she'd felt that if she were as cooperative as possible then DI Todd might leave her alone. She tried to answer the policewoman's questions about Jackie Wood and the article calmly, but Alex knew she had become uptight and defensive. What had she said? What the fuck had she said? She rubbed her eyes with her fists. She'd kept quiet about Malone, tried to say as little as possible about Sasha, then she had gone on about being under suspicion. There was no doubt she was bloody well under suspicion. She knew as well as anybody that the first people the police look at are the family of the murder victim – well that one was out, wasn't it? – and the next person is the one who found the body. That was her.

Taking a tissue, Alex rubbed the remainder of the ink off her fingers. She was absolutely sure she hadn't said anything that would lead the Detective Inspector to Malone, or Sasha – wasn't she?

She had to stop staring out of the window and go and see Sasha, do some work, something. Oh God. She dropped her head into her hands. The interview she had now with Jackie Wood was dynamite. Not what she wanted at all. Not as Alex Devlin, sister of Sasha and aunty to Millie and Harry. Maybe as Alex Devlin, journalist. But she couldn't do that, despite being the only bloody journalist who knew that the woman in the caravan who had been murdered was Jackie Wood. The only bloody journalist who'd known she'd been holed up in the caravan anyway. The police couldn't – and wouldn't, as DI Todd made clear – keep it under wraps forever. When she and Malone had left the caravan site, the local news organizations were already turning up. As soon as the body was officially identified, everybody would be descending on Sole Bay.

The journalist in her wanted to be the first to break the story. The sister in her wanted to protect Sasha from all the publicity that would surely follow. More opening of old wounds. More old pictures flashed on the TV screen. A happy Millie and Harry, dirty faces, grinning. Opening Christmas presents. Building a sandcastle. Sasha laughing. All that. More fending off calls. So, to be journalist or human? Fuck. Fuck. Fuck. She also had to make sure nothing about her and Martin Jessop came out. Even after all these years it would be a hell of a story, especially when news programmes had to be filled 24/7.

She drummed her fingers on the desk, trying to think everything through logically, but it wasn't working. She opened the desk and took out the key with its fob that Malone had handed to her.

Think.

Her phone suddenly sang out its grungy tune, startling her. She answered without looking, thinking it would be Gus or Malone.

'Alex Devlin?' The voice was young, polite, and vaguely familiar.

'Yes,' she answered.

119

'It's Ed Killingback. From *The Post*.'

She sighed, her finger reaching for the off button.

'Wait. Before you hang up, please listen to me.'

Something in his tone made her finger hover, just for a moment.

He went on quickly, as if he knew he was on borrowed time. 'I know the body in the caravan was Jackie Wood's. The woman who helped kill your niece and nephew.' He left a silence. An old journalistic trick; most people abhor a silence in a conversation and rush to fill it. That's how she often got some of the meatiest lines for her articles. He probably was just making some sort of guess and was waiting for her to confirm it, so she said nothing.

'Okay, fair enough,' he said eventually. 'But it was her, and I know you were there; you found her body. I haven't had any confirmation from the police, so all we have is speculation—'

Too damn right.

'. . . and the fact I saw you talking to DI Todd; but I am going to run with this tomorrow and thought you might like to talk to me. Give me your side of the story.'

'My side of the story?' Dear God, he knew something. She broke out into a sweat.

'Yes. How you found her, what you were doing up at Harbour's End, that sort of thing. Best to set the record straight.'

If that was the record he wanted setting straight, then maybe she should speak to him. However, she was curious. 'Why are you so interested?'

He chuckled. 'I have been interested in this case for years, since I was a journalism student, actually. It's fascinating. You know, the fact that Martin Jessop killed himself, that Millie's body was never found. Jackie Wood's role in it all. Whether she really did know what Jessop had done. It's like an unsolved murder mystery from the telly. And now she's dead. You can surely see what a great story it is. A great human story.'

She felt unbearably sad at his excitement. This was her life he was talking about, that he wanted to splash all over the paper, and she knew that next month most people would have forgotten all about it while she would be left to pick up the pieces of Sasha that remained.

'Alex? Alex? I'm sorry, I didn't mean to upset you.' How did he know? 'But I think we really should meet. You'll get a better press from me than you will from other tabs.'

Alex slumped in her seat. How could she be so naive as to think the whole thing wouldn't be splashed all over the papers tomorrow? Maybe even on the local news tonight. She hadn't been thinking straight. These days even the BBC went with 'locally named' rather than waiting for official confirmation – all in the rush to be first with the news. Sky – never wrong for long. They were all at it. And after being able to hide from it for fifteen years, now she didn't seem able to get away from being the news.

'Look,' she said, making a decision, 'I'll meet you, okay? I'm not promising anything, but I will meet you.'

'Really? Where?'

She thought for a minute, already regretting it. 'There's a café on the beach that's open all year round. It's called Jim's, it's just where the beach huts start.'

'I know the one, I'll see you there in what, an hour?'

Alex nodded, then realized he couldn't see her. 'All right. There's something I have to do first, but I'll see you then.'

'Okay. And, by the way. Did you know he had another lover, not just Wood?'

'Who did?'

'Martin Jessop.'

She pressed the off button without saying goodbye. She reckoned he'd gone beyond the need for pleasantries.

'You did what?' Sasha straightened up from her crouching position and threw the garden shears on the ground. She pushed her hair back off her face, leaving a grubby mark across her forehead.

Alex had gone round to Sasha's with her heart in her mouth, dreading having to tell her what she had done, and wondering what her reaction would be to the news of Jackie Wood's murder.

There was no reply when she knocked on the door, so she took out her key and let herself in.

'Sasha?' she called.

No reply.

She went through into the kitchen, resisting the temptation to look in the cutlery drawers or at the knife rack, but she did notice the dirty plates, the sink full of greasy water and saucepans, the sound of the washing machine. Peering through the window into the gathering gloom, she could just about make out Sasha in the garden, clearing weeds and the detritus of summer and autumn. On her good days it was her therapy. She said jobs in the garden helped her not think about anything else, provided a distraction from her thoughts, which was why her garden was always well kept, neat, and full of colour in the summer months. She liked spring for the explosion of new life. She said she wanted somewhere lovely to sit for when Millie came home. Alex wished she could spend some of that energy inside the house sometimes.

'Hallo, Sasha.'

Her sister was pulling up old grasses, chopping back others. She glanced at Alex, then went back to her work. Then Alex told her.

Now she faced Alex, her face a picture of disbelief. 'Are you telling me you actually went round to see that woman? Why, Alex? Whatever possessed you? Did you think she was going to tell you where Millie is buried or something?' She pulled her old duffel coat tighter around her body, but that didn't stop her shivering. Alex stamped her feet, trying to keep warm; the day's cold slithering into her bones.

'I thought she might, yes. It was for an article, Sash.'

'An article? A bloody article?' Sasha bent down and picked up the shears before slicing the tops off shrubs. 'You sold your soul for a bloody article.'

'Don't be so melodramatic, Sasha. I didn't sell my soul. I thought it would be a good idea to meet her, see what sort of person she was—'

'I can tell you what sort of person she was—' Sasha jabbed the shears towards her. Alex took a step backwards. 'She's poison. Scum. She should never have been let out. She deserves anything bad that is coming her way.' There was a smear of dirt down one side of her face. 'So what did she say, then, sister dear? Did she tell you where to go in order to find my daughter's body? Did she tell you so we could take her back and bury her next to her brother? Did she? Did she?' The pointed ends of the shears were getting closer and closer to Alex's chest.

She put up her hands as if to ward her off. 'Sash, don't. You're scaring me. Let me tell you what happened.'

'Do you know what?' Sasha's face was twisted with . . . what? Hate? Fear? 'I don't want to know what she said to you because I know it won't have been anything useful. She will never tell. She will defend her lover until she goes to her grave, which can't be soon enough for me.'

Her sister turned back to her shrubs and began hacking at them again, anger oozing from every pore.

She whirled round. 'I just want her dead, that's all. She killed my children. She did it. Nobody else. She's weird and evil and doesn't deserve to be on this earth. We're never going to find Millie so now the next best thing is for her to curl up and die somewhere.'

'She is,' Alex said quietly.

'What?' Sasha stared at her, a film of sweat on her forehead.

'Dead. Jackie Wood. That's what I came to tell you.'

Her sister crumpled in on herself. 'But I wanted to know, Lexie. Now she'll never tell us.' And she fell into Alex's arms.

Alex hugged her close, feeling the frailty of her body and smelling the grease in her hair, knowing how fragile she was when she used the childhood version of her name. 'Darling, I'm so, so sorry.'

Her shoulders heaved. 'Tell me,' she said. 'Tell me what happened.'

Alex rubbed her back through her coat. 'Sweetheart, it was when I went to see her for the second interview.'

Sasha drew away from her. 'Second interview?' Her voice was sharp. 'So you went to see the bitch more than once?' Alex was taken aback by the intense, feverish light in her eyes. 'Where was she living? A swanky hotel in London? A bed and breakfast, what? Where?'

'She was here.'

'Here?' Sasha blinked.

'In Sole Bay, yes.'

'Who let that happen, for fuck's sake? And you didn't think to tell me?'

Alex took a deep breath. 'No. I knew how you would react. I wanted to see what would happen before I said anything to you.'

'See what would happen? What do you mean? See if you could find out about Millie? What's this? Atonement? A hope that I might forgive you?' A glob of spittle landed on Alex's face. She wiped it away.

'No,' she said, as calmly as she could. 'I wanted to find out more about the woman, what made her tick, try and understand.'

'Understand? Understand? What the fuck do you mean? Understand what, exactly?'

Alex shrugged, trying to stay calm, telling herself that this was Sasha and she was hurting. 'Understand her thought processes. Then maybe I could find out about Millie.'

Her sister threw back her head and laughed. 'You poor cow. So bloody eager to make things right. You really think a couple of interviews for that excuse of a magazine you work for would get Millie back? You have no idea.'

'What do you mean, I have no idea?'

'Millie's gone,' she said, tugging the sleeves of her coat down over her hands. She noticed Alex watching her. 'Don't worry,' she snarled. 'I haven't been cutting myself again, I've been a good girl, a very good girl.' She sank back down on to the grass, the fight draining out of her. 'We're never going to see her again.' She sniffed. The end of her nose was red.

Sasha was exhausting; Alex didn't know which way to jump.

'Anyway,' Sasha continued, looking up at her. 'You said she was dead. How? Where?'

Alex crouched down so she was level with her, wanting to see Sasha's eyes as she told her. 'I found her in her caravan on the Harbour End site. You know, the one—'

'At the end of the harbour, yes, I know it. Go on.'

'She was lying on the bathroom floor.' Alex tried to stop the image of Jackie Wood coming into her head, but it was impossible. Again she saw her eyes, milky with not-being-there. Her clothes, covered in red. The way her body was twisted to fit into that small room. Alex swallowed. 'She'd been stabbed, Sash, stabbed many, many times.'

Sasha stared at her, then smiled. 'I'm glad she's dead.'

'Did you kill her, Sasha?'

'Wish I had,' she said.

Alex slumped down next to her on the grass and put her head in her hands. Did she believe her? She thought she did.

Sasha touched her arm. 'You believe I did it.'

Alex's head jerked up and Sasha laughed. 'Come on, Alex, you must know by now that I know the way you think. And I'll bet your first thought was that I had somehow known she was there and gone and murdered her. Well I didn't. I didn't even know she was back in Sole Bay.'

Alex nodded. 'I believe you. But now we're never going to find out where Millie's body is buried. And it's my fault.' She started to shiver with the cold.

Sasha rubbed her back with soothing, circular motions. The tension slowly drained out of Alex and she leaned into her sister. 'We were never going to find out, I realize that,' Sasha said. 'I've sort of come to accept it. I think I knew when Jessop killed himself.

And you know what? I'm so tired. So tired of living a half-life and wondering what happened to Millie. She's dead, her soul has gone, and wherever her body is doesn't really matter now, does it?' Her voice was soothing; her words were what Alex had been longing to hear. 'We've lived in the shadows for so long. That bitch Wood was only a minor player in the whole thing. Jessop was the driving force.' Sasha paused in the rubbing of Alex's back. 'Well, you knew that, didn't you?' She began to rub Alex's back again. 'Millie's a mermaid.'

'What do you mean?'

Sasha smiled. 'Just something I sometimes think, that's all.'

Alex felt the cold from the ground seeping into her bones. But the numbness she was feeling in her body was not just from the cold. She couldn't do the guilt any more. She heaved herself up.

'I've got to go,' she said. 'I have to meet someone.'

Sasha looked at her from under her eyebrows, then she stood up too. 'Okay,' she said, as if Alex hadn't said anything about the interview, about Jackie Wood getting murdered. She put her arms out for a hug. Alex folded herself gratefully into her.

'How could you do it?' her sister hissed in her ear.

Alex pulled away and left, not looking back.

15

'So nothing on CCTV?' Kate paced the floor of the musty smelling dump that passed for the incident room she'd been promised, trying to ignore the smell of hot dust emanating from the inadequate heaters. Two officers were tapping away at their computers while technicians set up the telephone lines to be manned after she'd done the press conference about Jackie Wood. Already satellite trucks were lining up along the road, attended by thin young men and women shivering in inadequate coats, gripping scripts or holding iPads, and harassed engineers, running around with microphones and talkback units – journos diverted from more mundane pieces to come and report on some real news. The newspaper reporters were the more hardened types, used to standing around passing the time in all weathers, and they were gathering in the police station car park. She would let them in to the warmth of the conference room when she was good and ready.

She suspected the Portakabin would become too small once the news got out about who the victim of the Harbour's End caravan site murder was, and she was sure Cherry would want to take the investigation back to Martlesham. Despite the cramped conditions of their temporary home and the damp, stifling air,

Kate preferred to be able to work close to her cases. She would argue the toss with Cherry later.

'No boss.' Steve wrinkled his nose. 'It was all for show.'

Kate had asked for Steven Rogers to be on the team; he was steady and reliable and could also provide the doughnuts.

'By "all" you mean that one sodding camera attached to wall of the toilets. Bloody hell, don't these people have any sense of security at all?' She sat down heavily on one of the hard chairs by the trestle table in front of the pinboard.

'It would seem not. No video in it, nothing.'

'It's a wonder anyone stays at that godforsaken place when they've got that level of security.'

Kate changed tack. 'What did you think of Alex Devlin, Rogers? Do you believe her story?'

Rogers loosened his tie and undid the top button on his shirt. 'I think she stuck to the truth. Mostly. But I don't think she told us everything. And that Malone character was a slippery piece of shit.'

Kate drummed her fingers on the table. 'You're not wrong there. There's something about him I really don't like. He was rude and obstructive. Not in the least behaving like someone who had been called by his girlfriend to the scene of a murder.' She stood up. 'Hasn't been in yet, has he?'

Rogers shook his head. 'Said he'd be in in the next day or two.'

'Very relaxed. I wonder what that says about him? As if I didn't know. Anyway. Alex Devlin. What did you think?'

'A bit ghoulish I'd say she was.'

'Why?'

'Wanting to interview one of the people who'd been done for the murder of her sister's children? If that's not ghoulish, then I don't know what is.' He shivered theatrically.

'I will remind you, Detective Sergeant Rogers, that Ms Wood had been let out on appeal,' Kate replied with mock seriousness, ignoring Rogers's snort of derision.

'Yes Ma'am. Sorry Ma'am.'

'Hmm.'

'She didn't mind having her fingerprints taken. Or DNA. And she came straightaway. Most people would leave it for a day or two.'

'A bit odd I agree,' Kate said, frowning. 'As you rightly point out, most people would want to go home after an ordeal like that. Have a cup of tea or whatever and come back in a couple of days. But then she's not most people, is she?'

'Ma'am?'

'Having a family member murdered must mark you, Steve, don't you think? Especially if it's a child.' Kate sighed and looked up at the board, which at the moment only had a map of the area pinned on it. Soon there would be a timeline charting Jackie Wood's whereabouts in the days and hours leading up to her murder, photographs of the caravan site; the caravan itself, and her body: photographs taken from as many angles as the police photographer could manage in the cramped area of the caravan bathroom.

'Maybe she just wanted to get it over with. I would in her place.' Rogers scratched the back of his neck. 'Though why we're bothering about the murdering bitch I don't know.'

Kate turned. 'Rogers, that is not what we think. Whenever a crime has been committed we want to bring the perpetrator to justice. Jackie Wood deserves our attention and hard work just as much as anyone. She deserves justice too.'

'Even though she didn't show any mercy towards those kids?'

'Do I have to keep reminding you that her conviction was ruled unsafe?'

'Huh.'

'We devote as much time and as many resources to catching her killer as we would for anyone else. Okay?'

'Okay.'

'She hasn't changed much,' said Kate after a silence. 'Just looks older.'

'Changed?'

She looked at Rogers. 'I found the little boy's body, Steve, but then I expect you knew that.'

'Aye, I did,' he replied. 'One of your first, wasn't it? Bodies that is? Never nice to find the body of a child.'

'Especially a murdered one.'

'No.'

She pushed away the picture of the little boy folded into the case, his eyes wide open and, she'd thought at the time, pleading with her. 'But none of us would be any good if we collapsed in a gibbering heap at the sight of a dead body.'

'You're right, Kate,' he said, gently. 'But we are human. If we didn't allow it to affect us in some way then I don't think we should be doing this job.'

She opened her mouth, then closed it again. She had almost been about to say that it had affected her, affected her greatly. The consequences of finding Harry Clements's body had reached out and clouded her life ever since. But she said nothing. Steve Rogers was a friend, a colleague, but she was a Detective Inspector and had to keep some distance. With responsibility came loneliness – she'd learned that one.

'What about the interviews?' she said, finally.

Rogers shook his head. 'Nothing much there, Ma'am.' He snapped back into policeman mode. He licked his finger and thumb and flicked through the pages of his notebook. 'Paul Herman in caravan twenty-eight said he and his wife were in the caravan but didn't hear anything.'

'And how far away are they?'

He consulted his notebook. 'Two rows away. To be honest, there weren't many people about. The manager of the site said the camp was only a third full.'

'But we need to speak to everyone.'

'Yes, Ma'am, I know.'

'Jim Cassidy was walking his dog at about eleven o'clock that evening but he didn't see anything either.'

'What about the caravan opposite Jackie Wood's?'

Rogers flipped over a few more pages. 'Nikki Adams. She said she was in all evening but didn't hear anything. Said she was watching television and went to bed early.'

'Anyone else nearby?'

'Nope.'

'What was this Nikki Adams watching?'

'*Emmerdale. Holby City*, and a documentary about dolphins.'

'The sainted Attenborough?'

'Probably.'

'Check it out, just in case.'

Rogers looked at Kate reproachfully. 'I will.'

She shook her head. 'Of course you will, sorry. No reason why her story shouldn't be kosher, but better to be safe.' She sighed. 'So we're not getting anywhere, are we?'

'Nope.'

'Okay, look.' She tapped her pencil on her front teeth. 'We need some bodies to go round the campsite again. I can't believe that everybody there was so involved with each other or their TVs. Somebody, somewhere had to have heard something.'

Rogers got up wearily. 'I suppose you want me to go now. I'll take Eve and John, shall I?'

The two officers in question heard their names and looked up from their computers.

'Thanks . . . yes, it'll save them from the cranks and the nutters who'll start to ring as soon as the press conference finishes.' A thought struck her. 'No. Don't go just yet. Wait till after the conference. I might come with you.' She smiled at Rogers, ignoring the resigned – or was it horrified? – look on his face. 'Come on, Steve, it'll be fun.'

'Fun? If you say so. But I thought elevated coppers like you didn't sully themselves with grunt work?'

She gathered up her papers. 'I like to keep my hand in, Steve, you know that. I spend enough time dealing with paperwork and our own nutters.' She pushed away the thought that perhaps the other reason she wanted to go out with Steve and the uniforms was to avoid getting home too early and having to speak to Chris.

'It'll be nice to have you along . . . Ma'am.'

Kate grinned, then looked at her watch. 'Now, it's time to go and face the wolves.'

16

Alex wished she'd never had the idea of interviewing Jackie Wood.

The wind off the sea was like a knife slicing through her clothes and scraping across her skin. The sun was going down over the water and threw ribbons of orange light across the grey canopy of sky. She hunched herself against the ever-present wind as she made her way through the sand dunes. How much more damage had she done to Sasha now? And what was she doing, handing herself over to the cops like a sacrificial lamb?

And DI Todd. There was a coincidence. She had changed, though, since she last saw her in that stifling courtroom. She remembered the police officer as a shy young woman with long black hair. No make-up. Not at all stylish. Now she had lost the soft lines of youth and was all angles and armour.

The sun had disappeared from the sky and the gloom pressed its heavy weight on her. The sound of the sea filled her head. Powerful; rushing onto the land, then sucking back out, pulling pebbles, rocks, detritus with it. She imagined the sea meeting the horizon, merging into a uniform grey. It was infinite, timeless, problems tossed on the waves.

Fingerprints, DNA, the whole bloody lot. How much had she compromised herself? She had an uneasy acceptance of

DNA databases – useful for solving cold cases, or even those that weren't so cold – but could they be trusted? Who knew who could have access to the information and how it could be manipulated?

She reached the concrete prom, with its line of jaunty beach huts with prosaic names such as 'Victoria' and 'Albert' and 'Sailor's Rest', and then round to Jim's Café, her way lit by the sodium lights on the road above.

Ed Killingback was sitting at one of the tables in front of the closed shutters of the café. There was a white light around him, like a halo. He looked about thirty, with dark brown hair that was in need of a cut – not that she could talk – and a rather smart pea coat that was doing the business because he looked warm. Alex knew her face was pinched against the cold and her lips were probably blue.

'Hello,' she said, as she sat in one of the chairs opposite.

'Hi.' He gave a wide smile and his eyes, a clear and piercing hazel, crinkled at the corners. If she hadn't felt so tired and worn out she might have thought he was flirting with her. 'Lucky I had a torch.'

'Sorry. I know I'm late. I—'. She stopped. Never apologize, never explain. 'I'm here now.'

Ed flipped over the cover of the notebook in front of him and took a pen out of his pocket. He looked at her again. 'I do admire your work in the *Saturday Magazine*,' he said, earnestly.

Alex rolled her eyes.

He laughed. 'Pretty cheesy, huh?' He had the grace to look embarrassed.

'Pretty cheesy, yes.' She smiled to take the sting out of her words. 'But thank you. If you really do read it.'

'I do. Honestly.' He shuffled in his seat. 'Sorry, I haven't got long. There's a press conference in about half an hour and I really need to be there.'

Alex's heart sank. Bloody hell, the press conference. The shit was really going to hit the fan now. She was glad she wasn't going. She'd been on the sidelines of enough of those when the twins had gone missing, when Jackie Wood and Martin Jessop were arrested, when they were sent down. She'd avoided the press when Jessop killed himself by taking Gus away on his first holiday abroad.

She shrugged; the scene with Sasha suddenly coming back to punch her in the stomach. 'Don't let me keep you,' she snapped. 'You'll probably do just as well going there, getting it straight from the horse's mouth. See how far they've got in their investigation.' She almost told him to run along, but bit the words back. That was just a bit too patronizing.

He looked straight at her. 'Call me Ed. And I didn't mean to irritate you, I'm sorry.'

What was she doing sitting by a café shut up for the night; on a deserted beach with a thirty-something journalist? Probably losing her marbles, that's what.

'So,' she said, 'what do you want to know? Not that I might tell you, you understand.'

'Okay,' he said, drawing out the word. 'You found Jackie Wood's body, didn't you?'

'Where did you get your information?'

'Sources,' he said.

'What sources?'

'Come on, you don't expect me to tell you that, do you?'

She looked out to sea. It was inky black now, and stars were just beginning to appear. She felt restless. 'I wish the café was open. I could do with a cuppa.'

He just smiled again, his pen hovering over pristine paper. 'So?'

'Look,' Alex said, suddenly impatient, 'I don't know what you want from me.'

He leaned across the table. 'Just a story I can use. Something no one else has got. Come on, I can help you. If you tell me what happened – on an exclusive basis, naturally—'

'Naturally.'

135

He didn't notice her sarcasm. 'Then I can tell your story. The true story.'

She sighed, feeling old. 'Don't you think I know how this works?'

'What?' he said, seemingly without an ounce of guile.

'I tell you my story, you write it up to fit the story you want to tell, and bingo, more lies are disseminated. Let me tell you, Ed,' she emphasized his name, 'you might like my writing, but I sure as hell don't like *The Post*'s.'

'Not the point, Alex – I write a good story and I don't make it up.'

'Maybe not. But then when the subs get hold of it, the story's mangled out of all recognition.' She knew very well that that happened; it had happened to her on more than one occasion to her cost. Irate interviewees on the phone. Telling them it was a sub-editor who changed the copy wasn't much of a get-out clause. They didn't want to know. Her name had been on the story, therefore, she was the one to blame. And she could understand that point of view. None of which was going to help her now.

'Look,' she said. 'Yes, I found Jackie Wood's body. I'd gone to interview her for a piece in the magazine I write for and found her dead in the caravan.' She swallowed hard, keeping her voice on an even keel. 'And that's all there is to it.'

'But she had served time for being involved with the murder of your niece and nephew. How easy was it for you to decide to interview her? And were you hoping she might tell you where they had buried Millie?'

She laughed, shaking her head. 'No, no, no. That's it, Ed. No more. Besides, you're now presuming she really was guilty and knew where Millie is buried.' She looked at her watch. 'Time for your press conference.'

He shut his notebook with a snap. 'You're probably right. But I'm not going to give up, you know. I told you, I've been following this case for years. I've done my research and I know there's more to all of this than meets the eye.'

'All of what?' Alex asked sharply. Too sharply. His interest was immediately piqued.

'Martin Jessop and Jackie Wood being done for the murders. It was all too neat, too tidy. Police accepted everything that was put in front of them. Don't you think?'

'A judge and jury found them guilty.'

'And Jackie Wood has been let out due to the old prof being found useless. And now they're both dead, and the dead can't tell tales, can they? Anyway,' he stood, 'you're right. I'd best get to the presser. But I really would like to talk to you again. Please.'

It was then she asked the question that had been burning at the back of her mind ever since he'd called her. The question she knew she shouldn't ask, had stopped herself asking, but which tumbled out of her mouth like a stream of vomit. 'You said Martin Jessop had another lover; a secret lover. How do you know?'

He put the notebook in the inside pocket of his coat, then swept his fringe away from his forehead. 'That can be for next time, can't it, Alex?'

She watched as he strode away, his feet crunching over the stones.

17

Kate drew her shoulders back and breathed. She hated doing press conferences – the feral, eager looks of anticipation on the faces of the journalists, all waiting to jump in with the smart-arsed question, all wanting to find a line, an angle. Then there was the clicking of cameras, being blinded by the flashlights, the banks of microphones in front of her. At least this time she didn't have to guide a grieving family through the process. That was the worst. Hollow-eyed parents clutching soggy handkerchiefs and each other. Relatives slack-jawed with the horror of it all. Often they put the relatives through the rigour of the conference if they had the slightest suspicion they might have been involved in the crime. It felt like a form of medieval torture for all involved.

It had been like that fifteen years ago, when they had paraded Sasha and Jez Clements in front of the cameras. So many pictures of the twins – in their best clothes, in fancy dress, with ice cream smeared around their grinning mouths – had been pinned to the boards behind the couple to bring home the point that two little children who had everything to live for had gone missing. Kate had been a bystander then, but she could remember the words of the DCI at the time, how he'd told the officers helping with the presser to watch the couple carefully, see how they reacted. And to watch any friends of the family.

Medieval torture.

'Ma'am?'

Kate was brought back to the present by the press officer, Helen Grant, sent from Martlesham to orchestrate proceedings. Kate didn't much like her – Helen enjoyed making the press wait for information, feeding them misleading stuff and generally being as obstructive as she could possibly be. Although Kate didn't exactly love the media – far from it – she did like to keep them onside because you never knew when they could be useful.

'Yes, Helen, I'm ready.' She tried to keep the dislike out of her voice.

'Good. I'll go in first, shall I Ma'am?'

Was she imagining it or was Helen being overly deferential, almost mocking?

'Thank you, Helen, if you would.' Two could play at that game.

Helen looked at her. 'You know I think we're going with this too early, don't you? We haven't got much to give them that they don't know already.'

'I'm aware of that,' Kate replied smoothly. 'But there has been a lot of public interest and her name is out there, so I think we should confirm that it was Jackie Wood who was murdered.'

'Which could lead to a whole lot of trouble for us.'

Kate marshalled her patience. 'Maybe, but as I said, the name is out there, and there was no next-of-kin to tell. We'll get more coverage if we just give them a little bit – it's the drip-feed of information to the press that's most helpful to us.'

'Ma'am, Kate, I think you should be careful here – it's a very sensitive subject. Questions will be asked.' She pursed her lips, which Kate thought made her mouth look like a cat's arse.

'Questions?' The woman was infuriating. As if she didn't know it was an awkward situation. She didn't need to be reminded of it, especially by Helen Grant.

Helen sighed, as if she were having to explain to a child, and it made Kate want to strangle her. 'You know the tabloids will go mad with the fact that a woman convicted in connection with the Clements twins' murder had been living back in the community,' Helen said. 'And not just any community, but where she used to live and where the Clements family lives. Imagine the *Daily Mail* headlines, for pity's sake.'

'I am imagining them, that's the trouble. And if we even try to wriggle out of it or cover it up, then we'll be in a worse situation than we are now.' She didn't have time for this.

'Well, don't say I didn't warn you.' Cat's arse mouth again. She pushed open the door of the conference room and disappeared inside.

Kate wondered whether she ought to take up yoga – all that deep breathing and concentration on 'mindfulness' – would surely help in situations when she wanted to scream. Loudly.

'Detective Inspector?'

Kate jumped as a man stepped out of the shadows. Jez Clements. He looked unkempt, his uniform grubby, shoes dusty. There were bags under his eyes and his skin was taut across his once-handsome face.

'Sergeant?'

'If you have a minute, Ma'am, I'd appreciate a word.'

She shook her head. 'Can't, I'm afraid. Got a news conference to attend. Shouldn't you be with your ex-wife now?' She deliberately made her voice cold. She had spent years avoiding this man in the corridors of the police station at Martlesham, not wanting such a tangible reminder of Harry Clements and his little body in the suitcase, and had been grateful Clements had never made it to the Major Investigation Team. She would probably have had to ask for a transfer if that had happened. Besides which, there was something she didn't like about him, something she couldn't quite put her finger on. An untrustworthiness, maybe? And she had heard he had a reputation with the ladies – a love 'em and

140

leave 'em – reputation. Was that part of her antipathy towards him? Then she felt angry with herself. Had the job taken all the compassion out of her? Clements had lost his whole family, he deserved her sympathy.

Something like hatred flashed in his eyes. 'I'm on my way to see her, Detective Inspector. But I wanted to know. About Jackie Wood.'

'What about her?' She made her voice more gentle.

'Do you know who killed her? Or why? Is there anything you're going to keep back that perhaps I should know about? Anything at all?'

She lifted an eyebrow. 'Come on, Sergeant. You know I can't give you that information.'

'Because you don't know.'

'Because I can't give you that information.'

He took a deep breath, and she saw the strain in his expression. 'Look, Detective Inspector, I'm sorry, I don't mean to be . . . rude.' He swallowed. 'It would just help to know how far on in the investigation you are. Rather than having to find out from the television or from reporters knocking on the damn door.'

'Surely the FLO—'

'Oh, for goodness' sake, you know how it works. No one's going to tell us a damn thing if they don't have to.' His voice shook. 'Ma'am.' He stepped forward and put his hand on her arm. 'Please.'

Kate heard the murmurings in the conference room. They were getting impatient. 'Look, all I can tell you is that, yes, it was Jackie Wood in that caravan and, no, we don't know who did it.' She looked at him, trying to understand what he was going through. 'Go back to Sasha, Jez. Go.'

She felt his eyes on her as she went through into the small meeting room of the Sole Bay police station, which was jam-packed with journalists, and with cameramen and women making last-minute adjustments to their equipment. She could smell damp clothes drying out and the warm musk of body odour. There was a knot of irritation in her stomach.

Standing behind a trestle table hastily erected for the occasion, with a clutch of microphones propped up in front of her like a group of furry guinea pigs jostling for position, she waited for the flash of cameras to die down and for Helen to do her introductory speech. All she had to do was to say that she, Kate, was going to speak. Bloody protocol; she could have done without Helen listening to every word she was about to say.

Helen was sitting down, smoothing her skirt over her knees. 'Where have you been?' she hissed. 'Everyone's waiting for you.'

Kate merely nodded to her, then looked around the room, making sure she had everyone's attention.

'Ladies and Gentlemen,' she began, putting her hands on the table and leaning slightly forward, deliberately looking down the barrel of a camera lens, 'following a very detailed investigation I can confirm that the body of forty-three-year-old Jackie Wood was found at half past nine this morning in a caravan at the Harbour's End caravan site in Sole Bay. She had suffered stab injuries.' She paused for effect. 'We have begun a murder investigation.'

A buzz went round the room like a Mexican wave.

'No murder weapon has been found. We would urge anyone who was in the area at the time or anyone who has any information to come forward. Any little piece of information could help solve this heinous crime (For Christ's sake - where had that come from? Heinous crime? This must all be affecting her more than she realized.)

She looked across at the array of reporters – wanting – needing their attention.

'We know that out there is someone who wants to call us, who's worried about something they saw. I say to you, call us now – you can be anonymous – simply tell us what you know. Please.' She allowed a few seconds silence to let the words sink in. 'Now, I will take some questions,' she said.

Hands went up.

Kate pointed to the reporter from the local BBC news programme, *Look East*.

'Can you confirm it's the same Jackie Wood as the Jackie Wood who was recently released from prison?' she asked.

'I can,' said Kate, nodding.

'Did you know she was in the area?'

'Yes.'

'And you didn't think you should have made that public?'

'Why?'

'In the public interest.'

'No.'

'No?'

Kate sighed. This was why she hated giving press conferences, especially about something like this, but she knew it was a necessary evil. And Cherry liked them. 'All good for public relations. Visible policing and all that,' he'd said.

'No,' she said. 'It would not have been in the public interest to know Jackie Wood was living in Sole Bay, any more than it would be in the public interest for you to know where Maxine Carr is living. Jackie Wood was given anonymity and a promise her new name and whereabouts would not be revealed. And we kept that promise. And you should know that's the way it works.'

The reporter arched her eyebrow. How she hated that supercilious look.

'So you would rather keep a promise to a convicted murderer—'

'Unsafe conviction,' she said, feeling unaccountably weary.

'You would rather keep a promise to a convicted murderer let out on appeal than keep the people of Suffolk safe.'

Kate stared at the young reporter. She'd had enough of this. 'Don't be so silly,' she snapped. 'She wasn't a convicted murderer. She'd been convicted in connection with the murders. Next question?'

'Penny Pembleton, *East Anglian*,' said a woman with a shock of frizzy ginger hair. 'Have you got any leads at all?'

'We are progressing with our inquiries.' Now who was being supercilious?

She took more questions – *Channel 4 News*, Channel 5, the *Guardian*, Sky, several of the tabloids – they were all there, determined to make something of the fact that Jackie Wood had been living in the midst of a law-abiding community. Kate wanted to sit down. Wanted a drink. Wanted to talk to Chris.

'Final question, please,' she said.

'Ed Killingback, *The Post*.'

'Yes Ed?' She steeled herself.

'Do the Clements know?'

'A family liaison officer is on her way round as we speak.' She looked around the assembled journalists. 'Now, thank you all for coming and—'

'Detective Inspector?'

'I said that was the final question, Ed.'

'Could Jackie Wood's death have any connection with what happened fifteen years ago?'

'We will be looking into that possibility, but it seems unlikely, at this stage. Now if I could give you all—'

'What do you have to say about the rumours that Martin Jessop had another lover? Not just Jackie Wood?'

A loud murmur went around the room and all Kate could hear was the scraping of pens on paper and the tapping of fingers on iPads.

Shit.

She wanted to rub the tension in her neck, but knew she had to nip this one in the bud or all hell would be let loose in the papers the following day. As for Killingback's rag – it was probably their front page exclusive splash.

'I don't know where you got that from, Ed?'

'You know I can't say. Sources and all that.'

'Well, I don't know what "source" that is, but I wouldn't rely on it if I were you. And I think it's unhelpful both for this case and for the Clements family for you to bring up some unsubstantiated assertion.' Steady. She had to be careful or else she would be seen as protesting too much.

'But—'

Ed's assertion had shaken Kate, but she tried not to let it show. Beside her, she could feel the heat of rage coming off Helen. 'If you have any evidence to do with a fifteen-year-old case,' said Kate, interrupting him, 'I suggest you get in touch with our cold case team. They would be very interested in what you have to say. In fact, if you have any new evidence, any new evidence at all, then we would like to hear it.' She stared at him, challenging him. 'Perhaps we could make an appointment for you to come to the station in the near future? Share what you have with us?'

He sat down, a slight smirk on his face.

Kate tried not to show any emotion at all. After giving out the phone number for the great British public to ring if they had any information, against a background of shouted questions and general hubbub, Kate gathered up her papers once more. 'I think that's all for now, ladies and gentleman. Meanwhile, we will put further updates on our website and Twitter feed. Any major news and we will call another press conference.' And she swept out, with Helen scurrying behind.

'That went well, Kate. Not.' Helen's mouth was in a straight line as she opened the door to the Portakabin for her.

'Quite.' Kate stopped and Helen almost cannoned into her. 'What was all that about Jessop and a secret lover?' She deliberately made her tone sharp.

'I have no idea,' she said.

Kate heard her press officer's voice shaking. 'Seemed to come from left field.'

'I thought you were supposed to cover all bases, know what the press is going to ask?'

'I'm not a mind reader, Ma'am,' she replied, her shoulders stiffening. 'Besides, are you sure you didn't have any idea about the lover development? Because if you know anything, I need to know. I'm going to have the press on my back from now until God knows when, so I would appreciate any heads-up from you. Ma'am.'

'It's the first I've heard of it. And if it were true, then it would have come out by now, wouldn't it? I suppose it's possible – just about – the investigating team had known something about it but decided it had no bearing on the case.'

'That doesn't help me, Ma'am.'

Kate just wanted to get rid of her. 'I'm sorry.' She looked at her watch. 'Time you were off home now anyway. The press can wait, or they can call whoever the duty officer is – for all the good that'll do them.'

'Thank you, Ma'am. Though the messages will still be there for me in the morning.' She turned on her heel and walked away.

Kate went through the door into the incident room and collapsed onto a chair. 'Bloody hell, why can't press officers face that lot, answer all the bloody questions, not just introduce you and leave you to take the flak. Isn't that what they're there for?'

'Because they'd be eaten alive,' said Rogers, looking up from his computer screen.

'You still here? Why aren't you knocking on caravan doors, finding our killer?' Kate eyed the doughnut on his desk wondering whether she could ask for a bite out of it.

'Waiting for you, Ma'am. You said you fancied an evening out.' He stretched, rubbing the small of his back. 'Need some new bloody chairs here.'

'It's your age.' Kate drummed her fingers on the desk. 'Rogers?'

'Ma'am?'

'You were around when Jessop and Wood were arrested, weren't you?'

'I was, yes. It was one of the biggest stories at the time.'

'And you helped on the case?'

'I did, but I was quite junior then – not as junior as you were, though Ma'am.'

'No, well.'

'Though you have climbed up the greasy pole a lot quicker than me.'

'Because I'm cleverer than you.'

'More clever. And a woman.'

Kate grinned, enjoying the banter. 'Now then, Rogers, I hope you're not going to go all resentful on me and play the sexist card?'

'As if I would, Ma'am.'

They both smiled at one another, having indulged in the game many times over the years.

'Back to the Jessop and Wood case – had you ever heard that Jessop had another mistress, not just Wood?'

Rogers looked down at his paperwork, picked up a pen. Kate watched as he ticked a box, then another. He turned a page over. Read it.

'Steve?'

'I wouldn't like to say, Ma'am.'

His shoulders were stiff, back rigid.

'Steve, I'm asking you as a friend, not as your superior officer.'

'Ma'am.'

She bit down a sigh. 'It could be important. And I won't say it came from you.'

Rogers put his pen down, carefully lining it up with the pad on his desk.

Kate looked around the small room. Eve and John were shifting in their seats, keeping their eyes glued to the telephone handsets in case they should miss them ringing. Or in case they should miss what Steve Rogers was about to say.

'I did hear something, yes.' He kept his voice low. 'Probably just office gossip.'

Kate's heart beat faster. 'What did you hear?' She knew gossip could have a kernel of truth.

He clasped his hands together. 'There were rumours – very quiet ones, you understand – that Jessop might have been involved with someone that we didn't know about. But they were squashed pretty quickly.'

'Squashed? Who by?'

He shrugged. 'I don't know. But one day one of the officers on the case said he had evidence, the next day he didn't. The whole line of inquiry was shut down.'

'What? That's nonsense. You must have some idea.'

He blew air out through his mouth. 'Word was that the mother's husband had something to do with it. And the officer in charge.'

'Wait a minute.' Kate held one finger up. 'Let me get this straight. You're saying that during the investigation of the murder of Harry Clements and the disappearance of Millie Clements, there was a rumour that Jessop had a secret lover and nobody looked into it?'

'Something like that.'

'No one looked into it because someone shut the line of inquiry down, and that someone was the detective inspector in charge?'

'Yes.'

'And the children's father – another police officer – colluded in this?'

Rogers nodded, looking uncomfortable. 'Jez Clements, yes.'

'Bloody hell.' She banged her fist on the table. 'He was here, just before the press conference. Asking about the case. Bloody hell.' Kate sighed. 'And no one questioned it? No one on the inquiry?'

'Well, you didn't, did you? Not at the time. You reckoned there was a good reason. And as I said, it was only a rumour. No one was sure that it happened. Perhaps there was no such line of inquiry. I don't know, Kate. It was just something that reached my ears after Jessop hanged himself.'

'Oh, I'm not blaming you, Steve.' She thought for a moment. 'Edward Grainger was in charge, wasn't he?' She remembered him well; a bluff copper who liked to do everything by the book, but with a reputation for basic honesty and a desire to see right done. 'I remember him. And I remember he left Suffolk as soon as Jessop and Wood were convicted.'

'Yes,' said Rogers. 'He was shipped off to Guernsey after that. I think he's retired now.'

'Still in Guernsey?'

'No. Came back somewhere round here I believe.'

'Hmm. And why would Jez Clements not want every avenue looked into? Want any line of inquiry investigated thoroughly when it was his children involved?'

'I don't know, Kate.'

There was certainly plenty to look into; now, there were other things to do.

'All right, Steve. I'll have to sleep on it, or something.' She gave him a tired smile. 'Now it's time to go and caravan-knock.'

She saw Rogers open his mouth to speak, and lifted a hand to stop him. 'I know it's late, but we've got a murderer to catch.' She took her coat off the back of her chair.

'So you're still coming with us, are you, Ma'am?' He shifted on his chair.

'Yes. Is that all right with you?'

She walked out of the door before he had a chance to reply.

18

'Here you go.'

Malone's voice pulled Alex out of a deep sleep that had been disturbed by dreams of Martin Jessop's bulging eyes as he hung from his top bunk, a knotted shirt around his neck. Jackie Wood had been in the dream too, smiling at her, blood dripping from her lips, hands beseeching. Alex was running away from them, down a corridor with a large, old-fashioned key in her hand. The corridor was endless, and Alex could feel panic rising in her throat. She was glad to wake up. 'Thanks,' she said, as he put a cup of tea on her bedside table, the feeling of terror gradually dissipating, her heart slowing down. 'You off out?' An unnecessary question as he had on his thick coat.

'Yep. Got a couple of bits and pieces to do.'

She struggled up and leaned back on the headboard, wishing her head didn't feel so foggy. The trouble was, when she got home she'd downed several glasses of white wine to dull the edges of the day. After meeting Killingback, she'd hesitated outside the police station, wondering whether to use her NUJ card to get into the presser, but had decided it was too dangerous. It was being held in a small room and she was bound to be noticed. Then, when she had got home,

Malone was waiting for her. One drink led to another, one kiss led to another, and before she knew it, Malone was staying the night. She put a hand to her forehead. Had she given him a front door key, too? Oh God. She was never going to drink again.

Alex damped down a wave of nausea and concentrated on stopping the room pitching and rolling around her. 'What sort of bits and pieces?'

She knew it sounded as though she was quizzing him, and she probably was. Malone wanted to move in with her, said they belonged together; fitted together. Alex wasn't sure he was right – how could she be – she'd only known the man for three months. But only a couple of days ago she'd been thinking he might be the one for her, so why was she hesitating now? There again, an in-depth interview for a magazine was hardly an application form for the role of boyfriend and surrogate father to Gus, was it? Because that's what she wanted as well. Not just someone to share things with, talk over things with, laugh with, but someone who could keep Gus on the straight and narrow. Or just any path, as long as it didn't involve the police.

And that was another problem. She knew, from the way Malone always evaded any poking into his past, that he wasn't exactly squeaky clean. Not such a good role model, then. On the one hand, she was so desperately lonely. On the other, she had always sworn she wouldn't introduce a man to Gus unless it was somebody she was serious about.

She could remember very little of Gus's father, had only a fuzzy recollection of his face, which she thought had been tanned and handsome. For that, read bland. She'd been in Ibiza with a dozen other hacks on her first press trip and spent the first twelve hours in a club high on vodka cocktails and freedom. She'd just dropped a tab of Ecstasy when he came up to her and began to chat. He might have been the DJ at the club, he might not have been. But she'd had a sort of recklessness about her at the time that made her go back to his flat and do things girls like her shouldn't. The next morning she tiptoed out of that flat without saying goodbye. Feeling a failure.

She hadn't even known she was pregnant for three months, and when it had finally dawned on her, made an appointment with a clinic in London to 'deal' with the problem. Then she was commissioned to write a piece about attacks on abortion clinics in the States and she'd had to look into the whole issue. What she found out made her cancel her date with the clinic, pack up the job, and go home to Suffolk.

Gus was the most important and precious thing in her life.

After he was born she vowed she would avoid relationships like the plague, but not long after, Martin Jessop had come along. She'd never really figured out what had made him different, why it had seemed right at the time, she just lived with the regrets.

Then when Millie and Harry were killed, Alex's emotions were all spent on her sister. But now the loneliness had kicked in, as well as the realization that she wasn't getting any younger.

And Malone made her laugh. But she still knew very little about him.

'Malone? What bits and pieces?'

He smiled and stroked her hair. 'Come on, sweetie, just stuff.'

'Are you ever going to tell me what stuff?' She realized her voice was shrill, but she had no idea what he did, where he got his money from; how he made a living now he wasn't being an undercover copper any more. 'I'll start to think you've got a wife stashed away somewhere.'

He leaned over her and planted a kiss on her forehead. 'I must go.' He turned towards the door.

'What about the police?'

He paused, his hand on the door knob and she could have sworn she saw his back stiffen. 'What about the police? I thought it was all okay.'

'It is. I just thought . . . I just thought you needed to go and do your statement, give your fingerprints and all that.' Alex's heart started hammering almost as badly as it had done during her dream and the nausea came back with a vengeance.

'I've done it.' He turned. 'So no need to worry, okay?' He patted his pocket. 'Don't worry, I can let myself in now if you're not home.'

'Okay,' she said. Damn, damn, damn.

She fell back onto her pillows. One day she would follow him, see where he went, what he got up to. She smiled. Now she really was going barking mad. The thought of even being able to follow him without him knowing was ridiculous. The thought of following him was ridiculous. Stupid.

But where did he go?

And had he deliberately ignored her jibe about a wife?

She shook her head, and waited for the room to stop spinning again. Waited for her skin to stop feeling clammy. Enough. She reached for her cup of tea and her hand brushed something metallic and cold. The key to the locker in Norwich.

Why would Jackie Wood have hired a left luggage locker unless she had something to hide? It wasn't as if she'd left stuff there during a day trip to the city, otherwise she would have got it out at the end of the day. No; there must be something in there she didn't want other people to know about. What other people? Alex wasn't sure, but one thing she was sure of: she had the key and she could find out what Wood was hiding. Perhaps. How she hoped it was the diary. What was it the reporter had said? Dead men tell no tales. Maybe not. But diaries certainly can.

An hour later she was up, showered and dressed, and eating dry toast in the kitchen with Gus, the hangover having retreated more than she deserved.

'What are your plans for today, love?'

He shrugged, smearing jam onto his piece of toast. 'Seeing the lads. Maybe a bit of footie in the park. Hang around, you know.'

She nodded. 'Great. But—'

He silenced her with a look. 'I'll be okay Mum, really.'

He reached across and rubbed her arm, obviously having sensed her doubt. 'I will, Mum, I promise. I won't spend the day at the amusement arcade or anything. I'll probably do something healthy like go fishing as well as have a bit of a kick about.'

She laughed. 'Fishing? I rather doubt that.'

He feigned a hurt look. 'Why?'

'First,' she ticked it off on her fingers, 'you don't have a fishing rod, and second, there is nowhere to fish around here – except the sea, I suppose – and third, you don't even like fishing.'

'Rumbled,' he said, getting up and putting his plate in the dishwasher. 'Mum, don't worry. A bit of footie really is on the cards and then we'll just hang about. Maybe do a bit of studying.'

She hardly thought studying fitted the agenda. 'And who is we?' she asked, not expecting much of an answer.

To her surprise he blushed. 'Oh, you know. Jack and the rest of the gang, and Carly and a couple of her friends.'

'Carly?' That was interesting.

He went to the fridge, took out a pint of milk and poured some into a glass. 'She was round here the other day.'

'Ah yes. The pretty girl with the bee-sting lips.'

He drank the milk without meeting her eyes. She could see him blush. 'I hadn't noticed.'

'Okay. Is she going skiing too?' She hoped she kept her voice casual.

'I think so.' Gus kept his voice casual too.

'Great.' Oh, the import behind the one-word answers. 'She seems nice.'

'Yep.'

Okay, warned off.

He put down the glass, and she longed to lean over and wipe the milk moustache off his top lip. But he beat her to it, dragging the back of his hand across his face. 'What about you, Mum? What are you doing today? Working?'

Alex thought about the Jackie Wood interview she should finish, and she thought about the key to the locker in the Forum nestling

154

in her pocket. She knew which she ought to do, but she knew what she was going to do. 'Actually, I think I might drive up to Norwich. I need a few things from Marks's.'

'Haven't you heard of internet shopping?' her son said, laughing. 'Save you the petrol and the aggro.'

'I know, I know. But I feel like a bit of a mooch around, treat myself to a bit of lunch or something.' The key was burning a hole in her pocket.

'Go for it, Ma.' He pecked her on the cheek. 'Gotta go. See you later.'

She might have been imagining it, but Gus seemed more relaxed, more in tune with himself. She rather hoped that Carly had something to do with it.

Alex arrived in Norwich as the sun struggled out from behind a slate-grey cloud and the pavements were just about dry.

Leaving her car in St Giles's car park, she headed down towards the market. How she loved its vibrancy. The colourful awnings; the buzz of chatter; the tangy smells of hot dogs and fish and chips vying with the aromas of freshly-ground coffee and frying Chinese noodles; stalls selling artisan bread and organic vegetables jostling for trade with those selling boiler suits or every part imaginable for vacuum cleaners. She wandered slowly, up and down the aisles, weaving in and out of the crowds and the pigeons strutting among the people and pushchairs; steam rising from the freshly cooked food and hot drinks. Putting off the moment when she would go to the Forum, frightened about what she might find – or what she might not find.

Enough.

She paused only for a minute at the second-hand bookstall and then almost ran up the steps and out of the market. There was the Forum; a great modern edifice of glass and steel, opposite the beautiful fifteenth century St Peter Mancroft Church. She loved the juxtaposition of old and new.

The powder-blue lockers were located inside the foyer near the stairs to the car park in full view of the people who'd gone inside to take shelter from the cold. She held the key in her hand – she didn't need to look at the fob to know the locker was number fifteen.

Standing in front of the locker, she tried to look as though she was meant to be there. Nonchalant, not shifting about looking guilty. Then she slid the key into the lock and turned it. The door swung open easily. Inside was a large brown envelope, which she pulled out and put in her handbag. Then she closed and locked the box, her heart beating hard.

Ten minutes later Alex was sitting in her favourite coffee shop, cappuccino in front of her, the tempting smell of Steve's sausage rolls wafting around. She opened the envelope.

Drawings. No notebook, no exercise book, nothing that could constitute a diary, just a sheaf of paper covered with childish drawings. Primary colours – red, green, blue – splodges of paint depicting . . . what? A house, a stick family, a tree, maybe grass. Another – yellow, brown all mixed up. A tail was there, maybe? She turned the paper over: *The Tiger Who Came To Tea by Millie Clements* written in a no-nonsense hand. A third piece of paper, just a long tail of green. *The Hungry Caterpillar by Harry Clements.* She turned over more and more sheets, all paintings, all by Millie or Harry. All so precious. She touched some of the paintings with her fingertips, thinking of the twins, imagining them flinging the paint on the paper. Why had Jackie Wood got these irreplaceable pieces of childhood? She slumped back in her seat.

A memory: she was round at Sasha's house, waiting. Her sister and the twins arrived back, laughing, cheeks flushed from the hot air outside. Millie and Harry were wearing matching Teletubbies' T-shirts and sun hats and were holding tight to Sasha's hands. It was one of Sasha's good days, when she was enjoying looking after her children, being a wife, enjoying her life. Her eyes were bright, without the unfocused expression that overshadowed many of her days, and her skin looked fresh and luminous, not the grey that so often characterized her appearance.

The twins scooted over towards Alex, calling her name in their high-pitched voices, and she scooped them up, one in each arm.

'Ooof,' she said. 'You're getting too big and heavy for this.' She set them back down on the floor.

'We've been to the sea,' said Millie, reaching up to drag her sun hat off her head, leaving her blonde hair sticking up in all directions. 'We paddled then we went clouring.'

'Paintin',' said Harry loudly, not to be outdone. 'Wiv paints.'

'Yes look.' Sasha beamed as she reached into her bag and brought out some still-wet pictures. 'We've been to the library and heard stories, haven't we darlings? And afterwards we sat and painted pictures about the stories.' She waved the paintings in front of Alex's nose. She could see that the different colours of paint had run into one another where they had been shoved any-old-how into her bag. 'We left some in the library to dry, but we brought— Oh.' Her face clouded over. 'They're ruined.'

'They're gorgeous,' Alex said. 'And I can't wait to see the others.'

Sasha started to shake. 'No. I've spoiled them.' She opened her fingers, and the paintings fluttered wetly onto the ground.

The twins stared, wide-eyed, thumbs in their mouths.

The memory dissolved.

'Are you all right?' One of the girls from behind the counter had come over, dishcloth in hand.

Alex looked up at her and realized she was crying. She managed to smile. 'I'm fine, thank you.'

'Your children's work?'

She shook her head. 'My niece and nephew.'

'Cute,' she said. 'If you're sure you're okay?'

'Yes. No problem. Thanks for asking.'

The waitress looked at her as if she didn't believe her, then nodded and walked off. 'Let me know if I can get you anything,' she called over her shoulder.

Alex knew there was no way the waitress could give her what she wanted. She slid the paintings back into the envelope. They must have been the ones that were left at the library to dry and Jackie Wood had kept them.

Weird. Why would she have done that? Had she been trying to hide from the police the fact that she'd taken them? Had she had an unhealthy interest in the twins?

And Alex still didn't have the diary.

19

Kate stood on the pavement and examined the house in front of her. Edwardian brick-built terrace with a small bay window upstairs and down, and another window over the front door. It was a house that had seen better days, with flaking paintwork and dirty net curtains at the windows. Perhaps she shouldn't be here. She should certainly have gone through the family liaison officer, but then she would have lost the element of surprise, and she really wanted to see Sasha Clements on home turf, as it were. There was something not quite right in Alex Devlin's account of her sister – the vehement denial that Sasha had anything to do with Jackie Wood's death before Kate had even said anything. And as for Alex's naive idea that Sasha wouldn't have found out about her interview with Jackie Wood, well, that was just ridiculous. She pushed away the thought that she should have been to see Sasha before, when Jackie Wood was first let out, whatever Cherry had said, but hadn't made the time.

She tugged at the gate that sagged from its hinges and walked up the short concrete path to the faded blue front door. Muted sounds from a television floated out on the crisp air. For once, the sky was blue and the sun was making a late showing, but nothing pierced the gloom that surrounded the house. She knocked.

After a couple of minutes the door opened a crack.

'Hallo?' said Kate.

The face peering out at her was thin and pinched, eyes wary. Sasha Clements looked nothing like how Kate remembered her from fifteen years before when her face had been everywhere – pale, high cheekbones, startlingly blue eyes, full mouth – the tragic beauty, she was labelled by some, though Kate couldn't remember who. But that beauty had fled, leaving behind a face full of sorrow and suffering.

Kate smiled in what she hoped was a non-threatening way while holding up her ID. 'Sasha? My name is Detective Inspector Todd. I wonder if I might have a word?'

For a few moments nothing happened, and Kate wondered if Sasha had heard what she had said, or even processed it, then the door opened wide. 'Come in. Please,' she said.

The house smelt fusty and unloved. The light was dim. As she followed Sasha into the main front room, Kate wanted to throw open the doors and windows and let the outside in. Clear the air of the dirt and the dust and the memories that lingered.

'Sit down.'

Kate sat on an old sofa that had seen better days – like most of the furniture in the room. An electric heater threw out a sliver of miserable warmth and the television was showing pictures of people dressed in red or blue sweatshirts racing round a flea market being harangued by an orange-faced presenter. Thankfully Sasha had turned the sound down. On every available surface there were photographs of the children, Harry and Millie. As babies. As toddlers. As growing up children. Her eyes alighted on one of Harry, obviously taken at Christmas as he was holding a pillowcase tied up with tinsel and there were paper chains hanging from the ceiling. He was beaming and wearing Thomas the Tank Engine pyjamas. Kate swallowed, the familiar tug of pain and doubt followed by certainty.

Sasha caught her looking. 'That's one of my favourite ones of Harry.'

Kate had never heard a voice so full of sadness.

'He was so happy. It was the first time he and Millie really, really understood what Christmas was all about.'

'Presents and family.'

Sasha nodded. 'That's right. You understand.'

Not really, she thought.

'They'd been so excited,' Sasha went on, 'and early on Christmas morning they'd come into the bedroom with Millie leaping straight onto the bed, snuggling in between Jez and me.' She stopped for a moment, ran a hand over her face. 'Then Harry came in. Beaming. I've never seen a beam like it. "He's been," he said. "He's been". Beaming.' Sasha sat for a moment, lost in her memories. 'Jez managed to find the camera and take that snap. Though Millie didn't like Jez getting out of bed. That's one of my favourite memories of him.'

'He was a beautiful child.'

'He was. And thank you.'

'What for?'

'For caring for him. When you found him, I mean. I haven't forgotten that.' Sasha jumped up off the sofa, suddenly all angles and energy. 'Can I get you tea? Coffee? Something stronger?'

'Coffee. Please.'

Kate could hear Sasha banging about in the kitchen, tried to imagine what she was doing – taking the cups out of the cupboard and banging the door shut. Turning on the tap and filling the kettle. Opening another cupboard. She had to concentrate on the noises otherwise she might have found herself undone by the photographs.

'Did you think I wouldn't recognize you,' Sasha said, as she came back bearing a tray complete with mugs of coffee and a packet of Rich Tea biscuits, its top torn open.

'I don't—', began Kate.

'Well, needless to say I did.' Sasha's eyes had changed from dead to bright, as if a switch had been turned on, lighting them from behind. 'And you were there, every single day at the trial. I noticed that you kept looking at them, but they refused to look at you. They were on their separate chairs, another chair between them.' She handed Kate a coffee. 'You know, I wondered why they didn't look at each other, never mind anyone else. I mean, you'd think they would, wouldn't you?'

Kate sipped the coffee. It was lukewarm, the water wasn't boiled. She could taste it.

'I tried to make them look at me too. Even when I was giving evidence. I just kept staring and staring hoping he would look at me and I could shout "You! You're the one! You are responsible!"' She shrank back in the chair. 'Do you see, Detective Inspector? Do you see what I mean?'

Kate nodded, not sure at all what she was agreeing with.

'I suppose you've come to tell me that Jackie Wood was back in Suffolk but is now dead. Dead as a fucking dodo. Thank Christ. I salute whoever did it. Anyway, is that why you're here? Don't worry; I've had one of your lot round already. Or two or three. And my sister. She went to interview her, did you know that?' Crumbs of biscuit sprayed from her mouth as she spoke. 'Yes, you did, you lot know what's going on everywhere, don't you? Everywhere. Did she kill her? Alex, I mean? Did she kill the bitch?'

Kate couldn't bear Sasha's manic movements any longer. She leaned across and put her hand on Sasha's arm. 'It's all right. I only wanted to make sure you were okay. It must have been a terrible shock: Jackie Wood coming out of prison and then being murdered.'

Sasha began to laugh; a laugh, which then got out of control and turned into huge sobs that wracked her whole body. She buried her face in her hands. 'I'm sorry, sorry, sorry.' She looked up, composed once more. 'It was a shock, I suppose.' She sighed. 'I thought it was all over. That, at least, I didn't have to think about her any more. But now I do.'

'Why?'

Sasha looked at her with surprise. 'Because she's still in my head, that's why. It's as if by letting her out of prison they let her back into my head and now I can't stop thinking about her, even if she is dead. She's there, all mixed up with Millie and Harry. I see her and I see my children.' Sasha lifted her arm to smooth her greasy hair, allowing the loose sleeve of her jumper to fall back. Kate saw the silver tracks of old scars, the raised pink skin of fresher scars and the crusty scabs of recent cuts. She understood that the hurt and pain Sasha must feel every day had to have an outlet.

She had to ask. 'Are you getting help?'

'What do you mean?' Sasha chewed her lip.

'For the self-harming, Sasha. There are plenty of organizations that can help you talk through . . . things. We've got leaflets back at the station. I could bring you some.'

Sasha's laugh was harsh. 'I'm fine, thank you. I've been to more counsellors and talked to more women with blue-rinse hair than you can imagine.'

'I think—'

'I think you should mind your own business, don't you?' She pulled her sleeves right down, catching and holding the edges with her fingers.

Kate drank some more of her coffee. 'Sasha, what were you doing the night Jackie Wood was murdered?'

Sasha shrugged. 'What do I do most nights? Read a bit. Watch telly – terrible programmes in the middle of the night. Sometimes I even go outside and do the garden.'

Kate stood up and went over to the window, moving the curtain aside. The garden was in stark contrast to the house inside: neat, tidy, colourful. Loved. 'In this weather?'

'Why not? It stops me thinking. And the cold can freeze the thoughts in my head.'

'Would you mind if I had a look around?'

Sasha scowled. 'What do you mean?'

'Just a look around the kitchen, the garden. That sort of thing.'

'Shouldn't you have a warrant for that?'

Kate tried to laugh. She was handling this all wrong. Her normal calm authority seemed to have deserted her. 'No. I just wanted an informal look around. For my own satisfaction. I'm not really here officially. I just wanted to see you, make sure you were okay. Maybe just get to know you a bit better.'

Sasha looked disbelieving, but then her face relaxed. 'Oh, go on then, have a nose. Look for clues. Though fuck knows what for, unless you think I killed her.'

'Did you?'

Sasha pretended to look thoughtful. 'Let's see. The woman who helped murder Harry and who probably has Millie somewhere has just got out of prison, but I don't want revenge. Oh no. I'm just prepared for her to walk around free while my little boy is rotting in a hole in the ground and Millie has floated away.'

'Floated away?'

Sasha punched her chest. 'From me.' Then all the fight seemed to go out of her. 'Go and look. I don't care. Maybe I did kill her, who knows.'

Kate stood and went out into the hallway. She opened a door that led into a small room that Kate guessed could be used as a dining room. But this one had a sofa in it, a small fireplace with a cast iron grate, and several boxes occupying the floor space.

'Been here twenty years and still haven't unpacked everything,' said Sasha, making her jump. She hadn't heard the woman come up behind her. 'Doesn't seem much point now. Can't be bothered. It's only spare plates and stuff, I think. We came here when we were first married, Jez and me. I was pregnant. Didn't know for ages it was twins, then we found out and we thought that would be great. Two in one go, how lucky were we? Get it over with. Two can't be any harder than one, and they'd be great friends. Best friends forever. I suppose they are now.'

Kate turned and looked at her, not knowing what to say.

'They'd be nineteen now, with boyfriends and girlfriends. Perhaps going to university and Jez and I would be worrying about them.' She gave a sad little laugh. 'I think about them all the time. Have you got children?'

'No, no I haven't.'

'My advice is . . . actually, I don't know what my advice is. I'd have willingly given them away when they were babies. Then I'd sometimes . . .' She shook her head. 'But now they've gone I want them back so much. So very much.' She seemed to be miles away but then, suddenly, snapped back to the present. 'Go on.' She waved her arm showing the scars again. 'Go and look. Where next?'

She'd had enough. The weight of dead children and lost possibilities was sitting heavily on her. She should have come here in a totally professional capacity, brought Steve with her, then she could have coped better. 'Just a quick look in the kitchen and then we're done, I won't take up any more of your time.'

'Doesn't really matter. I've got nothing else to do, have I?'

Kate made her way through to the kitchen, not really knowing what she was looking for. What was she expecting? A gaping great hole in the knife block – even supposing there was a knife block.

The kitchen was IKEA ordinary. Cupboards above a beechwood worktop. A toaster, kettle, mixer and yes, a knife block. She went over to it, lifted the knives out one by one.

'They're not a matching set.' Sasha had followed her in. 'We're not the sort to have matching Sabatiers. Or Jamie Oliver ones, for that matter. Does he do knives? He does everything else.'

A door slammed and Sasha froze for a moment, gripped the worktop with both hands.

'Sash? Are you there?' Kate recognized the voice of Jez Clements and all at once she didn't want to be there, didn't want to have to see this man again. 'I've brought you some food, in case you didn't have any in.'

'In the kitchen.' Sasha's face was strained and her voice was reedy. 'I think you ought to go.'

'Are you frightened of him?' Kate asked quickly.

Sasha shook her head. 'No, no, nothing like that. Nothing like that at all. Just go.'

Too late.

'What are you doing here?' His voice was hostile as he dumped two carrier bags down on the floor.

'She was only seeing how I was, that's all Jez.' Sasha didn't move.

Jez narrowed his eyes. 'You've never bothered about us before, *Detective Inspector*,' he almost spat out her rank, 'so I'm not sure why you are now. Unless you just wanted to poke around.' His voice shook and Kate regretted giving him the brush-off just before the press conference.

'No, Sergeant. I wanted to see how Sasha was doing.' He looked a mess. His hair needed a good wash and there was a couple of days' stubble on his face. His clothes looked as though he'd snatched them off the washing pile.

'Well she's doing fine, no thanks to you lot. No thanks to the help you don't give us. Can you tell me now how things are going? Or do I have to find out again from the tittle-tattle in the office?'

'Look, I know this isn't easy for either of you—'

'Isn't easy? No it bloody well isn't easy and you've been no help. You might think that officers would stick together.'

Kate gazed at him steadily. 'What do you mean by that, Sergeant?'

Jez met her gaze. 'I mean we should help each other, support each other.'

'Is that right? I heard you liked doing that, though I didn't realize you called it "help" and "support".' Kate heard her voice getting angry so she took a couple of deep breaths. This wasn't the time or place for that discussion. 'Anyway, I was concerned about Sasha.'

'So am I,' he retorted, seeming to ignore the anger and sarcasm in her voice and not reacting to what she had just said. 'But I don't see why you think it necessary to come and poke around. Unless you think we're responsible for putting that bitch down.'

Kate winced at his choice of words. Sasha was still gripping the worktop. 'I'm just trying to piece together what happened the night Jackie Wood was murdered. Where were you, as a matter of interest, Sergeant?'

'Me?' He laughed bitterly. 'Sitting in front of the TV with a microwaved meal, I expect. That's how I spend most evenings.'

'Come on, Jez.' This from Sasha. Wearily. 'You're not on your own very often, are you? Not these days.'

'Don't do this Sasha. Please.'

Kate watched the interplay between the pair with interest. Sasha's face was set hard; Jez looked almost pleading.

'Why not? You tossed me aside like I always knew you would.'

'I did not "toss you aside" Sasha . . . oh, what's the point?' He turned to Kate. 'If you must know, I was with someone that evening, but I'd rather not say who.'

Now Kate was interested. 'Why not?'

'Because.' He crossed his arms looking belligerent.

She sighed. 'You know the way it goes, Sergeant. You'll have to tell us eventually.'

'Maybe.'

'Because she's married, I expect', said Sasha with a sneer. 'That's the usual thing for you, isn't it, Jez? No complications, no involvement, no worry. That's how he likes it, Detective Inspector.'

Kate didn't want to be in the middle of an argument between this unhappy couple a moment longer. She looked at Jez. 'I think we need to talk again, don't you? I've got a few things I want to ask you about, okay?'

He looked defiant. 'Fine.'

Somehow Kate didn't think it was fine at all.

20

Another early morning and Alex's office was beginning to feel like a prison. Every time she went up there the guilt would rise in her throat. It was either about leaving Gus to his own devices over the half-term or knowing that she should write the article about Jackie Wood. That was what she was feeling most guilty about at that moment, because there, sitting in her inbox, was yet another email from her editor.

Alex – no preliminaries there then *– I know it's a difficult time for you but I need your copy asap. I want to put the magazine to bed and you're holding it up. Plus Fran wants to put a tease in the main paper so we can be the first to break it. Let me know if you can't deliver. If you can't I shall look the fool. I've trusted you on this, Alex.*

No signature. Not a good sign. And, 'can't deliver', not good words for someone who was essentially freelance. If she couldn't deliver on time, then she wouldn't get paid – obviously – but, more importantly, she would lose trust and probably wouldn't get any more work.

It had been hard enough to get Liz onside with the article. The phone call she'd made to her editor late the day after Jackie Wood's murder had been difficult, to say the least. Although, as Alex had expected, she was extremely interested, she'd had her management hat on when going through the ethics of the interview: the effects on Sasha, how Alex would feel seeing the interview in print. Alex explained it was all above board and all parties had agreed to the interview. And, she pointed out, you can't libel the dead. Eventually Liz had taken it higher and had got the okay.

'I want it quickly, Alex,' she'd said when she phoned back to tell her to go ahead. 'There'll be a lot of interest in the murder over the next few days and we can hit it at its peak if we get it in next week's magazine. I can hold it for you.'

But Alex had found it harder to order her thoughts than she thought she would.

She dropped her head into her hands. She still needed the money for Gus's skiing trip, not to mention the bills that needed to be paid. She rifled through the envelopes that had dropped through the letter box that morning. An ominous-looking one from the bank. Would be about a couple of direct debits she hadn't been able to pay. Her mobile phone bill. A credit card bill that she would have to shell out money for in the next couple of weeks.

There was always Ed Killingback's offer. She could spill her guts to him for an enormous fee. He would love that. But there was no way she was going to give him that satisfaction, especially as there was no reason why Killingback should even suspect anything about her relationship with Jessop. And besides, by writing it herself, she would have control over the content – she wouldn't trust Killingback not to put his own spin on it. And her work for the *Saturday Magazine* had been paying the bills for some years now and it needed to continue.

It had been three days since she had found Jackie's body and it was clear Liz would not wait any longer. Alex shook herself.

Enough. She had to get on with it. Taking out her notes, she opened a new document file on her computer and began to type.

Three hours later Alex pressed the 'send' button and was grateful for the whoosh that accompanied the email leaving her computer. She sat back in her chair and breathed a sigh of relief, hoping it would be okay.

She had written about the lonely woman she had found in that bleak caravan; how Jackie Wood was friendless with no idea how the world worked any more, how she couldn't even experience the simple pleasure of going out for a coffee and a cake in case she was recognized. She wrote about the effect Martin Jessop's crime had had on Sasha and the family, and how Jackie Wood had denied her part in it. She wrote about how she had hoped to get her to reveal where she and Jessop had buried Millie, despite her protestations of innocence, and she wrote of her shock at finding her dead. She wrote from her head, not her heart, and hoped it would satisfy Liz. She could see her editor's lips pursing in disappointment that she hadn't bared her soul enough. Tough. She had other things to worry about.

But in writing the article she had begun to feel almost sorry for Jackie Wood. She'd been a sad figure. Perhaps she'd always been like that? Alex pushed the thought away, and thought about Martin Jessop instead. How he had taken his own life, denying Sasha justice. At least, that's how the papers put it at the time. There was some truth in that. She'd certainly wanted to see him rot in jail for what he'd done to the family. How had his wife coped with it all?

His wife. She stood by him throughout the trial. Even spoke to the papers; protesting his innocence. Said they would be launching an appeal. Said she would be there for him when he got out.

Opening the drawer in her desk, she took out her old contacts book from the days when the computer didn't rule her daily life and flicked through its pages.

There it was. Martin's Cambridgeshire address where his wife and family had lived fifteen years ago. The village of Harpen. Did they move away? Or did they stay and brazen it out? Did she ever know about the affair she, Alex, had been having with her husband? She leaned back in her chair. The telephone number was familiar – mainly because, for days after the trial, Alex had been tempted to ring up Angela Jessop, just to have some sort of contact with Martin. But she never had. How could she? How could she still have had feelings for the man who had murdered her niece and nephew?

She drummed her fingers on the desk. Angela Jessop could have the diary. Did she phone or should she just turn up, not giving Martin's wife the chance to give her the brush off? If Angela Jessop had read the diary and Martin had written about his affair with her, about how they crept around, seeing each other without anyone else knowing, about how she'd had no compunction about taking up with a married man, what would his wife's reaction be on seeing her? Or had enough years gone by to soften the encounter? How would she feel about seeing Martin's wife? How would Martin's wife feel about seeing her? Round and round these thoughts went, until she wanted to drop her head onto the desk and sleep.

But she didn't. She got onto Google Maps and looked up Harpen. She reckoned it would take her a couple of hours to get there.

She clicked on Street View, and images of the road started unfolding. She wandered virtually through Jessop's village. It was not a chocolate-box place, and she liked that. There was a row of council houses, and at the end of the row, a village hall. A telephone box nestled in the hedgerow just passed it. She wondered if it still worked or if it was now some sort of art installation or library or just a piss box. She turned left by the war memorial and found herself in a country lane bordered by hedges. The Google car must have been making its journey in early summer as the verges were thick with cow parsley – she could almost smell the vanilla scent – and the farmer's tractor had not yet made its way along the lane brutally hacking back the brambles and the trees and the nettles.

The Jessops lived along this road somewhere. She moved the mouse forward to a wooden gate on the right. Whitehouse Farm. She willed Google to let her see over the hedge, through the gate, anything, anything so she could see Jessop's wife in the garden, perhaps deadheading some roses, the children playing a game of tag, shouting happily. It would be summer because the pictures looked bright and sunny and the family would be happy because nothing bad had happened to them.

She rubbed her forehead. What the fuck was she doing? Constructing a fantasy life for a family who'd had the heart ripped out of them. And there wouldn't be any children playing happily, not least, because they'd probably grown up and moved away from the shadow of their father being a murderer. She was losing touch with reality here. She had to get a grip.

'Hey, Mum? Are you there?' Gus called.

Reluctantly she put the computer to sleep and went downstairs.

'Hi darling,' she said, walking into the kitchen.

Gus was making beans on toast and a mess and Carly (Alex tried not to show surprise) was sitting at the table, her chin in her hand, auburn curls gathered in a messy bun on top of her head.

'Mum, I'm just making Carly and me something to eat, then I thought we might go into Norwich to the cinema or something. Can you give us a lift to the station?'

If she went to Cambridgeshire she could drop them there on her way. 'Yes, that would be fine. Are you meeting Jack or anyone?'

'No, just us Mrs Devlin.' Carly's voice was quiet and assured. 'I hope that's okay.'

Alex smiled, trying not to be unnerved by the poise of the girl – no, young woman. 'Of course it is, Carly. It's no problem at all. I have to go out myself anyway.'

'More interviewing, Mrs Devlin?'

Alex looked at her. Carly gazed back, a cool look in those almost violet eyes. She was beautiful, she had to commend Gus on his taste, but for some reason, Alex didn't immediately warm to her.

172

There was something a bit – what? – calculating in her manner. Something. She couldn't quite put her finger on it. Maybe she was just plain jealous. Carly was wearing black leggings and a lacy frill for a skirt. She had on a sheer chiffon blouse with some sort of tee-shirt underneath and long sparkling pendants in her ears and Alex wished she'd had the confidence to develop her own style at that age.

'Something like that, Carly. And do please call me Alex. Mrs Devlin makes me sound so old.'

'And you're not a Mrs anyway, are you?' she said, a slight smile on those enviable lips.

'No. No I'm not. Never married, Carly. I find it an overrated state.'

Gus was merrily slopping Worcestershire sauce over their beans and seemed unaware of the sudden tension that had permeated the atmosphere.

'I'm sure you're right. Alex.' She got up from her chair and went over to Gus, winding her arm around his waist, other hand cupping his bottom. Staking her claim. Alex's hackles rose, and jealousy surged through her. Then she told herself not to be so stupid. This was her son growing up, and she should be glad that a girl had taken an interest in him and she should not be jealous of that curvy figure. Carly nuzzled Gus's neck, which immediately blazed red.

'Not here, Carly,' he muttered in a low voice, but not so low that Alex couldn't hear.

She wondered if they had slept together and wished she'd had that talk with Gus that every parent avoids. But how could she have known? Ten minutes ago he was playing football with his mates. Five minutes ago he was in trouble for drugs and joyriding. So she should be grateful his tastes had taken a more mature turn. She should like this child-woman for his sake.

And she bloody well hoped she was sixteen.

So Alex swallowed her jealousy and laughed. 'Come on you two, hurry up and eat and then we'll make tracks, okay?' She went

173

over to her handbag, opened her purse and took out a tenner. 'Here,' she said, putting it on the worktop in front of Gus. 'Have this on me. I know it won't pay for everything, but it'll go some way towards the tickets.'

'Thanks, Mum,' he said.

'Yes, thanks, Alex.' This time Carly's smile was warm, as though she knew she had won the battle.

21

'So, let me get this straight.' Cherry leaned back in his chair, lacing his fingers over his stomach. 'You don't know who murdered Jackie Wood, why she was murdered, or when she was murdered? Is that about the nub of it? The gist of it, as it were?'

Kate tried not to shift in her seat. She wanted to appear as though she was in full control. No, scrap that, she didn't want to *appear* in control, she *was* in control. She tried not to look at her watch. It was late and her feet hurt. She just wanted to get home to Chris and a fire and to curling up in front of the television. But she had been called back to Ipswich by Cherry and knew that such a summons did not bode well.

'We know she was stabbed somewhere around midnight, but otherwise no breakthrough yet, sir. We're sifting through the phone calls we received after the press conference and we're hopeful we'll get some leads. We've also had a good response on Facebook.' She crossed her fingers out of sight of Cherry.

'Facebook. I think it's the only time people like us, isn't it, Detective Inspector?' He chuckled at his own joke, then became sombre again. 'Hopeful is not really good enough, though, is it?'

'No sir.'

'No. And the door knocking? I hear you went out and about with DCs Maitland and Evans.'

'I did, sir, and we're checking out a couple of leads from that.'

'I see. Slow progress.'

Kate gritted her teeth, determined not to let him get to her. 'Not slow, steady.'

'Hmm.'

Hmm, what did that mean? She did so dislike it when people chuntered an indeterminate word leaving their audience – her – in the dark.

'Meanwhile we have the press baying at our backs wanting to know why the woman was there in the first place. Why she was on our manor at all.' Cherry loved to use words like 'manor'; he probably thought it gave him some sort of street credibility.

'I dealt with the press conference, sir,' she said, knowing she had to be firm. 'I gave them enough information to keep them happy without giving too much away. It's essential to keep them onside. Sir.'

'Indeed. What do you think of my new painting, by the way? It's called *Rendlesham at Rest*.' He waved towards a canvas of a green mess that looked as though it'd had paint thrown at it – which was probably exactly what had happened.

Kate eyed it gravely. 'Very nice, sir.'

Cherry clicked the roof of his mouth with his tongue. 'Nice isn't quite the word I was looking for. Next you'll be telling me that you know what you like as far as art is concerned.'

'I do though, sir.'

Cherry leaned forward, his stomach grazing the edge of the desk. 'But that sort of attitude doesn't show true appreciation and understanding of art, does it?'

'I suppose not, but it's the best I can do. And I think *Rendlesham at Rest* is a brilliant interpretation of the landscape.' It was one of the most beautiful areas of Suffolk – with not only the forest but also the heathland and wetlands and its UFO trail – so to see it boiled down to a green splodge on canvas was a bit depressing. That was her actual opinion, but she wasn't going to tell Cherry that. 'And more a portrait of a place than a landscape.'

Cherry looked delighted. 'Splendid. We'll make an art critic of you yet. Now, back to the lamentable press conference, and Helen.'

At least she'd got away with being an art critic. 'I did what I thought was right as regards the press conference. And the press officer, Helen, is really only there to advise me and quite honestly hasn't got a bloody clue how the press work.'

'But you don't take her advice, do you? She tells you to go easy, answer as few questions as possible, and you get rings run round you by the BBC, ITV, Sky, et al.'

Kate bristled. 'I think that's a bit unfair, sir.'

He sighed as though he hadn't heard her. 'The powers that be were not at all happy about what came out during the conference. Not pleased at all.'

'What weren't they pleased with? Sir.' At some point Cherry was going to notice her insubordination and haul her over the carpet, or give her a ticket to his forthcoming exhibition.

'What you must realize, Detective Inspector, is that we were put in a very difficult situation when Jackie Wood came back to these environs—'

'I do understand that—'

Cherry held up his hand. 'Allow me to speak. And it needs careful handling.'

Kate resisted the temptation to sound sarcastic. 'I appreciate it needs careful handling, and whatever Helen says, I did a more than competent job at the press conference. And, as I said, we've got a couple of excellent leads.'

He leaned forward, and Kate could smell the coffee on his breath. 'Don't get distracted by the journalists.'

She folded her hand in her lap. 'What do you mean, sir?'

'I mean we are dealing with the murder of Jackie Wood, we are not looking at any past history.'

'I don't understand.' She was going to make him say it; say that they were asking about Martin Jessop's lover, because lurking in the back of her mind was Steve telling her about Jez being able to shut the investigation down with the collusion of a senior officer.

His lips became a thin line and Kate could hear the hum of the computer on his desk.

'Don't take me for a fool, Detective Inspector. I am not a fool.'

The hum became louder. Kate looked him straight in the eyes. 'I don't, sir.'

'Good. I'm glad we're both singing from the same hymn sheet. You've spoken to Alex Devlin?'

'I have.'

'I remember her as quite a composed young woman.'

Kate looked at him. He was a wily old fox, and certainly was no fool. 'She was quite shaken up at having found the body.'

'Is she a suspect?'

'Everyone's a suspect, sir. Including Malone, the man she was with, though we're still waiting for him to come down to the station for DNA and fingerprints.'

'But there's no suggestion he was there at the time?'

'No,' Kate admitted. 'And his alibis check out so we don't have any reason to bring him in. But—'

'But what?'

'Malone, sir.'

'What about him?'

'I don't trust him.'

Cherry looked at her. 'That's a shame. You're supposed to be able to trust him.'

'What does that mean?'

He leaned forward. 'I would try and leave him out of this as far as you can, that's all.'

Kate nodded, her suspicions about Malone and his undercover persona confirmed. 'As far as I can. But if it turns out he is involved with Jackie Wood's murder in any way, then I'm afraid—'

178

'The law must take its course?'

'Yes,' she said firmly.

'Hmm.'

She didn't like that 'hmm'. She cleared her throat. 'Any more news about Mr and Mrs Williams? And the . . . er . . . raid?'

He knitted his fingers together. 'Not yet, Detective Inspector. We have had a letter from their lawyers complaining about half-arsed amateurs – my words, not theirs'. He smiled; the old sod was enjoying her discomfort. 'But we are still hopeful we can draw some sort of line underneath the whole sorry business without it reaching the ears of our dear colleagues who uphold truth and freedom in our country.'

'I'm sorry sir?'

'Tut, tut, Kate, you'll have to be quicker than that. I'm talking about the parasites that stalk this land.'

'Right. The press.'

'I was thinking more of our dearly loved politicians. But the press also. So let's try and keep your name off their front pages shall we? Especially if it is to do with that abortive raid.'

'Yes sir.'

'Good. Now I have something else to ask of you, Kate.'

He was back to calling her Kate. That was something, at least. She allowed herself to relax for a moment.

'Sir?'

'I know you are the main officer on the Jackie Wood case—'

'Though you are the Senior Investigating Officer.'

'Indeed, Kate. It's a high profile case, needs a high-ranking police officer.'

'Right. Sir.' Kate knew she would be doing most of the legwork, the investigating. Cherry was there to take the glory.

'But,' he continued, 'I have an officer transferring up from the Met. He was on one of their MITs and I think he could be of use to you.'

Something leaden settled in her chest. If there was one thing she hated, it was having to work closely with someone else, particularly someone who had no experience. Particularly on this case, even though she knew she was getting too close to it.

Cherry must have been reading her mind. 'In fact, I did do battle with myself, wondering whether or not to take you off this case, Kate—'

She sat up even straighter. No, no, he couldn't do that. It wouldn't be fair. Not after all the work she had put in.

'But I decided it wouldn't be fair, not after all the work you had put in, so I would ask that you work with DI Glithro. I think it could be a very satisfactory outcome for all concerned.' He leaned back in his chair looking very satisfied with himself.

Buggering bloody hell. DI Glithro. His reputation had preceded him to Suffolk. Old school. Unreconstructed. Tough. Unsympathetic. Kate truly believed that, whatever Jackie Wood had done in the past, she deserved justice for what had happened to her now. Was Glithro the man to help do that? Would he just want to get the job done, not look any deeper, not want to look into the possibility Martin Jessop might have had a second mistress?

'Kate, we really can't get fixated on something that happened more than a decade ago.' He held up his hand, as Kate opened her mouth to speak. 'And I know that the presser threw up the possibility of there being another person of interest, someone who may or may not have had a bearing on the original case, but I cannot let that distract me from the job in hand, can I, Kate? And, quite frankly, we haven't got the budget or the manpower to chase after dandelion heads.'

'Sir, I believe I'm doing a good job on the murder investigation and I feel I don't need help. Perhaps DI Glithro could help someone else?'

He looked at her. 'I remember your involvement, you know.'

'Right.' Now what was coming?

'It's never easy finding the body of a child, particularly in such a high-profile case, as it was at the time, and still is.' His voice was gentle. 'I think you might be influenced by that involvement and

180

we should let Glithro cast an eye over the case. Be another pair of eyes and ears for you. Another point of view, perhaps?'

'I'm not influenced by my involvement, as you call it, sir.' She refused to think about Chris, about the pills in the back of her cupboard. 'It was fifteen years ago and I've handled worse cases since.'

'Really? Discovering a dead body can stay with you. It can seep into your soul and become a part of you.'

'I understand that, but what about the press? I've heard he's terrible with them, got no idea how to handle the modern media. Apparently, if you talk to him about Facebook or Twitter he thinks you're talking about a new band.'

'I'm sure Helen will be able to keep him on the straight and narrow.'

Kate wanted to bang the table in front of Cherry. 'Helen knows bugger all. She'd cancel all conferences if she had her way. She likes to treat journalists like mushrooms.'

'Mushrooms?'

'Yes, you know, keep them in the dark and throw shit at them.'

His mouth twitched. 'I must remember that one. But I'm not suggesting he take over the case, just be a sounding board for you. Obviously, you will still deal with the day-to-day investigation, the press et cetera, et cetera. You will be the eyes and ears of the operation. As SIO I am in overall charge. And I am expecting results, Kate, you know that?' He beamed. 'I think we've sorted that one now, haven't we Kate?'

Her shoulders slumped. 'Yes sir.' Oh God, could things get any worse?

They could.

'Good. Now then, on another matter, I am putting on an exhibition of my paintings and will be inviting a few of my senior colleagues to its opening. I look forward to seeing you there.'

'Right,' said Kate, knowing very definitely she would prefer carpet burns to paintings.

22

Alex had dropped the teenagers off at the railway station and was now driving into the village of Harpen, wondering what the hell she was doing. The whole journey, along the dull A roads, watching the countryside becoming flat and more windswept, passed in a dream, and she was almost hypnotized by the steady back and forth of the windscreen wipers. She couldn't believe she was actually doing this, and she had no real plan for when she got there, particularly if it did turn out that Martin's wife and family still lived in the same house. But the chances of that had to be minimal, surely? The house must have been besieged by reporters, television crews; ghouls who wanted to see where a murderer would live.

On the other hand, it was a small village and could have rallied round, protecting Martin's wife from people who wanted a piece of her and her family. Maybe she would have stayed because it was somewhere she felt safe. And her children had been teenagers. Maybe she would have wanted to keep them somewhere they knew and with their friends, rather than uprooting them to a place that was unfamiliar. Less disruptive. All these thoughts were milling around in her head until she didn't know what to think any more.

The village was different from the Google pictures: it was now two years on and midwinter as opposed to early summer. The council houses she drove past looked drab and utilitarian; their long gardens with grass that needed cutting and borders that needed tending. The village hall, that had looked charming on Street View, was on its last legs, with rotting window frames and peeling paint. Rain-sodden Remembrance Sunday poppies were scattered around the war memorial. She turned left.

The hedgerow was a collection of bare twigs and trees reaching up like skeletons into the sky. The rain had stopped falling. And there it was: Whitehouse Farm. Alex pulled up in front of the gate. That, too, looked as though it could do with a lick of paint. Then she put the car into gear again and drove on a little way, finding a farm track where she could park her car. She switched off the engine.

So. Here she was.

Still not convinced she was actually going to do this, Alex got out of the car and walked along the lane to the gate, avoiding muddy puddles as she went. The catch was easy to open and she found herself walking down the driveway. The garden either side was neat and well cared for. Martin's wife obviously liked her roses, judging by the well-pruned plants. The house was redbrick and solid, with sash windows, russet-coloured pantiles, and a solid, four-panelled front door. A comfortable family home.

God, what was she *doing*?

'Hello?'

A woman appeared from round the corner of the house. She was wearing black wellies and an old, comfortable anorak that was damp from the recent rain. In her hand was a small spade.

'Hello,' she repeated, pushing the anorak hood off her head. Her blonde hair was streaked with grey and gathered in an untidy bun on top of her head. 'Can I help you?'

Alex recognized her from the courtroom and the myriad of pictures that had appeared in the papers before, during, and after the case, though the well-groomed woman she remembered had been replaced with a more careworn version. Uncomfortably, she remembered some of the headlines: 'The Monster's Wife'; 'How Didn't She Know?'; 'She Lived With A Murderer', and some of the supposedly serious analysis all the papers filled their columns with for weeks – 'Can You Live With A Murderer And Not Know It?' – was the general tenor of such articles. Articles that could have just as easily referred to her, had the press but known it.

'Mrs Jessop?'

The woman's eyes narrowed as she looked at Alex. 'Who wants to know?' She cocked her head onto one side. 'Hang on, I do know you, don't I?'

Alex swallowed. 'Mrs Jessop, my name's Alex. Alex Devlin.' Her name hung in the air.

'I see.' A small frown appeared on Angela Jessop's face, as though she was trying to place the name. 'Sasha Clements' sister.'

'Yes.' Alex swallowed. Was she going to be told to go away? She looked around. 'You have a beautiful garden.'

'It keeps me busy.'

'It must do. There's a lot of work here.' Bloody hell, she really shouldn't have come.

'Did you want something, Miss Devlin?'

Alex shook her head, sudden tears in her eyes. She hadn't fully comprehended in all her Googling and fantasising just how damn difficult this was going to be. 'I'm so sorry; I'll leave you in peace.'

She turned to go when she heard a clatter on the stones as Angela Jessop dropped the spade. She felt a hand on her arm.

'I'm sorry. I'm being very rude. It's just that I'm very careful who I talk to these days, and . . .' Her voice was soft.

'I should have realized,' said Alex. 'I'll go.'

'No. No, don't go. Come inside. Please. I was going to make some tea anyway.' Her mouth seemed to force itself into a smile. 'I don't get much peace these days anyway, so don't be worried about that. And it would be interesting to talk to you. I expect that's why you've come here? To talk to me?'

'I . . .' She was lost for words. 'Mrs Jessop, I'm not really sure what to say. After all this time, I mean.'

'It should be me feeling awkward, not you. And call me Angela. If I may call you Alex?' Angela Jessop gave a wide smile that, just for a moment, swept away the cares of the last fifteen years and Alex saw what a beautiful woman she had been. 'Come on.'

Alex didn't want to go inside Angela's house; it would make the reason she had come here feel even more sordid. The woman seemed so nice, genuine, and all she wanted to do was to find out about the diary and cut and run. It was unworthy of her. No, there was no way she was going to be able to do this; she would leave now.

'Thank you,' said Alex, following her into the porch, where Angela hung her anorak on a peg and wrestled off her boots before going through into the sitting room. A fire was burning in the grate, and Alex sat down in an easy chair next to it.

'I'll go and make us some tea,' Angela said.

After she had bustled out, obviously glad of something to do, Alex looked around the room, interested to see where Martin had lived, wondering how much Angela had changed it over the last fifteen years. There were bookcases either side of the fire, and she stood up to see what were on the shelves. Poetry, biographies, and some books about gardening. Self-help books. Volumes and volumes of self-help books. No pictures of her children.

She wandered over to the window and looked out over the back garden, which was mostly lawn with curved borders stuffed full of shrubs and small trees. More shrubs stalked in a line, breaking up the expanse of lawn, giving the garden more depth.

'It's taken me along time to get the garden how I want it.'

She turned as Angela came back in, carrying a tray. 'Gave me plenty to do,' Angela went on. She put the tray down on a small occasional table. On the tray was a teapot, a jug of milk, and two cups and saucers. There was a plate of brownies that looked home-made. Alex shivered, taken back to when she'd been to see Jackie Wood not many days before.

185

'It's beautiful,' she said. 'The garden. I wasn't sure you would still be here. Whether or not you would have moved out.'

'Gone somewhere nobody knew us, you mean?' There was a bitterness to Angela's smile. 'Unless we'd gone abroad I don't think that would have been possible. And I didn't want to take the children away from everything and everyone they had ever known. The school was very good, though being teenagers they went through their own difficult phases. Whether what happened made them more difficult, I'll never know. But we managed.' She poured the tea.

Jackie Wood, Angela Jessop, both wronged women; both had their lives torn apart when the men in their lives were weak. Both pouring her tea, offering her refreshments. Her head began to ache again.

'They've moved away now. The children. Couldn't wait to leave, actually.' Alex remembered there had been no pictures of them in the papers, thanks to the judge. He had ruled they should be allowed their privacy. Allowed to grieve. It must have helped. 'James is abroad. Australia. He's a lifeguard. I hear from him occasionally.'

'And your daughter?'

'Bea? I have no idea. Brownie?'

'No, I'm fine, thanks.' Alex sipped her tea, wondering about Bea and why Angela's mouth had tightened at saying her name.

'What about you? Have you any children?'

'One. A boy, Gus. He's sixteen.'

Angela smiled. 'I'm glad. And your husband?'

'No,' she said, 'I'm not married. Though I do have a partner.'

'I've followed you over the years, you know. Read your articles. Seen your picture. You haven't changed a lot.' She smiled. 'I'm glad you were able to . . . well, get on with your life.'

'Yes,' Alex said, not knowing what else to say.

'And I see that the Wood woman is dead now.' She cleared her throat, pulling at her skirt. 'I saw it on the television.'

There was a silence Alex didn't know how to fill.

'I'm glad she's dead,' said Angela, fiercely. 'I saw her when she came out of prison, standing on those court steps, talking about compensation. Compensation.' The word was spat out. 'I hated that woman for taking everything away from me, you know.' She lifted her eyes and looked straight at Alex. 'You must know what I mean?'

Alex nodded, not trusting herself to speak.

Angela looked into the distance, rubbing the rim of her teacup with her forefinger. 'When he died – Martin, I mean – when he died they asked me where they should send his belongings. I said I didn't care what they did with them.' She shrugged. 'I sometimes wonder what happened to them. He used to wear a watch that had been given to him by his father. He always said he wanted James to have it when he died.' She kept rubbing the rim of the cup, round and round.

Alex remembered that watch. Martin used to wind it up religiously. It had a cream-coloured face with Roman numerals. The rim was silver, and the strap was a worn dark leather. It had suited his wrist.

'Anyway,' she went on, 'even if I had got it back from the authorities, there's no way James would have wanted it.'

'No,' said Alex. In silence, they both watched the flames dancing in the fireplace. 'So didn't you want anything back from him?'

Angela shivered. 'What do you think? Would you like mementoes from the husband who murdered two little children? Who didn't even have the guts to serve his sentence? Who took the easy way out and cheated all those who needed to see justice served, including me? As I said, I didn't care what they did with his stuff. Whatever it was.' She looked up from the flames. 'Why are you so interested? Sensing another story?'

Alex glimpsed the bitterness that must eat her soul every day. She knew that look. She had it herself. 'No. I'm sorry.'

Angela sighed. 'I'm the one that should be sorry. Sometimes I think I've got out of the habit of speaking to people, which is why I tend to say things out of turn. You know, I truly didn't know what

Martin was really like. I still can't believe it to this day. But it must be true, so I have to believe it.' She picked up her teacup and Alex saw that her hands were shaking. 'I've often thought about contacting you and your sister, but my nerve failed me every time. I thought I wouldn't know what to say to you, that you wouldn't want to see me, that I would bring back too many bad memories. But all I really wanted to say was just that: I am so, so, sorry. And if I could change the past I would.' She shrugged. 'I know. It's not enough.'

Alex felt ashamed. Here was Angela, face contorted with shame, apologising, unwittingly showing the pain and suffering she'd been through the past fifteen years, and all she, Alex, had come for was to find out about a fucking diary.

'Your sister?' Angela hesitated. 'How is she?'

Alex thought of Sasha, still caught in her own private hell. 'She's coping,' she said at last. 'I know it seems a long time ago, but for her it's like yesterday.'

Angela hung her head. 'I can't imagine.' Then she looked up. 'Why did you come today?' Her forehead creased with a frown, as though she had just realized there was no real reason for Alex to be there. She was right, there wasn't. 'I mean, I've told you that I wanted to see you, but you weren't to know that. And it's been fifteen years. Why did you choose today?'

Alex opened her mouth, but no words came out.

'It's all right,' she said. 'I think I understand.'

'You do?'

'I think seeing Jackie Wood out of prison opened the way to wanting to see me. Perhaps to lay some ghosts to rest.' She leaned forward and put her hand on Alex's knee. 'Maybe your sister could see her way to paying me a visit? Would that be asking too much?'

Yes it would, far too much. She should tell her, extinguish any hope that she might get some forgiveness from Sasha.

'I don't think she will. But I'll certainly try and ask her.'

Angela sat back once more. 'Thank you,' she said. 'You see, it's been good for me. To be able to say sorry at least to one of you – even if it took you having to come to me rather than the other way round.'

There was nothing more Alex could say, so she put her cup and saucer down and stood. 'I ought to be going, Angela.'

'Yes, you must be busy.' Angela put down her own cup and saucer and stood too. 'I'll see you out.'

They walked to the door. 'Thank you for coming, Alex. I do appreciate it. I've often wondered what it would be like to be able to talk to you. Now I know. And it has made me feel better.'

Alex felt Angela's eyes on her back as she walked down the path. Even if the problem of the diary hadn't been solved – and maybe now it never would be – at least Angela Jessop might sleep a bit easier in her bed tonight. She damped down a sudden flare of resentment. As she reached the gate she turned to wave, and imagined she caught a look of pure hatred on Angela's face before it was replaced with a smile. Alex shivered.

Alex climbed into the car and a great deluge of tiredness washed over her. All she wanted to do was to lean back and sleep. What had been the point of the afternoon? It had been obvious right from the start Angela didn't have Martin's diary otherwise she wouldn't have been so accommodating.

And, there was always the possibility that there was no diary, that Jackie Wood had been playing with her. But then, she couldn't afford to take that chance.

Ever since Jackie Wood had come out of prison Alex had been on a feverish spiral down into places in her head she hadn't been to since the twins went missing. And that was probably the other reason she went to see Angela. Because for fifteen years she'd refused to acknowledge that she'd done Martin's wife any wrong. And yet she had. A great wrong.

By seeing his wife she was making herself bleed.

23

'You sure you want me to stay in here?' He peered through the windscreen at the tall green pines that were waving in the wind, at the grey skies that seemed to be pressing down on top of them, and at the drops of rain that occasionally splattered onto the glass.

Kate nodded. 'Please, Steve. I think I'll get more out of him if I speak to him on my own.' She tried not to smile or feel irritated at Steve's subtext: she would need brawn to deal with Jez Clements.

Steve Rogers shifted his bulk behind the steering wheel. 'If you say so, Ma'am.'

'I do.'

They listened to the sound of the wind.

'So Glithro's coming on board then?' said Steve.

Kate rolled her eyes. 'Seems so. God, things don't get any easier, do they? Bloody Glithro.'

'Hmm. He's not a bad copper.'

'If you were policing in the last century.'

Steve barked out a laugh. 'I know what you mean – he doesn't have a lot of time for the pc brigade but he's got good instincts. It could be worse.'

'How?' she asked gloomily.

'The Artist might have wanted to get his hands dirty.'

Kate shuddered. 'Get more involved you mean? Thank Christ it hasn't come to that is all I can say.'

'There you are, you see. Could have been worse. Here's Clements now.' He pointed as another car drew up beside them in the car park. 'I'd rather you didn't venture too far though; I don't trust him further than I could throw him.'

Kate laughed. 'I think you'd have to get in better shape if you wanted to throw Jez Clements anywhere.' She pulled on her gloves before opening the car door and getting out, gathering her trench coat around herself in a vain attempt to keep out the cold.

'Maybe. He patted his not inconsiderable waist. 'But at least the padding keeps out the cold. Look, he's a slippery bugger. And why he wanted to meet here in the forest is beyond me.' He shook his head in disbelief.

'Neutral territory, Steve. Not the office, not the town, or anywhere we might be seen. That was the deal. I think he already feels compromised and being seen with me could put the final nail in his coffin.'

'Hmmph. As I said, be careful, Ma'am. It gets a bit isolated once you get out of the car park area.'

Kate looked up at the trees that surrounded them. 'I know. It's almost like something from Stephen King, but don't worry I will be fine – I'm not sixteen anymore, you know.' She grinned as she shut the car door, then turned to meet Jez Clements.

He had obviously scrubbed up for his meeting with her – clean jeans, walking boots, a decent duffel coat. He'd had a shave and washed his hair, and Kate could see what it was that women liked about him.

'Thanks for agreeing to meet here, Detective Inspector.'

Even his manner was different – less confrontational, more deferential. 'That's okay. I can understand you not wanting to meet at HQ or in Sole Bay.'

'Thanks.'

191

'And you may as well call me Kate while we're out here.'

He nodded. 'Okay. What about the goon?'

'The goon?' Then she realized who she meant, particularly, as when she glanced over Steve was glaring at them. 'He just likes to look out for me, that's all. Says if I'm not back before dark he'll come looking for us. Just so you know.' She gave him a brief smile, then looked around. 'Shall we go up this path here? If we follow it round we'll eventually get back to the car park.'

The forest-floor detritus crunched beneath their feet and the wind whistled through the trees as they walked.

'I love it here,' said Kate eventually. 'You sort of feel as though you could get lost but you don't really because all the paths eventually lead to a road. Sometimes you see deer, too.'

'And you get ticks from them that suck your blood.'

She glanced across at him. 'Well, yes, I suppose. I don't tend to think about that.'

'Ah, well, Detective Insp . . . I mean Kate . . . for every good thing there is the opposite. I've learned that over time.'

'Look,' she said, stepping over a pile of horseshit and thinking she might as well get on with it, 'I'm sorry you feel that you have been kept out of the loop. That's what you said, isn't it? That nobody was telling you what was happening?'

Jez put his hands in his pockets. 'It's bloody freezing here, isn't it.'

'Yes. Well?'

Jez stopped, looked up at the sky. 'Have you got children, Kate?'

Her heart gave the familiar clench that happened whenever she was asked that question. 'No.'

He turned and looked at her. 'Pity. Might make you less hard.'

She blinked at him. Was that how she came across? Some sort of hard bitch? She had never imagined herself in that way. 'Really?' She tried to inject sarcasm into her voice, though she wasn't sure whether she succeeded.

'You're known as the ball-breaker by some, did you know that?'

'Really?' she said again. 'I think that's their problem, not mine. Next time you hear that, tell them to look at their own inadequacies.' For fuck's sake, this was the twenty-first century; she couldn't be doing with those sorts of views. She thought they'd got past that – evidently not.

'If you did have children you might know something about what we felt, what we still feel. About Harry and Millie.' He walked on. The noise of the wind changed from a whistle to a moan and the sky looked even more threatening. 'You don't know what it was like, what it's still like. The questions, the memories. I not only lost the children, but I lost Sasha as well. I loved those children. Loved them. I would have died for them. Now there are no birthdays to celebrate, no weddings to plan or partners to like or hate.' He shook his head. 'You lose your future when you lose your children.' There was raw suffering on his face.

She didn't say anything.

'Sasha's parents didn't approve of me, you know.'

'Oh?' She wanted to let him talk.

'No. We met while Sasha was still at school. I'd been going out with Alex. Not in any serious way. Her parents had tolerated me because she was going off to university and they thought it would fizzle out. And it would have done. But then I got with Sasha. She was fed up of having to follow in Alex's footsteps, of Alex being held up as an example to her, a goody two shoes if you like, so she latched on to me.' He laughed humourlessly. 'I was from the council estate and wanted to be a copper. Her parents went apeshit and did their best to dissuade Sasha from being with me—'

'But the more they tried, the more she wanted to be with you.'

Jez looked at her. 'Yeah. How did you guess?'

'It's an old story, Jez. Trying to dissuade your daughter from being with the bad boy drives her even further into his arms.'

'That certainly happened. Then she got pregnant and . . .' He fell silent.

'And?'

'Nothing. And nothing.' He shook himself. 'Look, I get that you're sorry if me and Sash feel out of the loop. The truth is, we do feel as though things are going on and nobody's telling us. Maybe we don't really have a right to know how the investigation into Wood's murder is going as it's probably got nothing to do with what happened fifteen years ago.'

'Are you sure about that?' Kate said sharply.

He stopped. 'What do you mean?'

How much of her hand to show? 'I heard that Martin Jessop had another lover, mistress, whatever you like to call her, and that there was a cover-up so that the fact didn't get out into the public domain. I heard that you were involved in the cover-up.' All her hand, obviously.

He laughed and shook his head. 'I don't know where you've got that one from, I really don't, but it's bollocks. Me involved in a cover-up? I was just a green constable then, how could I have done that?'

'Is it bollocks?'

'Complete and utter bollocks. And why would I want to cover anything up anyway?'

'That's the question I've been asking myself, Jez. What is it you wanted to keep from people?'

'I didn't want to keep anything from anybody you stupid—' He managed to rein himself in. 'All I wanted was to bring the murderers to justice. But then Jessop topped himself and fifteen years later Wood gets let out on a technicality. What do you think that's done to Sasha? And now you're accusing me of some sort of cover-up. Though what Martin Jessop having some other fancy woman besides that bitch – if he even did – has got to do with anything, I don't know.'

'It's the cover-up I'm most interested in at the moment.'

'What fucking cover-up? Who was the sad fuck gave you the idea there was any cover-up in the first place?' He wouldn't meet her eyes and she thought he protested a bit too much.

'I have it on good authority,' she said patiently, hoping she didn't sound too pompous.

'Fuck that.'

She sensed she wasn't going to get any further with that line of attack so tried a different approach. 'Jez. I want to help you, I really do, but I can't unless you give me something. If you are involved then, well, perhaps there's a good reason. But I can't help you and Sasha unless you tell me.'

'Leave Sasha out of this.' He was breathing hard now.

'I will as far as I can, but I can't promise anything.'

'This has brought back all the bad memories for her, you know.'

Kate thought of the cuts on Sasha's arms, of her hollow eyes and haunted look. 'Do you really think they ever went away?'

He walked on ahead of her.

Bugger. She wasn't handling this at all well. 'At least give me the name of the woman you say you were with on the evening Jackie Wood was murdered,' she called.

He stopped, turned and walked back, taking his phone out of his pocket. He thrust it underneath her nose. 'There it is, there's the number. And I don't *say* I was with her, I bloody well was with her. You can call her now. Her name's Alice, Alice McSweeney. And then let that be an end to it because I don't want her name dragged through the mud.'

She looked at him. 'Don't be stupid, Jez, it doesn't work like that as well you know. She could say anything over the phone, I'd still have to send someone round to see her. You need to tell me where she lives. If you're telling the truth and she's telling the truth then we can rule you out of the list of suspects for Jackie Wood's killing.'

'Fine. It's The Lodge on the Leiston Road. You can't miss it. Please be discreet, for her sake if not mine. Her husband's a councillor or something.'

'We will be. Thank you.'

'So you haven't got anyone for the murder then? No one's in the frame? Not that I particularly care. Better now she's dead.'

'She was innocent.'

'Good old British justice, hey?'

'We will find who killed her.'

'Good luck with that.' He stamped his feet. 'Are we done now?' Their walk had brought them back round to where the cars were parked. 'Unless there's anything else you want to tell me? Anything that might help?'

'No.' He pointed his key fob at his car, unlocking the doors, and began to walk towards it.

'What about Edward Grainger?' she said to his departing back.

Was it her imagination or did he break his stride? 'What about him?' he asked, getting into his car.

'He tried to bury the fact that Jessop had someone he was seeing. In secret. You helped him, I heard.'

'Bollocks, Detective Inspector.'

'I don't believe it is.'

'Tough.'

He drove off.

24

It was a miracle that Alex managed to drive back to Sole Bay without crashing into anybody or being stopped for careless driving, such were the myriad of thoughts going round and round in her head. There was one sombre moment when she found herself drifting into oncoming traffic, and it was only the screeching blare of a horn that made her wrench the wheel over at the last minute. She had to stop by the side of the road then, body drenched in sweat, heart racing, unable to stop thinking about Angela Jessop. All these years on her own, bringing up two children, coping with the stigma of having a murderer as a husband. And the diary – what had Martin written in that goddamn diary? What secrets might it reveal? Not just about their relationship, but the things she used to tell him. Maybe he'd written those down too.

She was still in a world of her own when she pulled up outside her house, the streetlight reflecting off the wet pavement.

'Mum.' Gus hissed at her as she opened the front door. 'We've got visitors.'

'Visitors?' She hung up her coat and gave Gus a kiss on the cheek before he could flinch away. 'Who's that? Carly? Did you have a good time? What did you see at the flicks? How did you get back?' She gave him what she hoped was a bright smile, wanting to banish the dark thoughts from her head.

'We walked from the station. Look Mum, never mind that. It's that journalist guy who stopped me when Jackie Wood first got out of prison. And some woman who says she knows you from the caravan site. Who are they Mum? What are they doing here?'

Alex's heart began to flutter and she felt sweat on her palms. 'Ed Killingback?'

'Yeah, that's his name. He wanted to speak to me but I told him to fuck off.'

'Gus.'

'Sorry, Mum, but that's what you'd have said. Anyway, he said he'd wait for you.'

'And he's in there with that woman Nikki?' At the thought of the woman from the caravan opposite to Jackie Wood she felt sick. Her stomach swooped and dived. Alex had known at the time she hadn't heard the last of her, and now Nikki Adams was here, closeted in her house with a fucking tabloid journalist.

'She didn't tell me her name. Mum, are you okay? You've gone as white as a sheet. What are they doing here, Mum?'

'Did they come together?'

'What do you mean?'

'It's a simple question, Gus.' Fear made her short-tempered. 'Did they arrive together?'

'No, I don't think so. The journalist guy came in a car – I saw him park it – and I think the woman walked here. Said she'd found the house easily.'

That was something, at least. 'Where's Malone? Have you seen him?'

'Yeah. He's in there with them.'

Her heart settled down to a less frantic beat and she began to breathe more easily. He would keep the lid on things.

'Mum? What is it? You're scaring me.'

Alex looked at his anxious face and found her voice. 'I just don't like journalists bothering us at home, especially not him. He's a parasite and I don't trust him. He keeps wanting my story, our story, and I'm not giving it. Thank God Malone's there. Were they on their own for long before Malone arrived?'

Gus shook his head. 'No. He came in a couple of minutes after me and Carly got back.' He blushed furiously.

'That's all right, darling. Are you two okay?'

'We're just upstairs listening to some music.'

Alex narrowed her eyes. 'Gus?'

'It's cool, Mum. Please don't worry – Jack arrived about ten minutes ago. He's going to have a look at my computer.'

'Your computer?'

'Yeah. Remember I told you I had a couple of corrupted files. Jack's gonna see if he can fix them. So don't worry.'

No, actually she wouldn't worry; she had other, more pressing things to worry about than her son's relationship with a girl. And Jack had turned up too. So she rubbed the side of his arm and sent him back upstairs.

Malone came out of the sitting room and grabbed her wrist. 'Where have you been?' he hissed. 'You've got a couple of visitors and I don't want to play nursemaid to them. One's a bloody reporter.' The tension radiated through his arm and shoulders.

'I'm sorry,' she said. 'I had to go and see someone; I'll tell you about it later.' She thought she must have looked pained or affronted or something because he let go of her arm, rubbed the side of his face.

'Now I'm sorry,' he said. 'It's just I don't trust you lot as far as I can throw you.' His Irish accent was more pronounced than ever.

'You lot?' She smiled at him. 'Cheers, Malone.'

'You know what I mean. I don't really include you in that, you know.'

'Oh really? Sounded as though you did.'

'Though I didn't realize you knew Ed Killingback,' he went on as if he hadn't heard her. 'You didn't tell me you met him the

199

other day, before the press conference?' Malone's subtext: what have you been saying to a reporter?

She looked at him. 'I don't really know him. As you rightly point out I only really met him at the press conference. He has phoned a couple of times, but I've ignored him.' When lying, she'd learned from the master himself; it's always best to stick as close to the truth as possible. 'He wanted me to tell my story to him. You know, finding Jackie Wood and all that.'

'He's too late for that, isn't he, being as you've already sent a story about Jackie Wood to the magazine.'

'Yes.' She didn't want to think about that, not now. 'What does Nikki Adams want?' Her back was sticky, she wanted a shower.

'Fuck knows. Just go in there and act naturally. Don't give her anything to feed any suspicions she may have, okay?'

'Suspicions?'

He planted a kiss on her forehead, sweetness and light again. 'Just be careful. That Killingback is sly.'

'I'll get rid of them as soon as I can.'

'Would you like me to stay tonight?'

A conversation she didn't want to have. 'Perhaps tomorrow?' she said, with as bright a smile as she could muster.

He nodded, turned on his heel and collected his coat, jamming his beanie hat on his head. She watched as the door closed behind him and wondered if she'd done the right thing by sending him away. After all, he was always good to talk to, to bounce things off. He'd been fantastic when she'd come back from the Forum having discovered the paintings that Jackie Wood had kept in the locker, though he did question why she put them back, hadn't brought them home, thought it was a bit odd Wood had hidden them there. She couldn't give him an answer. It seemed like the right thing to do at the time, that was all.

But tonight Alex wanted to think.

She took a deep breath, practised a smile, and ventured into the lion's den.

The fire was lit and casting a warm glow into the room. Ed Killingback and Nikki Adams were sitting in armchairs either side of the fire. She almost expected to see them with shoes off, feet curled up. It all looked very cosy.

'Have you got a drink?' she asked.

Ed Killingback held up a wine glass. 'Yep. Your friend – Malone, isn't it? – provided us with a pretty decent Sauvignon, thanks. The bottle's over there.' He nodded to the table that sat in the bay window. 'Nikki and I have been having a good chat, haven't we, Nikki?' He smiled over at her.

Alex went over to the table and poured herself a glass. 'Good,' she said. 'Glad he was looking after you.' She wasn't going to rise to the bait.

Nikki nodded. 'Yes. I've got a bit fed up of going from one dead-end job to another the last few years. I've always thought I'd like to be a journalist, and Ed's been giving me some good tips.'

'I bet he has,' muttered Alex, taking a swig of the wine.

'I hope you don't mind me calling in like this,' Nikki said with wide eyes, 'but I wanted to make sure you were okay. You know, after finding the body and all that.'

Was it her imagination, or did Nikki subtly emphasize the word 'finding'? Or was she being paranoid? Was Nikki's accompanying smile just a little too knowing?

'Yes, Nikki was telling me how upset you were that day.' Killingback looked at her over the edge of his glass.

'Well, anyone would be, wouldn't they?' What a bloody nightmare. Nikki Adams, who she'd virtually asked to lie to the police. Actually, there was nothing virtual about it. What did the woman want? Why was she really here? She wanted to ask her and be damned with the consequences.

'Why are you here?' she said, addressing Ed Killingback instead. 'I'm really not happy about you ambushing my son again, trying to get him to talk.'

'Ah, sorry about that. But if you won't talk to me . . .' He spread his hands and smiled as if it were all a game to him, which it probably was. 'Though perhaps your sister would like to unburden herself?'

'Sasha?' Alex's voice came out as a squeak. 'Talk to you? Unburden herself? Is that why you called round here today?' She took another gulp of the Sauvignon. 'Sasha is still hurting, still grieving for her children. I don't care what any Appeal Court says – the woman who helped kill them just came out of prison and was murdered before she could say where one of Sasha's children is buried. The other one, in case you'd forgotten, having been found in a suitcase dumped in a lay-by. Not good, Ed, not good.' She threw the wine down her throat.

He looked taken aback by her onslaught.

'I'm still trying to find out who Martin Jessop's other mistress was,' he said, looking straight at Alex.

'Yes,' said Nikki Adams. 'Ed just mentioned that to me. Have you any idea about the woman?'

The one thing she had to do was to appear calm. 'Why the fuck do you think I would know about some murderer's mistress?' she said, trying not to shake as she went over to the table and picked up the wine bottle. 'More, anybody?'

'Sorry, sorry,' Nikki said, looking stricken. 'I don't know why I asked. It's just that when Ed mentioned it I thought . . .'

Alex shook her head. She had to slow down, gain control of the situation and herself. 'No. Forgive me, Nikki. I've had a long day and the last person I wanted to see was Mr Killingback, especially as I've got a bit of headache coming on. And he's just after a story to fill his paper. Whatever he says, he doesn't care about you, or your life, or your family.' She put the wine bottle down. The only taker had been her. She took a deep breath, managed a smile. 'It's late and I've got a fair bit to do, so, if you don't mind?'

Killingback stood up. 'Okay, I get the hint.'

He placed his glass on the mantlepiece. 'I'm sorry to have intruded. I didn't mean to upset you or your family. It's just that, after our little chat the other night, I thought—'

'Whatever you thought, you were wrong,' Alex interrupted. 'Please go.'

Killingback raised his eyebrows. 'I will. But I'm not going to stop looking for the other woman.'

Was that why he'd come to the house? To warn her? To say in some oblique way that he knew she was involved? She put her hand to her head. It had really started throbbing. She should be getting used to these headaches by now.

'Oh, I'm sorry,' said Nikki, not getting up from her chair. 'You are tired, and the last person you wanted to see today was me, to remind you of that dreadful morning when you found poor Jackie.' She tutted. 'It must have been so horrible. Finding her like that. Not knowing what to do or who to tell. It must have taken you ages to get yourself together.'

Alex didn't believe her look of concern for one minute. 'It was,' she said. 'And you were so helpful.' She hoped she'd said it in a meaningful way. Nikki seemed to slightly nod, so maybe she had got away with it.

'As I said.' Killingback made his way to the door. 'You and your sister know where to find me.'

'As do I, Mr Killingback,' said Nikki, looking from Alex to the reporter. 'When I need any advice about journalism.'

'Yes,' he said. 'Any advice. And any new thoughts you may have about the murder, you know, I'd be glad to hear them.'

'And you won't need to pay me a penny,' she said, sweetly. Alex swore Killingback's ears went red and she wanted to laugh before the thought came to her that Nikki probably didn't need to take money from Killingback because she was going to demand it from her.

'I'll see myself out,' he said.

'And I've warned you,' said Alex.

'What?'

'Stay away from my son. He doesn't want to speak to you. If you ambush him again I will have you for harassment. Okay?'

Killingback nodded. 'Fair enough.' Then, as he reached the door, he turned. 'Malone.'

'What about him?' she said.

He pursed his lips. 'I've seen him somewhere before, I'm sure of it. I know that voice, too.' Then he winked at her and left.

Oh God.

But Alex couldn't feel even a small sense of relief that at least Killingback had left, because Nikki was still ensconced in front of the fire, still sipping her wine, still smiling at her in a mildly superior way.

'He's a slimy bugger, isn't he? Though pretty good-looking.' Nikki crossed her legs, settling in for the long haul. 'I hate the press anyway. They give you nothing but shit.'

Alex was surprised. 'I thought you were interested in becoming a journalist?'

She shrugged. 'Not particularly. And if I was, you could help me, couldn't you? But those sorts of people like to puff themselves up and believe they're something special, don't they? And they're more likely to let something slip if you massage their fucking great egos. Anyway,' she put down her glass and for one glorious minute Alex thought she was about to leave, 'I did just want to see how you were. Honestly. I meant it when I said the whole thing must have been quite a shock for you. Especially as . . .' She left the sentence hanging.

'Especially as I said she had a migraine when she was actually lying there dead, you mean?' The words tumbled out.

Nikki smiled. 'I did wonder.'

'I really didn't know what to do when I found her; I was shocked, you know, worried, disorientated, I suppose. Just wasn't sure what to do.' She had to stop gabbling.

'You panicked. Anyone would be the same. Anyway, I didn't tell that police detective woman anything about that. After all, you didn't kill her, did you? Just said I didn't hear anything the evening before because I was too busy watching telly, and the next morning I had a half shift and then went shopping. That's all.'

'Half shift?'

'Yeah. Stacking the shelves ready for the hordes. I had to leave home bloody early.'

'How early?'

'What?'

'How early did you start?'

'I left the caravan about half past four. Sodding freezing and miserable at that time, I can tell you.'

'And you didn't see or hear anything?'

'What are you? The bloody police?'

Alex laughed, an unnatural and forced sound. 'Sorry. No. Just wondering, that was all. But thanks for not saying anything.'

She sniffed. 'That's okay.'

They both stared into the fire, at the orange-red flames that were licking the sides of the grate, listened to the crackle of the wood.

'It's hard.'

'Hmm?' Alex got up and poured them both another glass. If the wretched woman was intent on staying then she might as well have some alcohol to dull the pain, she thought.

'Working. At Tesco's. Doesn't bring in a lot of money. And, as I said, I'm fed up of doing a succession of dead-end jobs.'

So this was it. 'Really?'

'Ed Killingback said his paper could pay me if I remembered anything, well, juicy was the way he put it.'

'I thought you didn't like Killingback? And that he was "a slimy bugger"?' Alex stopped herself making commas in the air. She drank her wine quickly. Put the glass on the floor. Picked it up. Wondered if she should have another glass. No, Nikki had barely drunk any of hers.

'I don't.' Nikki shook her head. 'I really don't.'

Alex wasn't going to make it easy for her, so she looked at her watch and sighed. 'Look, I'm really sorry, but it's been a long day, as you said, and I need to have some food and get to my bed.'

'I'm sorry. I wasn't thinking.'

Oh, what a game they were playing.

'But,' she continued, 'as I said, Tesco's doesn't bring in a lot and . . .'

Alex reached into her bag for her cheque book.

25

'Mmm, something smells good.' Chris came into the kitchen from his workshop and stopped to give Kate a kiss on the back of her neck as she stirred the sauce. 'Sorry I've kept you up so late.'

She leaned her head back into his chest, glad to feel the solidity of him, inhaling the smell of him, linseed oil and resin fighting with the aroma of basil and tomatoes and mushrooms filling the kitchen. 'That's okay. It feels like it's been ages since I've seen you, awake that is. And ages since we've been able to eat together.' She needed to reconnect.

'True,' he said, burying his face into the soft skin of her neck. 'We've been like ships that pass in the night, as the saying goes. If I didn't know you better I'd think you were avoiding me.'

She wriggled out of his hold. 'Don't be stupid,' she said, guilt making her words sharper than she intended. 'Anyway, it's just spag bol, I'm afraid,' she said. 'How's it going?'

Chris was finishing an oak table with eight chairs – a commission for a local farmer – that had taken him a great deal of time and effort, but the result was looking beautiful. His craftsmanship was impeccable – he lavished care and attention on all his furniture and had built up an excellent reputation in the area.

Kate couldn't tell him that she had gone into his workshop one day when he was out to look at some of his pieces. The table took pride of place in the centre of the room, with four of the finished chairs along the wall.

Then she'd spied it in the corner – a baby's crib. She went over and stroked it. The lines were smooth, the wood warm, she could feel the love Chris had poured into it radiating out into the air. Her heart constricted. She knew she couldn't tell him she'd seen it.

'Do you want to grate some Parmesan?'

'No problem.'

She watched as he washed his hands and dried them on a towel before reaching into the fridge for the cheese. He smiled across at her, and began to grate the Parmesan. Smiling back, she tried to shake off her usual feeling of irritation knotted through with guilt. And where was the love? Had she lost it amid the not-wanting to have children? Surely, if she loved him enough, she would want to have his children, whatever it took? If she loved him enough she would be able to overcome her feelings of fear, inadequacy; the sheer *hopelessness* she felt when she looked at him.

'Have I got a spot on my nose or something?' he said, rubbing the side of it to make the point.

'No.'

'It's just that you were looking at me rather intently.' He laughed. 'Maybe I've grown another head.' He carried on grating.

Kate thought that if he wasn't careful he would grate his fingers. 'That's enough, darling, really.' She began stirring the sauce again, this time a bit too vigorously, as some splashed onto the side of the cooker. 'Damn and blast,' she said, wanting to bang the wooden spoon down on the worktop and wanting to cry at the same time.

'Okay.' He put the hunk of cheese and the grater down. 'What's bothering you?'

'I . . .' Kate said the first thing that came into her head. 'It's been difficult.'

'Cherry?' He had been ambushed by her boss at a drinks do. Knowing that Chris was, as he put it, 'a creative', he'd banged on about art and life and ended up inviting Chris to view his paintings – an invitation Chris hadn't yet got round to accepting. 'You mustn't worry about him.' He went up to her and put his arms round her, pulling her close. She tried to relax into him. 'He's not giving you grief about the drugs raid, is he?'

'Not exactly.' She sighed. 'It's not just that, though Chris. He's brought in a Detective Inspector to help or hinder me, I'm not sure which, on the investigation.'

He kissed the top of her head. 'Is that such a bad thing?'

'Only in as much as he acts as though he's a reincarnation of Gene Hunt and I don't trust him.'

'Ah. Not so good, then. But Kate, you're a fantastic officer. Impressive. You'll sort it.'

'Do you really think so?' She hated her own neediness.

'Yes, yes I do.' He peered at her. 'You look tired.'

Kate sighed. 'You know what, I am.'

'You sit down and I'll pour you a nice glass of wine, then you can tell me about your day – and the last few days as we don't seem to have seen much of each other – while I put the spaghetti on and make the salad, okay?'

Kate nodded, feeling overwhelmed. What had she done to deserve this good man? That was the problem, though, wasn't it? He deserved someone who could give him what he wanted.

She sat down at the table, and Chris set down a glass of red supermarket plonk in front of her. Her favourite. She enjoyed the mellow taste on her tongue and the liquid warmth as it slipped down her throat.

Kate watched as Chris busied himself with a pan, water, and spaghetti. 'So is that the only thing that's bothering you?'

She opened her mouth, wanting to tell him, talk to him properly, not just about the case, and the desperate sadness that surrounded Sasha and how Jez was a slippery eel and she wasn't sure how to handle him, but needing to tell him about the visit to the doctor's, the real reason why she wasn't falling pregnant, maybe even discuss the counselling option, see what he thought about that.

The moment passed.

'I went out and did some proper plod work the other evening,' she said, hating herself for the evasion. 'It was all a bit pointless though.'

While Chris got on with making a salad and a dressing to go with it, Kate told him about the determination with which the four of them – her, Steve, John, and Eve – had set out. A bit of door-knocking seemed infinitely preferable to sitting in front of mounds of paperwork or sifting through photographs of Jackie Wood's dead body. There were definite disadvantages to climbing up the greasy pole, and desk work was certainly one of them. She couldn't understand how Cherry stood all that, as well as the interminable meetings he had to go to. She felt she might get somewhere doing some honest police work.

But it hadn't turned out like that. It was very much see no evil, speak no evil, hear no evil. The man who'd been walking his dog – Jim Cassidy – had seen absolutely nothing, heard nothing, and was very definitely saying nothing. Had seen a light in what may or may not have been Jackie Wood's caravan, but hadn't seen anyone going in or out. They knocked on doors, but were mostly greeted by silence or by other people who'd seen nothing, for whom it was 'none of their business'. There had been several empty vans in the vicinity of Jackie Wood's caravan, and the one that did have an occupant, one Nikki Adams, said again she had been watching television all evening. They had yet to check on the programmes. Kate had barked at Eve to get on with it as soon as they got back to the station.

'This Nikki character,' said Chris, draining the spaghetti, 'she sounds someone worth looking at a bit more?'

'Maybe.' She tried not to feel irritated that Chris was putting his tanks on her lawn. 'We've certainly got to see if she really was watching television.'

'It just seems odd that she didn't see or hear anything when her caravan is right opposite, you said. There isn't much distance between them.'

'Hmm, maybe. How's supper coming on?' she said, wanting to get off the subject of her police work before she snapped at him for interfering.

'Just about ready.' He began ladling thin strings of pasta and dollops of sauce onto the plate. Kate knew by the set of his mouth she had hurt him.

What the fuck was wrong with her? She sat down and sprinkled Parmesan on top of the bolognese before beginning to fork twists of spaghetti and sauce into her mouth. 'There is something a bit odd that I found out.'

'Oh?' Chris poured her another glass of wine before topping up his own. 'What's that?'

'Martin Jessop had another lover.'

Chris frowned. 'Martin Jessop? He's the guy who was—'

'Put away for the murder of Harry and Millie Clements. Killed himself in prison.'

'Another lover? You mean . . .'

Kate nodded. 'Not just Jackie Wood. Maybe not even Jackie Wood.'

'And this mistress stashed away on the side, that hasn't come out before? Not at the trial or anything?'

'No. And I hadn't heard a whisper until recently. But more worryingly—', she reached across and poured herself another glass of wine, 'it's said the detective in charge of the investigation knew.'

'And who was that?'

'A Detective Inspector Edward Grainger. He's retired now. I do remember meeting him, though, just briefly, before I went to court.'

'To court?'

'Yes, you know, when I had to give evidence about finding Harry Clements.' Damn, how had she let that slip out?

Chris stared at her. 'No, I didn't know. You've never told me about that.'

'Haven't I?'

'No. Not that you actually found the little boy.'

She waved her hand, closing that compartment in her mind. A splodge of spaghetti and sauce landed on the floor. 'I'll tell you about it sometime. Anyway, Grainger knew about the lover and the investigation was closed down – with the help of Jez Clements.'

'What do you mean?'

'Just that – Clements apparently managed to get any lines of inquiry into whether Martin Jessop had another lover closed down. Shut off. Grainger obviously didn't look into it any more.'

'But from what I remember you telling me', Chris wrinkled his brows, 'was Jez Clements nothing more than an ordinary PC at the time?'

'Yes, you're right. Nothing more than that.'

'So how could he have had any sort of influence over that sort of investigation? And surely, as the father of the twins he was part of it all? Too close to be involved?'

'Yep. And that's the fifty-thousand dollar question, Chris. Except, I suppose, it's obvious really. He must have had some sort of hold over Grainger for him to be able to do something like that.'

She put her chin in her hand. 'Of course, this is all supposing the rumours are true. I mean, I've got no evidence, just this gut feeling.'

'Copper's instinct?' He smiled.

'Don't knock it. It's solved many a case. I don't know, Chris. I tried to talk to Clements about it today, but he wasn't giving an inch. And I suppose part of me does feel sorry for him. But if it did happen, it's plain wrong, that's the point. Whether or not it would have had any bearing on anything is not the issue. It might have done. It should have been part of the investigation and it wasn't.' She smoothed her hair down with both hands. 'It matters, Chris, it really does.'

Chris put down his spoon and fork and put his hand on her arm. 'That's what I love about you, Kate. You always look for the truth.'

Now she wanted to cry. Guilt gnawed at her stomach. She couldn't tell him, give him hope.

'I went to the doctor's the other day.' The words spewed out of her mouth.

She could hardly bear the way his face lit up.

'Why didn't you tell me earlier? And? Did you ask about tests?' He chewed his lip. 'You know I don't mind doing more of that if it would mean our own children.' He took a gulp of his wine.

Kate thought about the antidepressants hidden away at the back of her cupboard. How bad did she have to feel to allow herself to start taking them? Was this it? This cloak of doom that had settled on her shoulders and grew heavier by the day? She'd spoken to people with real depression, how everything looked bleak, how they could hardly bear to get up in the morning – if they did at all – how worthless they felt, and how they were sure the world would be a better place without them. She didn't feel like that. She just had a weight on her shoulders and the relentless rolling of anxiety in her stomach.

And it was self-inflicted. If she could give this kind, generous man what he wanted then she felt certain the cloak would lift, the fog clear, and the knot in her stomach dissolve. But how could she, when every time she thought about holding a baby in her arms she saw the little body of Harry Clements, his limbs bent at an angle so he could fit inside the suitcase? Why couldn't she tell Chris this? Did she think he wouldn't understand? But telling him would mean confessing to all the lies by omission she had told. All those times when he'd lamented their lack of fertility because there might be something wrong with one of them and she'd stayed silent. The lies would destroy him . . . them. What did that say about her? Shame washed over her.

'I know you don't, Chris,' she said softly. 'I just feel—'

'Look,' he said, a note of desperation in his voice. 'You don't have to say anything now, don't have to tell me what the doctor said.'

'But I want to, Chris.' She swallowed. 'We didn't talk about tests just yet. She wondered if there was some psychological reason for me not getting pregnant.' Okay, she couldn't quite get the words out, couldn't make herself, but at least she was giving him a version of the truth.

'Psychological? What, it's in your head?'

Why was he being so obtuse? 'That's generally what psychological means, yes.'

'Like what?'

Now was the time to tell him. How involved she'd been in the case. How she'd held that poor, broken body after her colleagues, the pathologist, after everyone else had had their little piece of him. The feeling of lightness in her arms, the sense of a life cut short before it had even begun. The insistence to everyone that she was fine, she was okay, she was a police officer and would have to deal with that sort of thing for the rest of her career convinced everyone she was coping. And she had thought she was. She went to serious car accidents and saw the mutilated bodies of the victims and didn't have nightmares. When she moved to serious crimes she saw her fair share of murder victims – shot, stabbed, bludgeoned – you name it, she'd seen it. But when it came to children she was a mess.

'That there's something about the pain, about having to look after a small human being that scares me.' She twisted some more spaghetti onto her fork.

'Sweetheart, you wouldn't be on your own. I'd be with you every step of the way.'

She rested her head on her hand. 'I know you would.'

'I'd come to every ante-natal class, every hospital visit, every time you were sick, when we have the baby—'

'When I have the baby.'

He looked stricken. 'Sorry, I didn't mean ... oh, you know what I meant, don't you?'

She managed to smile. 'Of course I did. But that's what I mean; I'll be on my own then.'

'And then there's afterwards.'

'Afterwards?'

'Yes, when the baby grows into a child, then a teenager, then an adult. How am I going to keep him or her safe then?'

'Sweetheart . . .' He ran his hands through his hair. 'That's what it's all about. They have to learn, make their own way in life. We can only help and then we let them go.'

'I'm not sure I can do that, Chris.' This was the nearest she had come to telling Chris what really bothered her, about the crippling fear she felt whenever there was talk about having children, of having to suffer the pain she saw in Jez Clements's face earlier.

'I'll be there with you. All the way.' His smile was crooked. 'You have to trust me.'

She reached out, touched his arm. 'I do. Please, just give me a bit more time.'

He nodded.

26

Alex closed the door on Nikki Adams and breathed out a huge sigh of relief. At least flourishing her chequebook meant that she could get rid of her; it was almost worth the money. But she could hear Malone's voice in her head when she told him. He'd be bound to tell her she should have waited. Now, he would say, Nikki had the power, knew she was frightened about her talking to the police, and would almost certainly be back for more. Yes, Alex knew all that, but right at this moment, as she trudged up the stairs to Gus's room, she had no regrets.

Knocking on his door, she could hear the drone of some game on the computer and a lot of shuffling and giggling.

'Come in, Ma,' he shouted.

She put her head round the door. 'Hi. I just thought I'd tell you the visitors have gone now, if you wanted to come downstairs.'

Gus fiddled with his computer. Carly was lying on his bed propped up by a couple of pillows, twirling some of her Pre-Raphaelite hair between her fingers. Jack was lounging on the floor, back up against the cupboard, flicking through a computing magazine.

'It's okay, Ma, we're going over to Jack's and I'll probably stay there, if that's okay?' He stood up, holding his hand out to Carly to pull her up off the bed. Jack stood too and stretched.

'Sure,' Alex said, worried about where Carly was staying but not liking to ask. 'Um, don't forget you've got that assignment to do for tomorrow.'

Why oh why did she have to bring that up? Ever since her own mother had come bursting into the sitting room brandishing a hot-water bottle, when she was having a perfectly normal conversation with a new boyfriend, and saying she was about to boil the kettle, Alex swore she wouldn't embarrass her own children in front of their friends. Not that much anyway. And now look at her.

Gus, to his credit, just rolled his eyes. 'I hadn't forgotten. I'll do it later.'

'Great,' she said. 'I found that article about prison reform you wanted, so I'll print it out and leave it on your desk.'

'Cool.'

'I wish my mum helped me with my essays,' said Jack, looking up from his magazine.

Alex laughed. 'What's the point in having someone who writes for a living if they can't get their hands on some info. It's an interview I did with the governor of a prison in the north a couple of years ago. He was done for abuse eventually.'

Jack nodded slowly. 'Wow. Heavy.'

'I think that's great, Alex,' said Carly, smiling warmly. 'Helping Gus. And thanks ever so much for having us.'

She waved her hand. 'I haven't done anything.'

'I'm glad you got rid of those two, though, Mum. I don't like that journalist – I think he's a creep.'

'You're not wrong there,' she said. Nikki Adams wasn't any better, but she couldn't tell him that. She suddenly had a picture of her folding up the cheque and putting it in the back pocket of her jeans with a smile that said 'gotcha'. She shuddered.

'You okay, Mum?'

She blinked. 'Yes fine. Off you go.'

'Okay,' he said, pulling Carly behind him.

Jack raised his eyebrows. Alex smiled. 'Young love,' he said.

'See you tomorrow, you lot.'

'Bye, Mum.'

Carly waggled her fingers. Jack smiled. Once again, she was glad to see the front door close.

An hour later she was lying on the sofa, her head on Malone's lap, the fire dying down. He was stroking the hair off her forehead. Her headache was beginning to go and she could feel her shoulders relax, the tension draining away.

'Don't say it again, Malone.' She closed her eyes.

'What would that be?'

'I told you so.'

'As if.'

'I'm glad you came back, though. From wherever you went earlier.'

'Just a walk.'

Frustratingly, he wasn't giving anything away.

'And I'm glad I'm here even if you don't want to get too involved or you worry too much about Gus's sensibilities.'

She snorted. 'I think I'm going to have to accept that he now has a girlfriend, with everything that entails.'

'I hope you're not expecting me to give him the birds and the bees talk. Probably too late for that anyway.'

She opened one eye. 'You think?'

'Come on, Al. What d'you reckon?'

'Hmm. Maybe.'

They sat in companionable silence, listening to the hiss and the spit of the fire. She refused to worry about Sasha and she didn't want to go over what Angela Jessop had said. She wanted to relax, just for a minute, enjoy Malone's company. Surely that wasn't too much to ask?

'By the way,' he said, stroking her head softly.

'Mmm?' She was feeling pleasantly sleepy.

'You know I said I'd find out if Jessop or Wood had said anything in prison about this diary you're so exercised about?'

'Mmm.' Not listening properly.

'He definitely did have one.'

As Malone's words sank in, she struggled up, all thoughts of sleep banished. 'And?'

'And what?'

'He used to write in it every day when he was on remand, according to my source.'

'Who is?'

'You don't want to know. Anyway, the source said he was writing in the diary through the trial as well.'

'Does "your source" know what happened to it?'

Malone shook his head. 'He said the last time he saw Jessop with the diary was a couple of days before he strung himself up and just before some policeman visited him.'

She had reached for the wine bottle – the second of the evening, she thought – and was about to pour herself a glass. She stopped. 'Policeman?' She had a feeling she knew where this might be going.

'Apparently he wasn't in uniform but my source recognized him in the visitor's room. He was the sort of bloke who would have a run-in with a little old granny, apparently.'

'Jez.' It had to be.

'Jez as in Sasha's husband, Jez?'

'I reckon so. It was something he said at the time, about going to find out what sort of man would kill children. I don't know how he wangled the visit, but I reckon it must have been him. Plus he's not well thought of in the force, so it's said.'

'So it's said? Don't you know? He is your brother-in-law after all.'

'Ex. And yes, I do know for sure, I was just trying to make myself feel better. I also try not to have too much to do with him these days. He hasn't got a good reputation.' Plus it was too hard, just too hard.

'Sounds like he might be worth a chat to.' Malone was now stroking her arm, causing delicious sensations up and down her skin.

She shivered, though whether it was from Malone stroking her arm or the thought of talking to Jez in a meaningful way she couldn't be sure.

'Tell me about Sasha and Jez. What sort of people are they?'

'Oh, Malone, we would be here all night.' But she was grateful for the slight change of direction.

'Just the potted version then.' He got up and threw another log on the fire. 'There, we've got a bit of time.'

The log caught, she watched the red and yellow flames flicker around it, devouring it slowly. She sighed. 'Sasha was always jealous of me. Felt that our parents loved me more, all that sort of stuff. I was going to university, she didn't get in, so she got married.'

'A bit drastic?'

Alex grimaced. 'Wasn't it just. She enjoyed the shock of it, running away and then coming back with a ring on her finger. She always had to go what she thought was one better than me.'

'Sounds like she had some serious issues.'

Alex settled herself down with her head on Malone's lap once more. How could she make him understand about Sasha's completely unbalanced view of herself? How she never felt good enough, that she felt so inferior to everybody that, somehow, she couldn't cope with her life? That she struggled with bulimia, anorexia, any kind of eating disorder you care to name; that she cut herself; that their parents had looked on in bewilderment?

'When we were young,' she began.

'Sounds like the start of *Winnie the Pooh*,' said Malone with a grin.

She laughed and poked his arm. 'I wish it were so innocent. I mean, it is innocent, it's just, well—'

'Spit it out sweetheart.'

She knelt up on the sofa. 'When we were young,' she began again, wanting him to understand. 'I think I was about eleven and Sasha was ten, it was Christmas time—'

'Oh no, I feel Hollywood schmaltz coming on.'

220

'No,' she said. 'Just listen. At Christmas we had one big present from my parents and lots of little ones. I opened my big present first. Before Sasha, I mean.'

'Okay, I get it. You both have big presents and you get to open yours first.'

She ignored him. 'Usually we opened them both together because they were always the same thing. This particular year, though, something felt different, so I opened mine first. Well, more quickly than Sasha, really. I just couldn't wait I was so excited. My present was a magic set, full of card tricks and magic wands and special string with a ping-pong ball that looked as though it was balanced in mid-air. I had so wanted that magic set. So had Sasha. We'd both been asking for one for months. We wanted to learn tricks, dazzle our parents, make them smile. Sasha wanted to make them see how clever she was.' She paused.

'And? What happened?'

The flames danced in the fireplace, the fire's warmth stealing around her.

'When Sasha opened her present, it was a doll. One of those that sucked on a bottle and cried and peed. It had a horrible squashed-up face.'

'She didn't like it, I take it?'

'No. If anything, she'd wanted a magic set more than me. But Mum and Dad thought she wouldn't be able to do the tricks and she'd lose the bits and that she'd really prefer a doll. But she did want a magic set, so badly.' She chewed at her bottom lip. The memory of Sasha's face when she opened the present and it had been that bloody doll still etched on her memory. 'And, being the older sister and having got my heart's desire I promptly locked myself in the bathroom until I had perfected the tricks and then I put on a show for the parents. I refused to tell Sasha how the tricks were done.'

Malone cupped her face in his hands. 'That wasn't very nice, Miss Devlin.'

'I still feel ashamed of myself now.'

He let his hands drop on to her shoulders. 'What happened?'

'She pulled the legs and arms off her doll, and then one day, when I was over at a friend's house, she found my magic box, stamped on the wand and the ping-pong ball. She tore up the cards, instructions, destroyed everything she could get her hands on. Mum and Dad punished her. Sent her to bed without any supper, I think. But she'd had her revenge.' Alex looked at Malone, saw his mouth twitching. She punched him gently on his arm. 'Hey,' she said. 'It's a serious thing when you're eleven years old, you know.'

'I know, I'm sorry.'

'I suppose what I'm saying to you, Malone, is that Sasha's always been fragile.'

'Fragile? Mental more like.'

'Maybe.'

Malone got up and went to the kitchen to fetch yet another bottle of wine. Alex stared into the fire and could almost see Sasha's defiant but pleased face when she'd cried and screamed at her sister after finding out what she'd done. Then Sasha leaning into her just before Mum dragged her off to her room. 'Now, neither of us can play,' she'd breathed into her ear.

'Look,' said Malone, sitting back down and pouring them each a glass, 'I don't really see what all this about magic tricks and dolls has any bearing on Sasha as she is now.'

'Think about it, Malone. She has always felt inferior to me. Always felt she's had to battle to be recognized for who she is. So when Jez took an interest in her she fell for him; hard, really hard.'

'And where did she meet him?'

She gave a short laugh. 'He was my boyfriend. She seduced him to punish me for being me, I think. The thing was, Jez and me had run our course anyway, so it didn't really matter. And by the time Sasha realized that, it was too late. She'd married him. But the irony was . . . is . . . what she could never quite realize, was that Jez was crazy about her.'

'Ah.' He sipped his wine.

'Her next trick was to get pregnant; it was a sort of putting two fingers up to me. She was married, had a family, and was nicely settled. I was still chasing dreams. At least, that's how it looked to her. Then when I did get pregnant a few years later she could really flaunt her respectability.'

Malone looked confused.

'I was a single mother who had no intention of getting married to the father,' Alex explained. 'In fact, looking back, it seemed as though Sasha was at her most settled around that time; a happy mother. After all, she had it all now and I had nothing – or very little anyway. No husband, no father for my child, no job. I'd come back from London with, as she saw it, my tail between my legs. She was the nicest she's ever been. But . . .' She paused, trying to think what it was she wanted to say. 'There was always a darkness underneath.'

'What do you mean?'

She searched for the right words. 'I think, looking back now, a lot of her happiness was a bit of a show. Putting a brave face on things, and that maybe things weren't as right in her world as she made us think.' She downed her glass, indicated she wanted another one; felt she was turning into an alcoholic, but at least the wine was dulling the edges.

'Depressed you mean?' Malone filled her glass.

'Maybe. Probably. Jez was fiercely protective of her. I wonder if he thought his little family might be taken away from him. I should have tried harder. Then the children were taken and our lives changed irrevocably. Neither of us slept for weeks, at least, not until Jessop and Wood were put away. Now she sits in that house surrounded by memories and waits for Millie to come home.' She gazed into the fire.

'Does she really think Millie is still alive?'

'I don't know, Malone. I really don't.' She closed her eyes, weary of talking.

'So what about Jez?'

'What about him?' She was too comfortable to let her erstwhile brother-in-law inside her head.

'Do you see him much?'

'Not if I can help it.'

'Why?'

'Oh, you know. It was so difficult.'

'That's not unexpected, but he is . . . was . . . your brother-in-law, the father of your niece and nephew. You were all tied together in that vile event, surely that makes you closer, doesn't it?'

Alex laughed. 'Come on, you must have read the statistics. Loads of marriages fall apart after the death of a child, never mind two. I also think Sasha went to a place where he couldn't reach her any more.'

'Ah.'

They sat in silence for a moment.

'Perhaps,' said Malone, his fingers idly tracing circles on her arm, which was warm from the heat of the fire, 'perhaps Jez knows where this mysterious diary is? It seems he's the last person we know who saw Jessop alive. Perhaps he's even got this diary himself.'

Alex tried to stay relaxed but went cold inside. 'Maybe.' If Malone was right, Jez would know if Jessop had written anything about Millie and where he had hidden her body. He would have acted on it; she would have known about it. And Jez would also know if Jessop had written anything about her. Oh God. Surely if he had the diary, and if Jessop had charted her affair with him, Jez would have said something? No. Either Jez had the diary and it said nothing or he didn't have it. There was no getting away from it; she still had to know.

'What is so important about this diary?'

'It might tell me about Millie.' Lying by omission. She felt rather than saw Malone nod.

'Okay,' he said. 'So. Jez doesn't have the diary; Jackie Wood didn't have it. Angela Jessop doesn't have it. Who's left?'

Alex sat up straight. 'Oh my God. How could I have forgotten that?'

'What?'

'When I went to see Jackie Wood she mentioned having a boyfriend.'

'She did have a boyfriend. Martin Jessop.'

'No, don't you see? She's always denied that she was having an affair with him, but she's never said anything about having a boyfriend before. It was like a throwaway line when I talked to her.'

'Perhaps she was trying to impress you.'

Malone tried to pour her another glass, but she stopped him. Her head was swirling enough as it was. She uncurled her legs and stood up.

'I'm just going to go and have a look at my notes, make sure I'm not imagining it.' She attempted to walk in a straight line to the door, hearing Malone chuckling softly behind her. 'I'm perfectly fine,' she said, turning slowly and smiling at him. 'Perfectly fine.'

'Good,' said Malone, chuckling turning into laughter.

'Bastard.' she smiled.

She was right.

When she brought up the transcript of the interview on the computer, there it was in black and white. Helvetica font, anyway.

JW: You know, I was quite happy, in my own world. I even had a boyfriend.

Surprised you . . . not Martin Jessop, whatever papers might have said.

Me: Who was it?

JW (looks out of window at this point) I didn't say anything about him then, and I'm not going to now.

Me: Come on, Jackie. It's fifteen years. (Note - have never read anything about her having a b/f before apart from MartinJ)

JW: It doesn't matter who he was. He wasn't involved, wasn't around when it was all happening. (harsh laugh) Certainly didn't want to know when I was arrested.

So, could this boyfriend have something to do with the disappearance of the diary? And if so, how was she going to find the boyfriend, never mind anything else? It was all so bloody hard, and she felt as though she was going round in circles. She might have to throw herself on Malone's mercy again, see if any of his 'friends' had heard Jackie talking about the boyfriend, the diary.

Alex was just about to leave when she remembered the article she'd promised Gus she would print out for him. She went back to her computer and searched her documents until she found it.

As she picked it up off the printer she heard the faint ringtone of Malone's phone downstairs and him answering, before she went into Gus's den – not something she liked to do uninvited.

Okay, so it wasn't that bad, not really. After she'd switched on the light and winced at the sight of what looked like a small army of empty mugs – could be worse, could be beer cans – and various items of clothing lying discarded on the floor, she went over to his desk and put down the sheaf of papers.

She felt happy, mellow. Relaxing with Malone and a drink or three was A Good Thing.

She turned off the light and went downstairs.

The fire was warm and welcoming, music was playing softly in the background, the air smelt of woodsmoke and Malone's tangy, lemon scent, and Malone was pacing up and down talking on his mobile phone.

He saw Alex and ended the call, smiling at her, eyes crinkling, and she wondered if she had imagined the anger on his face a second ago.

'Who were you talking to?' she asked.

He shook his head. 'No one you need worry about.' Again the smile.

'Really?' She arched an eyebrow, hoping she looked seductive rather than demented. 'Come on, Malone, you can tell me. We're an item. Together. You've got a key to the door. My door.' She lurched towards him. Christ, she must be more drunk than she'd realized.

'No need to worry your pretty little head.'

Red rag to a bull, patronizing git. 'Oh really?' She lurched towards him again and he put out an arm to steady her while she snatched the mobile out of his other hand.

'Hey, what do you think you're doing?'

'Nothing,' she sang, as she weaved out of his way. 'Just seeing if you've got another fancy woman tucked away.' She tried to focus on the screen.

'Well I haven't, okay? Give me the phone.' He wasn't smiling now.

'No,' she said, scrolling through his recent calls. She found it, squinted at the names and the times of calls. And there it was, the same name, same number over and over again. *Gillian Home.* 'Who's this? Gillian? And why "home"?'

He sighed. 'It's not what you think.'

'And what am I thinking?' Suddenly she wasn't feeling relaxed, or drunk.

He gazed at her.

'You're right.' She nodded, wishing she could rewind, go back to before, not be stupid and take the phone. 'I am thinking that. I am thinking Gillian is your wife and you have been phoning home and she's been phoning you for cosy chats. Am I right?' She put up her hand to stop him speaking. 'And please don't patronize me by telling me she doesn't understand you.' She heard the fire

227

crackling and the rushing sound of disappointment in her head. 'So in what way is it not what I'm thinking?'

His eyes glittered. 'Leave it, Alex.'

'Leave it? Leave it?'

'It's none of your business.'

'Oh just a minute, Malone.' She could scarcely get the words out over the tide of anger that threatened to engulf her. 'I think it is my business . . . it has got a great deal to do with me. You come in here, into my life, into Gus's life and we accept you at face value. I believe I have found someone strong and faithful and good and it turns out you have another *life*? Do you really not think it is my business?' She had never felt such fury. It coursed through her body and she realized she now knew what was meant by blood boiling. That's how it was. As if her blood were shooting through her veins, hot and at speed. She felt at once dizzy and energized. She found herself bouncing on the balls of her feet. 'Who the hell are you?'

Malone breathed deeply before pinching the bridge of his nose between thumb and forefinger. 'I'm an undercover detective. You know my life isn't easy, you knew things wouldn't be as simple as with another man, a boring man; but Alex, you have to know that I care about you. Deeply.'

'Care about me?' she said, bitterness waiting to choke her. 'Oh boy.' She thought about how she had trusted him with her secrets, her son, her life, even. And then she thought about how he had not hesitated to come to her when she found Jackie Wood's body. How he had helped her then, how he had listened to her, and the anger drained away and sadness filled its place. 'Just go, Malone.'

'Gillian is my wife in name only. Home is home in name only.'

'Really? Is "Gillian" someone you fucked to get information from, then? Someone you *befriended*? Does she know who you are? Coppers like you have been prosecuted for that. Maybe I'll tell her who you really are.' She made as if to press the redial.

He lunged towards her, grabbing her wrist, twisting it, the phone clattering to the ground.

Malone looked at her, his face stony. She cradled her wrist with her other hand. She would not cry.

'Fuck you, Malone. Fuck you.'

His phone began to ring. *Gillian Home* flashed on the screen.

27

As Kate looked round at what passed for the incident room in Sole Bay – the hastily assembled trestle tables and the uncomfortable plastic chairs – she wished she had taken up Cherry's offer to move the whole motley crew back to Ipswich. He'd said it would be easier for her as the murder investigation went on. But since he'd foisted Glithro on her, and an invitation to his bloody exhibition, she had argued that she would be making regular trips back to Ipswich anyway, and she was always at the end of her mobile phone. So he'd agreed to let her stay at the scene of the crime.

She had been pleased with her victory then, but standing now in the temporary cabin that had seen better days and wishing she had worn a thicker jumper, she wondered if, indeed, Cherry had been right to want her back at the Martlesham headquarters, if only for the warm, clean comfort it afforded. And where there was a proper coffee machine.

'Right, let's have a look at what we've got.'

Kate faced her small team who'd congregated early in the morning, and took a sip out of the, frankly, disgusting plastic cup of coffee. She made a mental note to bring in a kettle and a decent jar of the stuff. The team included DS Steve Rogers, DS Eve Maitland, and, of course, DI Glithro. He was sitting with his arms folded and a 'come on, impress me' look on his face. He was late forties with steel-grey hair buzz-cut close to his head. He kept himself fit and he dressed well, wore good shoes, Kate noticed. If it wasn't for his black eyes that simmered with aggression, Kate would almost call him good-looking. She knew he'd been divorced three times and had two children he never saw, so was the sort of copper that was married to the job rather than to anyone or anything else.

Cherry was also there, having travelled from Ipswich that morning just to see 'how you're getting on, Kate, and I am SIO'. It was all she needed.

She told herself to ignore Cherry and pointed to the pictures of Jackie Wood stuck to the wall behind her: pictures that showed Wood lying dead on the caravan bathroom floor, as well as photos that had appeared in the press on the day of her release.

'What do we know? We know from post-mortem results that she died sometime between midnight and seven in the morning on that Thursday. There was no sign of a break-in so she probably let her killer in. Most of the blood was found in the bathroom, some traces in the main part of the caravan itself, probably spread by the killer.'

'So she was . . . what . . . followed in there and stabbed?' This from DS Maitland.

Glithro snorted. Kate glared at him. 'Yes, Maitland. Not so much followed in, more likely chased – she had defence wounds on her hands. Multiple stab wounds to the chest and neck. One of the chest wounds probably killed her, according to our pathologist. The killer would have been covered in blood.'

'Weapon?' Glithro asked.

'Kitchen knife, six-inch serrated blade, not found at the scene. Still looking for it.'

'River and sea nearby, though, Kate?'

'Yes sir.' Cherry had just stated the obvious. 'We have been looking in nearby ditches, fields, sand dunes, of course. The trouble is, if he threw it away—'

'He?' Glithro again.

Kate glared at him. 'It could be a she; Jackie Wood wasn't very heavy, could have been overpowered easily, especially if it was unexpected; but for the purposes of the meeting we'll call the suspect "he", okay?'

Glithro shrugged, and not for the first time Kate had the thought he had been put on the earth specifically to annoy her.

'As I was saying,' she continued, 'if the murderer threw the knife into the river or the sea then we'll never find it – the currents will have taken it. You know what they're like round here. Anything can be taken by the sea and not be found for months, years, if at all. And it would be the most likely way of disposing of it, if he had any sense.' She drew a breath.

'Footprints?'

'No, DI Glithro. No bloody footprints. Because of the confined space in which Wood was stabbed our killer managed to avoid treading in significant amounts of blood.'

Glithro nodded.

'Rogers,' she went on, 'if you could get us all up to speed with the people you've spoken to, please.'

'Yes, Ma'am.' He shifted about on the uncomfortable chair that did not quite accommodate his bulk and looked at his notes. 'Paul Herman in caravan twenty-eight said he and his wife were in the caravan the evening or night Wood was murdered but didn't hear anything.'

'Where, in relation to Wood's caravan, is caravan number twenty-eight?' asked Cherry.

'Two rows away, sir. We spoke to about three couples in their caravans – it's not exactly fully booked this time of year – and to a Jim Cassidy who was walking his dog about midnight, but he neither saw nor heard anything.'

'Did Nikki Adams's alibi, such as it is, check out?' Kate began to draw lines on the whiteboard with coloured pens, trying to establish connections with the people they'd interviewed and Jackie Wood. She felt like a toddler with crayons. She tried not to think of the high-tech equipment back in Ipswich.

'Nikki Adams?' interrupted Cherry.

'She is staying in the caravan opposite to Jackie Wood. Came to the town to find work and does some shifts in Tesco's.'

'Hmm. At least she's not a sponger, I suppose.'

'No, sir,' said Kate, wishing Cherry would leave her to it, but she could see he was settled in for the long haul.

'Well, that's the odd thing,' went on Steve Rogers, 'her alibi does check out – in as much as *Emmerdale*, *Holby City*, and a documentary about dolphins were on the telly that night—'

'I enjoyed that one,' said Cherry. 'Old Attenborough at his best.'

Rogers acknowledged Cherry's interruption with a polite nod. 'Indeed sir, I enjoy a bit of Attenborough myself. But then she says she went to bed to get some kip before her shift at Tesco's started, and we only have her word for that. However . . .' He drew a deep breath and looked around the room. 'Ms Adams isn't quite who she seems.'

Kate nodded at him. 'Go on.'

'There was something about her I couldn't quite put my finger on – her eyes were a bit shifty, Ma'am –' he ignored the sigh from Glithro, '– so I asked about her in Tesco's, wanted to see her records, if you like.' He put his hand up. 'I know, I know, Data Protection and all that, but they were most helpful and the young woman in the office offered to show me Ms Adams's file, I didn't have to ask, and as she was being so helpful I didn't like to say no.'

'Had the young woman in the office taken a shine to you then, Steve?' asked Eve Maitland to general ribald laughter around the room.

Rogers went puce.

'Oooo, have you asked her out?' Maitland was not going to let him off the hook.

If it were possible, Rogers went an even deeper colour. 'None of your business,' he said.

Kate held up her hand. 'All right, all right, let's hear what DS Rogers has to say or we'll be here all day talking about his love life.' She nodded at him once more. 'So what did you find out?'

He looked at his notes again, though Kate suspected it was more for show than anything else.

'She calls herself Nikki, and all the staff there know her as Nikki. But her real name is Beatrice Nicola Jessop. Adams is her mother's maiden name.' A hum went around the room. 'And she hasn't been at the caravan site or working at the supermarket for long; she hired the caravan the day after Jackie Wood arrived.' Rogers looked around, pleased at the effect he was causing.

Kate gave a low whistle. 'Bloody hell, Steve, that's one hell of a find.' Kate felt that familiar tightness in her gut that told her they were getting closer to some sort of answer.

'Just police work, Ma'am,' he said modestly.

'Bloody good police work. Jessop's daughter renting a caravan opposite Jackie Wood, under an assumed name, that's one hell of a coincidence.' Kate drew a line in red between Nikki Adams's name and Jackie Wood's picture. 'Enough to get a warrant to search the caravan. Rogers, take a couple of uniforms with you and go and talk to Miss Adams, see what she has to say for herself.' She tapped the pen against the whiteboard. 'I think I'll visit Angela Jessop, see if she knows what her daughter is doing. And I want to talk to both Sasha and Alex Clements. DS Maitland—', Maitland looked up, an eager expression on her face, 'I would like you to talk to Jez Clements.' Maitland gave her a sullen look. 'I know, I know, he's a sleazeball but he needs talking to and we also need to check out his alibi.' She looked at her notes. 'He says he was with an Alice McSweeney. Mrs Alice McSweeney. And I also want to know if he was involved in any sort of cover-up at the time of the trial.'

Cherry leaned forward on his chair. 'Cover-up, Detective Inspector?'

'I want to cover all avenues,' replied Kate without any hesitation. 'I also happen to think . . .' She hesitated, not wanting to antagonize Cherry further. 'I also think that what happened years ago has some bearing on this case.'

'I would imagine it does,' said Cherry, picking an imaginary piece of fluff off his immaculately pressed trousers, and immediately making her feel stupid, 'that's why Jackie Wood was murdered. Revenge.'

'I think it goes deeper than that, sir.' Kate was not going to be put off.

'Oh?'

'We have always thought, though it was never proved, that Jessop and Wood had an affair. But what if there was someone else? Another lover? Maybe even the only lover? What if there was someone else but it was brushed under the carpet during the investigation?'

'Brushed under the carpet?' Cherry's tone was that of someone who could scarcely contain his incredulity. 'What evidence have you got for this?'

'There have been persistent rumours and—'

'Rumours?' said Cherry, smiling like a shark. 'Is that all? May I remind you we are dealing with a murder here.'

'But it could have some bearing on it.'

'Detective Inspector, let's concentrate on finding Jackie Wood's killer, shall we? We do not have the budget to do anything else, much less chase about after rumours.'

'Sir—'

'And,' he was on a roll now, 'I have to see the AC later and I don't want to have to tell her that (a)' – he jabbed his finger towards her– 'we have got nowhere on this case, which will not be good news because as you know there is a great deal of media interest in the murder, or that (b) we are wasting precious resources chasing a rumour' – he made it sound like a dirty word – 'that has no substantiation in the real world. After all, there is the possibility that

Wood's murder had nothing to do with who she was or what she had done in the past, but was the result of an opportunist, *n'est pas?*'

'It's possible.'

Cherry stood up. 'So, can I advise you to get on with the job in hand and find Jackie Wood's murderer before we all look silly.' He swept out, the floor of the Portakabin creaking under his footsteps.

Kate turned back to her team. She drew a breath. 'Okay. So Rogers, you'll go and see Ms Adams – or Ms Jessop – or whoever she may be. Find out why she changed her name, why she took a shitty job in Tesco's, and why she happened to rent a caravan opposite Jackie Wood.'

'Not much to go on there, then?' Rogers grinned.

'Quite. Number one suspect at the moment, but I suspect that nothing about this case is going to be simple. DS Maitland, you get along to see Jez Clements; find out when he's next on shift so you can talk to him away from the station. The rest of you,' she nodded towards the three other detectives in the room, 'carry on bashing the phones, checking Facebook, Twitter, and all that. I shall go and have a word with Mrs Jessop, and the Clements.' She gathered up her papers and began to walk out of the room.

'Kate.' Glithro caught up with her. 'I know you don't want me here.'

'Oh?' Kate kept on walking. 'Not totally insensitive then.' She could smell his slightly spicy aftershave and sense his strength beside her.

'It's obvious, isn't it? You haven't assigned me a job.'

'I thought that, as you were a DI, you might have some thoughts in that direction,' she said smoothly.

'I have as a matter of fact but first I want you to tell me why it's significant that Martin Jessop might have had a tart that wasn't Jackie Wood? After all, it's a long time ago now—'

'Fifteen years, that's all.'

'Okay, fifteen years isn't that long in the scheme of things, but two people have been tried and found guilty of the murders of the twins. Cherry's right. We really should be concentrating on Jackie Wood's murder. And it is, you have to concede, most likely revenge.'

Kate knew he was right. Knew that it was more of a personal thing for her, this need to find out about this mysterious person. She had an irrational belief that it could be the answer to finding Millie Clements's grave after all these years. And if she did that, then maybe, just maybe, she might find a little bit of peace inside herself. Though she couldn't tell Glithro this.

'I'm sure you're right,' she said crisply, carrying on back to the box room in the main building that passed for a temporary office for her. 'Nevertheless, I want to take a look at this claim that was never investigated.'

'Why?'

'Because I feel it's worth looking into.'

Glithro shook his head. 'No, no, why was it never investigated? You said in there,' he jerked his head towards the Portakabin, 'that the line of inquiry was squashed.'

'That's right.'

They had reached Kate's office and she sat down behind her desk. Glithro filled the rest of the space with his bulk and his Italian suit and his fancy scent. She had never seen such a well-dressed copper.

'Do you know who by?'

She picked up a pen and started doodling on the pad in front of her. 'By whom. Strictly speaking.'

'Now you're sounding like Cherry.' He grinned, and leaned back on the doorjamb, arms folded. 'So?'

'Rumour has it that it was Jez Clements.'

'Right. Who was in charge of the original case?' He appeared unfazed.

'A Detective Inspector Grainger. Now retired.'

237

'Live locally?'

'I believe so.'

'Then that's where we go.' He pushed himself off the doorjamb and jangled his car keys. 'No time like the present.'

Half an hour ago, Kate would have bristled at the suggestion of Glithro accompanying her, now she thought that maybe it would be a good idea. Alex and Sasha Devlin could wait.

28

If Edward Grainger had known this was to be his last day on earth then maybe he would have tidied up a bit. Then again, maybe he wouldn't. Ever since Jill had died he couldn't be bothered with crap. Crap like cooking for one, or cleaning for himself, or going out on his own, talking to people, *interacting*.

He stroked the stubble on his face, looked down at the slightly stained dressing gown he was still wearing even though it was what? – past ten o'clock. Everything was so much effort. Jill would be so disappointed in him. He could hear her voice in his head now. *'Come on, Teddy. What do you think you're doing? Do you think I wouldn't like to stay in my jim-jams till lunchtime? Get off your arse now!'* If he closed his eyes he could see her, standing in front of him, that slight smile on her face as she berated him.

He sighed. But Jill wasn't here, was she? The cancer had carried her away so quickly they'd hardly been able to draw breath between diagnosis, prognosis, and death. Came back to Suffolk as soon as they could. Jill wanted to die where she was born and he could hardly deny her that, could he? No excuse that she could know about anyway. The trouble was, now he was rattling around in this perfectly nice chalet bungalow that didn't feel like home and probably never would, despite Jill having fallen in love with it as soon as they had driven down the bumpy track and seen it squatting among the sand dunes. He'd tried to talk her out of it. After all, it wasn't near a town or even a proper village and the neighbours were second-homers. But Jill had been adamant. This was where she wanted to spend her last days.

Now he was alone. He picked up the whisky glass. Empty. But the bottle was close to hand, with plenty in it. He unscrewed the top.

He looked out of the window, across the flat sand to the sea beyond. Normally he loved the sea, whatever the weather. He loved that the horizon stretched away as far as the eye could see. It was eternal, changing only with the weather. It usually gave him a sense of well-being when he sat and watched it, but today he was feeling restless and couldn't get Jill out of his head. He sipped the whisky.

It began to rain in that miserable way only the East Anglian clouds can produce. He watched it as it swept in over the sea like an opaque sheet blowing on a washing line, blotting out the view, coursing in rivulets down the window. It had been a mean February.

Edward ignored the ringing of the front doorbell when it came. He had no time for people these days, no need for them. There'd been enough of that when he was in the force; having to kow-tow to authority, be polite to toerags because of their bloody 'rights', which they shouted about every five minutes. He was glad to get out of policing when he did. Things were getting more and more skewed towards the criminal's interest. Even in quiet old sodding Guernsey.

The bell rang again. Who the fuck was it? He didn't usually get salespeople this far along the track, and even Jehovah Witnesses wouldn't come out in this weather, would they?

A third ring. Bugger it.

He heaved himself out of his chair and went to the door. They'd just have to put up with him in his dressing gown and stubble. Designer stubble, maybe.

He slipped the chain on the door before opening. Couldn't be too careful, not after some low life had tried to rob him a couple of days ago. Woken up in the middle of the night by noises downstairs. Little scrote had buggered off through the back door before he could get to him. Must get the man in to do the window locks.

'Hello?'

He was talking to someone's back. For goodness' sake.

'Parcel for you,' said a voice.

Parcel? He sighed and took the chain off the door.

Mistake.

The visitor turned round. The first thing Edward noticed was the balaclava, the second thing was the gun, pointing directly at him. The eyes staring out from the balaclava were cold.

An old grievance, was Edward's first thought. Someone he'd put away who now had come back to take revenge. Or maybe a robbery. He'd give them the bit of money he had in the house then they'd bugger off.

'Now, look here,' he blustered, 'you'll just get into more trouble if you use that thing.' He pointed to the gun, which he could see was being held with a slight wobble and the safety catch off, neither of which inspired confidence.

'Maybe.'

Edward swept his hand back. 'I haven't got much, but you can take what you want. Take it all.'

'I will.'

'Look.' Edward tried again, fear building up inside him at the implacability of his visitor. 'Why don't you put that thing away?' He pointed to the gun. 'Then we can go inside and talk.' He could see the mouth behind the balaclava shape into some sort of smile.

'Good idea. But I'm not putting the gun down. Just let's go inside quietly otherwise I will shoot you in the kneecap and drag you inside. Is that clear?'

The most frightening thing of all was that the voice that came through the cloth was almost normal, pleasant, if slightly muffled.

Edward had to fight the urge to laugh. But the gun was still aimed at him; despite his years in the force and the number of stories he told about fighting crime and arresting scumbags and toerags, he'd never actually had a gun pointed at him at point-blank range. His stomach started to dissolve. He tried to get a grip. Do as they asked and it would all be over soon.

His visitor stepped forward and Edward had no choice but to move backwards, inside the house.

'That's it, Detective Inspector Grainger, let's go in and sit down.'

A jolt of unease, to put it mildly. So this most unwelcome person knew who he was. Had to be something to do with someone he'd arrested, someone he'd put away. A relative perhaps? His mind raced around furiously, examining options, looking for answers.

They went into the front room. Edward looked out of the window, hoping against hope there would be someone walking on the beach. But the rain was still sheeting down, and Edward knew none of his neighbours would come to their holiday cottage in the middle of the week.

Edward sat down in one chair, his visitor in another, still holding that stretched smile, gun held a little steadier now, but still pointing right at his guts.

'Now then, Detective Inspector Grainger . . . actually, I think I'll just call you Teddy. Is that all right?'

No, it wasn't all right. That's what Jill called him; she was the only one to call him Teddy. He didn't want this . . . this person, this terrorist, to call him Teddy. He clenched his fists. 'I'd rather you didn't.'

His visitor shrugged. 'Teddy. You know why I'm here.'

Edward leaned forward on the chair. 'Actually, I don't. But perhaps we can work something out. I have a little bit of money, but no real valuables in the house. Why don't you just take what you came for and leave? Please?' He hated the pleading note in his voice, and he wanted to wipe his sweaty palms down the sides of his pyjama bottoms.

'Oh, I will Teddy. How about if I say the name Martin Jessop, hmm?'

Edward rocked back in his chair. That was a name he'd been trying to forget, been told to forget, for fifteen years. He closed his eyes, clenched his fists.

'I see you know who I'm talking about then, Teddy.' The voice was amused. 'And I don't think you like remembering.'

'Martin Jessop is dead. He hanged himself. He was a murderer.'

'Yes, I know that,' his visitor hissed, voice changing from a tone of quiet amusement to one of menace. 'Jackie Wood's dead too.'

'I know. I read the papers, watch the television,' said Edward, trying to inject some spirit into his voice. He'd been pleased when he'd learned about her death. Another loose end tied up, after all this time.

'My, my, clever man. And I expect you're clever enough to know that Martin Jessop didn't kill those little children?'

'He was tried and convicted.' He tried to appear calm – unclench his fists, breathe normally. The visitor was still wearing the bloody balaclava; that was a good sign. There could be a way out.

His visitor bounced out of the chair, began to walk around the room, gesticulating. 'This bungalow. Nice. Nice area, too. Can't have been cheap.'

'Sold my house on Guernsey.'

'Even so.'

Edward watched carefully for any sign the gun might waver again. Nothing, it was steady, as though his visitor had gained confidence.

'So, Teddy, why did you do it?'

'Do what?'

'Keep quiet about Jessop's mistress?'

'Don't know what you mean.' His stomach was knotted; he began to pray.

'Come on, let's not tell lies, not at this stage.' His visitor tore the balaclava off. Edward closed his eyes.

'Look at me,' the visitor said.

Edward opened his eyes. 'I know you,' he whispered.

His visitor sat down in the chair again. 'Yes, you do.'

Edward couldn't say anything. It was a bad, bad sign. No balaclava. There was no saliva left in his mouth. He licked his lips.

'Dry?' His visitor leaned forward, face almost eager, smile menacing. 'Let's get you a drink.' The visitor stood, gun still trained on Edward, and picked up the whisky bottle on the table next to him. Not good. The visitor was wearing thin surgical gloves. Poured a glass.

'Drink up, Teddy.'

'I don't—'

'I said, drink up. Please.'

Edward lifted the glass to his lips, but his hand was shaking so much some of the amber liquid slopped on to the front of his dressing gown.

His visitor tutted. 'Butterfingers, Teddy. Pour yourself some more. Not too much, though. We don't want to vomit now, do we?'

Edward poured some more liquid into the glass.

'Now drink it.'

He downed it in one gulp, grateful for the burning in his throat and the warmth that suffused his body.

'So, Teddy. You didn't answer my question. Why did you keep quiet about Jessop's girlfriend? And why wasn't Jessop's alibi looked into more rigorously?'

'His girlfriend was Jackie Wood, and I didn't—'

'Stop it, Teddy. Tell me the truth. You might as well, after all these years.'

His visitor was shouting. Edward downed his whisky before pouring himself more, liquid slopping onto his legs. He didn't want to think back to that time, how easily he had been persuaded to turn a blind eye to what was going on. Easily persuaded? It had been more than that. Jez Clements had thrown him a lifeline. Said he'd keep quiet about the kickbacks he was getting from some of the scrotes and gave him money to pay off his gambling debt. Don't know where he got the money. Probably a loan or something; it was worth it for him, gave him leverage. Jill had never known how close they had come to losing it all. So yes, he not only turned a blind eye to any evidence that might throw Jessop's guilt into doubt, he actually ignored it; 'found' the evidence to blow Jessop's alibi apart and squashed any rumour of a secret mistress. In fact, actually encouraged the thought that Jackie Wood was his other half. All it had needed was a word here, a sentence there. People saw what they wanted to see, believed what they wanted to believe.

'Was it worth it?' The visitor's voice was soft now.

Had it been worth it? Edward drained the glass. His eyes misted over. No. It hadn't been worth it. Not now; now that Jill was gone. He'd give it all up, confess to anything if he could have his Jill back.

'Never had children, did you?'

What? Edward jerked his head up. 'What's that got to do with it?' he asked, feeling the familiar twist of hurt when the subject of children came up, even though it was years too late for them.

'Good job, Teddy. Life's hard with kids. Especially . . . well, they wouldn't have liked you. Liked what you became.'

'What?'

'Look at you.' The visitor gently guided Edward's hand as he poured the whisky. 'Sitting there in your pyjamas and dressing gown in the middle of the day. What would Jill think of you?'

He drank, his head beginning to feel pleasantly fuzzy. Perhaps this was a joke or a hallucination? 'Jill?' His tongue was thick and the word filled his mouth.

Laughter came from a long way away. Edward raised the glass to his lips again, wanting to feel the alcohol warming him once more.

'Yes, Jill. She loved you, and you loved her. But then you lied to everybody. You lied to your colleagues, to the court, got rid of evidence about Alex Devlin. Closed down the investigation. You betrayed her, didn't you?' The visitor's voice was insistent.

Edward nodded, gulping back the tears now. 'Yes,' he said. 'Betrayed. I'm so sorry. So sorry, Jill.' If he hadn't been holding his glass he would have put his head in his hands and sobbed.

'Why did you do it, Teddy?' The voice was gentle and kind and made Edward sob even more.

'I had to,' he said. 'Had to. I needed the money. Or we would have lost everything. I'd have lost Jill.' Tears and snot ran freely down his chin. 'And I couldn't go to prison. They hate coppers in prison.'

'Now, see,' the visitor's voice was still kind. 'You're upset. Here, take these.'

'What?' Edward looked up to see two faces. Two noses. Four eyes. Two smiling mouths. Where had they all come from?

'Pills, Teddy, they'll help you relax.'

He felt the tears running into his mouth, the snot on his chin. He wanted to cry.

'Teddy, come on, swallow them down. Have a bit more whisky.'

More whisky. Yes. But – he struggled, tried to clear his foggy, befuddled mind – there was something, something bothering him. Something that didn't make sense. He shook his head, trying to clear a space in the fog.

'More whisky, Teddy.' The voice was impatient.

'How . . . how d'you know 'bout Alex Devlin?'

'What did you say, you old fool?'

'Devlin. The girl? How . . .' The effort was too much. His chin sank onto his chest.

Suddenly his head was wrenched up by fingers pulling on his chin. 'How did I know?' Edward flinched as spit flew in his face. His visitor's eyes were blazing. Edward never understood what that meant until now. Blazing.

'We found the diary. When we came to your house the other day. Broke in. Searched for it while you were off out buying booze and finally, we found it. Martin Jessop told us all we needed to know. Now do you understand?'

The fingers let go of his chin. Edward nodded, tears flowing freely.

'Now.' The voice was tender again. 'Have some pills. They'll help.'

Edward nodded and scrabbled the pills from the outstretched hand.

'That's it, carefully now.'

He felt the hand guide his own to his mouth. He could smell the latex and powder of the surgical gloves. He parted his lips and swallowed the pills. They made him want to gag. The gloved hand was stroking his throat, helping the pills down.

'There, that's better.'

'I'm sorry,' he heard himself mumble. 'Jill, I'm sorry. Sorry. Sorry.'

'Have some more, Edward. Just a couple more pills.'

'You know I'm sorry, don't you?' he whispered as the pills went in his mouth. Somewhere in his brain he knew he had to make his visitor understand. Somewhere he knew it was important that they should know he was sorry, for all of it. All of it.

'That's right, Teddy. Soon you'll be able to forget. No more painful memories, hmm? That's what you want, isn't it?'

Edward opened one eye. Took effort. Tried to open the other. Couldn't. Saw a large plastic bag. Heard a tearing, snapping noise. A hiss like gas escaping from a balloon. Wanted to say he would put things right. Too much.

The darkness closed around him as he heard a whisper of movement in the air.

29

'Damn. Fuck. Shit. Bollocks.' Kate banged the steering wheel with the palms of her hands making them sting.

'That looked as though it hurt,' said Glithro, his voice mild. 'And a nice array of swear words there, Detective Inspector.'

Kate turned to him. 'There goes our fucking lead.'

'A lead, Kate. There'll be more where that came from.' He smoothed the hair on the top of his head.

They were sitting in the car outside Grainger's house, letting the forensic team do their work. It was fuggy, and the windscreen had steamed up, blotting out the dismal view of rain and sea and more rain.

'I don't know where you get your optimism from.' She sighed, aware she was sounding especially grumpy. 'Sometimes, in the winter around here, I fantasize about working in a hot country like Spain or somewhere. Sunshine all day long. Arresting expat crooks.' She grinned. 'I reckon I could enjoy that.'

'No you wouldn't.' Glithro unwrapped another piece of chewing gum. 'You'd be bored witless after a while and very sunburnt. Your skin's not made for constant sunshine. And besides, those crooks abroad are very stupid. All they want is a big fuck-off villa and some arm candy and to boast about what they've done. They're an easy catch.'

'Then why haven't more been caught? Oh, bloody hell.' She banged the steering wheel again. 'Why the fuck did he kill himself now, of all times?'

Glithro laughed. 'It was very inconvenient of him, I must say. He could have waited an hour or two.'

'It's no joking matter.' She groaned. 'We could only have been minutes too late.'

'True.' The muscles of his jaw worked slowly. 'Haven't seen an exit bag suicide for years.'

'How do people know how to use those things?'

'Come on, Kate, it's all over the internet. Plenty of advice about how much helium to let flow into the bag to make you drowsy enough not to want to pull the bloody thing off your head. Plenty of places to buy bags with the Velcro to do them up with. Christ, there are forums that can tell you what poisons to cook up to kill yourself successfully. You know that as well as I do.'

'Depressing.'

'Some people are that desperate.' His voice was sharp enough to make Kate look across at him, but his face was immobile. Then he seemed to shake himself. 'And Edward Grainger was obviously that desperate.'

There was silence in the car, broken only by the sound of the rain on the roof. 'All a bit pat, though, isn't it?' said Kate. 'Could have done it any time over the last fifteen years.' She could feel the frustration bubbling up inside.

'No obvious note.'

Kate leaned back and closed her eyes. 'No note. Dies at a rather convenient time. Let's not presume anything.'

'So, if we're not definitely coming down on the side of suicide, could he have been murdered?'

'Precisely.' Kate opened her eyes.

'And if he was murdered—'

'Who did it?' Kate finished for him.

'More than that, Kate, why? And why now? Has someone got wind of the fact that we're looking into Jackie Wood's murder and are looking back into the past?' He turned on the seat to face her, his face animated. 'Someone's frightened.' He wrinkled his nose. 'Or he could have killed himself. Maybe it was just coincidence that we were coming up to see him on the very day he decided to top himself. There was no sign of forced entry. No sign of force at all. He just looked as though he'd gone to sleep.'

'It's the helium that does that, isn't it?' said Kate, thinking of the bottle of gas with the tube snaking into the plastic bag over Grainger's head. 'Makes them docile so they don't try to claw the bag off. And he'd been drinking.'

'Clements. That's who we've got to talk to next, isn't it?'

'Can't talk to Grainger.'

'Obviously.' Glithro grinned.

'Are you interested then, Glithro?'

'Interested?'

'In something that happened fifteen years ago?'

He shut his eyes as if he were thinking. 'It's all happening at once, isn't it?'

'Meaning?'

'First, Wood gets released from prison, then she's murdered – found, coincidentally, by the murdered children's aunt – then Grainger's found dead. I mean, what's next and why now?'

There was a knock on the side window, and Kate pressed the button to open it while breathing a silent sigh of relief. It was the pathologist smiling her usual sunny smile.

'Jane,' she said by way of greeting. 'How goes it?'

Jane lifted her umbrella high and bent her head into the window. 'Fancy seeing you here, Katie. Bloody miserable,' she smiled. 'Poor guy didn't look after himself well, and what a way to die. Brrr.' She shivered and the rain dripped down her face.

'Do you want to hop in the car?' Kate felt as though it was the least she could offer.

Jane shook her head. 'No, want to get off. Just thought I'd tell you that it looks like suicide.'

'Looks like?'

'Not convinced, despite the bag over the head and the helium. Have to do some more tests. Toxicology and all that, though there's enough booze and pills lying around to kill an army. Hey ho. I'll let you know. If you want to come along to the post-mortem you'll be very welcome.'

Kate thought about the low, dark building with its pure white interior that smelt of death, however antiseptic Jane kept it. 'I'll let you know, Jane, okay?'

'Sure.' Jane straightened. 'Your guys are still in there nosing around, but I'm off. Toodle pip.' She banged the top of the car before walking away.

'"Toodle pip".' Glithro shook his head. 'I've heard it all now.'

'Come on, you know Jane. She loves her work.'

'Hmm. I count myself lucky not knowing her. I bet she's a lesbian too.'

Kate remembered why she hadn't liked Glithro in the first place. 'Does it matter?' she said, coldly.

Glithro banged the back of his head on the seat. 'Oh God, I'm in a car with a card-carrying feminist.'

'Oh, don't be so stupid. What are you doing? Hankering for the seventies or something?'

'Just making an observation.'

'Well keep your ignorant, ill-informed and, frankly, offensive observations to yourself.'

'What? Just because I said our lovely Jane was a lesbian? Some of my best friends—'

'Are lesbians,' she finished off his cliché. 'I know; that's what they all say and it really doesn't cut it, so just keep quiet.' Kate was furious with herself for having begun to like the man.

251

They sat in silence for a few minutes.

'Along with that,' Kate continued as if there hadn't been a break in the conversation, 'if you have a problem with gay people it's because you feel your masculinity's being threatened.'

Another silence ensued. Kate breathed deeply to try and defuse her irritation.

Then Glithro smiled. 'You're awfully easy to wind up, you know.'

'What do you mean?'

He shrugged. 'I'm not really bothered whether Jane is gay, straight, or bi, I just enjoy teasing you.'

Kate couldn't think of anything to say to that.

'Look, do you want to find somewhere to eat?' he asked.

'Why?' She still felt antagonistic.

He looked at her. 'Why not? I'm hungry. Katie.' He grinned.

Not being able to think of a good reason why not, half an hour later Kate found herself sitting opposite Glithro in a small café on the side of the coast road. The tables were covered in oilcloth and there were black and white photographs of fishermen and their nets and boats on the walls. It was just the place to thaw out. Kate felt herself relaxing as they tucked in to an enormous plate of fish and chips, with a pot of builder's tea on the side.

'So, you must have been quite young when you found the little boy in that suitcase.' The batter on Glithro's fish cracked as he sunk his knife into it.

'Thanks, Glithro. No pleasantries from you, then.' Her fish was soft and fresh inside its batter coating.

Glithro chewed and swallowed. 'Man, this is good. I believe in getting straight to the heart of the matter.'

Kate nodded. 'Okay. I was young, yes. It was horrible. Why can't you hold on to your wives?'

He looked at her steadily and she realized what a coal-black colour his eyes were. 'Truth is, I should never have got married in

252

the first place. But each time I thought I would get it right. This time I would be a good husband. Didn't work though.'

'And the children?'

He speared some chips. 'Ah. Biggest regret. Biggest joy. Regret because I suppose I should never have brought them into the world. Regret because I hardly ever see them.' He smiled ruefully. 'Perils of the job. And joy because, well they are, aren't they?'

She swallowed. The fish was dry in her throat. 'I wouldn't know,' she said.

'Ah.'

'What do you mean, "ah"?'

'I just mean I've obviously hit a bit of a nerve.'

'Nope.' Kate squirted some sauce out of the giant plastic tomato. It looked like a dollop of blood on her plate.

'Okay.'

They ate in silence for a few minutes.

The compulsion to talk became too much. 'When I found Harry, Harry Clements, he hadn't been dead that long. I mean long enough to have lost the rigor mortis and for some putrefaction to have set in – it was a hot summer – but not so long that he didn't still look like a little boy. I was eventually allowed to take him out of the suitcase. But not until he'd been photographed and examined and generally gawped over.'

'Who told the parents?'

She shook her head. 'Anna Lord. She was a good copper. She went along with her partner, DI Bishop. I was there too. Insisted on going, seeing as I'd found him.'

'It's the worst part of our job. Taking away the hope.'

'But at least Sasha Clements knew what happened to Harry. She's still left wondering about Millie. Even now she's left wondering about Millie.' She managed to swallow some of her food. 'Then there was the trial and the sleepless nights, the worry about putting over the evidence in the right way, and then the satisfaction that Jessop and Wood were put away. I was so naïve.'

'How so?'

'To think that it could all be wrapped up as easily as that. That I could forget about it.'

'The child. Harry. He died from drowning, didn't he?'

Kate nodded. 'That's what the post-mortem said. Though when he was found he was wearing brand new pyjamas. Nothing fancy, only chain store ones.' She had a sudden flash of blue, of Thomas the Tank Engine. 'He was nice and dry. Just dead.'

More silence. Sounds of knives and forks scraping on plates. Glithro taking a drink of tea. The sound of him drinking magnified.

'I've never wanted children since,' she said casually, dipping a couple of chips in the tomato sauce and feeling as though a great rock in her stomach was starting to dissolve. The very act of telling someone the truth without excuses was . . . liberating, that was the only word for it. She felt giddy. Excited. She tried not to think why it was Glithro she'd decided to confide in; the one copper she thought she didn't like. Turned out maybe she was wrong about him.

'And what does your partner think of that?' Those black eyes, looking steadily at her.

She was going to say he was fine about it, didn't mind. Was willing to wait until she was ready. 'My husband doesn't know,' she said. 'He doesn't know what I really think.'

'Ah.'

The sound of her phone ringing broke the tension between them. It was DS Rogers. She listened to what he had to say, then cut the connection. She picked up her tea and drained the cup. 'Time to get back, DI Glithro. Steve has had a tip-off from the boys at the Grainger crime scene.'

'It's a crime scene now is it?'

'Oh yes,' said Kate, putting some money down on the table, 'suicide note on the computer.'

30

The lights were off as Kate pulled up outside the house. Chris was probably absorbed in his work in the studio. Maybe putting the finishing touches to the table and chairs. She stretched as she got out of the car. Things were beginning to come together.

The suicide note on the computer was obviously false.

I'm sorry. I can't go on any longer without my Gill. Forgive me.

Yeah, right. Nobody wrote their suicide note on a computer that they then switched off. And the clincher was one of the officers who'd been first on the scene. An old mate of Grainger's who'd known the couple and who had been to his wife's funeral. 'Her name was Jill with a "J", not a "G",' he said. 'Grainger would never have got that wrong, however far gone he was.'

Then when they got back to the station, Rogers had turned up a report about an attempted burglary at Grainger's house, which Kate thought was too much of a coincidence not to have been related. And now that they had two murders in a quiet Suffolk town in the space of a week, she had to get answers before she had Cherry – and the press – baying for blood.

255

'Look,' she told her team, 'get onto any cameras in the area – you never know – they could have been speeding off somewhere. Bound to have come in a car, the place is far too isolated to walk to. Something tells me the robber came back. Why, I don't know. Yet. And my gut tells me that if we find Grainger's killer, it could give us some clues to Jackie Wood's murderer. I'm convinced the two are linked. Too much of a coincidence not to be.'

'Hi darling, I'm back.' She took off her coat and hung it over the banister. The house was cold, unwelcoming, as if no one had been in it all day. Strange. Chris normally left a dimmed lamp on for her even when he was working. Must be totally absorbed in what he was doing.

She went upstairs to get changed, looking forward to a glass of wine and a chat with Chris – she wanted to tell him about the day, how she felt they could be getting closer to the killer of Jackie Wood.

She switched the light on in the bathroom.

The doors of the cabinet above the sink were wide open. Bottles of bubble bath, mouth wash, and shampoo lay cracked and broken on the floor, their contents merging into one lurid blue swirl. Tubes of toothpaste, cans of deodorant and shaving foam littered the floor, too. In the basin were assorted bubble packs of pills.

Pills.

A crawling dread went down Kate's spine. She picked up the packs. Her contraceptive pills and the pills Doctor Bone had given her for depression. The contraceptive pill packet half empty, the pills for depression full. She put her hands either side of the basin and bowed her head. Chris had found them. She kept them both right at the top and back of the cupboard underneath bars of soap and aspirin. What the fuck was Chris doing? He never rooted around in the cabinet, never. His stuff – toothbrush, toothpaste, shaving stuff – were all on the bottom shelf on the right-hand side. Not at the top. Not at the bloody top. Why hadn't she been more careful?

She took a deep, shuddering breath and scooped the mess out of the basin before splashing her face with cold water. The crap on the floor would just have to stay for the moment.

The night was clear, a frost in the air. With the moon lighting her way, Kate went down the path and pushed open the studio door. Chris had finished the table and chairs and they stood in the middle of the room, the moonlight making them gleam. They were beautiful. Kate ran her hand over the wood. It was smooth and hard and somehow living under her touch. The chairs were simple, the lines clean and pleasing. She walked around the furniture and saw a pile of what looked like kindling in the corner of the room. She swallowed and went over to the pile and knelt beside it. She could see it was the remains of the beautiful baby's crib Chris had been making. She picked up a couple of pieces of the splintered wood and hugged them to her chest.

'It was a surprise. For you. For our baby.' His voice came from the corner of the studio and a light snapped on.

Chris looked at her, his face stony, eyes red-rimmed, skin pale. 'Did you hear me? Kate? For our baby. The one I thought we'd have eventually. The one we'd have when you'd finally found the courage.'

'Chris . . . I . . .' She was crying.

'The baby we'd have because we love one another and I thought that one day, that would be enough. That I would help you over whatever it was stopping you from completely committing. That's what I thought.' He sniffed and wiped his nose with the back of his hand.

Kate's heart was breaking. 'I'm sorry. I didn't mean—'

'You didn't mean me to find the pills did you? The ones for depression, well, I could understand that. I could even understand why you might not want to tell me about it. Especially as you obviously thought you didn't need them anyway. But the contraceptive pills. Why, Kate? Why?'

Kate gulped down a sob. 'I told you it was difficult for me, that you had to give me time—'

The sound of Chris's fist on the desk beside him made her jump. 'Time? I was willing to give you all the fucking time in the world. I'd've waited forever. I'd have done anything for you, Kate, anything. But this. You lied to me and lied and lied. Why couldn't you just tell me the truth and tell me you didn't want children?'

'You'd have never married me then, would you Chris?' She was shouting now, heedless of the tears pouring down her cheeks. 'You made it perfectly clear that you wanted a family. I tried to tell you I wasn't sure—'

'Wasn't sure? I knew you weren't ready. That's what you told me. I knew I'd have to wait. Plenty of couples don't have children until they're in their forties. I thought that was us, Kate, I thought that was us.'

'My job—'

'Oh, your bloody job. That's what matters, isn't it? Not me and you. Not our lives together, but your bloody job.'

'You know it's important to me, it's part of who I am. I can't just give it up to have babies.'

'Don't even try that one.'

'What do you mean?'

'Kate, it's the twenty-first century. There's such a thing as paid maternity leave now. Paternity leave too. We would have managed. We would have been a family.'

Kate recognized that he was speaking in the past tense. 'I'm sorry.' She bowed her head.

'Finally she says "sorry". But I think the job is your baby. And your partner. I don't think I can compete.'

'Chris, that's not true.'

He looked at her sadly. 'You deceived me. And what lies were you spinning the doctor for him to give you pills for your . . . depression?'

'Her.'

'What?'

'The doctor was a her. And I wasn't lying. Not completely. I—'

He held up his hand as if to ward her off. 'Enough Kate. I don't think I can take any more. The table and chairs are finished and Mr Betts is sending round a van for them sometime this week. I'll come back and let them in when I know what day they're coming.' He heaved himself out of his seat like an old man.

'Where are you going?'

He shrugged. 'I don't know, Kate.'

She couldn't bear the defeat in his face. 'Are you leaving me?' Her voice was a whisper.

He stood in a silence that seemed to her to go on forever. 'I trusted you and that's gone. I thought we were a team, but it seems we're not. I need some time to think.'

'"Think"?' He wasn't going, wasn't leaving. She couldn't let him; she loved him; she'd do anything for him. Even have his babies? That quiet but insistent voice in her head. She pushed it away. 'Chris, there's a way back from this, I know there is. Let's talk about it. Have a drink, something to eat.'

'Talk about it? Oh Kate, I've been trying to talk to you about it for months. You haven't wanted to listen. Why should it be any different now?'

'Please, Chris. I will listen. Give me a chance. Please.'

Chris closed his eyes for a long moment. 'Kate. Give me a bit of time, please. Then we'll talk. I promise.'

Kate didn't trust herself to speak so she nodded.

'Thank you,' he said, before walking out of the door.

Kate put down the splintered bits of wood she'd forgotten she was holding. One of the pieces of wood had dug into her palm, causing it to bleed. She stared at the red drops of blood.

31

The shadow through the door gave her one hell of a fright.

Alex had spent a second night, tossing and turning until the duvet was a knotty tangle around her body and the pillow a lumpy mess under her head, thinking back to that bloody awful evening.

They'd both stared at the phone as it kept on ringing, until 'Gillian' left a message. He'd tried to tell her again that Gillian was work, nothing to do with them and their relationship.

'What do you mean, "work", she'd spat at him. 'Is she or isn't she your wife?'

Malone was inscrutable.

She grabbed the phone off the floor and looked at the number, trying to commit it to memory. 'Malone. Is Gillian your wife? It's a simple question.'

'Yes.'

Her anger drained away. The niggling suspicions she'd had, that she'd pushed to the very back of her mind, had proved to be true.

He took a step towards her. 'Alex. You must understand—'

'I understand all right.' The anger was back.

'No. You don't. I married Gillian as part of my work. She was a major player in a radical environmental organization and—'

'And that makes it better does it?'

'She knows who I am now. What I am.'

'So why hasn't she divorced you?' His patient voice was irritating her.

'It's going through. That's what she was ringing about.'

'Really? Come on, Malone. Why should I believe you now? You've lied to me all through our relationship. I let you into my life and Gus's life and you do this to me.'

'No.' His voice was quiet.

'Yes.'

'I love you, Alex.'

'I don't think you even know what that means.'

She told him to leave.

Now her clock told her it was half past five and she was thankful to be able to get out of bed and drag herself to the shower. It was supposed to revive her – and to that end she used litres of her favourite shower gel and stood under the boiling hot water for as long as she dared. But it wasn't working. That heavy, nagging feeling in the pit of her stomach refused to go away. It was going to be difficult to get Malone out of her system, she knew that. He'd infiltrated himself into her head and into her family and now she felt let down. Betrayed. The trust she'd had in him smashed into a million little pieces. There was a pricking at the back of her eyes and her throat was rough and sore. She stepped out of the shower, dried herself and got dressed. She was making herself a black coffee while forcing down a piece of toast when the doorbell went.

She hurried towards the door and froze. Through the glazed window she could see the outline of a man. Her heart swooped and sank. Something to do with Gus. She hadn't checked whether he was home. Perhaps he'd been out all night. Been to a rave. Dropped some E or whatever it was these days. Ketamine perhaps. Legal highs. Or maybe he'd been run over and was lying dead in a country lane. That bloody Carly had left him on his own. Jack probably couldn't be relied on either. Or maybe he was in hospital having his stomach pumped. Oh God. Something had happened to him. Had to be a police officer at this time of the morning. She found herself walking slowly, trying to delay the inevitable, tasting fear in her mouth.

'Jez,' she said as she opened the door, hanging onto it to keep upright. Why had they sent Jez round? And why was he wearing jeans, heavy boots, and a thick coat? A scarf obscured his chin, mouth and nose, but his eyes stared at her. Why wasn't he in uniform? 'What are you doing here? Is it Gus?'

'Gus? No. Why should it be?'

'Because—'

He held up his hand to cut her off. 'Look, Alex, I haven't got much time.' He jerked his head. 'Come for a walk with me. Please.'

'A walk? But it's not even gone six yet and it's still dark.'

'I know. I need to talk to you, though.'

'But Jez I—'

'Now, Alex. Please.'

There was an urgency in his attitude that made Alex realize this was important.

She grabbed her coat.

They walked down the street and turned into the nearby churchyard of St Mary the Virgin. Fog swirled around them, damp settling on her hair and shoulders. Alex very rarely entered churches these days, but just occasionally she would slip into this one and breathe in the scent of candle wax and incense, and it would soothe her soul.

They sat side by side with careful distance between them on a bench overlooking a row of well-tended graves. She could feel its wooden ridges and the cold and wet seeping through her coat. It was a long, long time since she had spent any meaningful time alone with Jez, much preferring to deal with him on the phone, usually to ask him to be with Sasha when she was in one of her downward spirals. To be this close to him, alone, made her nervous.

'What the fuck were you doing?' Jez looked straight ahead and his voice was quiet, muffled by the scarf. He took his tobacco tin out of his pocket and busied his hands making a roll-up. Alex waited until he had finished and, pulling the scarf down off his face, lit it, cupping his hands around the flame of his lighter. There were heavy nicotine stains on his fore and middle fingers.

'What do you mean?'

'Jackie Wood, that's what I mean.'

'I was trying . . .' She looked up into the sky. It would soon be dawn. 'I am trying to make amends.'

Jez blew out smoke. 'That doesn't mean you had to go and chat to Jackie Wood though, does it? Christ, you've just about crucified Sasha, bringing it all up again.'

Now she turned to look at him. 'Bringing it all up again? It's always there, Jez, you know that. Even if you don't live with her you know how she suffers every day.'

She watched him bite down hard on his lip. 'We all suffer. I miss those kids, you know? No, you can't know. You don't really know anything.' He looked into the distance. 'I miss Sasha. I really loved her, Alex, really loved her. I still do.'

'Oh, let's not go through this again, Jez. I know life was difficult afterwards, there's no doubt about that. It wouldn't have been anything else. I just wish—'

'What do you wish?'

'That you two could have stayed together. That's all. I think she loves you, Jez and always has.'

His laugh was bitter. 'Oh she loved me all right. Too much. That was the problem.'

Alex looked at him for the first time, seeing the deep grooves either side of his mouth, the greying stubble and the frown lines on his forehead. 'What do you mean?'

'Nothing.' He pinched the end of the roll-up, picked a shred of tobacco off his tongue, and tried to light it again.

'Come on, Jez.'

'You don't want to know. Look, we've got to keep Sasha away from stories about Wood, about Jessop. It makes her worse.' He inhaled deeply. 'The press are bound to dredge it all up again. Well, they've started, haven't they? Poring all over it. I hate them, Alex. Hate them. That bloody Ed Killingback keeps on my fucking back.' He laughed tonelessly. 'Killingback on my back. Yeah, right. Says he's searching for the truth. He doesn't want to know the truth. Nobody does.'

'We know the truth,' said Alex.

Jez turned to her. He smiled, but it didn't reach his eyes. 'Alex. You don't know the half of it.'

'Then tell me, Jez. Please.'

He leaned forward, putting his elbows on his knees, smoking slowly, carefully. He shook his head, eyes closed.

Alex took a breath, feeling as though she was about to jump into a pit. She had to ask.

'Jez, do you know anything about a diary?'

His eyes snapped open. 'Diary?'

She searched for the right words. 'When I went to see Jackie Wood she told me Jessop had written a diary.' She swallowed. 'I've been looking for it in case it said anything about . . . about where Millie might be buried.'

The clock chimed the quarter hour.

'No it doesn't.' His voice was a monotone. 'It says nothing about Millie. It was all about you and Jessop.' He looked up at Alex. 'What? Do you think I didn't know? I've always known.'

Her heart was thumping. 'Why have you never said anything?'

'Because I care about Sasha. She is all I care about. And I had to keep the truth about you and Martin from ever coming out.' He stared into the distance. 'God, if I'd known about the two of you while I was trying so fucking hard to get them banged up—'

'What do you mean?'

He took a deep drag of his roll-up and threw it onto the ground. The tip glowed, then faded and he ground it underfoot. 'They were being so slow. The police. I just helped them along a bit. Planted the clothes in the bin. Put some soil and sand and stuff in the communal area of the flats. Got into Jessop's flat when they were out searching for my kids. It's easy if you know what you're doing.'

She put a hand up. It was all too surreal. 'Hang on. Are you telling me you planted the evidence?'

'Why not? I needed them put away.'

'Because they were guilty?'

'I needed them put away.'

It was too much to take in. Alex hugged her stomach. 'Why did Martin never say anything about me? At the trial, I mean? It would have helped his case.'

'He loved you, that's why.'

Alex sat back on the bench. 'Oh.'

'But then I heard through the grapevine he was going to bring up your relationship for his appeal, so I went to see him in jail.'

The air around them grew still.

'And?' she prompted, knowing this was all leading to the diary.

'And he showed me his diary.'

Her whole body tensed. She stopped breathing.

'It was all there, Alex. Every meeting you'd ever had, the feelings he'd had for you. He told me he'd kept quiet because bringing you into it wouldn't have helped him. Not then. At first, I tried to persuade him it wasn't going to help at that time either, but he wouldn't listen.'

She didn't want to hear any more. 'So what did you do?'

'So I told him he was right and that it was time the truth came out. I said I would take the diary and put it in a safe place. And then I asked someone to take care of him.'

'Take care of him?' She was confused 'What do you mean?'

'What do you think I mean?' His laugh was bitter. 'For fuck's sake, grow up Alex.' There was despair on his face and anger behind his eyes and all at once she understood.

'My God. He didn't hang himself, did he?' She looked up at Jez. 'Did he?' Her voice was loud.

Jez ground the roll-up under his foot. 'No.'

'My God,' she said again. Sadness and sorrow and anger for what they had all lost welled up inside her and she blinked hard. 'And the diary?'

'What about it?'

'Where is it now?'

'I had to use it as part-payment.'

'Part-payment?'

He turned to look at her, his mouth in a cruel smile. 'How do you think I got DI Grainger to bury the fact that you were screwing the murder suspect? Do you think I just asked nicely? "Oh, excuse me sir, but my sister-in-law's been shagging Martin Jessop and if my wife knew it would kill her so please could we keep that quiet?" Do you think that's what I said? No, for fuck's sake. He needed money and he needed me to keep quiet about some dirty dealings so I paid him off, putting myself in debt up to my eyeballs, and I kept quiet. And he had the diary as insurance.'

Alex stepped back, letting go of his arm. 'Insurance?' she whispered.

'Grainger wanted to make sure I kept in line. Didn't want me to tell his superiors about the bribes he took from me or anyone else. Said if he had the diary he could destroy you if he needed to.'

'And has he still got it?' She was amazed her voice sounded so normal, amazed that the sky wasn't full of thunder and lightning.

'He's dead.'

'What?'

'Grainger's dead. Killed himself. So I don't know what's going to happen now. Don't know if he hid it, if he still had it, if the investigating cops have found it. I don't know. I guess we hope that if anyone does find it no one will realize its significance and it gets bundled up with his stuff and goes to whoever is his next of kin.'

Jez looked so defeated she almost wanted to put her arms around him.

'And I've had DI Kate Todd on my back and some young copper called Maitland around quizzing me about Jackie Wood; where I was when she was killed.'

'And where were you?'

Jez looked at her. 'Don't worry. I didn't kill her. It was tempting though.'

'What do you mean?' Alex pulled her coat around her. The air seemed to be getting colder.

He sat back down on the bench, took out his tin, and tried to make another roll-up, but his hands were shaking so badly he had to give up. 'I went to see her.'

'What?'

'I found out where she lived – people get careless in the office – and went just to talk to her, find out how long she was going to stay in the area, make sure she wasn't going to come anywhere near our family. Put the frighteners on her. Little did I know you were going to interview the bitch. Anyway, she knew where the diary was – apparently Jessop had left a letter with her solicitor, Danby, that told her Grainger had the diary.'

'Danby? That sly bugger.' She thought about her search for the diary – how she had even got Malone to look in the caravan after she found Jackie Wood. The trip to the Forum. The paintings by the children that she'd found there. And all the while the diary had been with a bent copper.

'Yeah. Anyway, she tried to shake me down. Wanted money to keep quiet. Everybody wants fucking money. Until I realized she hadn't got a clue what was in the damn diary. When I told her about you and Jessop, she didn't know a thing about it.'

'It was you who told her about me and Martin? Just recently?'

'She was going on and on at me about how she knew all about the diary, how she and Martin had been so close, but not lovers, but that he told her everything. On and on she went until I just wanted to shut her up. Told her she hadn't had a clue what was going on under her nose in those flats.' He looked across at Alex.

'Don't worry. I told her I could have her thrown back into jail again so fucking fast it would feel as though she'd never been out. I tell you, whoever killed her did us a fucking favour. Was it you?'

'No.' She shook her head, still shaken by the vehemence in his voice. 'No, no, don't be so bloody stupid. What do you take me for?' Angry at him for even thinking she was capable of such a thing.

He shrugged. 'Could have done. I don't know.'

'I did wonder if Sasha had stabbed her.'

'Nah. She'd have told me. I hear the murder weapon has never been found.'

'No.' Alex couldn't look at him.

'Did you have anything to do with that?'

'No. There's something wrong here, something I'm not seeing.' She put her hand over her mouth. 'My God, maybe he really was innocent. Maybe they both were. Have we been wrong all these years?' She felt sick at the thought.

How had her life come to this? Sitting on a bench in a church-yard dispassionately discussing whether her sister had murdered another woman. Or even contemplating that Martin didn't kill the twins. She looked at her hands, at the skin that was just beginning to lose its elasticity and at the nails kept short to enable her to type. She thought about Jackie Wood, her loneliness and her sense of righteousness when she had come out of prison. She thought of Martin and how she thought she had loved him; the bitterness and anger that had filled her when he had been arrested. The guilt she had felt – still felt – for bringing him anywhere near her family. How she had ignored his pleas for her to listen to him, how she had thrown away every letter he had written to her.

Then she thought of Martin protecting her, not saying anything about her. Keeping her safe. But how the temptation had become too great when he thought it might help with his appeal. She tried to imagine his life in prison, imagine his fear when Jez visited. His terror when someone, somehow, made him hang himself – or did the job for him. How she had been on a relentless search for a diary that may or may not incriminate her. How her sister bounced from despair to greater despair. How she could never recover, never live with the fact her babies had died. How she, Alex, had been living a half-life for the last fifteen years.

She looked up at the church and wondered if she could believe in God.

'Jez, were Martin and Jackie Wood even guilty?'

Her brother-in-law looked at her, and she was shocked by his haunted expression. 'Al. Don't even go there. They were arrested, convicted, and found guilty.'

'On the planted evidence,' she whispered.

He turned away from her. 'They would have got to them eventually, I sped the process up, that's all.'

'And then Jackie Wood had her conviction quashed.'

'Shit happens. All I want is to keep Sasha safe. It's all I've ever wanted.'

'Jez, look at me.'

He didn't turn his head. Alex ploughed on. 'When the twins were alive Sasha wasn't well, was she?'

'She had me.'

'That's not what I asked. I know I had my own problems so was pretty preoccupied and didn't see her and the twins as often as I'd have liked. So tell me, was she properly ill even then?'

'I could look after her. I wasn't going to let anyone take her away from me.' He jumped up. 'I've got to go. I'm due at work.' He started to walk away.

The clock struck the half hour.

'Jez.'

He turned. 'Yes?'

Her throat was full. 'They had done it, hadn't they? Jessop and Wood. You knew that for sure?'

He shrugged. 'Hardly matters now. They're both dead.'

She stared numbly at his retreating back. It did matter. It really did.

269

32

There was a buzz of anticipation in the small conference room born of optimism that a breakthrough was imminent. Kate felt a tingling in her blood. This is what it was all about, this was what she lived for. If only she could dissolve the brick of loneliness in her stomach.

She put her papers down on the rickety table and looked at Glithro who was leaning back in his chair, a slight smile on his face. Suit as sharp as ever, shoes a soft, polished leather. 'You look like the cat who's got the cream, DI Glithro.'

He gave a lazy smile. 'That's one way of putting it.'

'We've got them, Ma'am,' said Rogers, practically rubbing his hands together with glee. 'We've bloody got them.'

'So I gathered from DI Glithro.' She almost laughed at the disappointed look on Rogers's face. 'It's all right. He's left the glory for you. That's why we're here at this godforsaken hour.' She was, in fact, glad to be up and about by seven; she hadn't wanted to stay in the house a moment longer than was necessary. It was lonely when the only company she had was guilt. She'd even thought about getting a cat. 'So show us what you've got.'

'Okay.' Rogers moved the mouse on his computer. 'This is what the guys sent over a couple of hours ago.'

'My, you must have influence in the right places.' This from Glithro.

'Somebody I used to know. She owes me a favour or two.'

'Bloody hell, Steve. Talk about a girl in every port. This is a girl in every police department.' Eve Maitland rolled her eyes as she spoke.

Even Kate found herself laughing at this. 'Okay, okay. Come on Rogers.'

They gathered round his desk.

'Your instincts were right, Ma'am,' he began, 'there was a speed camera – not on the small road where Grainger's house is – on the road out of the village. They've had a lot of problems there with speeding drivers, particularly near the school, so they lobbied for a camera and got one.'

'And it works,' said Glithro drily. 'Wonders of wonders.'

'Not only that,' – Kate was positive she could see Rogers's chest puff up with pride – 'but it's one of those new ones that takes a picture from the front. It's forward-facing you see. No more couples getting off fines and penalty points by claiming they couldn't remember who was driving.'

'Oh God. The public are going to love us even less,' said Glithro with a groan.

'It's all right, Detective Inspector,' said Kate. 'You can update our Facebook page. Tell them all about it.' This drew titters from the other officers and a sour look from Glithro.

'Anyway,' continued Rogers, 'this is what they sent over. The picture.' Everyone leaned forward. 'See. It's two women.'

'Three quarters of an hour before we found Grainger,' said Kate, pointing at the time and date stamp on the screen. 'If we'd been a bit quicker, Glithro, we might have caught them at the scene.' She peered again. 'My God.' The younger woman in the driver's seat was easy to identify. She'd interviewed her only the week before over the Jackie Wood murder. 'Nikki Adams. Nikki bloody Adams. Or should we say Nikki Jessop. Or Bea Jessop or whatever

271

the fuck she wants to call herself. And who's the older one?' She leaned in even closer, narrowing her eyes, thinking she might have to give in and get some glasses. A familiar woman. Older, yes, but with a resemblance to Nikki and she was familiar too. 'Angela Jessop,' she breathed.

'Martin Jessop's wife and daughter,' said Rogers, rather unnecessarily.

Glithro whistled. 'And doing forty-eight miles an hour in a thirty zone. Three points and no speeding course for them. Could do them for careless driving too – I mean, look at the spray thrown up.'

Kate looked at him sharply. 'You're showing your traffic cop credentials. If you're not careful I'll have you busted back there.'

Glithro looked at her, a smile hovering at the corner of his mouth. It made her feel unsettled. She cleared her throat. 'This isn't proof that the Jessops had anything to do with Grainger's murder,' she felt it best to ignore the snort of derision from Glithro, 'but it certainly puts them close.' She thought for a moment. 'Right. Rogers, go and see if Nikki is hiding out in her caravan; I'll get onto Cambridge Police and get them to send someone round to Angela's house. We don't want them doing a moonlight flit somewhere.'

'And will you go to Cambridge to talk to her?' asked Rogers.

She shook her head. 'No. I'd rather have them both in the same place. Get the Cambridge boys to bring her here. Maybe even let them see each other. I know we should go to the custody suite at Martlesham, but I want them on our territory. Unsettle them a bit. They might give up more then. There is no way they're not involved in what's going on, it's too much of a coincidence.'

'Let's hope we don't get any drunks or fights in the town tonight or there'll be nowhere to talk to them. We've only got two interview rooms. Suites is putting it a bit strong, I reckon,' observed Rogers.

'Well the town drunk can go to Martlesham. He won't know he's born when he sees that luxury.'

Rogers's phone rang. 'I'll just get that, Ma'am.'

Glithro sat back down and folded his arms. 'All we've got, Detective Inspector, is two women being caught by a speed camera.

272

How can you leap from that to them killing Grainger? Another fact we haven't actually established?' He picked an imaginary piece of fluff off his immaculately pressed trousers.

Kate looked at him, feeling tired and crumpled. His black eyes bored into hers. She ran her tongue over her teeth. Furry. Her mouth tasted of stale coffee. 'Don't spoil the party, Glithro, I do realize that.' Now she was cross with him, showed it in her voice. 'I'm just wanting to talk to them, you know? See if they've got anything to say for themselves. That's all.'

'Be careful.'

She gritted her teeth. 'I know how to do my job,' she replied.

Rogers put down his phone. 'That was news from Jane Blake. Grainger had enough drugs in his system to kill a dozen horses. Antidepressants or something, some long name anyway. Plenty of drink, too.'

'So, no evidence of murder?' Kate could scarcely hide her disappointment. Perhaps she was on the wrong track after all.

'Not as such.' He grinned. 'But she did find fresh bruising on his chin and dried saliva on his face. That's gone to forensics for DNA. She also puts the time of death about an hour before you found him. And the computer guys said there was no evidence of him having bought the helium and all that stuff on the internet. Or anywhere, for that matter. Nothing on his computer, nothing on his bank statements or credit card bills to suggest it. So unless he paid cash—'

'Someone else bought it,' she finished. 'Thank you Steve, I could kiss you.'

'Steady Ma'am,' he said, turning a deep shade of beetroot.

33

The fog had lifted by the time Alex reached home, her head full of Martin and everything he had meant to her. Everything she must have meant to him. She thought back again to those days when he had been like a drug in her system; nothing and no one else mattered. He had filled her head and her life revolved around him – wondering what he was doing, being jealous of the people who could spend time with him openly, hating his wife, and planning the ways and means of seeing him secretly. What a selfish person she had been. Still was.

Before she did anything else, she ran up the stairs and quietly opened the door to Gus's room and peered in. As her eyes became accustomed to the gloom she could see a Gus-shaped body snuggled under the duvet and hear the reassuring snuffly sounds he made when he was asleep. Thank God, there was no sign of Carly.

In the kitchen the toast she had made earlier, before Jez arrived, lay congealing on the worktop, her half-drunk cup of coffee cold beside it. She filled the kettle again. What she could really do with was a drink, but therein did lie destitution and madness. Any more thoughts like that and she would have to join Alcoholics Anonymous. Actually, not a bad idea for a series of features

– Addictions of the Famous. Probably been done before though.

The kettle boiled and she put a teabag in the cup before pouring the water onto it. The not quite boiling water, which would mean a not quite good enough cup of tea. She put down the kettle and leaned over the worktop, her heart feeling sore, quite literally sore. She hadn't known that was possible.

Could she have been wrong? Could Martin have been an innocent victim in all this? Could she have had a part to play in his death? And Sasha. Poor, weak vulnerable Sasha. Everything done to protect her. For a moment she felt a shaft of pure rage that she damped down quickly. She couldn't allow herself to go there. The protection of Sasha had always been the number one priority for her parents, and by way of osmosis and necessity had become number one priority for her too. If she stopped to analyse it too much she would go mad.

Bad choices. From Gus's father to Martin to Malone she had made bad choices.

And the diary. The fucking diary. Even though she knew where it was she was still no closer to getting her hands on it. Nothing about Millie in it. Her affair with Martin exposed – she had been right to be worried. Now what?

She jumped as her phone suddenly rang out its grungy tune. Her editor, Liz. Calling this early did not necessarily mean good news. She wouldn't answer it.

'Hallo,' she said.

'Darling,' gushed Liz. 'Loved your Jackie Wood article. Well thought out. Well written.'

Alex could sense a 'but'.

'But I'm not sure you've quite managed the personal touch. It's a little . . . detached.'

She wedged her phone under her chin, picked up her tea, and started up the stairs to her study.

'Liz,' she said, sitting down in front of her computer, 'I'm the only journalist she spoke to. No one else. As I said to you, it's an exclusive.'

'I know darling, even so. I wasn't quite feeling it. What do you think? A bit more heart in it, maybe?'

The heart that hadn't been in the article sank. 'Oh,' was all Alex could think of saying.

'Look, let me send it back; I've added some thoughts to it. Have another look at it, have a tinker – I think you'll see what I mean – then get it back to me asap.'

'Asap. Okay. I'll have another look at it.'

'Good.' Liz had her brisk, no-nonsense tone going on. 'Send it as soon as. Later today. Don't want to miss the boat.'

'As soon as. Later. Right.'

'Thanks, Alex. *Ciao.*' The phone went dead.

'*Ciao.*'

The doorbell sounded.

No, she wasn't going there.

Whoever was pressing the bell was leaning on it.

'Mum?' Her son's strained voice sounded from downstairs.

Sighing, she pushed back her chair and went onto the landing.

'Alex, I'm sorry for bothering you.'

Ed Killingback. The last person she wanted to see, which, considering she hadn't wanted to see anyone put him in a very special place indeed.

Gus, still in his pyjamas and with his hair standing in tufts hopped from foot to foot behind him in the hallway. 'Mum? I'm so sorry, really sorry. I answered the door and he sort of barged in. I couldn't stop him. Sorry.'

'That's all right, Gus. Don't worry about it. Go back to bed. I'll deal with Mr Killingback.'

'May I come in?'

'Looks like you already are in, and actually I'd like you to go out again, please,' she said, astonished at his gall.

'I know you're not my number one fan, and you're going like me even less when I tell what I've come for, but I am trying to be fair.'

How had she ever thought he was good-looking? He looked like a ferret, grubbing out stories from wherever he could. She came down the stairs and stood in front of him.

'You found Jackie Wood's body, didn't you?'

'You know that,' she said testily. 'Now, either tell me what you're here for or get out. I've got work to do, a living to earn.'

'Sorry, yes.' He smiled. She didn't like the look of that smile. 'Shall we go and sit down?'

She led the way into the kitchen.

'You may remember, when we met, before, I said it was a good opportunity for you to tell your side of the story.'

What a smarmy bastard. 'And I told you, I didn't want to and I wasn't going to.'

'You also asked me how I knew Martin Jessop had a lover.'

'He did. Jackie Wood.'

He wagged his finger at her. 'Now, you know what I mean, a *secret* lover. He was a busy boy.'

'And you're going to enlighten me.' Alex tried to keep her face neutral.

'Any chance of a coffee?'

'No.'

'Fair enough. It was guesswork, really. From an article I dug out of the newspaper archives. It was written by a reporter on *The Post* who'd talked to Jessop before he was arrested. Just when people were starting to put two and two together about him and Jackie Wood. In the article Malcolm had written – now, how does it go?'

Alex had a pretty shrewd idea that he knew exactly how it went.

'Let me see – "People think me and Jackie are an item. We're not. I have a lovely wife and two children at home. I've already hurt them once, I don't want to do it again."'

'That doesn't say anything, though, does it? He always denied the rumours of anything between him and Jackie.'

'True. And there was never any proof of anything else. That's the one slip he made: "I've already hurt them once" – "once", he said. Because Malcolm was a bloody good hack he knew that meant something and kept digging, but he couldn't make anything stick. But now,' he leaned forward, 'I do have proof.'

Alex raised an eyebrow. 'Oh?' she said, trying to ignore the prickle of sweat on the back of her neck.

'A diary.' He pushed an A5-sized blue hardback book over the table to her; the sort of hardback notebook that could be found in any stationers.

She swallowed, trying to get saliva into her mouth. She looked at the diary, but didn't dare touch it. This was it, then. The diary she had spent so much time looking for.

'I see,' she said quietly. 'And where did you get that?'

Ed tapped the side of his nose. 'Sources. You know.'

The diary. She thought that, if she could just find it, all would be well. She pulled it towards her and opened it. There was her name. Very first entry.

Alex. I just like saying her name over and over in my head.
I daren't say it out loud in case someone asks me who she is.
And how could I say that she is the love of my life, that I'd
give anything to be with her.

She shut the book quickly and bowed her head. She didn't need to see any more. He had protected her. No matter what she thought about him and his betrayal of her, and of his wife and children, he had protected her. And she had done nothing for him.

'So what do you want from me?'

He smiled. It looked like a shark's smile. 'Nothing.'

She jerked her head up.

'Nothing?'

'No. This is just a courtesy call.'

'What do you mean?'

'I'm publishing it.'

'What? You can't.' She tried to snatch the diary off the table but he was too quick for her.

'No you don't, this is mine now.'

'No it's not. If anything it belongs to the Jessops.'

'Exactly. They, the Jessops – well Jessop's daughter, actually – said I could use it how I wanted.'

'Daughter? Bea? I thought no one knew where she was?'

'Bea? No, she's here all right.' The shark's smile again. 'Though you know her as Nikki.'

She closed her eyes for a moment, exhaustion filling her bones. What a fool she'd been. Nikki Adams or Bea Jessop or whatever her sodding name was must be laughing all the way to the bank. 'How much do you want? And how much does Nikki want?' she asked wearily, wondering how she could manage it.

'Money?' He shook his head. 'Bea doesn't want money. She wants justice.'

'She was happy to take money when it was offered. Now she wants justice – also known as revenge – and you? What is it you want?' She looked at him carefully. 'You want a chance to make your name. The big story. The one everyone wants.'

'It's not a bad one though, is it?' He grinned and Alex wanted to punch his sneery, smiley mouth.

She drew patterns on the table with her finger. 'You'll destroy me. And my family,' she said quietly.

'You destroyed Jessop's family.'

'How did I do that? He did it all by himself.'

Ed sat back in his chair, crossed one leg over the other. 'Are you sure about that?'

'What do you mean?' Her heart began to beat faster.

'Look, as I told you before, I've made a study of this case and something doesn't add up.'

'Now you're sounding like someone in a bad movie.'

He shrugged. 'Maybe, but think about it. Why would your brother-in-law go to so much trouble to cover-up the fact that you had an affair with Jessop?'

'He wanted to protect me and his family.'

'He went to great lengths to do that, didn't he? Did you know he bribed a senior officer to shut down any investigation into rumours that Martin Jessop had another mistress, lover, call it what you like?'

Alex looked at him.

'Edward Grainger, his name was.'

'Was?' She was not going to give him anything.

'Dead. Killed himself. Recently. But you see where I'm coming from? A lot of effort went into "protecting" you, and I wonder why?'

'Not just me. To protect the family. And my sister. Which is why you mustn't use the story. It'll crucify her. She didn't know I was in a relationship with Martin.'

Alex jumped as Ed banged the table. 'Oh, wake up and smell the coffee, will you!'

'There you go again, sounding like a bad actor in a bad movie.'

'Listen to me. There's more to it than that, there has to be.'

She pounced on his words. '"Has to be"? Because you want it so, is that it?'

'No. Listen. Did you have any idea at all that Martin – already the father of two children – would be capable of killing your sister's children?'

'Evidence was found—'

'Evidence can be planted. False evidence found. Look at what happened to Jackie Wood. I'll ask you again, did you have any idea?'

'No. None. I was more than surprised when he was arrested.'

'If you read the diary you'll see that there is no evidence at all in there, no evil thoughts towards children. All he writes about is that he loves you. He details the places you go, the things you do. Then, when he's arrested, on remand, he talks about prison. His wife. His children. Hardly the ramblings of a murderer.'

'How would you know what the ramblings of a murderer would be?' She felt desperate now, was trying to push away thoughts of Martin, of Jez, of the doubts starting to overwhelm her.

'Look.' His voice was gentler now. 'I just want the story. And I'll write it, whatever. I'm giving you the chance to give your side of it, that's all. I don't expect to unmask the real killer, not now. Though you never know.' He got up. 'Think about it.'

The door slammed.

34

Kate shut the door of the interview room behind her. As rooms went, it was a bit newer than most, less graffiti on the magnolia walls, but it still had the smell of defeat permeating the air; the window was set high up in the wall and the plastic table and chairs bolted to the floor. She put the coffee down in front of Angela Jessop, who was dressed in a black, long-sleeved jersey dress, quite expensive from the look of it. She had silver studs in her ears and a long, bright orange and cream scarf around her neck. Her hair was swept up into a bun, her make-up was enough and not too much.

'Do I need a lawyer?' Her tone was even, but there was intent behind her eyes.

Kate smiled pleasantly. So, Angela was on the offensive. Not uncommon for people when they end up in the interview room, but still. 'I don't know. Do you?' She didn't want her to say yes, not yet, otherwise she wouldn't get anything out of her.

'What am I here for then?'

Kate indicated the plastic coffee cup. 'Sorry about the coffee, but it's the best I can do. I've tried bringing my own coffee maker but health and safety wouldn't let me plug it in. So we've had to make do with the vending machine.' She set her own cup down and sat opposite Angela Jessop. 'And if you don't mind, I'll just turn on the recording. Is that okay Angela? May I call you Angela?'

Angela nodded.

'And standing in the wings over there,' she pointed to Eve Maitland who was by the door, 'is Detective Constable Maitland.' Kate turned on the tape machine, and gave her name, together with Eve's, and the date and time.

Angela put both her hands around the coffee cup. 'Why have you brought me here?'

'For the tape, Angela, could you state your name please.'

'Angela Jessop.' She sighed. 'I ask you again, why have you brought me here?'

'Just for a bit of a chat, really. You're free to go if you want, you're not under arrest or anything—'

'You could have fooled me. Those plods in Cambridge made me feel like I was some bank robber.' She ran her hands through her hair. 'They told me they wanted to clear something up and it would be easier if I came to the station. I didn't realize I was going to have to come here. I thought I would just go to Parkside. I've been there often enough in the past.'

'Yes, I'm sorry. It must all bring back memories.'

'It does. And not good ones, as you can imagine.' She looked up at the strip lighting, then around the room. 'They all feel the same, smell the same, these places. And although I've spent fifteen years trying to erase them from my memory, it's all come flooding back.' She shuddered. 'They questioned me for hours, you know.'

Kate did know, she had read the transcripts. Some of the questioning had seemed brutal, as if they truly believed she had helped her husband kill the babies. How she held out, Kate didn't know, especially when they'd gone down the road trodden by some of the tabloids at the time. How could you live with a murderer and not know? was the easiest of the things she was asked. For a minute Kate felt sorry for her, then she remembered the sight of

Grainger's face in the plastic bag – the swollen tongue, the bulging eyes – and she didn't feel sorry for her any more.

'Sorry about that.'

'Sorry? That's not much comfort, you know.'

Kate nodded. 'Things are a bit different today.'

'Really? You could have fooled me.'

'I saw my daughter here too. Just now as I was coming in. PC Plod wouldn't let me talk to her though. What is she doing here?'

Kate made a show of opening up a cardboard file and looking through some papers. 'You mean Bea Jessop?'

'That's right.'

'Yes. Though we seem to know her as Nikki.'

'Why do you want to talk to her? She's done nothing wrong.' She began to pull at her scarf with her free hand.

'I'm sure she hasn't,' Kate continued smoothly, 'we just wanted to talk to you both. As I said, clear something up.' She looked down, as though considering her notes. 'Actually, that's something that's puzzling me. Why did she change her name?'

Angela gazed at one of the magnolia walls. 'Why does anybody? To become someone else. To get away from the shame of being her father's daughter.' She looked at Kate again. 'When they questioned me – then, I mean – it felt like days. I'm sure you lot were convinced that I had to be his accomplice. When they found those clothes in Martin's bin, that's when they really went to town. Showed me pictures, terrible, terrible pictures.'

Kate remained still. She knew those pictures, too. Had looked at them often over the years, though in reality she didn't need the photos; she had a perfect, sharp photo of Harry in her head.

'Who questioned you at the time? Can you remember?'

Her mouth twisted. 'How could I forget. Grainger. Detective Inspector Edward Grainger. Self-satisfied sod that he was.'

'Have you seen him recently?'

'Grainger?'

'Yes. Edward Grainger.'

284

'I thought he'd gone to work in Guernsey?'

'No, he came back here, when his wife fell ill. She died about a year ago.'

'I'm sorry.'

I'm sure you are, thought Kate. 'Grainger was murdered yesterday.'

'Murdered?'

She wasn't a bad actress. The strip light flickered. A tic appeared in her cheek.

Not a bad actress. But not great.

Kate put her elbows on the table and clasped her hands together. 'He was fed whisky and pills, then someone put a bag over his head, pumped helium into it, and murdered him.'

'That's awful.' She blinked three times. The light flickered again. A strand of hair came free from her bun.

'The thing is, Angela, you were caught on a speed camera about three quarters of an hour before he was found. On the road leading away from his house.'

'A speed camera?'

'Yes.'

'On the road leading away from his house?'

'Yes.' Kate tried to stay patient.

'Is that why I'm here? Because I was "caught", as you say, on a speed camera on a road near his house?'

'Shortly before he was found, yes. And shortly after he died. And it wasn't just you in the car. Your daughter was with you.'

'What?' Her lip curled. 'And one fuzzy dark shot from the back showed you all that?'

Kate pulled the speed camera photo out from her bundle of papers and slid it across the table to Angela, who picked it up and studied it.

She put it back down on the table. Her complexion was pasty. Both hands were playing with her scarf, twisting it round and round. 'So? It doesn't prove anything.'

'What were you doing near his house on the day he was murdered?'

'How do you know he was murdered? Sounded more like he killed himself.' She looked at Kate defiantly. 'The cowards, they always find the easy way out. Leave a note saying they couldn't take any more. Even Martin. Did you know he had a lover?'

Kate closed her eyes briefly and tried to damp down the excitement. The note. Nobody had mentioned a note. And finally, something about the lover.

'Angela. Tell me about the mistress, lover, whatever you want to call her.' She was getting close to knowing more about what happened fifteen years ago, she could feel it.

'Bitch, I call her. If it wasn't for her Martin would still be alive.' Angela abandoned her scarf and began to pick the sides of her thumbs. 'It was that damn diary. I didn't even know it existed, not until Bea told me about it.' She laughed. 'I'm sorry, I can't get used to calling her Nikki. Just like I couldn't get used to thinking of her stacking shelves in Tesco's. "Bea," I said to her, "can't you find something a bit more suited to your qualifications?" She trained as a teacher, you know.'

'Whose diary?'

'Martin's.' She seemed surprised at the question.

'And it told you about the mistress?' Kate knew she had to go carefully here; she didn't want Angela Jessop to clam up.

'I wonder now if she had something to do with, you know, what happened.' She looked at Kate, her eyes had gone back into their sockets. 'Do you think it could?'

'I don't know, Angela. Tell me.'

She gave a deep, shuddering sigh. 'Martin's lawyer was a friend of the family. He played golf with Jonny Danby.' A smile twisted one side of her face. 'Old boys' club, eh? It was easy enough to keep in touch with Jonny over the years, get a bit close to him. I wanted to keep tabs on the Wood woman in prison. See what was happening to her. Thought it might be useful, and it was.

286

Jonny Danby had been Martin's lawyer as well as Jackie Wood's.' She picked at the skin on the side of her thumbs. 'He told me about the appeal and that she was most likely going to be freed. He said he didn't think she would go and live at the other end of the country. It was just a matter of a bit of research to find out that her parents had died and that they'd had a caravan in Sole Bay. That the caravan hadn't been sold. Good old internet.' She shrugged. 'Bea went to Sole Bay and rented a caravan on the same site just after Wood moved in. It was a stroke of luck that it was right next door to Wood's. Then, when Wood came to the caravan a couple of days later, Bea helped her move in. She told me she had some plan to make Wood pay for what she had done to our family. She never believed her dad was guilty, you see.' She smiled. The skin on the side of her thumbs was raw.

'What about you? Did you believe Martin had killed those children?'

Angela Jessop gave a sigh from the depths of her soul. 'At first I didn't know what to think. I loved him. Oh, I knew he'd strayed,' she waved her hand as if dismissing the hurt. 'After all, he gave that interview to *The Post*. I hated him after he killed himself. But then . . . then I realized that he would never, ever have hurt those children. Never.'

Kate nodded. 'So, the diary?'

Another sigh. 'They got chatting and Wood told Bea all about the diary. Said Martin had even written it in prison, but a policeman had taken it off him. Said Edward Grainger had it. Said it was "explosive". That was her very word. "Explosive". Then that woman came along. Alex Devlin.'

Kate thought about the burglary. 'So Bea went looking for the diary one night, did she?'

'Well, she could hardly go and ask the bugger could she? So yes, she did. And found it. Could I have some more coffee, please?'

Kate nodded. 'We'll take a bit of a break.' She switched off the tape recorder.

Eve Maitland slipped out of the room, coming back a couple of minutes later with the drink.

'So,' said Kate, switching the tape recorder back on and announcing all their names again, 'Bea found the diary?'

'You were there, weren't you?'

'When?'

'When they found Harry. You found Harry.' She grimaced. 'It must have been . . .' She shook her head. 'Oh, I don't know, horrendous.'

'Yes.' Kate refused to let the images that haunted her into her head. 'The diary.'

'It described everything. The times they met. Where they met. What they did.' Her expression was filled with disgust. 'Creeping about. Sex in anonymous hotel rooms to start with, then she found him the flat in Sole Bay. So very convenient.'

Even now, Kate could see the hurt on her face, hear it in her voice. 'Does it say where Martin buried Millie?'

Angela looked at her, surprise on her face. 'No, no.' She shook her head. 'The diary said nothing about any of that, just about her. And when he got to prison, how he felt he couldn't betray her, that it wouldn't have done any good. It would have done me some good, though.' She looked at Kate, her eyes shining with tears. 'He did talk about me and the children, too. He still loved us. I can hang on to that.'

'Who was she?'

'She?'

'The mistress?'

'Didn't I say? Alex Devlin, that's who.'

The sides of her thumbs began to bleed.

35

For the first time in what seemed like months the sky was clear and the sun was shining as Alex walked up the path to Sasha's house. It was time to find out the truth; there was no more hiding. She knew there was nothing to stop Ed from writing his story, putting all his speculation out there. Perhaps it would reopen the case into the twins' murder, and maybe then they would find out where Millie was buried, but somehow she doubted it. Life didn't work like that, not in her experience.

She knocked on the door.

Jez opened it. He was pale and looked as though he needed to sleep for a week. 'Alex.'

'Is Sasha okay?'

'Yes, why?'

'Well, you're not normally here and I thought for a moment—'

'That she'd been cutting herself again? No more than usual. What do you want?'

Alex was taken aback. 'I want to see Sash, if that's okay with you.'

'Sure.' He opened the door wider and she tried to push past him to go through to the sitting room.

He grasped her arm and she resisted the urge to shake it off – she was becoming sick of people trying to stop her doing things – and contented herself with a glare. 'I want to see my sister.'

'There's something you should know.'

'The diary. I do know. Ed Killingback thoroughly enjoyed telling me he had it.'

'*He* had it?'

'Yes, why?'

'Because it was stolen from Grainger's house a few days ago, just before he was killed.'

She laughed. 'I can't believe Ed Killingback stole it.'

'No. Bea Jessop did.'

'Bea?'

'Apparently so. I think Angela and Bea are both involved in Grainger's death. That's what I heard down the station anyway.'

Alex leaned against the wall. 'Oh, God. It really is all unravelling, isn't it?'

'Hey, Lexie, what are you doing here?'

If Jez looked as though he needed to sleep for a week, Sasha looked as though she needed a month's worth. Her hair hung lankly across her shoulders; her face, a light shade of grey, was all sharp angles. She held a stained dressing gown closed with one hand, the other was scratching her head, her neck, her arms. Gone was the woman who had seemed to be trying to get it together when she came round to tell her about Jackie Wood. God, how could she tell her about Martin and the diary and all the publicity that was about to blow their lives apart again?

'You were just going, weren't you?' said Jez, still holding on to her arm.

How easy it would be to say yes, to turn away and go out into the sunshine again and carry on with her life, maybe leave town until the papers were in cat litter trays.

'No,' she said. 'I want to talk to Sasha. It's important.' She looked at Jez. She could have imagined it, but she thought she

290

saw him flinch. 'Something else happened the day the twins disappeared.'

'C'mon through, Lexie, c'mon through,' said Sasha, in the sing-song voice Alex knew of old; the voice Sasha used when she was on the edge. She giggled. 'That sounded a bit like that game show, didn't it? You know the one . . . c'mon down. What was it called Jez?'

Jez ran his hands over his head. 'I have no idea, Sasha.'

'Oh don't you? That is disappointing. Anyway, Alex, I want to talk to you too. I want so, so much to talk to you.'

The sitting room was airless and stuffy, as usual. Alex sat down on the sofa and patted the seat next to her. Jez stayed in the doorway, almost as if he were blocking her exit. 'Come here, Sash,' she said. 'I've got something to tell you.'

Her eyes narrowed. 'If it's about Martin Jessop then don't bother. I know all about you and him. Always have done.' She waved her hands about aimlessly. The dressing gown fell open to reveal a stained nightie.

Alex tried to breathe. She had always tried to protect Sasha. Jez had always tried to protect Sasha. But she had always known.

Sasha sat down and patted Alex's knee. 'Always known. I came to see you one day, at your house. Let myself in. I saw him with you. I saw you with him.' Her face twisted. 'I saw your lover. You brought Jessop into this family. And do you know what? When I went to see him—'

'You went to see Martin? Oh my God, when? He never said.'

'Darling, I can't remember when, I just *did*. But, do you know what? He didn't want to know me. Not at all.'

'What do you mean?'

She started to cry then. 'He said he found me cheap. Ugly.' She looked at Jez. 'Just like you do; you find me cheap and ugly.'

'I've told you over and over, I love you Sasha, I always have.'

She looked at him, horror on her face. 'Have you?'

291

'You know all this, Sasha. You know all this.' He put his head in his hands.

Alex felt ill. She took hold of Sasha's hands. 'Sash?'

'Mmm?'

'What really happened the day the babies were taken?'

36

FIFTEEN YEARS AGO

Sasha had managed to escape to the bathroom for a wee on her own, without curious toddlers wanting to know what she was doing, why she was doing it, why, why, why. Now she wanted to have a shower, again on her own, while Jez was looking after Harry and Millie. She'd hated asking him, knowing the look of impatience tinged with disgust at her sour-smelling body that would appear for nanoseconds on his face. But it would be there.

She looked at herself in the mirror. White, washed-out face, stringy hair, breasts that drooped. That was why she woke up every morning with a heaviness, a blackness in her mood. Lately, she'd thought about running away, escaping her responsibilities.

Maybe, just maybe, today might do the trick, because she was escaping. Getting on the train to Norwich and just wandering around. She'd probably sit in Waterstone's and have a coffee, read a new book that she might buy. Have lunch somewhere . . . Frank's Bar, maybe. That would cheer her up.

Her shoulders slumped. Cheer her up. Some hope when it sometimes took a gargantuan effort even to turn on the shower.

It seemed to take an age to take off her clothes. She stepped into the shower and looked at the taps for one minute. Two. Three minutes. Try to think about the sunshine outside. The fact that she was going to have a day all to herself while Alex looked after her children, and Gus would be there as a playmate. Maybe her sister would take them down to the sea, or to the park, or the library. Yes, that would be good, the library. They loved the books and the stories there. She frowned. But that Jackie Wood was odd. She was sure the librarian kept some of the paintings the children did at story time. And one day she'd followed them home. Oh, she thought Sasha hadn't seen her, but she had. On second thoughts, perhaps she should tell Alex to give the library a wide berth.

She felt her mood beginning to lift and she straightened her shoulders and turned on the water. Wash it all away. Wash all the rubbish that was in her head away. Rubbish float away on the water.

Half an hour later she was clean, hair dried, and dressed in what she thought of as her going-out clothes. She had quite a few of those, barely worn as her normal uniform was tracksuit bottoms and some sort of sweatshirt, or, on a bad day, her nightie and dressing gown. Today she'd even made the effort and put on a bit of make-up.

'You look fantastic,' said Jez, smiling at her, a child hanging off each arm. 'Bloody gorgeous.'

'Sssh,' she laughed. 'Not in front of the children.'

He laughed with her, and Sasha felt on top of the world. She was going to have a great time; she'd even do a bit of shopping.

'Here love,' said Jez, holding out three twenty pound notes, 'get yourself something nice. A handbag, new dress, whatever it is that you women want. Shoes maybe.'

'Red shoes with an impossibly high heel?'

Jez nodded. 'Red shoes with an impossibly high heel.'

She nodded, her head feeling clearer than it had for months. At times like these she really believed Jez loved her, that she wasn't second best to Alex. Yes, Jez said that she was the one he wanted, that when he saw her, Alex faded into the background. But could she really tug of worry. Alex had been his first love; she knew that for a fact. She could still see them entwined on the sofa in their small sitting room, her sister looking up and smiling a Cheshire Cat smile. She had resolved to wipe that smile off her face, to make her sister suffer. So she went out of her way to flirt and pout her way into Jez's psyche until she was sure she had him hooked. Line and sinker.

After that, it hadn't taken long to lure him away from Alex. At first it had been like a game, brushing passed him in the hallway; asking him to help zip up her dress; wanting his opinion on her clothes, what film to watch, what book to read. All so very obvious but tried and tested and it worked.

The consequence of her plan was that, somehow, she could never quite believe, in spite of his continual reassurance, that Jez really wanted her, really wanted to be with her. 'Do you really love me?' she would plead, until he was driven to distraction and would walk away, leaving her feeling even more insecure.

She felt she had to work extra hard to keep him.

Then she fell pregnant, and for a short while dared to feel happy and contented, secure even. It helped when they found she was expecting twins. Even Alex hadn't been able to compete with that. But somehow that sense of well-being didn't last and she slowly descended into the not-quite-good-enough area of her mind. It was as though there was a mist slowly swirling around in her head rendering her unable to think or act clearly. She fumbled her way through life.

But today was going to be okay. A day out. A day to buy red shoes with an impossibly high heel.

The doorbell went.

'That'll be Alex,' she said. 'When are you off to work, Jez?'

He smiled at her and she wanted to believe he loved her. 'I've got time for a quick coffee with your sister, then it's off to the fun factory.'

Alex gave her a brief kiss on the cheek as she let her in. 'You go now,' she said, balancing a gurgly Gus on her hip. 'The twins will be perfectly safe with me. Don't worry about a thing.'

'Thanks, Alex. I'll be back about five?'

'That's fine. Go on. I'll see you at my house then, okay?' Alex gently pushed her out of the door. 'Take advantage of my generosity.'

The sun was warm on her head as she walked down the path and opened the gate. A perfect summer's day. She glanced back. A tableau – Jez and Alex laughing; Alex leaning forward tickling Harry; Gus pulling at her hair; Millie clapping her hands, reaching out to her father – a family together. Sasha turned away.

She'd had a good day, with the dark thoughts only beginning on the way home as she stared out of the train window. Had Jez actually gone to work, or did he stay with Alex? She knew he'd said he was going, but people didn't always do what they said, did they? Did Millie and Harry love Alex more than they loved her? However many times she told herself to stop being stupid, she couldn't get the bad thoughts out of her head.

Her feet started to drag as she reached Alex's road, the energy draining out of her body. The carrier bags looped over each hand were becoming heavier, their handles tighter. She was late. The thought of two kids wanting to crawl all over her because she'd been away for the day and then having to walk them home and get them ready for bed was too much. They were bound to be hyper after being with their Aunty. She'd have fed them sweets and ice creams and fuck knows what. And she'd bet any money that Alex would have let them have a good long sleep this afternoon. They didn't usually need a nap these days, but they were bound to have had one today. And Alex wouldn't have to deal with the consequences. Whereas she would have to pick up two grizzling kids and take them home. Then Jez would be wanting food and she'd start worrying all over again about what he'd been doing and who he'd really been with.

Her head ached.

She stopped in front of the gate.

Her children were playing in the little front garden on their own. Anything could happen to them. They could be snatched. They could open the gate. Run off. Get hit by a car. She clenched her fists. How could Alex do this? Leave them outside on their own?

There was a car on the pavement. Probably that Martin Jessop's car. No wonder. No doubt they were inside going at it like rabbits while she was out here watching her children playing without any supervision.

Oh, she knew all about Martin Jessop. Alex didn't realize that she knew, but she did. She'd seen them together one day and confronted him in the street later, wanting to know who he was, what he was like, why he wanted to be with Alex, of all people. Her sister, who couldn't remember shagging the father of her son. Alex who had been with Jez first. Before her. But he'd looked at her like she was something he'd found on the bottom of his shoe. Arrogant tosser. He thought he was oh-so-arty, so clever. He'd even come on to her. Well, she soon put a stop to that. Then he'd said how he knew she got depressed and sometimes neglected the children and poor thing could he help in any way? She'd been angry then, shouting at him in the street. He'd called her a fishwife, she told him he was a wanker.

At least that's what she thought happened. Maybe she didn't speak to him at all. Perhaps he looked at her, or through her, or passed her as if she was nothing. She shook her head to try and clear it. Whatever. He shouldn't be there when her sister was supposed to be in charge of three children. Of Harry and Millie.

At that moment they turned round and saw her.

'Mummee, Mumeeee!' shouted Millie. Harry came running over on his chubby little legs, Millie following. Sasha dropped the carrier bags and held out her arms. Harry flew into them. His body was solid against her own, but she knew the bones were fragile. Like a little bird. Easily broken.

She buried her face in his hair. My beautiful babies, she thought.

Suddenly she didn't want to talk to Alex, go home with the twins, put the supper on. The evening was still bright and warm. The beach, the sea. That's where she would go. She always felt better there; the waves and the sea spray. She would forget about Alex and Martin and Jez and just enjoy being with her children.

'Come on,' she said excitedly to Millie and Harry, 'let's go and get an ice cream.'

The twins wriggled out of her arms. 'Yes please, Mummy. Ice cream,' said Millie.

'Yesss,' said Harry.

That's it, ice cream; then she wouldn't have to go through the exhausting ritual of cooking them any tea. Ice cream would fill them up. And they would love it.

She took them over the sand dunes and down onto the beach towards Jim's café. There were still a few people around. A couple on those funny half-deckchairs reading the newspaper. A man on the shoreline casting a line into the sea. Another couple throwing sticks for two bouncy, dripping Labradors. Even a family having a barbecue. A soft breeze blew off the sea, the salt catching on her tongue.

They were too late, the café was shut.

She sat down at one of the tables and wanted to cry.

'Ice cream, Mummy?'

She stroked the top of Millie's head. 'Not today, darling.'

'But you promised.' This from a whiny Harry.

'Promises are always broken,' she snapped. 'Never rely on promises.'

Neither of the twins spoke, they just watched her.

She stood. 'Come on, let's go to the beach hut.' She set off at a run, the twins trying to keep up.

Sailor's Rest. The hut that had been in the family forever. Sasha had memories of family picnics on the beach – egg and cress sandwiches, sausage rolls, Madeira cake, lemonade – all coming with a coating of sand. Had they played games with their parents, beach cricket, making sandcastles, digging deep holes and watching the water flood into them – or was that something she only thought she remembered?

She threw open the doors of the hut to let in the evening sunlight. 'Come on,' she said excitedly. 'Let's get the deck chairs out. Mummy'll make us all a drink and we can watch the sun go down and maybe build some sandcastles. What do you think?'

'We haven't got our spades,' said Millie.

Stupid child, always putting obstacles in the way. 'They'll be here.' Sasha opened up the cupboard in the corner of the hut and started pulling out old cushions, newspapers, discoloured plastic plates and cups from ancient picnic sets, a battered kettle, a couple of dog-eared paperbacks. Finally she admitted defeat and sat back on her heels.

'Where are our spades, Mummy?' asked Millie.

'And bucket?' said Harry, putting his thumb into his mouth.

Sasha jumped up. 'Look, never mind about that. We don't need buckets or spades; we'll have a drink instead. Squash. There'll be some orange squash in the cupboard on the wall.' She reached up. Yes, there it was. Half a bottle of squash. No water. She'd have to go to the standpipe and fetch some. She grabbed three beakers, poured some of the squash into them, and set them down on the little trestle table.

'Stay there,' she said. 'I'm just going to get some water.'

She grabbed the water carrier and ran across the sand to the standpipe.

'Here we are,' she said when she got back, 'nice juice for us. I'll have one too.' She smiled, feeling her face stretch in an unfamiliar way. The twins hadn't moved. 'Come on, have a drink.' She pushed the beakers towards them. They looked at her. 'Drink,' she said, rubbing her hands together. 'Just drink it, will you.'

'Mummy,' whispered Millie, 'the cups are dirty. There's black bits in there.'

299

Sasha giggled. 'Bit of dirt won't hurt you, Millie. Look, Mummy's drinking hers.'

'Don't like it,' said Harry.

'For God's sake, Harry, just drink it will you.' Honestly, she was trying to make the day fun. Have some fun with the twins. Better fun than they'd had with Alex. Couldn't they see that?

Harry's lip wobbled.

'C'mon Harry,' said Millie. 'Look I'm drinkin'.' And she took a sip from the beaker.

A big, fat tear rolled down Harry's cheek. 'Don't want to.'

'Oh, for God's sake stop whining, Harry.'

Her harsh voice made Harry cry properly, with Millie watching him, shuffling from foot to foot.

Sasha glared at the twins. 'So bloody ungrateful,' she muttered, folding her arms across her body.

Now what?

She jerked her head up. 'Let's go and watch the sun on the water. We might even see it go down. What do you think?'

Millie nodded, the expression on her face doubtful. Harry didn't say anything, just carried on sucking his thumb. Then: 'I'm tired, Mummy. Harry's tired.'

Another shovelful of guilt filled the space in Sasha's chest. 'I know, but we'll remember this for the rest of our lives.' She scooped him up into her arms, picked up her bag, and strode out of the hut, with Millie following behind.

The sun was beginning to bleed into the sky. They'd walked a long way along the beach. In the distance she could see the fisherman packing up his bag. The couple with the dogs had already left, and she watched as the family shovelled sand onto their barbecue, the faint smell of charcoal mingling with the sea air and the salt. The three of them sat down on the shingle bank. Sasha watched as the waves rushed in and then pulled out. Rushed in, pulled out. The gentle sucking of the stones, the occasional cry from a

300

gull up above. The twins were playing; trying to dig a channel in the sand between the shingle. Sasha hugged her legs and put her chin on her knees.

She wanted to run.

How could one day on her own in Norwich make any difference? She just wasn't a good wife, and Jez was bound to leave her one day for someone more vibrant, capable, likeable. And what would she and the twins do then? What would their lives be like then?

And she would never be able to protect her children from the bad things that were inevitably going to happen to them.

The sea carried on its hypnotic push and pull.

The beach was empty now, the light fading fast. The sea was flat calm. The sky washed down into the horizon. It was peaceful.

Inviting.

Sasha knew what to do.

She lifted Harry into her arms and took Millie's hand. 'Come on darlings. Swim time.'

'But Mummy, I'm tired,' said Millie.

'So am I, sweetheart.'

She led her daughter forward until the grey sea lapped around their ankles.

'It's cold, Mummy,' Millie started to cry.

'It won't be cold for long, I promise. Now hush, sweetheart. Just do what Mummy does, come on. And let's sing.'

She gripped Millie's hand harder, singing about her favourite things, and walked further into the sea, pulling her daughter behind her with a strength she didn't know she had.

Both children were crying now as she pushed on further and deeper.

She felt a current drag her under. She opened her eyes and saw Millie beneath her. There was no noise. Even the constant chatter in her head was quiet. She still had Harry in her arms.

37

Jez ran through the dunes and onto the beach, heart pumping. breath coming in shallow gasps. She had to be here.

The light had almost gone and he could scarcely see anything – even the moon had taken against him by staying behind clouds. He'd brought a torch with him from the car and he shone it along the shoreline.

There she was, sitting with the sea lapping around her.

He ran, and slithered down beside her.

She was holding Harry in her arms. He was wet and blue and dead.

Sasha turned to him. 'I couldn't do it, Jez.'

'Where's Millie?'

She smiled. 'Gone to be a mermaid,' she said.

38

NOW

Alex hadn't realized Sasha had a clock. She could hear its loud tick-tock cut sonorously through the silence in the airless room. Sasha hadn't moved throughout Jez's account. Jez was looking straight ahead, not looking anywhere or at anyone; his voice was unemotional.

'So,' said Alex, feeling unnaturally calm, 'what happened then?'

She remembered, on that day, she'd said goodbye to Martin, cleared up some of the mess the children had made, and looked at her watch, thinking Sasha should have been home an hour or so before, but was hoping she'd been having a good time. Then she looked into the carrycot where Gus was sleeping. It was getting too small for him; she would have to—

That was when she realized something was missing. Any sound from the children. Nothing. She walked quickly outside, trying to breathe normally.

The gate was shut, but the twins were nowhere to be seen. A terrible tide of fear was rising up inside her – she couldn't think straight, didn't know what to do. The light was beginning to go.

She hesitated, heart hammering, looking back at the house. Once Gus was asleep, it took an earthquake to wake him. Without stopping to think any more, she ran up the road, round the corner. Back down the road again, into the next one. No sign. Back to the house where she stabbed Martin's number into her phone. Could he have heard them as he left? Must have. No answer. No fucking answer.

Jez. She phoned Jez, who'd just finished his shift. He told her not to worry, that Sasha had probably picked them up and taken them home.

'Without telling me?' she'd screamed at him.

'You know what Sasha's like,' he said. 'Let me check. I'll be back soon. Don't worry.'

But she had worried. The whole time. And the worry deepened when she found two carrier bags shoved in the hedge, one containing a pair of red shoes.

'What happened then,' said Jez, 'was a nightmare.'

He told Alex when he had found Sasha and Harry he had taken them both home by cover of darkness and had dressed his little boy in his favourite Thomas the Tank Engine pyjamas. He cried for Millie, lost in the sea, and knew the currents would carry her body far, far away from the shore.

'Then I sat down to think. But I couldn't think straight. My stomach was churning; I was sick, crying, a mess. I had lost my children and was about to lose my wife. But I couldn't lose them all, that's what I felt; I didn't want to lose them all. I was mad with grief. I loved them. I loved Sasha. Do you understand?'

Alex shook her head. 'No. Sasha needed help.'

'She would never have got help. Not then. She'd have been put away for years, you know that. She'd have been seen as a monster.'

'But you were happy to let Jackie Wood be seen as a monster?'

'She wasn't my wife,' he shouted, making Alex jump. 'See, you don't understand, and if you don't, how would anyone else?' He took a deep breath and closed his eyes. He opened them again. 'And she was creepy enough. Always hanging around the children – not just Harry and Millie either. Hiding their paintings away.

304

Following Sasha to the playground because she wanted to see the children on the swings. Always on her own. I didn't think they'd arrest her as well. That was just a bonus.

'She was just lonely, that's all.'

'She was plain weird.'

'And why Martin?'

'Sasha told me how Martin had tried to seduce her while he was having an affair with her sister, with you.' He shouted at her.

'I don't believe you,' said Alex. 'He loved me, he said so.' She didn't want Jez to take that away from her.

'Not according to Sasha. No one tries it on with my wife and gets away with it. And he was stopping you from looking after the children properly that day. You were in bed with him when Sasha turned up, weren't you? You might as well admit it.'

'Yes,' she whispered. The guilt was roaring in her ears. 'So you should blame me.'

'Oh, I do,' he replied bitterly. 'But you're Sasha's sister and she loves you. Martin was a piece of dirt. I mean, didn't he even realize the children weren't in the garden when he left you?'

'He went out the back way.' Guilt, shame; all cascading over her.

'So he wouldn't be seen.' His face was twisted in anger, then it relaxed. 'Anyway, things spiralled and soon I was in too deep. There was no way back. And I found a sort of peace. I suppose I had buried my grief as far down as it would go.' He shivered. 'Now you know it all, Alex, what will you do?'

She looked at Jez, his face ravaged by loss and guilt, at Sasha who was quietly humming to herself while picking at the scabs on her arms. She vaguely recognized the tune as something from *The Sound of Music*. She felt strangely calm.

'You framed an innocent man, Jez, and then you had him killed. You framed an innocent woman and she spent some of the best years of her life in prison. You know what I'm going to do. I think this has gone on for too many years, don't you?'

39

She'd had to get out of the station, so had grabbed her coat and walked down into the town to her favourite tea shop, where she was drinking a pot of the tea she favoured when she needed to think – Assam with a pinch of lapsang souchong. That it was her favourite was a secret between her and the tea shop owner. She didn't want to appear posh in front of her colleagues.

'Can I join you?' Glithro stood in front of her.

'It's a free country,' Kate said, then immediately regretted her churlishness.

Glithro nodded at the china teapot and the porcelain cup. 'Do you always drink tea?'

'No. I like coffee too.'

Glithro made a movement with his hand as if he were batting away a fly. 'I didn't mean that. I meant, do you ever drink? Alcohol? You know, beer, wine, cocktails?'

Kate narrowed her eyes. 'Why do you ask?'

'Might be interesting to see you let go.'

'Then the answer is no.' God, why did he always make her feel as though she was some sort of uptight virgin?

He smiled wolfishly. 'Just wondering.'

'Well don't. So what's happening?'

'We've arrested Nikki and Angela Jessop and have got a warrant to search both Nikki's caravan and Angela's house.'

'Bea, her name's Bea.'

Glithro smiled. 'It might well be, but I can't get used to calling her that.'

'I can see why Bea killed Grainger, but why Wood?'

'It was always said she'd had a relationship with Jessop, maybe she thought that had been part of the reason he'd been found guilty and been taken away from her. Maybe she threatened Wood and lost her temper. Maybe we'll never know.'

'I don't like that.'

Glithro grinned. 'What? The never knowing? It happens.'

Kate sighed. 'Where does that leave us, Glithro?'

The waitress turned up with a huge slice of passion fruit cake that Kate had ordered.

'I'll have one of those, too, please,' said Glithro.

'Too much sugar is not good for your heart at your age, Glithro.'

He looked at her. 'I'll manage. Don't you worry about me. And in answer to your question, let's wait for the DNA results. They might show us something.'

'Maybe.'

'Tea smells interesting.'

'Thought you wanted alcohol?'

'Not in the middle of the afternoon. And I was only asking if you ever drank, that was all. Don't worry about it.'

'I'm not.' She tried to smile and hoped it was working. 'Would you like a pot? Of tea?'

'No. Far too posh for me.' He grinned. Then his expression became serious. 'Anyway, About those results – what's the betting there'll be a match for the DNA we found in Jackie Wood's caravan?'

'Bea's DNA will probably be in there, won't it? She had at least one conversation with her.'

'Bathroom?'

'That might be more of a result.'

'But Alex Devlin, Glithro. Jessop's mistress? There's something odd about all this.'

'Look, you had a hunch that the murder of Wood had something to do with what happened years ago, and I think you were right. I'm coming down on the side of revenge, pure and simple. I mean, imagine what it must have been like for Angela Jessop all these years, having to live with the fact her husband was a murderer. Imagine how twisted the children must have become. The son buggered off abroad, didn't he, leaving the daughter – Bea, Nikki, whatever you like to call her – to bear the brunt of the mother's disappointment with life.'

'Disappointment?' Kate cut a piece of her cake with the edge of her fork. 'That's a bit of an understatement, wouldn't you say?'

'Yeah, probably.' The waitress brought his cake and set it down in front of him. 'Thanks, love,' he said.

'Love?'

'What's wrong with that?'

'She's not your "love".'

'Oh, get over yourself, Todd.' He grinned as he got stuck into the cake. 'And you're not going to change me now anyway. What about Alex Devlin? Could she have killed Wood?'

Kate shook her head thoughtfully. 'My gut reaction – and before you say anything, I believe a lot in gut reaction – was that she was genuinely shaken up at the scene. I saw her, remember? But I suppose anything's possible. Though—'

Glithro lifted an eyebrow. 'Though?'

'When I spoke to Alex Devlin she said something about Jackie Wood being stabbed "with a bloody kitchen knife". How did she know that?'

'I'd say that, either she did kill her, or she got rid of the weapon, for some reason or other.'

'Correct.'

'Okay. So why not our Alex as the mistress?'

'I never said that, Glithro,' she said irritably. 'I said I found it odd. I suppose what I'm thinking is; what was it about Alex Devlin that made Jez Clements and Grainger go to such lengths – ,' she pointed her fork at him, '– lengths, I might add, that got two people murdered – to cover it up?'

'Perhaps we'll know that soon. I've sent DC Maitland and DC Evans to pick up Devlin and Clements, as you wanted.'

'Thanks.'

They ate their cake companionably for a few minutes.

'How's life generally?' asked Glithro.

'What do you mean?'

'Forgive me for saying, but you do seem a bit distracted, and I know things haven't been easy at home.'

'Oh, you know, do you?'

'You sort of said as much last time we ate.'

She put down her fork carefully because if she didn't she would stab the interfering bugger with it. 'Well. My husband found out that the reason I wasn't getting pregnant was because I was still on the pill and not because there was something wrong with one of us, so he smashed up a beautiful crib he had made for our baby and walked out and I don't know where he's gone. Curiosity satisfied now, Glithro?' She kept her hand steady as she picked up the fork again.

'Okay. So what are you going to do?'

It would not be a good idea to show too much weakness in front of a colleague. Not a good idea at all. Bad enough she spilled her guts in what was colloquially known as a moment of madness. She looked up at the ceiling, opening her eyes as wide as she could. Always guaranteed to stop tears. Then she looked directly at Glithro. 'How many times have you been divorced?' She kept her voice hard.

He inclined his head. 'Point taken. Not the best person to give advice.'

309

'No.'

'And thank you for not stabbing me with the fork.'

'I was tempted, Glithro.'

He gave her a smile that was not appropriate.

'So, since you asked, I'm going to find out where's he's gone and try and talk him round. There will be a way through this.'

'I see.'

The old-fashioned bell on the tea-shop door rang again.

'Thought I might find you in here, Ma'am.' Rogers appeared at the table.

'Sit down, why don't you,' she said, wearily. 'Let's have a tea-party. What is it?'

Rogers sat, looking longingly at the cake. 'All those doughnuts I've shared, Ma'am—'

Kate found herself laughing in spite of herself. 'All right, all right.' She signalled to the waitress. 'More cake, please.'

'So, Rogers, what brings you here?'

'Well, Ma'am. I have good news and bad news and pretty bad news.'

'Let's have the bad news first.'

'Firstly, Jez Clements's alibi checks out with the McSweeney woman. Nice house too.'

'Right.' Why did she want him to be guilty of the murder?

And secondly, the tests have come back and there was no DNA on Jackie Wood's body or clothes. No fibres, hair, anything that could lead us to the killer.

'Bugger'

'But the good news is we have a match for the DNA found in the dried spittle on Grainger's chin.'

'And?' asked Kate. 'Don't keep us in suspense.'

'Angela Jessop.'

'Bingo,' said Glithro.

Kate thought he looked so pleased he was about to rub his hands together with glee.

'Enough excitement, Detective Inspector Glithro. We've got them for Grainger's murder but not for Wood's. I'm not convinced about Bea Jessop. We will, however, bring her in for questioning, but we'll also review the evidence, cast the net wider.'

'She might cough to it.'

'She might not.'

'Perhaps we should make her.'

'Really, Detective Inspector? And how would you propose to do that? Rough her up a bit? Threaten her? Threaten her family?'

He pursed his lips. 'If it works, then . . .' He shrugged.

Kate leaned towards him. 'I've got news for you, Glithro,' she said through gritted teeth, 'we don't do that here. Not these days, not ever, do you understand me?'

He shook his head, laughing. 'You are still so damned easy to wind up.'

The waitress put a plate with an enormous slice of passion fruit cake down on the table. Kate quite wanted to lift up the plate and grind the cake in Glithro's face.

'Er, now do you want the pretty bad news?' said Rogers, smiling nervously, looking from one to the other.

'Go for it,' she said, realizing Glithro wrong-footed her all the time and she didn't know whether to be plain annoyed or to smile sweetly. She reckoned the smiling would annoy him more.

Rogers took an envelope out of his pocket. 'The Artist wanted me to give you these.'

Kate took the envelope and opened it. Inside were two tickets to an art exhibition. Cherry's art exhibition. She groaned. 'Bloody hell. Now I'm going to have to make polite comments about twenty-five bad paintings instead of just the one.'

Glithro laughed.

'And you can stop laughing, Glithro,' she said. 'There are two tickets here.'

She was glad to see the smile wiped off his face.

40

ONE WEEK LATER

A shaft of late afternoon light through the high window lifted the gloom of the crematorium chapel as Kate walked out. There had only been two other mourners there: Alex Devlin and a man of about sixty in a smart black coat.

The service had been short and perfunctory. Just one bunch of flowers from Alex Devlin, lying on top of the coffin. No one to give a eulogy, no sense of occasion as the coffin creaked its way behind the curtains, and no grieving family to mark Jackie Wood's passing.

Kate went up to Alex, who was just shaking the hand of the man in the black coat. They hadn't had much contact since that surreal day in the café when the mystery of Edward Grainger's death had finally been solved and she had turned up, whey-faced, talking about her sister and Jez Clements and how there'd been a terrible miscarriage of justice. Kate knew how much courage it had taken for Alex to face up to the truth – she'd been doing a bit of that recently herself.

'It was good of you to come, Joseph,' Kate heard her say. The man nodded, put his hat back on his head, and left.

312

She touched Alex lightly on the back. 'Hallo. Not much of a turnout for Jackie, is it?' She could see her breath in the air. Although the seemingly relentless rain had stopped earlier, it was still cold, even for the time of year.

Alex turned and looked at her, a small smile on her face. 'No. But I felt I ought to come, after everything. You know.'

Kate did know. 'And that man, I presume was the penfriend?'

'You knew about him?'

'Oh yes, we had to find out about all of Jackie's acquaintances as well as her family.'

Alex smiled ruefully. 'Funny, isn't it? Jackie told me she had a boyfriend and I thought it was going to be a big thing, a big reveal, you know? But no, just a penfriend.'

'Yes, you wouldn't think they still existed, would you? But apparently they belonged to a penfriend club before emails became the only way of communicating. Seems he wrote to her in prison, as well.'

'He seemed nice, and he came all the way from Preston.'

They stood in silence for a few moments.

'And how's Sasha?'

Alex shrugged. 'Oh, you know. Getting the help she needs anyway, but I'm not sure a court case will be good for her.'

'They might find her unfit to plead, or the CPS won't prosecute her because she was suffering from delayed postnatal depression at the time the children died,' said Kate, gently, seeing the tears behind her eyes.

'I guess. It's just so hard. I tried to do my best for her, over the years, you know, but all the time I was making things worse. If only I'd known then how bad she was.'

'They both hid it from you very well, didn't they? You can't blame yourself for that.'

Alex shook her head. 'No. I should have known. But I'm just going to have to live with that, aren't I?'

Kate made her voice hard. 'What Jez did was wrong. And selfish. He was only seeing it from his point of view, and not even from Sasha's.'

Alex shook her head. 'No, no, he loved her so much he couldn't bear to see her going to prison for what she'd done. I mean, there was plenty of that going on fifteen years ago, wasn't there? People going to prison for killing their children and then it turned out to be cot death, all that sort of thing. But by the time that was found out they'd been inside too long; they couldn't cope. Or had lost their family. I suppose it's better these days.'

'Perhaps.'

'I thought that, after all this was over, I might go away somewhere, you know, with Gus; make a new start. If I can tear him away from the new girlfriend, which doesn't seem very possible. I mean, I can freelance from anywhere these days, it shouldn't be hard. If I don't get sent down for perverting the course of justice or something.'

'I think after all this time, you're more likely to get a suspended sentence, particularly if you've got a good lawyer.'

Alex looked up at the sky. 'And thanks for getting the diary.'

'Ah, well, that's evidence, isn't it.' Kate smiled. 'It was rather good watching Killingback seethe, very satisfactory. But there's nothing he can do, not at the moment anyway.' She hesitated. 'How about you, Alex? Now you know what really happened, are you feeling, I don't know—'

'Less guilty?' Alex shrugged. 'Possibly, maybe. I don't know. Like I said, I should have noticed what was happening to Sasha, but I was so caught up in my sordid affair with Martin that I was blind. And two innocent people died.'

'Hey, Martin loved you, you know. It's all there, in the diary.'

'Maybe. I don't know if that's enough.' She looked at her watch. 'I'd better be getting back otherwise Gus might start to get worried. He's getting ready for his skiing trip and I think his mate Jack will be at our house. They'll both be wanting food – that I do know.'

'He's a good boy, Gus. Even I can see that.'

'Even you?' asked Alex.

'It's a long story. Maybe I'll tell it to you one day. Just one more thing . . . Malone . . . are you still seeing him?'

314

'Not at the moment.'

Kate sensed she didn't want to say any more. 'He's a slippery customer, that's for sure.' She paused. 'We never did find the knife, you know.'

'The knife?'

Alex's innocent look didn't quite work, thought Kate. 'From the scene of Jackie's murder. It's still an open case, and one day we will find the killer.'

Alex nodded. 'I hope you do,' she said. 'It's the least she deserves.'

'No wake for Jackie, then,' said Kate, smiling.

'Didn't seem appropriate somehow. Besides, there was only you, me and Joseph. That would have been a lot of dog-eared sandwiches and vol-au-vents to eat.'

'Here,' said Kate, rooting around in her bag and coming up with a business card. 'In case you ever need me. If you have anything more to say. Perhaps you'll remember something about the knife.'

Alex stuffed it in her coat and held out her hand. 'It was good to see you again.'

Kate shook the offered hand. 'And you.'

Alex Devlin cut a lonely figure as she strode down the crematorium path, thought Kate, and she wondered what the journalist had ahead of her with her broken family. Hopefully, her son could be her solace so she wouldn't be alone. She looked up at the sky. The low sun and custard-looking skies spoke of snow in the air. Then she turned round. 'I know you're there. You can come out now,' she said.

Malone stepped out from behind a line of trees near the door of the crematorium. 'How did you know?' A wry smile lit up his face and his eyes twinkled at her. Lord love us, twinkled. What was she like?

'For an undercover policeman you don't stay very undercover.'

'Ex. I really am done with that now. She didn't see me though, did she?'

Kate shook her head. 'No. Too busy thinking about Jackie and talking to the friend.'

'Friend?'

'The only other mourner; the guy in the nicely cut coat.'

'Ah.'

'What happened to you two?'

'Happened?'

'You were as thick as thieves when I first saw you outside Jackie Wood's caravan.'

He shrugged. 'Yes, well . . .' His voice trailed off.

'Ended badly, did it?'

'Maybe a man like me isn't supposed to fall in love.'

Kate looked at him. 'Maybe you're right, Malone. And she's had enough heartbreak in her life, she doesn't need any more from you.'

'I thought . . .' He sighed. 'Doesn't matter. Thanks for not giving me away. It was nice to see her, just one last time anyway.'

He left, walking down the same path trodden by Alex minutes earlier.

Another lonely figure.

Alex was glad of her warm coat as she made her way home along the beach, watching the waves come in and go out and wondering if Millie's body would ever be washed up. Perhaps it had been, on some far distant shore and was lying in a morgue somewhere, unclaimed. They would soon know though, if that were the case, then they could bury her next to Harry.

Home and family, that's all that mattered really. Not even work so much, although, to see Gus's face when she told him he could go skiing and damn the expense had made revamping the article about Jackie Wood worth it. The only trouble was, her editor Liz had been on her case, wanting the story about Jez and Sasha from her point of view. Maybe she would write it one day, but it would be on her terms and no one else's.

She trudged up the beach and found a bench to sit on. *In Memory of Elsa Who I Loved For 50 Years* went the inscription on its back. Lucky Elsa. She took out her phone and stared at it for a few minutes. Gillian. The other woman. Were they really getting divorced? How could she believe anything Malone said? And if he was lying, did Gillian deserve to know about his duplicity? It would be so easy just to key in the numbers that were burned on her memory, and Gillian's life could come crashing down. Perhaps she ought to know she was living a lie. But could she do that? Was it so important for her to know the truth? Perhaps she did know and just didn't want to see it. Her finger hovered over the keypad.

She put the phone back in her pocket.

THEN

It was dark and it was cold but her little torch led the way along the roads between the caravans at Harbour's End. A weak light shone from behind the thin curtain hanging at the window of the caravan. She knew it was the right one. Following Alex this morning had been the right thing to do. Call it a hunch, an instinct, but somehow she'd known Alex was going to see the woman. The killer. The way she had buried herself in her coat, looked around, hurried away. Alex had a secret, and she thought she knew what it was.

And she was right.

Creeping forward, she kept to the shadows not wanting some busybody to see her.

She pressed herself against the side of a caravan as a man went by, whistling to his dog who stopped to piss up against a car.

Almost there.

The knife was snug in her pocket.

She hated Jackie Wood. She was to blame for everything that had happened in her life, everything she had lost, everything she had done. The only thing that had kept her going these last fifteen years was the thought of her inside. Banged up. Suffering.

She wanted her to suffer, like she had wanted everyone to suffer.

She climbed the steps and with one gloved hand knocked softly on the door.

The stupid bitch opened it.

Jackie Wood peered at her. 'I know you,' she said.

Sasha pushed her inside.

Acknowledgements

For her support, advice and belief in me, many, many thanks to my agent, Teresa Chris. Also thanks to Sarah Hodgson and all at HarperCollins for their wisdom and enthusiasm.

Thanks also to Susan Rae for the loan of her BBC Radio 4 name and for all her support, and to Julia Champion, who's lived up to her name since we first worked together on radio, and to the Swaffer family and Sue Welfare for just being there.

To Bernardine Coverley: wish you could be here now, you would be so proud for me.

A special mention for Melanie McCarthy who has been at my side for more years than I care to remember, and a big thank you to Sarah Bower and Jenny Knight for their friendship and encouragement. And, above all, thanks and love to my husband, Kim, and children Edward, Peter and Esme. I couldn't have done it without you.

KILLER READS

DISCOVER THE BEST IN CRIME AND THRILLER.

SIGN UP TO OUR NEWSLETTER TO KEEP UP TO DATE WITH OUR LATEST BOOKS, NEWS AND COMPETITIONS.

WWW.KILLERREADS.COM/NEWSLETTER

Follow us on social media to get to know the team behind the books, hear from our authors, and lots more:

 /KillerReads

 /KillerReads